A RESTLESS EVIL

A RESTLESS EVIL

Ann Granger

headline

First published in 2002
by HEADLINE BOOK PUBLISHING

10 9 8 7 6 5 4 3 2 1

ISBN 0 7472 7472 X (hardback)
ISBN 0 7553 0295 8 (trade paperback)

Typeset by Avon Dataset Ltd, Bidford-on-Avon, Warks

Printed and bound in Great Britain by
Clays Ltd, St Ives plc

HEADLINE BOOK PUBLISHING
A division of Hodder Headline
338 Euston Road
London NW1 3BH

www.headline.co.uk
www.hodderheadline.com

ACKNOWLEDGEMENTS

With grateful thanks to Tim Buckland BDS for his
expert advice and help on dental matters in this
and previous books.

Map of Lower Stovey

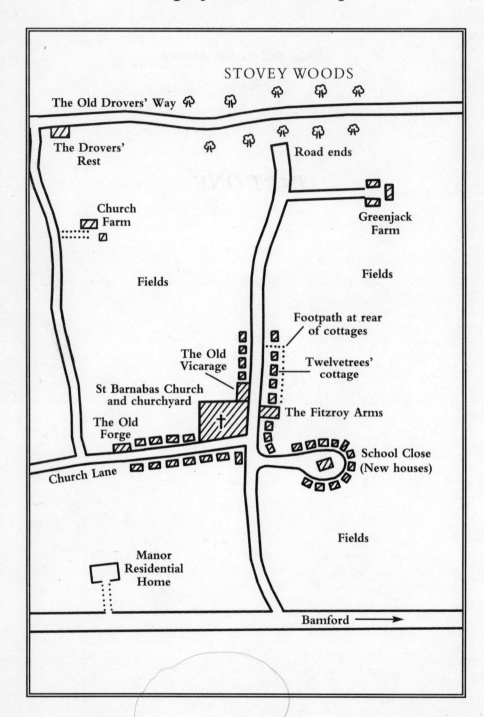

STOVEY WOODS

The Old Drovers' Way

The Drovers'
Rest

Road ends

Church
Farm

Greenjack
Farm

Fields

Fields

Footpath at rear
of cottages

The Old
Vicarage

Twelvetrees'
cottage

St Barnabas Church
and churchyard

The Fitzroy Arms

The Old
Forge

School Close
(New houses)

Church Lane

Fields

Manor
Residential
Home

Bamford →

PART ONE

Chapter One

The pub was called the Drovers' Rest. Its faded sign creaked monotonously back and forth, depicting a flock of sheep and a figure in a smock. The sheep were shown too big, or the shepherd too small, depending how you looked at it. Guy Morgan looked at it for no longer than he had to before he slipped his rucksack from his shoulders and straightened up with a sigh of relief. A number of bicycles were propped against the mellow stone walls. He wasn't the first to stop for a midday break.

Guy hadn't walked very far that day but the weather had sapped his strength and made his legs feel as if they were weighted with lead. The dust which had filled his nostrils had parched his throat and given him a raging thirst. It was all the fault of that same wind which played with the pub sign. April is normally a time of squalls and showers and buffeting winds interspersed with spells of sunshine. But this was a variety of the south wind which goes by different names in parts of Europe and is blamed there for any number of ailments from general lassitude to depression. It had no business here at all on the rolling Cotswold hills. It was a child of the desert which had taken the wrong turning and after sweeping across the Mediterranean and Europe, marauded over the English countryside for twenty-four hours as unpredictable and merciless as a Rif tribesman.

High in the sky, birds struggled to maintain their course against its wayward currents. From early morning when he'd set out, Guy had felt himself besieged by it. It had ruffled his hair and puffed its dry warm breath disagreeably into his face. He pushed open the door, glad at the prospect of being free of his tormentor for an hour.

Inside he found himself in a long, low-ceilinged room which ran across the building from one side to the other. It was partitioned by a lath and plaster wall pierced by an opening between massive oak uprights. He guessed that once this had been part of a more formal division of the room into two. Beyond the opening, to the right, the cyclists had taken up residence. They huddled over the tiny tables, quaffing strange-looking liquids, making short work of various high-energy snacks. Guy had nothing against cyclists but tended to avoid them at these often shared halts. They hunted in strung-out packs, human greyhounds, swooping past him crouched over their handlebars in an extremely uncomfortable posture. Their legs and torsos were clad in figure-hugging lycra and their shins were shaved to glossy smoothness. Some of them affected peaked caps, the peaks turned upward. In their minds they were tackling not just this dusty country track but some Pyrenean col. Guy acknowledged fairly that they, in turn, probably looked on him as a heavy-booted technophobe, as archaic in this millennium year 2000 as the smocked rustic of the inn sign. Guy exchanged a nod with the nearest cyclist and moved away to lean on the bar. The landlord appeared before him and said amiably, 'Hello, there.'

'Hello,' returned Guy. 'I'll have a pint and your bar menu, if I may.'

'You may, indeed.' The landlord produced a plastic folder.

Guy opened it up and read the list of offerings. It seemed somewhat elaborate for such a traditional-looking establishment in such an out-of-the-way place. Even the Ploughman's Platter boasted Brie.

'Haven't you got any Cheddar?' he asked.

'If you want it,' said the landlord.

'It doesn't say so here.'

'Yes, it does, look, right there.' A stubby forefinger pointed at the foot of the page where Guy read the words 'A selection of English cheeses available'.

'What other English cheeses have you got?'

'Only Cheddar.' The landlord added reproachfully, 'It's the beginning of the season.'

Guy settled for the Cheddar Ploughman's and his order was shouted into a back room. The landlord returned to the bar.

'Walker?' he asked.

'Yes. Just taking a break for a couple of days.'

'All on your own?'

'A colleague was coming with me but had to cry off.'

'Oh, right.' The landlord pursed his lips. 'How much further are you going?'

'As far as Bamford and from there I can catch the train back to London.'

'Ah, London, is it? Well, you might be lucky.'

Guy wasn't sure what this meant. 'No trains?' he ventured.

'Oh, you'll catch a train all right, once you get to Bamford. You might get a bit wet before you get there.'

'It's been as dry as a bone all morning,' objected Guy. 'Just very breezy.'

'Weather's changing. It's already tipping it down in Wales and they're threatened with floods in Devon. It's coming this way. I saw it on the telly.'

'I'll just have to walk a bit faster, then, won't I?' retorted Guy, annoyed by the landlord's evident satisfaction.

The door opened and another pair of cyclists came in. The landlord abandoned Guy for the newcomers. His parting shot was, 'You want to get a bike, like them.'

A gum-chewing girl bearing a plate of salad appeared from the back room and looked at Guy with a mixture of doubt and assessment.

'You the Ploughman's?'

He took his lunch from her and retreated to a far corner where someone had left a tabloid newspaper. Guy settled down to his lunch, his beer and scandal. As he got to the end of all three, he became aware of a shadow across the printed page and the faint warmth of another human being nearby. His ear caught a noisy intake of breath. He looked up.

The adenoidal girl stood by his table, watching him in a curiously unsettling way. She stretched out a hand to his plate. Her fingernails were bitten short and on the middle finger of her right hand she wore a cheap ring. Instinctively Guy felt himself throw up the defences. He knew her type.

'You finished?' she inquired.

'Yes, thank you,' Guy told her.

She picked up the plate but instead of moving away, stayed rooted to the spot, the plate held in both hands.

'Walker?'

He managed not to snap back that wasn't it obvious? He confirmed it in as discouraging a voice as he could.

She was impervious to subtle hints. 'All on your own?'

He'd explained this already to the landlord and he was blowed if he was going to explain it again to this predatory female. He nodded curtly, not giving her the satisfaction of a proper answer which would keep the conversation, such as it was, going.

'Shame,' she said. 'Can't be much fun all on your own and that. No one to talk to. Where are you staying tonight?'

'I'm not sure,' he told her, evading the trap.

'The Fitzroy Arms in Lower Stovey does rooms,' she offered.

'I hope to get a bit further than Lower Stovey.'

'Pity,' she said. 'I live there.'

He was rescued by the landlord who surged up and ordered, 'Come on, Cheryl, get going. Don't stand there nattering.'

'He might have wanted some afters,' Cheryl defended herself, adding in a sing-song voice addressed to Guy, 'We've got apple pie, lemon lush pie and ice-cream.'

He declined. 'I've got to get on.'

'Please yourself,' she said and flounced off towards the kitchen.

The landlord observed, 'Anything in trousers, that one.' He lumbered back to his bar.

Guy saw now how empty the place had become. He was the sole visitor. The cyclists had prudently got on their way long since. Glancing guiltily at his wristwatch, he realised he also should have moved before this. He grabbed his rucksack and strode through the door.

Outside there were distinct signs that the landlord's forecast was to be proved correct. The vexing wind had definitely fallen and a grey rash on the horizon heralded a depression spreading eastward. Already a misting of rain veiled the furthermost hills. Guy set out, refreshed and clinging to an optimistic hope he could keep ahead of the weather.

For twenty minutes he made good progress, even though he was now walking uphill. Then a large fat drop of water landed splat in the dust in front of him. In the past few minutes, the grey mass had raced across the intervening sky. Guy swung his rucksack to the ground and delved in it for his map and waterproof cape. He looked around him. He'd not yet crested the summit but even so, from up here he had a fine view all around. The hills were a subtle patchwork of varying shades of green enlivened by patches of bright yellow under the shadow of the now overhead rainclouds. Sheep and their lambs clustered in ragged white groups under stone walls. His eyes also sought shelter. There was a farm in the distance, he judged at least a mile and a half across the fields, too far. He could turn back to the pub, but it went against the grain to retrace his steps and even more to face the grinning landlord. Never admit defeat.

Guy ran his finger across the dotted line on the map which marked the old drovers' way. Far removed from the modern ribbons of asphalt which criss-crossed the country, it was no more than a stony track but it ran as straight as a die. Some said it had been laid down by the Romans, who were famous for that sort of thing, as the legions moved northward in their conquest of Britain. What was certain was that as long as the history of the area had been recorded, it had been marked as a drovers' path. Once traffic had been plentiful: herders driving cattle to the towns for slaughter; country folk going to and from market, driving their flocks of sheep ahead of them and burdened with baskets of farm produce; strings of pack-ponies taking goods to isolated hamlets or bringing the packs of wool to the town. Then the wool industry had dwindled. Many of the markets had vanished or survived in a new form without animals. The drovers' way was no longer needed. Today it was travelled by ramblers, like Guy, cyclists like those he'd encountered at the pub and horse-riders.

Occasionally, to the annoyance of all three of these groups, a roaring destructive motorbike blazed its unwelcome trail across the hills. At its widest the drovers' way was about ten feet across. In parts it narrowed to admit only a pair of walkers in comfort.

Guy opened out the map. The wind, to prove it still had breath in its body, caught it and rattled it in his hands so that he couldn't read it and it threatened to rip free. He squatted down and spread it on the ground. Another raindrop fell, plumb in the centre of it as he held the paper flat with his palms. The village of Lower Stovey was the nearest hamlet, but that was another good two miles and meant going out of the way. Moreover it was where Cheryl lived. He didn't know what hours she worked but it was likely the afternoon was her free period and he'd no wish to come across her again. He wondered how she got to and from work and vaguely remembered a small motor scooter parked at the side of the pub.

However, there was another haven. Just over the crest of this rise he'd see lying below him Stovey Woods.

Guy folded the map hurriedly, creasing it, and jammed it back in his rucksack. He slung the straps over his shoulders and pulled the hooded waterproof cape over his head and the pack. The rain was falling faster now, striking malicious pellets against his face and bare legs. The dust puffed up where the drops landed. Slowly the spots blended with adjoining ones as the dry ground slaked its thirst. Soon raindrops would turn to puddles, earth to mud. Guy strode out briskly.

As he topped the rise and started down the other side towards the dark stain the woods made on the landscape, he heard a rumble of thunder. As he'd done when a child, Guy began to count in his head. *One – two – three – four –* The lightning burst across the sky in a sudden flash which hurt his eyes. Four miles away. He had a brief sensation of heat on his face and he thought, blimey, it must've been closer than that!

He began to jog down the hill. Received wisdom was that you shouldn't shelter under trees when there was lightning about. Guy hoped that meant you shouldn't shelter under the one tree around in open land. In a wood, surely, the odds against your tree being the one struck had to be in your favour.

The nearer he came to the woods, the more they struck him as a black, impenetrable mass. He felt a twinge of atavistic alarm. The forests had always been places to be feared, the haunt of elves and witches, bandits and wild beasts. Not now, Guy consoled himself. Not in this day and age when we were free from medieval terrors. No elves, no witches, hopefully no muggers and no —

'Hell's teeth!' Guy heard himself exclaim. 'What the dickens is that?'

Something, some sort of animal, had been lying in the long grass at the edge of the wood. At Guy's approach it rose up. He thought at first it was a large dog, but the dark outline was all wrong for a dog. Was it a goat? Impossible. No, it was a small deer – a muntjak. He laughed aloud in relief. The muntjak, disturbed by his arrival, trotted away from him, ears laid back, into the woods.

Guy followed it. The track which was the old road ran between trees on either side. This part of the woods was Forestry Commission land. The planting was of pines. To either side of the track was a grassy verge, beyond that a deep ditch before the trees began. Guy scrambled across the ditch to the right and stumbled into the darkness – and dryness – among the regiment of straight, uniform trunks.

Beneath his feet the carpet of pine needles was soft and spongy. The scent of resin was heavy on the air like incense after mass. There was a cathedral stillness, a holding of breath, a waiting for the moment of revelation. There was no sign of the muntjak. He couldn't hear it. He couldn't hear the crunch of his own feet. He couldn't hear anything except the patter of the raindrops falling on the pine branches.

There was a track among the trunks and he followed it automatically.

9

It was narrow, made by the regular passage of the deer not by man. It twined capriciously, as no Roman road ever did, weaving to the left around this tree, to the right around that one, making him perform manoeuvres he associated with country dances. Occasionally his ear did catch the brief sound of a rustle, not made by the rain, up in the branches overhead. A pigeon, perhaps, or a woodpecker. Like him, the birds kept a silent watch, waiting for the rain to cease and life to begin again as normal.

There was some kind of clearing up ahead. He made for it out of curiosity, just to see what it was, not to step into it and the rain. On the edge of it, he stopped.

He stood atop a sort of rampart. It dropped steeply and at the bottom, in the clearing, grew a tangle of bramble bushes, nettles, dock, cow parsley and puny saplings of native trees sprung from seeds blown there, carried there on the hide of the deer, excreted in animal droppings, or scattered by the birds. Beyond it rose a corresponding bank, completing the saucer-like depression. Guy, standing by the first line of pines ringing the area, thought it formed a natural amphitheatre. He ought to be looking down at some spectacle, a show. Curious about the nature of the rampart, he scraped at it with the heel of his boot to little purpose. To excavate this would be a major archaeological task. When he got home, he'd look it up in the library. Find out if anyone else had made note of this place, had any theories.

The rain was easing. His curiosity now had overcome his first instinct to keep dry. He began to negotiate his way down the slope. He needed to take care. Underfoot it was loose, unstable. Tree roots poked through forming treacherous snares. Nettles nipped his bare shins spitefully. Brambles reached out and scratched at his unprotected skin. Nature, allying itself against him, driving back the would-be intruder.

The muntjak must have been sheltering here but he hadn't seen it. Now it saw or smelled him. Without warning, it dashed out of the tangle of undergrowth, sprang up the slope on the further side of the clearing and disappeared among the trees. Startled, even though he now knew what it was, Guy stopped short, slipped, felt the earth give way beneath his foot and fell.

Over and over he tumbled, scrabbling in vain for a handhold, brambles tearing at his flesh, until he came to a stop, on his stomach, face down in the rotting vegetation. It smelled foul from underlying stagnant water which had drained down into the basin. He moved cautiously, a limb at a time, checking for breaks and sprains. Everything seemed OK. He'd been lucky but he'd have a sore back from the rucksack bumping against it on the way down.

He got to his feet and turned to make his way back by the route he'd come. Then he saw that, in his descent, he'd disturbed the tangle of greenery which had been covering the entrance to an animal lair in the side of the bank. Too big, he thought, for the entrance to a rabbit warren. A fox-hole possibly, or even a badger's entrance to its set. He knelt and scraped away some more debris and peered in. A stale, fetid odour oozed out. He muttered, 'Faugh!' and was about to pull back his head when his eye was caught by an object near the mouth of the den.

Guy stared down at it for a moment. Then he picked it up, examined it carefully, uttered a low whistle and put it gently back on the earth. Sitting up, he divested himself of his cape, unslung his rucksack and searched in it until he found his torch. Now he lay down again on his stomach and, heedless of the smarting nettle-stings and protesting bruises, carefully shone the beam of light into the tunnel. The excavation ran back some way between twisting roots before turning to the right but the torchlight clearly picked up a higgeldy-piggeldy scattering of objects of different shape and size near the entrance.

Guy put down the torch and stretched in his arm as far as it would go, searching with his fingers until they touched something small and dry. His face was pressed against the damp musty soil surrounding the opening. Earth crumbled and fell into his hair and eyes. He was hardly aware of it. Eventually he withdrew every one of the objects he could reach. They were yellowish-brown in colour and appeared to have been there some time. Some were broken. One or two showed signs of having been gnawed, though the teethmarks were old. He had no doubt as to what they were. They were human bones.

Now that he was satisfied he'd retrieved all he could, Guy took out his mobile phone and called 999. 'No Network Coverage' the screen informed him obligingly. He cursed softly. He was in a dead spot. An unfortunate phrase, but apt.

He searched in his rucksack for something to wrap the bones in. The only paper he had was his map so he sacrificed that. Then he climbed up the bank, followed the deer track back to the main dirt road, plodded through the trees until he reached the far side of the wood and tried his mobile again. This time he was successful.

'Which service do you want?' enquired a voice.

'Police,' said Guy. There was nothing an ambulance could do for the owner of the bones.

He was connected with the police. He gave his name, his home address, explained that he was on a walking holiday and he had found human remains, bones, after falling down a slope.

The new voice, tinny and a little weary, asked where he was. He told it, Stovey Woods, or just outside.

'And these bones, sir,' said the voice. 'You just fell over them, you say?'

'No,' corrected Guy. 'I said I fell over. I disturbed the nettles covering the entrance to the burrow in my fall.'

'Burrow?' said the voice. 'Most likely animal bones, then, sir, don't you think?'

'No, I don't think,' said Guy. 'If I thought that, I wouldn't have rung you.'

'People often think they've found human bones,' said the voice. 'But it's nearly always animal, a fox's dinner. Are they very small, like a rabbit?'

'No!' snapped Guy. He was beginning to think this the most irritatingly complacent voice he'd ever listened to. 'Some are damaged and some are incomplete, a lot are missing. But they include a clavicle, parts of two ribs, three or four vertebrae, a badly-chewed tibia and an entire mandible with most of the teeth still in it. Some of the teeth show dental work. That should be helpful to you. Unfortunately, the rest of the skull is missing. Of course, there might be more further back in the tunnel.'

There was a silence. He thought he could hear the person at the other end talking to someone. A new voice came on, deeper, more authoritative. It, at least, wasn't smug. It was suspicious.

'This is on the level, sir?'

'Absolutely!' Guy was finding it difficult to control his frustration. 'All I'm asking you is, what do you want me to do? Bring the bones in to the nearest police station or wait until you can get someone out here? I don't know how you'll get here,' he added. 'I'm on the old drovers' way.'

'We can get there, but you'll understand we don't want to be brought all the way out there on a wild-goose chase. Not accusing you of anything, sir, but you could be mistaken. This dental work, as you describe it, might just be discoloration. Old bones go a funny colour. So is there any other thing which makes you think these are definitely human?'

'Why do I think they're human?' howled Guy. 'How many times do I have to tell you? Because I recognise them!'

'Not many people could do that, sir. Why're you so sure?'

'Because,' said Guy, breathing heavily, '*because I am a doctor*!'

'This is it,' said Alan Markby, trying not to sound as dismayed as he felt.

Beside him in the car, Meredith Mitchell shuffled the estate agent's brochures and found the one she sought.

'Former vicarage,' she read aloud. 'Early nineteenth century. Five bedrooms, three reception, stone-flagged kitchen. Outbuildings. In need of some restoration work.'

They both peered through the windscreen at the house.

'A lot of restoration,' she said doubtfully.

'Nice big garden,' he pointed out.

They clambered out of the car and opened the creaking gate. A path which had been gravelled, but was now almost entirely overgrown with weeds and pitted with rain-filled depressions, led to a front door curiously scarred as if someone or something had been kicking or scraping at it. Markby pressed the bell-push.

In response a furious barking broke out from inside the house. There was the sound of scrabbling claws on parquet and a woman's voice. Some sort of tussle seemed to be in progress. Eventually a door inside slammed and to an accompaniment of laboured breathing, the front door creaked open.

The woman who appeared before them was tall even wearing flat walking shoes over dark woollen tights. Her untidy grey hair was nearly shoulder-length and her angular features devoid of make-up. She did, however, sport jewellery in the form of dangling earrings which looked home-made, each a grape-cluster of coloured glass beads.

She placed a hand on the doorframe to support herself and, fixing Markby with a direct look, gasped, 'It's Roger.'

'No, it's, I mean, I'm Alan Markby,' he replied, taken aback. 'I rang to arrange a viewing.'

'Yes, I know that's who you are!' she retorted. She'd got her breath back now and took her hand from the doorframe. 'I meant my dog, Roger. He makes a racket but he's a silly old thing really. Wouldn't do any harm. Likes visitors but jumps up at them. Not everyone likes it. So I've shut him in there.' She pointed at what looked like the door of a cloakroom.

On cue, from behind it, came a lugubrious howl.

'Roger doesn't like being left out of things,' said his mistress. 'Are you coming in?'

They stepped dubiously over the threshold. Roger whined and scratched at the door which held him prisoner. It rattled on its hinges.

'Too big for me now,' said the woman.

'The house? Roger, the dog?' Meredith whispered wickedly in Alan's ear.

He mimed her to silence but the other woman hadn't overheard.

'Can't afford to keep the damn place up. That's why I'm selling and why it's going cheap.'

Markby, mindful of the price, tried to hide his scepticism by asking politely, 'You are Mrs Scott?'

'Of course I am. But you wouldn't know, would you? I might be the housekeeper. Well, I'm not!' She gave a surprisingly deep bellow of laughter.

Markby caught Meredith's eye again and they exchanged furtive grins. Mrs Scott was leading the way, her long, drooping skirts swaying. She wore a hand-knitted sweater. Markby wondered if it had been created without benefit of a knitting pattern. He was no expert on such matters but there was an air of bizarre improvisation about the garment. It was banded in strata of rose-pink, navy-blue and orange. In places the colour ended mid-line and the next colour began as if that was the point at which the knitter had run out of wool. Back and front sections were square and the sleeves stitched on clumsily raglan-style. They were tubular and cuffless. With that and the bead earrings she was certainly colourful.

'This is the main reception room,' Mrs Scott said, throwing open a door. She stood aside for them to enter.

It was a spacious room with attractive mouldings round the ceiling but it didn't appear to have been decorated in years. The door paint was yellowish, perhaps once white, and round the handle dark and greasy. Its panels were scratched, too. Dust lay thick. Some quite nice antique silver on a table was black with neglect. An old sofa bulged in all the wrong places, a little like Mrs Scott herself, and strands of coarse shiny horse-hair escaped from holes in the fabric. Dog hairs clung to everything. Roger had left his mark. There was an insidious musty smell, a little like rising dough mixed with wet wool.

'You have central heating,' remarked Alan. He was staring at a huge ancient radiator with misgiving.

'We've got it, but it doesn't work,' said Mrs Scott honestly. 'Needs a new boiler.'

The other rooms were in pretty much the same state. A small dingy retreat called grandiosely by Mrs Scott 'the study', was crammed with dusty Victorian furniture, some of which looked as though it might have been brought from elsewhere in the house to be stored there. Meredith, always curious to examine books, had sidled off to peer into a huge glass-fronted oak bookcase crammed with leather-bound volumes. Markby scanned the spines briefly over her stooped form. They appeared to be mostly works of theology. The bottom shelf, however, was given over to a set of the Victoria County History and a fat tome entitled *Man and Myth: The Legacy of Pre-history*. On the far wall an ebony and brass crucifix loomed above an oak desk. On the desk lay an appointments diary white with dust and an old briar pipe resting on a worn tobacco pouch. There was still a faint odour of pipesmoke in the room, absorbed by the furnishings over many years. He felt a prickle run up his spine as if a ghostly hand had touched it. Good Lord, he thought, it's the same. It's just the same.

'You don't use this room much now?' he heard himself ask.

'It's as he left it,' was Mrs Scott's reply.

Alan Markby said, 'Yes, it is.' He was aware of the sudden, surprised look Meredith turned on him. He should have explained to her before they came. Now explanations would have to wait.

The kitchen was huge, a cavern of a place, with the old range still in place, pitted and rusted, alongside a fat-spattered gas cooker. Upstairs, someone had made an effort to brighten up the master bedroom with liberal amounts of sky-blue paint and very little talent with the brush.

'Nice room, this one,' said Mrs Scott. 'Got a good view of Stovey Woods. Come and see.'

They followed her to a sash window which she pushed up with an effort. 'Bit stuck, most of them are.'

They peered out. They could see the road which led through the village, winding towards the distant dark mass of the the wood.

'We're a dead end,' said Mrs Scott. 'No through traffic. Nice quiet village, this. No one comes here who hasn't got business here. It's popular with the second-homes crowd. When they're not here, you hardly see a car. Well, I'm blowed. That makes me a liar, doesn't it?'

16

A car had appeared as she spoke and not just any car. This was a marked police vehicle. It cruised past as if uncertain where it was going. Markby leaned out as far as he could and watched it wend its way towards the wood.

'What do the cops want, do you think?' asked Mrs Scott. 'Someone loosing off a shotgun in the woods, may be? Haven't heard 'em. Would only be after pigeons, anyway. Nothing for the police to worry about. Bit of deer poaching?'

'Alan?' Meredith touched his arm.

He pulled in his head regretfully. 'What? Oh, yes, could be anything. Well, is there anything else we should see, Mrs Scott?'

'Only the downstairs cloaks where Roger is.'

'We'll give that a miss,' Markby said hastily. 'Would it be in order to look round the garden?'

'Help yourself.' She clearly didn't intend to accompany them.

As they strolled down the path between abandoned flowerbeds and overgrown vegetable patches, Meredith asked the question which had been hovering on her lips since the study.

'Why didn't you tell me you'd been in that house before?'

He hesitated. 'It was a long time ago. It was still a vicarage then and I had reason to call on the incumbent. Police business, you know, routine stuff.'

'Was that Mr Scott, by any chance?'

'What? Oh, no. It was a chap called Pattinson.'

'Is that why you wanted us to view it? Because you knew it already? Why didn't you say?'

'I don't – didn't know the place. I wasn't shown over it back then. I was shown straight into the vicar's study and after I'd spoken to him, I left. I didn't even see into the other rooms.' He added, 'It's in a bit of a state, I know.'

She did her best to put an optimistic gloss on it. 'It's a beautiful big drawing room. Expensive to heat, though. Did it look better, smarter, when you saw it years ago?'

'I told you, I only saw the entrance hall and the study. It looked all

17

right. Not that I was paying much attention then. I'm pretty sure that bookcase and the desk in the study were there then, and the crucifix, but polished up and clean.'

'She's a nice woman, batty but nice.'

Markby stopped and turned towards her. Her face was hidden by her ruffled brown hair. She'd pushed her hands into her jeans pockets and was idly manoeuvring a broken piece of ornamental edging with the toe of her trainer. He caught her lightly by her upper arms. 'Don't pretend. You make me feel guilty. It was a mistake coming, all right? I know you don't like it. Just say so.'

'Well, I – oh, all right.' She tossed back her hair, slipped her arms free and began to number off the points on her fingers. 'The heating's broken, the windows stick and I wouldn't lose my money if I bet there was something wrong with the plumbing. Against that, it has large rooms, some lovely period features like the mouldings, and the garden is your dream, I know that. But,' she sighed. 'The village does look a teeny bit, well, dead. I'm sorry. Perhaps you'd love the place. I wish I could tell you that I did. But I don't. You did ask,' she finished defensively.

She reached out to squeeze his hand reassuringly. 'We'll find the right house if we keep looking.'

'And then we'll get married?'

'Then we'll get married. I'm not backing out, Alan.' She was looking up at him anxiously under the heavy fringe of hair.

'OK,' he said, kissing her. 'Just so I'm sure. It's not me, it's the house.'

'It's not you. The house is like Dracula's weekend retreat.'

He laughed and they set off back towards the gate.

'I wonder what that squad car was up to?' Markby mused.

'Nothing for you to worry yourself over, Superintendent. Do you think Mrs Scott knows you're a copper?'

'I didn't tell her when I rang. I don't go round announcing myself. Hey, I'm a policeman! It doesn't go down well.'

They got back in the car.

'We could,' Markby said tentatively, 'just drive down to the woods and take a look.'

'At the woods or at whatever has taken the police down there?'

'Both.'

'Go on,' she said resignedly. 'You won't rest until you know. But count me out. I'll go and take a look at the church, if it's open. I'll wait there for you, anyway. Pick me up on your way back from your busman's holiday.'

Chapter Two

As Markby's car neared the woods, the road, or what passed for it, grew worse. Only a remnant of its original asphalt surface remained, cracked and weed-strewn. The edges had broken away and he rattled and shook his way in a wavering middle course over potholes filled with water from the afternoon's downpour. He hoped he didn't meet the police car careering towards him. Here and there parts of the dry stone walls lining the road had crumbled and sent mini-avalanches of lumps of yellow stone to encroach on the track. No one had troubled to remove them. No one, he guessed, came down here in a car. *What, never? Well, hardly ever.*

'*I am the captain of the Pinafore . . .*' he hummed in an out-of-tune way. He was as near tone-deaf as made little difference. He regretted it. He'd have liked to enjoy music. He did enjoy Gilbert and Sullivan's operettas but for the lyrics rather than the tunes.

He fell silent and thought back to the house-viewing. That had been a notable lack of success. He should, perhaps, have mentioned to Meredith that he'd been in the house before. But it had been so long ago and as he'd tried to explain, the only room he'd seen had been that claustrophobic study. Yet it hadn't been an unfriendly place. Rather pleasant, as he recalled it. The vicar, Pattinson, had been an elderly man, a little on the dithering side and vague, but sharp enough when defending his flock. The book which had lain open on the vicar's desk

21

on that occasion, Markby recalled, had been that massive volume on myths which he'd glimpsed still there in the bookcase. 'It is by way of being a little interest of mine!' the vicar had said apologetically.

Living in Lower Stovey, a man would need a few interests to pass a long evening. Markby had to confess it was rather more cut-off than he remembered it. Surely, there had been more people about when he'd come here many years ago? There had been children running home from the village school. Women had stood gossiping outside a shop. Someone had run a shoe and bridle-repair business from a delapidated lean-to by his cottage. Perhaps the lean-to had finally fallen down. There was no sign of it now. Also gone were school, store and inevitably children, as young families moved out given the lack of the first two. It had left a deserted wasteland of a place. An inhabited wasteland of second homes and prosperous two-car commuter couples, yet a wasteland nevertheless.

They had an agreement, he and Meredith. They'd find a house and then they'd get married. At the moment he had a Victorian villa in Bamford and she had an end-of-terrace cottage. They'd tried living together in his house and it hadn't worked. She was adamant it wouldn't work in her house, either. It was that much smaller than his. They'd fall over one another at every turn. Yes, clearly the answer was to look for a new house, but where to find one both of them liked? So far they'd viewed five. Not many, Markby supposed. But enough to be discouraging. For that reason, he'd pinned his hopes on the old vicarage at Lower Stovey. First sight of it today had disposed of his sanguine expectations. He didn't blame Meredith for not fancying it. He just wished he could quell the secret suspicion he harboured that she might have another reason other than the house's obvious flaws. She might, just might, be playing for time.

He'd told himself this thought was unworthy and should be dismissed out of hand. It was preposterous. And yet he knew that the idea of marriage made her nervous. It had taken long enough to get her to say yes. He sighed. All he wanted was to pop over to the local registry office and sign on the dotted line. She had at long last declared herself willing to do the same. They were held up simply because they couldn't find a house. Or not one they wanted to live in.

He jolted to a stop and peered through the windscreen. The road had run out. It shouldn't have come as a shock. Back on the main highway, where the turning for Lower Stovey was marked, a large and prominently placed sign warned the traveller *No Throughroad*. But the abruptness with which the surfaced road ended was still quite startling. Before him was a patch of rough grass and a gate. Beyond the gate lay the trees. In the silence and stillness, the years slipped away. Twenty, no, twenty-two, years ago. So long? Yet little had changed here. It wouldn't take much to make the dark mass of trees seem scary, looming as it did over him, even without memory to colour his imagination. He remembered the first time he'd been here, at this very spot, and gazed at the same scene. The memory was so sharp, crystal-clear, it did indeed seem like yesterday and the emotion he felt hadn't changed. He had never then, nor ever since, been anywhere which had so much inclined him – the most practical and in some ways unimaginative of men – to believe in magic. Not the beneficent magic of fairy godmothers and glass slippers, but the dark magic of lost arts and old gods.

The years between had passed with frightening speed. What on earth had possessed him to return to Lower Stovey? To view a possible property? Or the promptings of his sub-conscious, even a morbid curiosity or the old, fatal lure of unfinished business? When he'd seen the police car pass by on its way to the woods, his pulse had raced and he'd felt the thrill of the chase and something more, a twinge of something like anticipation, even hope. Hope that an old secret would at long last be revealed. Was it possible, he asked himself, that after so long the Potato Man was back?

Markby had been no stranger to the general area even twenty-two years earlier. He'd known the old drovers' way, even walked it with a couple of friends as a teenager. He was aware it passed through the woods. But Lower Stovey itself, that had been a new place to him, and he'd been brought here by the Potato Man.

Markby had then been a newly-promoted inspector, as his junior colleague Dave Pearce was now. Like Dave, his new rank had sat uneasily on his shoulders like a new coat. He'd been anxious to distinguish himself and determined not to make any mistakes. His superintendent had been Pelham, elderly, wily as an old dog-fox, resentful of his approaching retirement.

'There's no shame in making a mistake,' he'd told Markby, 'provided you learn by it. It's only if you go on making the same mistakes and never learn that you ought to be asking yourself if you're in the right job.'

As it turned out he'd made mistakes a-plenty over the intervening years but he still didn't believe he'd made any on that case, not that he could think of, looking back. Yet even doing everything right, by the book, hadn't produced success. Perhaps he'd been too young and inexperienced to dare to throw away the book and strike out on a line of his own. He sighed as another memory was dredged up.

Also like Dave, Markby had been newly-wed at the time. He hoped Dave's marriage lasted longer than his had done. But he thought it probably would. Dave and Tessa gave every sign of being a well-matched couple who would survive the stormy seas of marriage's early years. Unlike Rachel and himself. Their boat had sunk practically in the first gale.

Yet here he was seeking to be married again, married to Meredith. What made him think that, having failed so dismally at the first attempt, he'd do better the second time around? Perhaps only the memory of Superintendent Pelham and his homespun wisdom. Markby hoped he had learned by his mistakes. Perhaps even in the matter of marriage practice made perfect.

Stovey Woods and the Potato Man, the first case handed entirely to him in his new rank. 'See what you can make of this, Alan,' Pelham had rumbled. 'The blighter's got to be caught.'

But, to Markby's great dismay, they didn't catch him. He'd chalked up a failure on his very first case. Talk about omens. Luckily, he'd not been superstitious, though he had wondered if some jinx haunted Stovey Woods and not just the Potato Man. Perhaps that was why he hadn't mentioned being here before to Meredith. He associated his previous visit with a bitterly felt sense of having been outmanoeuvred by a mind more cunning than his own.

Over the years he'd tried to console himself whenever his thoughts turned back to that case, as they persisted in doing from time to time, despite everything. He told himself those had been the days before DNA revolutionised the way the police went about identifying the criminal. Nor had offender profiling yet reached out beyond metropolitan areas. Given these weapons, which now everyone took for granted, he might have got his man.

For the Potato Man had been a serial rapist. They didn't know how many victims he'd had because, as is the way in such cases, they only knew of the women who'd come forward. Again, twenty-two years ago, women had been more hesitant to tell their story, fearing unsympathetic police officers and a society which was inclined to blame the victim rather than the perpetrator. 'What was she doing, wandering about up in those woods on her own?' had been many people's response on hearing of a new victim. The lack of cooperation on the part of the very people who should most have wanted the rapist caught, the villagers themselves, had been one of the most frustrating aspects of the whole case.

The first victim the police had known about was a girl called Mavis Cotter, described in popular parlance as 'a bit simple'. Getting her story out of her hadn't been easy. Her vocabulary was limited and she had been in deep shock. She wasn't used to answering questions of any kind and she could neither read nor write with any competence. As her tale emerged over several frustrating interviews, she'd gone to the woods because there were blackberry bushes on the outskirts. She'd worked her way round to the far side and decided to cut home through the woods as being the quickest way.

She hadn't heard him. She hadn't seen him. Without warning something had been thrown over her head and trapped her arms. The only detail she could give was that she'd noticed an earthy smell. At first they hadn't paid too much attention to that because after all, lying on the woodland floor, she might be expected to smell earth. There had even been some who'd questioned that any of this had happened as Mavis told it, suggesting that Mavis had agreed to intercourse but taken fright afterwards and made up the story of the attack.

But Markby had been inclined to believe her because he didn't think Mavis had the mental agility to think up her story or to stick to it once she'd told it, and she certainly had answers to any sceptical questions (when you eventually got them out of her).

Why had no cloth or covering been found at the place she said the rape took place? Because he'd taken it with him. Then why had she not seen him as he ran away? Because he'd pushed her face down into the leafmould and told her not to move or he'd kill her. His voice had been gruff, sounded funny. She hadn't recognised it. Terrified, she'd remained lying there for some time, she didn't know how long, before getting the courage to look up, see she was alone, and run home. Also he'd stolen her necklace. Just a string of cheap beads but it had been Mavis's pride and joy and she'd wept as much for them as for her lost virginity – the implication of the last had not come home to her. Had she not just lost the beads, unaware the string broken? No, insisted Mavis tearfully. He pulled the necklace from her and it had hurt her throat as the string broke. Marks on her neck seemed to bear this out. Nevertheless, the villagers of Lower Stovey had generally been of the opinion that you couldn't believe anything Mavis Cotter told you because she wasn't right in the head and never had been. Only the girl's mother had insisted her daughter had been violated.

They had, however, been obliged to believe Jennifer Fernley the second victim. Jennifer had been a student and a keen walker. She'd started off to walk the Bamford way with a friend but early on the friend had twisted her ankle and dropped out. Jennifer had walked on alone. She had been passing through Stovey Woods, keeping to the marked track, when attacked. She had heard running feet behind her. What kind of running feet? Oh, not a light athletic run, more a heavy clumsy galumphing along. She'd half turned to see who it was, been aware only of a dark shape, and then he had thrown something like a sack over her head, blinding her and trapping her arms. It had smelled earthy. After the attack, he'd pushed her head into a bramble thicket, leaving her face a mass of bleeding scratches, and ordered her not to move or she'd die. His voice had been gruff and peculiar. And he'd stolen something from her. Her wristwatch.

'The bloke's a collector,' said old Pelham on being informed of this. 'He takes something from his victims as a souvenir. He's probably got a box full of trinkets at home and takes 'em out of an evening and gets off again, handling them.'

It was Markby who had suggested that what might have been thrown or pulled over the victims' heads could have been a potato sack, accounting for the earthy smell. After that, the Press had called the rapist the Potato Man. Some joker had even drawn a sketch and pinned it on the wall of the incident room. The drawing had shown a headless oval body with stick arms and legs, eyes, nose and mouth drawn in the centre of the oval. Above it was printed WANTED. Markby, angry, had torn it down.

So that was how he'd come to pay his call on the Reverend Pattinson, vicar of Lower Stovey. He'd been forewarned that Pattinson was a scholarly sort of fellow, a bit out of his time, in Markby's informant's opinion. The type happy to live among his books and take a couple of services of a Sunday and more suited to an eighteenth-century parsonage than a twentieth century one. Nevertheless, as Markby had soon discovered, Pattinson had had firm ideas about his flock and refused even to consider a rapist might be among them. They were all family men, respectable to the core, he insisted. The village was small. Everyone knew everyone else. If there was a violent psychopath living among them, someone would know.

In vain, Markby had pointed out that someone generally did know. They just didn't tell. He also drew the vicar's attention to the description they'd had of the attacker's voice: gruff, funny, peculiar, 'like an animal's, if an animal could talk', said one village woman, the third victim. It was Markby's opinion this indicated the attacker had disguised his voice and why would he do that unless he feared it would be recognised, either then or at a later date?

The vicar was adamant. Whoever the attacker was, he wasn't a Lower Stovey man. Many people walked the old drovers' way. Besides the hikers, there were tramps, New Age hippies, gypsies, wanderers of all kinds. The police should be looking among these.

There had been two more reported rapes after that, one another village woman, the other a young woman cyclist on the old way who had stopped at the woods to answer a call of nature. In the first case, the Potato Man had taken a single pearl clip earring and in the second, a copper bracelet.

And then he'd gone to ground. There had been no more rapes. The Potato Man passed into local legend, become unreal except in the memory of his victims and in the minds of the police who knew they'd lost him. Perhaps the Reverend Pattinson had been right and the man had been a wanderer who had set up some temporary home in the woods and then, when police investigations grew intrusive, had moved on. As abruptly as he'd appeared, the Potato Man had vanished.

Markby stirred in the cramped confines of the car seat and dragged his mind back to the present. He could see the police car parked on the grass, but there wasn't a soul about. Had the officers gone into the woods like the kids in the fairy-tale and were unable to find their way out? No friendly woodcutter around here to rescue anyone. Who was he, anyway, in those stories, that woodcutter? asked Markby of himself as his mind made a lateral leap. What did he represent? A woodland spirit almost certainly. And the Potato Man, what had he been?

He got out of the car and found his feet sinking into soft ground. The trees still dripped the recent rain. He squelched forward, his shoes collecting a thick clagging of mud.

As he reached the gate he heard voices and three figures emerged from the dark regiment of pines. Two were in uniform, the third mishapen by a large hump bulging on his back and clad in startling yellow.

They met up by the gate. He let them through and then held up his ID. 'Blimey, Superintendent,' said one of the patrolmen in awe. 'They sent you out here for this?'

'No,' he told them. 'I was in the village and saw you go past. It's just curiosity on my part. What have you got there?'

The uniformed man was carrying a badly-wrapped package suggesting a fish and chip supper which it manifestly wasn't. He looked down at it. 'Bones, sir.' He began to open it up carefully.

Markby recognised the paper as a crumpled ordnance survey map. The man held it out to him. A jumble of brownish objects nestled in the cup formed by the officer's hands and he could see one of them was a jawbone. Markby fought to keep his face free of expression. Could these be the bones of the lost rapist – or of one of his victims? Had one of them raised her head and seen him and met death?

'Pretty old,' he said. Yes, lying bare for twenty years or more at least. He looked at the young man in the yellow waterproof and made a guess. 'Did you find them, sir?'

'Yes,' returned the young man. 'I fell down a slope and there they were.'

'This gentleman is Dr Morgan,' explained the other officer. 'Being a medical man he knew what they were. We had a look round, just in the area where they were found. We couldn't find any more, not just in a quick search.'

'I'll see someone gets out here and has a better look.' Markby glanced at the woodland. 'But it will be difficult to search the whole wood.'

'Pity you didn't leave them where you found them, sir,' said the other officer to the young man in the yellow cape. 'You are sure you took us back to the right spot?'

'Yes, I'm sure,' said Dr Morgan testily. 'You saw for yourself the marks where I rolled down the slope. I didn't leave them there because something might have moved them before you got here. I couldn't stay with them. I told you, the mobile didn't work in there and anyway, you'd never have found me. I had to come out here and wait for you.'

'Well, you'd better come with us and make a statement,' said the first officer. He cast a slightly apprehensive glance at Markby.

'Thank you for reporting your find, Doctor,' Markby said to him politely. 'Spoiled your hike, I expect.'

'No sweat,' said the other with gloomy resignation. 'This walking break has been pretty well jinxed from the start.'

'Stovey Wood is an unlucky place,' Markby replied and the other three looked at him, startled.

They parted company. Dr Morgan divested himself of his yellow cape, revealing the hump to be a rucksack which he unslung before climbing into the back of the police car. Alan returned to his car, opened it up and leaned in to take out a newspaper. He spread a layer of sheets on the car floor. He wasn't a finicky person but there was no point in making work. He scraped some of the mud off by rubbing his sole on a tussock, sighed and clambered in behind the wheel.

Their small convoy set off, lurching back down the pot-holed track to the village. As they reached the church, Markby tapped his horn to let the men ahead know he was leaving them there. He pulled up by a lych-gate and watched the police car until it was out of sight.

Chapter Three

Ruth Aston perched unhappily on a rickety stepladder, cleaning Sir Rufus Fitzroy's memorial with a bright green feather duster.

The Fitzroy monument, as the leaflet giving the church's history called it, gave the impression of having been an expensive piece of sculpture in its day. The leaflet, however, repeated the tale that the sculptor had been down on his luck and done the work for a song. He'd been an Italian who'd arrived in Britain hoping for commissions from wealthy patrons. He had been reduced to making nymphs and satyrs for landscaped gardens when asked, almost in passing, if he couldn't produce a suitable memorial for a gentleman. Nevertheless, the result was one of the tourist attractions of Lower Stovey's parish church, in as much as it had any. Architecturally, it was no different to a host of other late medieval churches. It had lost its original stained glass when Cromwell's soldiers knocked it out with Puritan zeal. They'd pulled down its carved statues of the saints on the façade and smashed them. The only one left was one they couldn't reach, an unknown bishop high on the west front where nothing could get at him but the jackdaws.

The Victorians, with their own brand of pious hooliganism, had remodelled the chancel, taken out the fourteenth-century font and replaced it with a Gothic-style version by a follower of Pugin. They had also taken out the eighteenth-century boxpews and put in oak benches nowadays occupied by, at best, a congregation of fifteen souls on a good Sunday. The villagers, both indigenous and late-comers, weren't religious and the weekend visitors, second-home owners, spent their Sunday mornings soaking up rural atmosphere in the village pub and their afternoons getting ready for the drive back to London.

In these circumstances, Lower Stovey no longer warranted its own priest or even a weekly service. It got whoever could be spared from duties at other churches in the area on a monthly rota, though technically it was in the care of Father Holland at Bamford.

But its church did have a few interesting features and Ruth, who had made it her task to dust them off from time to time, knew them intimately.

The Fitzroy memorial displayed the deceased's periwigged marble profile held aloft by a pair of cherubs. The sculptor had chosen a side view, presumably, to make the most of the dead man's distinctive features. He had probably been thought handsome in his day with his thin face, hooded eyes and aquiline nose. Beneath the sculpture was an inscription listing his virtues, which had been many; his achievements, which had been noteworthy; his learning, which had been extensive; and the dutiful sorrow of the nephew who had inherited his fortune. To the left of the inscription was the figure of the Grim Reaper, partly veiled. He leaned on his scythe, left skeletal leg straight, right one crooked nonchalantly across it resting on its bony toes. He had the air of someone contemplating another job well done. To the right of the inscription, completely veiled, was a mourning female figure in classical robes, one finger pointing up at the portrait above lest any onlooker fail to get the message, even after all the rest.

Ruth didn't care for the Fitzroy monument. It seemed to her both ghoulish and smug. She doubted Sir Rufus had been the paragon it made him out to be and she had her doubts about the nephew's motives in having the thing put up.

Ruth herself was a small-boned woman with a tip-tilted nose and widely-spaced green eyes. Her fair hair was streaked with grey but because it had always been an ashen blonde, it looked little different now to when she'd been younger. She'd been a pretty child, a pretty young woman and now, at fifty-seven, was still attractive. At the moment she was wearing denim jeans, sensible flat shoes and a much washed-out man's rugby jersey which had belonged to her late husband. Because the jersey was way too big, the cuffs were folded back and the rest of it flapped round her sparse frame, giving her, as she put it, plenty of room for movement. It was her church-cleaning outfit.

She'd been alone in the church and liked it that way. But now behind her back came the creak of the North door opening, a burst of birdsong from the churchyard trees and the tap-tap of a stick. She knew who it was. She had no need to turn round. He'd seen her car parked outside from his cottage just a little further down the street on the opposite side. He never failed to come across for a chat. The conversation pretty well always went the same way. She'd no reason to think today would be any different. Ruth suppressed a sigh and waited for the inevitable opening question.

'Are you all right up there on that ladder, Mrs Aston?'

'Yes, thank you, Mr Twelvetrees.' Her reply was automatic. Her eye had been caught by a small greyish area on the plastered wall high above Rufus Fitzroy's head. It couldn't be accounted for by the shadow thrown by a wooden beam or carved corbel head. Surely not a damp patch? That was a problem they'd been spared so far. If it was, it would have to be reported to Father Holland.

'That don't look too good a ladder to me. You wants to get on to the church to buy a new one.' The newcomer tapped the ladder with his stick.

Fat chance, thought Ruth. She really couldn't ignore that grey patch. Someone would have to inspect it but she couldn't reach up so far from her stepladder nor did she fancy teetering up there at that height. She'd ask Kevin Jones if he'd bring a long ladder from the farm and climb up and have a look. Kevin was very obliging about that sort of thing.

'The rain's stopped. Fair old downpour, wasn't it?' Her visitor persisted in his side of the conversation despite the lack of response.

'I was in here,' mumbled Ruth.

He changed tactic. 'That's a fine bit of marble.'

Ruth surrendered. She paused in her labours and climbed half way down her stepladder to where she could turn her head without unbalancing herself.

There he was, William Twelvetrees, Old Billy Twelvetrees, so-called because there was a Young Billy, his son, even though Young Billy no longer lived in the village. Old Billy was broad as he was tall and as sturdy as this old church. He had a thick shock of white hair despite his fourscore years. He was red-faced from a lifetime in which every working day had been spent in the fields and every evening in the snug of the Fitzroy Arms. Old Billy's only infirmities were a dodgy hip, hence the stick, and an occasional spasm of angina which gave him the excuse not to attempt anything strenuous, however minimal. He raised the stick now and pointed it at the monument.

'I don't like it much,' she said. 'It's too fancy *and* morbid.'

'They knew how to do a proper monument in those days,' said Billy reproachfully.

'How are you today, Mr Twelvetrees?' asked Ruth, refusing to be drawn into a discussion on Georgian funerary art.

'I still get them twinges.' Billy tapped his chest. She was spared more detailed medical information because, as it turned out, Billy's mind was on something else. 'You seen the police car?'

Ruth stared at him. 'Which police car?'

Though he was pleased that she'd not yet heard the news and he'd be the first to tell her, yet there was a petulance in the way he spoke, as if his daily routine had been upset by the unexpected event with its unknown origins. 'He come out of the blue, roaring past, near on an hour ago and he hasn't come back. There's a speed limit in this village, police or no police. What do they want here, anyway? I looked over and saw you hadn't left your little house yet. I see your car wasn't parked out front here, so I reckoned you might not know.' He put one gnarled finger alongside his nose.

Ruth, who was a retired teacher of English, thought crossly that of course you couldn't see something which wasn't there.

Old Billy was still grumbling.

'He ought to be reported. He drove through the village like a bat outa hell. Why ain't he come back?'

Ruth glanced apprehensively towards the chancel and murmured, 'Perhaps you oughtn't to use that expression in here, Mr Twelvetrees.'

He brushed this aside. 'They've gone up to the woods, that's my reckoning. Don't know what they want up there.'

'Are you sure?' Ruth asked sharply. She tried to drive away the unwelcome feeling of something bad about to happen.

'There's only one road, ain't there?' he sulked. 'It leads to the woods and stops there. I waited by my door to see if they'd come back driving the same speed and if they had, I'd have reported them. What do you think is keeping them there, Mrs Aston?' He peered up at her. There was something grotesque about his round red face with its stubble of white whiskers and snub nose, as if one of the corbel heads above had returned to life from the hands of the medieval mason.

Ruth put out a hand and grasped a cherub's head to steady herself.

'Here, you sure you're all right, Mrs Aston? You've gone quite pale.' He moved closer, fixing her with his shrewd little eyes beneath the thatch of shaggy white brows.

'I'm all right!' Her voice was shrill in her own ears. 'I'm sure it's nothing serious.' She sought an explanation. 'Perhaps someone's lit a fire in the woods. People do silly things like that.'

'Then it'd be the fire engine, wouldn't it? Not the police.'

'If you go back outside,' said Ruth with quiet determination, 'you'll see the police come back eventually. They have to come this way. They might stop and tell you or ask you something.'

For a moment she hoped the ploy had worked. He turned as if to go and she thought she was rid of him. But the North door creaked open again and a splash of watery sunlight fell across the flagged floor. A dark silhouette framed by the Gothic arch moved and descended the two worn steps into the church. Behind the newcomer, the door closed.

Ruth's heart had given a little hop, anticipating the new arrival would be one of the policemen seen by Billy. But she could now see it was a woman and not in uniform. A stranger, which wasn't that unusual. They did get people to see the church. The woman was tall, mid-to-late-thirties, with thick brown untidy hair. Not a pretty woman, thought Ruth, but a striking one. Her features were regular, her eyebrows arched over fine eyes, possibly hazel. She wore jeans and a pale yellow cotton shirt.

'Am I disturbing you?' she asked.

'No,' Ruth replied gratefully, clambering the rest of the way down from her stepladder. 'Have you come to see the monuments?'

The visitor looked surprised. 'I didn't know there were any. Are they famous?'

'I wouldn't say famous, but they do get the odd mention. I'm Ruth Aston. I'm a churchwarden here.'

Old Billy cleared his throat loudly and tapped his stick on the flagstone.

'And this,' said Ruth resignedly, 'is Mr Twelvetrees who's lived in the village longer than anyone else.'

'S' right, I have,' said Billy.

'My name's Mitchell, Meredith Mitchell,' said the young woman. 'My partner and I are house-hunting. We've just been to see the old vicarage.'

'Mrs Aston can tell you all about the vicarage!' said Billy.

Ruth glared at him. 'Why don't you go and watch for the car coming back?' she urged again. 'I'll just show Miss Mitchell round our church.'

Billy was torn between two subjects of absorbing interest but plumped for the police car over a tourist. He muttered, 'All right,' and stomped out.

Ruth heaved a sigh of relief. 'He waits till he sees me come in here and always comes over for a chat. I suppose he's lonely, but after you've had the same conversation with him for a few times, it gets a bit much.'

She gestured at the interior of the church around them. 'The reason he said I could tell you about the vicarage is because I used to live there. My father was the last incumbent. We don't have our own vicar now, the congregation is too small. But the older locals, like Old Billy Twelvetrees, still think of me as "the vicar's daughter". Hester, the friend who shares my home, and I act as churchwardens and keep an eye on things. I feel my father would've expected it of me.' She grinned wryly.

'We haven't made any decision about the house,' said Meredith quickly. 'We just came to look at it.'

'It's in a bit of a state, isn't it?' Ruth asked sympathetically. 'It used to be very nice. The garden did, anyway. Muriel Scott isn't a gardener and that wretched dog of hers has dug holes everywhere. Did you meet Roger?'

'No, he was shut in a closet.'

'Avoid him, if you can. He slobbers. Sorry if I seem nosy, but have you got a family? I mean, the vicarage is on the big side.'

'We don't have any children. I agree, it's probably far too large. My partner came with me to see it today but he's driven up to the woods.'

Ruth eyed her with sudden suspicion. 'Why?' she asked tersely.

Meredith looked a little embarrassed. 'We saw a police car go up there earlier. Alan's a policeman himself. He had to go and find out.'

Ruth said dispiritedly, 'Oh, yes, the police car. Old Billy saw it, too. Everyone will have seen it.' She shook herself. 'Well, this is the Fitzroy monument. He's an ancestor of mine on my mother's side. Several other memorials are to Fitzroys. It's like visiting elderly relatives when I come in here. I feel they don't quite approve of me. Though quite why they should disapprove of me when they were such a disreputable bunch, I don't know. The reason the church is so big is that it was built with blood money.'

The visitor's eyebrows twitched. 'What sort of blood money?'

'Oh, well,' said Ruth. 'That's what I call it. Hubert Fitzroy gave the money to rebuild the original small church on such a grand scale after the suspicious death of his wife, Agnes. She fell from a window but there were rumours she was dead before she was pitched over the sill. The authorities must have heard the rumours but Hubert was the king's man and loyal and a woman's life had little value then. The bishop made a bit of a fuss because Agnes had been a kinswoman of his, but he quietened down when Hubert promised him this church. Hubert and

Agnes have a tomb over there, if you're interested, with their effigies on top. Hubert's is defaced. Agnes's isn't. I've often wondered about that.'

Ruth paused. She couldn't help it. The thought of the police car up there by the woods crowded everything else from her mind and jabbering away about wicked old Hubert didn't help.

She tried another ploy. 'There's no Upper Stovey, by the way. You'll have noticed that, perhaps. We're called "lower" because we're below Stovey Woods. At least, that's what people think. When I was very young, it was mostly native trees. Then the Forestry Commission moved in some time in the sixties and planted conifers.'

'Did you play up there, when you were a child? It must have been tempting,' Meredith asked her.

Ruth shook her head. 'I never liked the woods. As a schoolgirl they scared me and I never went in there unless I went with my mother to walk the dog and look for interesting bits of greenery to decorate the church. Other village children went there but I believed I might meet the Green Man.'

'I've heard of him,' said Meredith. 'He was a forest spirit, wasn't he?' She looked at Ruth, slightly puzzled. 'Is there a legend about him hereabouts?'

'Come outside,' Ruth said suddenly. 'I want to show you something on the wall under the eaves.'

Outside the church the sun had come out and was doing its best to dry up the rain. It had its work cut out in the churchyard which was covered with long grasses and self-set bushes and generally unkempt. Poking up among the grass-stalks and between the irregular humps of the old burials were the tall plants of honesty, with spade-shaped leaves and clusters of purple flowers. Meredith remarked she'd seen the same plant growing profusely in the vicarage garden and they agreed it must have migrated from there to colonize the churchyard. Tombstones and monuments emerged from the jungle of weeds and flowers, lichen-encrusted and lop-sided. An angel on a nearby pillar looked about to topple full-length at any moment, weighed down by its useless stone wings. A solitary magpie, which had been perched on the stone head, flapped away at their approach.

'One for sorrow,' Ruth said aloud and looked around almost desperately for a second. Two for joy? No, just the one.

She thrust the superstition from her mind and began to apologize for the state of it all as the two of them picked their way round the building. 'We used to pay Old Billy to tidy it but then he couldn't do it any longer because of his hip and his angina. It looks just terrible. No new burials take place here, although I suppose if any of the really old villagers, Billy for example, expressed a wish to be buried here we'd try to find a spot. Father Holland always says we should respect a wish for a person to be buried among his own kin.'

They stopped and she pointed upwards. 'Do you see up there, the gargoyle?'

Meredith looked up in the direction of her pointing finger. Some kind of mythical beast formed the waterspout. She said, 'The dragon thing?'

'Yes. Now look to the left, along the gutter and down a bit.'

Meredith looked as directed. 'Oh,' she said. 'There's a carving, a face, on the side on the church right up under the eaves.'

Ruth said soberly, 'That's him.'

A ray of sunlight caught the carving as she spoke, enabling them to see more clearly a cunning face peering from a thicket of leaves.

'Some people,' said Ruth, 'think he's a Celtic god, Cernunnos, but my father believed he was part of a far older tradition, before even the Celts, perhaps neolithic. There's another line of thought which links him with the rites of Dionysus, a sort of west European version of them. My father was doubtful about that. At any rate, the woods are of ancient origin. My father's researches told him they'd always been a sacred place. There's a sort of earthwork in there, mostly overgrown, which my father believed might have been a place of sacrifice. There are plenty of roof bosses and pillar capitals in other churches which show foliate heads, as my father liked to call them, to distinguish them from the real Green Man. It became a fairly common decoration, just a flight of fancy in many cases. But the original Green Man, whatever he was, lived on in people's subconscious. The men who built this church believed in him all right, the masons and workmen. They knew that this church, representing the new beliefs, challenged the old ones. So they put the Green Man up there, where he looks out towards Stovey Woods, his domain. Inside the church, he's always a sort of trespasser. But when we go to the woods, then we're the trespassers.'

She saw that the visitor was looking at her a little strangely and Ruth forced a laugh. 'Sorry to go on so. It was a particular interest of my father's so I was brought up on all this. I don't believe in him, of course. It's just that Stovey Woods have a reputation. Over the years things have happened there, not nice things. That's why I didn't like it when Old Billy told me a police car had gone there. I hope it doesn't mean more mischief.'

She had intrigued her visitor who looked as if she was about to ask what kind of mischief. Ruth bit her tongue and wished she hadn't been so garrulous. What had led her to burble on about the woods? The reason, she supposed, was that they were never far from her mind. They were part of that jumble of suppressed memories which lurked like a fishy monster in a lake, surfacing when least expected. But she was in luck. Her companion had been diverted and instead of putting the dreaded question, was pointing up the road which led to the woods.

'The police car's coming back,' Meredith said. 'And there's Alan's car behind it.'

The two women began to walk towards the lych-gate, Ruth trying to look natural, not to hurry, not to seem eager to hear any news. And I don't want to hear bad news, I couldn't bear it, she thought desperately. What shall I do if . . .

The police car rattled past without stopping. There was a youngish man, in his thirties, sitting in the back of it. What had he done? wondered Ruth. The following car, however, slowed and drew up. A tall, thin, fair-haired man in a pullover and chinos got out. He came towards them, smiling.

Meredith said, 'Ruth, this is Alan Markby. This is Mrs Aston, Alan. She's the churchwarden here and her father was the last resident vicar. She grew up in the vicarage.'

Ruth found herself blushing. 'I was just showing Meredith our church. It's not very active, I'm afraid.' She drew a deep breath. He looked a nice man. He'd tell her, wouldn't he? 'What happened?' she asked. 'Up at the woods?'

The man shrugged his shoulders and a fringe of fair hair fell over his forehead. He bore, thought Ruth, a superficial resemblance to old Sir Rufus with his thin features and patrician bearing.

'Nothing to get excited about,' he said. He spoke with that kindly firmness which Ruth associated with those who carry their authority as if it were natural to them. She found she was both relieved and disappointed. That was policemen for you. Like doctors and priests, they were custodians of other people's secrets. They never parted with information. She should have known. She felt embarrassed because she knew she shouldn't have asked.

But Meredith beside her had no inhibitions and urged, 'Oh, come on, Alan. We're dying to know.'

'You are, you mean,' he replied good-naturedly. 'Keep it to yourselves. A hiker sheltering from the rain found some old bones.'

Ruth heard a gasp escape her lips. She faltered, 'Bones? What kind of bones?'

'Not a skeleton, nothing like that. Just a few and we'll have to wait and see what the experts make of them.'

'How awful, do you mean, not animal?' Things were going from bad to worse. Ruth thought her horror must show in her face to a degree which even he must think was more than might reasonably be expected from someone hearing the news.

'Unlikely,' he said. 'Human, all right. But as I say, pretty old and not many of them. I doubt they'll be easy to identify. We'll try, naturally.' He must at last have taken notice of her pale face and gaping mouth. 'It may be an archaeological find,' he said. 'These things turn up from time to time, unearthed by wildlife.'

Ruth pulled herself together. 'Oh, well, then that's what it probably is. How – how interesting.'

'Ruth's been telling me about the woods,' Meredith told him. 'And how very old they are.'

Ruth wondered whether the man called Alan heard her. His mind seemed to be running on something else. He looked at both of them for a moment quite blankly, then blinked and said rapidly, 'If you've finished here, Meredith, perhaps we should be getting back.'

'Yes, sure,' Meredith said, sounding a little surprised. 'Thank you for the guided tour, Ruth. It was really fascinating.'

'Not at all.' As they started to walk away, Ruth called after them on impulse, 'If you come back to Lower Stovey, to take another look at the vicarage, please come and have a cup of tea with us. My cottage is at the end of Church Lane. It's called The Old Forge because once it was a forge and I share it with an old friend. Do come, Hester and I don't get many visitors.'

They promised they'd come. She watched them get into the car and drive off. It was a nightmare. After all these years, how could it have happened? Why had she asked them to come and see her? To learn what the police found out? The man wouldn't gossip, not him, not a police officer himself. But the woman, Meredith, might. Then there was Hester. What would Hester say when she heard the news? She'd been asked to keep it to herself but she'd have to tell Hester.

There was a movement to her right in a bushy young yew. Its sprays of dark green needle-like leaves quivered and parted. A wreathed face with small malicious eyes and a snub nose appeared. Ruth gave a little shriek.

The face vanished. The bush shook again and Old Billy Twelvetrees emerged from his hiding place. She'd quite forgotten him but she should have known he'd be hanging around.

'I heard 'un,' he said. His tongue ran over his withered lips and his expression had grown thoughtful. 'Bones, eh? Human bones.' He drew a deep rasping breath and looked down at the grassy strip between two graves where his own stout boots were planted. 'That's a turn-up for the books, ain't it?'

42

* * *

'Bones?' Meredith ventured as they drove back to Bamford.

'Bones. The countryside is full of them. It doesn't have to be sinister.'

'You don't sound as if you believe that.'

His manner was too off-hand by far, she thought. You don't fool me, Alan Markby, what's going on here, eh?

'I don't disbelieve or believe anything,' he was saying virtuously. 'The bones were found by a young doctor walking the old drovers' way. He turned off into the woods when it started to rain, fell down a bank and *voilà*! Found himself looking at a mixed collection of odd bones which he recognised as human.'

Meredith thought about it. 'It seemed to upset Ruth.'

'Who? Oh, Mrs Aston. She's old Pattinson's daughter, you say? Perhaps I should have mentioned I met her father years ago.'

Meredith, glancing at him, said, 'I'm sorry if I seemed to make a big deal out of your being here before.'

He shook his head. 'I should have told you. You were right about the old vicarage. I don't know why I brought you out to view it. I knew it was a big place, too big.'

'I'll go back to the estate agents,' Meredith offered. 'There must be other houses.' She leaned back in the front passenger seat. 'Did you get a look at the church when you were last here?'

'Is it interesting?'

'Oh yes. There's a carving on the outer wall of the Green Man. That's what we'd been looking at when you came back. Ruth's father was very interested in the legend.'

'There's a farm,' Alan said suddenly. 'It's called Greenjack Farm. It's back there alongside the woods. I went there when I came before. The Green Man legend must be connected with the name.'

There they left the subject, Meredith with a half-resolve to visit the public library and look up the Green Man, Markby clearly with things other than myth on his mind.

Chapter Four

It was no great distance from the church to Ruth's house. She would have walked it, had she not needed the car to transport her own vacuum cleaner to push over the vestry carpet. She gave a little snort as she struggled to wedge the unwieldy old machine across the back seat. Carpet indeed! It was hardly worthy of the name. It was just a layer of backing threads with traces of blue and red wool marking a lost pattern. It had been down there in her father's day and probably in his predecessor's. There was little chance of it ever being replaced now. Perhaps she and Hester ought just to roll it up and burn it.

But she knew they wouldn't. The vestry carpet symbolised, for her, Lower Stovey and its resistance to change. Some people liked being stuck in a time-warp. Ruth didn't. She saw it as a rejection of enlightenment and hope. Bit by bit, far from being preserved, they were being eroded away to nothing of any real meaning. Perhaps they'd turn into a community like Brigadoon, only coming to life once in a hundred years. Sometimes, when in philosophical mood, she wondered whether they all existed, or only dreamed they existed, like the Chinese sage and the butterfly her father had told her about when she was a child. Am I a man dreaming I am a butterfly? Or a butterfly dreaming I am a man? But Ruth knew she was real, Lower Stovey was real. It existed because the woods existed. Nothing that was the cause of such torment could be anything less than reality.

She drove the short distance at a sedate pace, turning into the drive at the side of the Old Forge. She stopped, got out and dragged out the vacuum cleaner again, leaving it standing like a solitary sentinel on the path while she put her car away. She intended to carry it indoors, but somehow, after closing the garage door and lugging the vacuum cleaner as far as the back door, she abandoned it once more to walk to the far end of her tidy garden and stare over the hedge at distant Stovey Woods. She often found herself doing this. The woods exerted a horrid fascination over her. She felt their pull. On rainy days like this they looked nearer. Their dark mass nestled in a dip in the landscape. Like a sump, Ruth thought, into which everything bad, everything nauseous, everything shameful had drained.

Beneath her feet, the ground was wet and grass trailed watery fingers around her ankles. Everything had a fresh-washed look and was cool after the recent stifling heat. It smelled different, too. Damp earth. Sodden leafmould. Churchyard smells. Smells of the grave.

'Ruth? What are you doing?'

She jumped at the sound of the voice and turned guiltily. It seemed to be her day for having people jump out of the greenery at her. Hester had emerged from the further side of a privet hedge where she'd been working unseen. Her arms were filled with red rhubarb stalks and their huge dark green leaves like a grotesque bouquet.

'I've pulled these because they've grown so big. After all this rain there will be more tomorrow. I've been thinking I might make rhubarb and ginger jam. Not with this lot, though. I'll make a pudding with this.'

Ruth was relieved to hear it. They had more jam of all varieties than they could possibly eat as it was. Making jam was one of the things which Hester did to show her gratitude for being allowed to live here with Ruth. Theirs was a long friendship. They'd been students together as young girls, sitting up half the night to discuss obscure authors, dishing the university gossip, planning stupendous futures. And this is how we've ended up, thought Ruth. The pair of us, stuck out here in this neck of the woods, with teaching careers behind us and in front of us, what?

46

What, indeed? Before Billy Twelvetrees had arrived with his disconcerting piece of news, she would have said nothing lay ahead but a humdrum retirement. It had been enlivened to date by occasional outings to Oxford for old time's sake or to Cheltenham for the National Hunt racing fixtures. They were modest gamblers, really only flutterers, but they enjoyed looking at the horses and mixing with the crowds of Irish visitors who always thronged the spring festival. The buzz of excitement was infectious. They rarely went to London. Its roads were clogged with traffic and fumes, its pavements peopled with hurrying pedestrians, pale of face, blank of eye, stressed of manner. The joy of the racing crowd was totally absent. If London crowds were aware of anything it was time's winged chariot. Ruth and Hester had reached the stage of their lives when they no longer had to make time their master.

They hadn't always shared a home, she and Hester, but they'd kept in touch throughout their careers. Hester hadn't married. Ruth had married late. It was the death of her husband which had brought Hester to Lower Stovey, at first just to stay for a few weeks and keep her company. It had been during a summer. Hester was still teaching at the time and her school on holiday. But she'd longed to take early retirement. She'd had enough. So somehow it had been agreed that Hester would give in her notice when she returned to her school and at the end of the following term return to Lower Stovey for an unspecified period until she sorted herself out. The sorting out had resolved into a permanent niche at the Old Forge.

Occasionally, Hester would say with a nervous giggle, 'Really, Ruth, it's about time you chucked me out!'

Ruth could always read the fear in her eyes when she said it. She knew what Hester wanted was reassurance and she always gave it.

'Nonsense, what should I do without you?'

Relief would surge into Hester's plain, weather-beaten face and that evening she'd cook some complicated dish as a thank you. She was a very good cook. Ruth, a slap-dash worker in the kitchen whose sponges left the oven as flat as biscuits and whose pastry required a breadknife to cut it, appreciated that Hester had taken over the cooking. It was just that Hester didn't always know when to stop. French sauces and savoury curries, followed by confections of cream or meringue, were all very well but sometimes Ruth did long for sausage and mash or good old beans on toast.

'Crumble would be nice,' she said now.

Hester beamed at her. 'Then crumble it shall be. I'll just chop the leaves off and chuck them on the compost heap. They're poisonous, you know.' She shook a stick of rhubarb topped with its umbrella of a leaf at Ruth.

'Rhubarb?'

'Not the sticks. Just the leaves. You mustn't eat the leaves.'

'Who'd want to?' asked Ruth logically.

'You'd be surprised what people do,' returned Hester in a sinister voice. 'Do you remember that awful row there was a couple of years ago at the garden show when someone entered rhubarb as a fruit and someone else objected and said it was a vegetable. Then the first person, who was it? I do believe it was Evie at the pub. She said how could it be a vegetable when you ate it for a pudding? I think they solved the problem by putting it in a class on its own in the end.'

Ruth smiled at her. It wasn't only being relieved of the cooking chore which made it nice to have Hester there. She shared the running costs of the house and the car, both of which were useful. She was someone to talk to of an evening in the relaxed manner of old friends. Ruth was fond of Hester and, though it referred to a time she tried to forget, she owed her a debt which could never be repaid. She'd left the Old Forge to Hester in her will in case she pre-deceased her friend. It seemed only fair and anyway, there was no one else, was there? No one else to leave anything to.

'What are you looking at?' asked Hester, clumping towards her in her sensible shoes. Her baggy corduroy trousers, damp-stained at the hems, flapped around her ankles.

'At Stovey Woods.'

There was a moment's silence. Hester asked gruffly, 'Why?'

'Old Billy Twelvetrees came into the church and told me the police had gone up there. It seems someone found some bones.'

'Animal,' said Hester.

'No, human.'

'Old Billy's got it wrong.'

Ruth shook her head. 'There was some sort of policeman and his girlfriend who'd come to look over the old vicarage. The woman came into the church and later the man came to join us and told us human bones had been found. Old Billy overheard him, worse luck.'

Hester came closer and said fiercely, 'They'll be historical. You know how ancient the old drovers' road is. It runs slap through the woods. Some animal, digging around, has dug up a medieval peasant or old gypsy burial, you'll see.'

Ruth turned towards her and smiled again. 'Yes, Hester, you're probably right. I couldn't help but wonder, you know, just for the moment, whether they might have found Simon.'

They stared at one another. Then Hester rallied and said, 'Nonsense.'

'He has to be somewhere, doesn't he?' Ruth replied.

'He doesn't have to be in bally Stovey Woods!'

They'd had this argument before. Ruth abandoned it, not because she admitted Hester might be right, but because she knew she, Ruth, was and she didn't need Hester or anyone else to agree.

They were walking back to the house. Ruth let Hester proceed her into the kitchen and watched her run the tap over the rhubarb stalks.

'You wouldn't think they needed any more washing after that rain,' Hester said in an attempt, Ruth knew, to turn the conversation away from the grim discovery.

It would take more than that to wipe it from Ruth's mind. But thinking of Billy Twelvetrees, she suggested, 'If you do make jam with the rest of the rhubarb, why don't you give a couple of jars to Dilys or drop them by old Billy's place when you're passing? I'm sure the old fellow would like some.'

It had been a spur of the moment suggestion and it left her feeling she was somehow trying to buy the old man off, which was stupid. Or was it?

'Oh God,' she burst out and put her hands over her face.

'Come on!' Hester was there, comforting, awkward and sincere, patting her with wet hands. 'The chances of these wretched bones being – being *his*, are a million to one. You don't even know – no one knows – where *he* is.'

'I've always known where he was,' said Ruth, taking her hands from her face. 'He's been in Stovey Woods, all this time, waiting for us to find him and now, someone has. You'll see.'

The discovery of the bones meant there was something Ruth had to do. Something she should have done years ago. She left Hester happily turning the rhubarb into crumble for lunch, their main meal of the day. Ruth slipped into her bedroom and took a small rosewood box from the recesses of her wardrobe.

It was a pretty little object, a Victorian traveller's companion, originally with various compartments to hold the necessary ointments, panaceas and other medical necessities of the day. It had belonged to her father and it must have been he, she supposed, who'd removed the internal compartments, leaving the stripped box to be used as a receptacle for papers. He'd kept bills and receipts relating to the fabric of the church in it. She set it on her bed and retrieved the key which she kept under a vase on her mantelshelf. She unlocked it and opened it by the brass handle on the middle of the lid. A familiar faint odour rose into her nostrils compounded of memories of its original use, a tang of sal volatile, a heavier sickly whiff which might, she supposed, have been laudanum, the sweetness of lavender oil, sharpness of peppermint and an exotic hint of oil of cloves. It still held papers, envelopes, worn by much fingering, yellowing a little.

Ruth took them out and spread them on the duvet cover. The sight of the handwriting in which the words *Miss Ruth Pattinson* were scrawled, caused a hard lump to form somewhere in her midriff. It wasn't grief that she felt, that had died long ago. It wasn't anger, that had died too.

The effort of keeping its flames burning had been too much. So, was it shame? Or just something as mundane as embarrassment? Never underestimate embarrassment as an emotion, she thought ruefully. More actions had been undertaken – or failed to be taken – because of it, than many a better respected motive.

Her fingers moved as if of their own impulse, picking up the nearest envelope, slipping the letter from inside. The pain in her midriff grew worse. How eagerly she'd torn open the envelope the first time, all those years ago. How desperate to read its contents, interpreting every word as a word of love and devotion, believing its casual assurances that she was the only girl he cared about. In her own mind, then, these shallow efforts had ranked with the great love-letters of history.

'Stupid, stupid, stupid!' she whispered.

Not stupid, not back then. Just naive and in love and wanting something so much she'd convinced herself it was real. For a long time now she'd read these words for what they really were, spur of the moment declarations inspired by hormones, not love. A young man's words, a young man at heart still a boy, wanting to be in a man's world but loath to quit the freedoms of youth, to accept the responsiblities a man's world brought with it. In addition, a young man deeply flawed, selfish and spoiled.

There were takers and givers in this life, so her mother had once told her. There'd been a streak of cynicism in the late Mrs Pattinson, perhaps derived from long years with an unworldly husband for ever trying to see the best in his unpromising flock. Ruth knew her mother had been right in this. Ruth had been a giver but he – oh, he had been a taker, all right.

Ruth shoved the letter back in its envelope and gathered it up with the others. She couldn't burn them in the house, Hester might walk in and see her doing it. Hester would understand but she didn't want Hester to know. She'd burn them in the garden. It was wet underfoot out there, but that didn't matter, a few papers needed only a match put to them.

She slipped past the kitchen. From within came the sound of a wooden spoon being scraped round a bowl and Hester humming to herself. Out the front door Ruth went, round the side of the house, scurrying down the garden path, behaving like a sneakthief on her own property. Behind the privet hedge she set to work. It wasn't as easy as she'd thought it would be. Just putting a match to an envelope and its contents resulted in the corner smouldering, turning brown, going out. She had to take each letter from its envelope. The first single sheet she set match to, floated up into the air to her alarm and still burning, fluttered across the sky towards the house.

'Damn!' said Ruth aloud.

Each sheet had to be separated, screwed into a twist. She piled them up and finally managed to set light to the lot. They burned satisfactorily, though blackened wisps still floated away, betraying her presence and activity. She just hoped Hester didn't look out of the kitchen window.

Hester hadn't, but someone else had. Someone she'd quite forgotten.

'What are you doing there?'

The voice came from close behind her. Ruth jumped, squeaked, and spun round.

A solid figure in a quilted nylon coat and Crimplene trousers stood watching her. Dilys Twelvetrees, a middle-aged female version of Old Billy. Her broad face, normally devoid of any expression, was alive with curiosity.

'Burning rubbish,' said Ruth firmly.

The expression on Dilys's face turned to one of cunning. 'Burning old letters,' she said.

Ruth wanted to snap that it was none of her business. Instead she muttered, 'Old receipts and business stuff.'

Dilys rightly dismissed this pathetic invention. She put her head on one side and contemplated Ruth. 'You got left, didn't you?' she said.

'What on earth do you mean?' Ruth heard herself ask.

'You got left,' repeated Dilys patiently. 'Like me. Your feller left you, too.'

'Nonsense,' said Ruth. 'You knew my husband. He died.'

'Not him,' said Dilys scornfully. 'Before him. A young feller.' She glanced at the patch of blackened scraps and feathery pale ash. 'Surprised you kept 'em so long,' she said.

With that, as if she knew she'd uttered an unanswerable statement, Dilys turned and plodded off on her way home.

How could she know? How could the woman know? Was it just by some instinct or – Ruth's heart pounded at the thought – had Dilys found the key, worked out that it opened the box and read the letters? She hadn't thought Dilys had that much curiosity in her. Now she wasn't sure.

Drat the woman, thought Ruth. Drat the whole Twelvetrees clan.

Dilys was employed by them as a cleaner for the 'rough work', the scrubbing of the ancient flags on the kitchen floor, the cleaning of windows, the taking up of rugs and beating the living daylights out of them in the backyard. In winter, Dilys cleaned out the log-burning stove in the sitting room. Dilys was good at peeling spuds and carrots, releasing Hester for the making of her complicated sauces.

Of course, Ruth and Hester could easily have managed all these things between them. But what other work would Dilys have found in Lower Stovey? Employing Dilys was what the Reverend Pattinson, Ruth's father, would have called an act of Christian charity. What was more, the link between their two families covered two generations.

Many years ago, Dilys's mother had been employed by Ruth's mother to scrub the vicarage floors. Dilys's brother, Young Billy, had mown the vicarage lawns before he left the village to make his way in the outside world. When Ruth and her late husband had returned to Lower Stovey to set up home in the Old Forge, Dilys had turned up on the doorstep on their first morning there, stolidly announcing, 'You'll want me to do for you, will you?' Not a question, just a statement.

So why was it, then, that the sight of Dilys's shapeless form and work-worn hands added to that sense of guilt which Ruth seemed to have been destined from birth to carry around with her, weighing down her shoulders and unable to be shed. Sinbad had the Old Man of the Sea and she, Ruth, had Dilys.

Ruth could remember, as clearly as if it had happened yesterday, the very first time she'd set eyes on Dilys Twelvetrees. They'd both been five years old and it had been their joint first day at school.

The school, of course, had been Lower Stovey Church Primary School. It no longer existed as a school. Dwindling numbers had led to its closure some years back, followed by sale and redevelopment. The buildings had been converted into a close of maisonettes, done rather cleverly. The people who lived in School Close were not villagers, although they were residents. They commuted to jobs in Bamford or elsewhere. They might show their faces occasionally of an evening in the Fitzroy Arms, but otherwise they were invisible, taking no part in village life. Or, as Ruth phrased it to herself, what passed for life in Lower Stovey these days.

The Reverend Pattinson had believed it right and proper that his daughter should attend primary school with the other village children. The inevitable boarding school would come later. This wasn't because her parents couldn't bear to send her miles away. It would be nice to think that, but untrue. Had they considered it the right thing to do, they'd have ferried her back and forth to some private school. But they had considered it right she should attend Lower Stovey Church Primary. Possibly they'd also been happy to save on fees for a few years and the chore of the daily school run. But chiefly the vicar (more than his wife who knew the village rather better than he did) believed that Ruth would learn from mixing with the village children and they from association with her. Moreover, the parents of the children would see that the vicar and his family were approachable, human, one of them.

Which they weren't and couldn't ever be, thought Ruth crossly. Her four years at Lower Stovey Church Primary had been wretched. Good intentions don't always result in good outcomes. From the start she'd been an outsider and an oddity, held by the other children in contempt. She talked posh. Her father didn't work with his hands at a proper job. He was a Holy Joe who sat in his study among books. In Ruth's hearing at school, the children, quoting their parents and finding the words hilarious, referred to their spiritual leader as a bit of an old woman.

But his wife, now, that had been a different matter. Ruth's mother, prior to her marriage, had been Miss Fitzroy, last of that line. She'd grown up at the Manor, (nowadays a retirement home for the well-heeled elderly). Older villagers, ignoring her marriage, had continued to address her as 'Miss Mary'. The vicar's wife drove a car, which none of the village women did fifty years ago. She drove it once a week to Bamford to have her hair washed and set at a proper hairdresser's, and twice a year made an expedition by train to London where, villagers whispered in awe, she had her hair cut in Harrods' hairdressing department. The village women gave each other home perms which, in damp weather, frizzed and made the wearer look as if she'd had an electric shock.

On her first day at school Ruth had been confused at midday by being told it was now dinner-time and if she wasn't having her dinner at school, she could go home, returning by two o'clock. At the vicarage they ate dinner in the evening. She caused hilarity by saying, 'Oh, you mean lunch.' Only she'd probably said 'luncheon' because the vicar was fussy about details like that. It was one of many *faux pas* Ruth was never allowed to forget.

On that first day she'd been seated next to Dilys Twelvetrees and been distressed by the strange odour emanating from the other child. Later she was able to identify this odour as being compounded of rancid chip fat and cabbage water, the smells of which clung to Dilys's clothes which were seldom washed. As was Dilys, come to that. To be fair, the majority of village parents wouldn't have dreamed of sending their offspring to school other than clean and tidy, the boys with hair cut to military shortness and girls with tightly-braided pigtails. But the Twelvetrees family, Ruth had soon discovered, was not as other families. They were regarded by other villagers with mistrust and unease. They, too, were outsiders of a kind and Ruth sometimes wondered if the class teacher had seated the two little girls together for that reason, calculating that individual isolation might cause them to strike up a friendship. If so, it hadn't worked. Dilys might be one of 'them Twelvetrees lot' but she joined in the general contempt of Ruth.

Also at the school, but older and in senior grades, were Sandra and Young Billy (already so-called) Twelvetrees. Ruth had little to do with Young Billy who was an amiable, unteachable ten-year-old, given to 'skiving off'. Sandra and Dilys were poorly nourished and badly dressed. Dilys was the worst dressed because she had to wear Sandra's cast-offs and they'd already been cast off by someone else. On one terrible day, Dilys had appeared in a last year's cotton dress of Ruth's, bought for a few pence at a church jumble sale. It was too tight in the bodice and where the hem had been let down it was a different colour. Ruth had been embarrassed by this, but Dilys had hated her for it and contrived to spill green poster paint over Ruth's laboriously just-finished painting of the Queen in her Coronation Coach. In winter, the Twelvetrees sisters wore knitted pixie hoods. Their shoes were never cleaned, neither were their teeth. Which is why, thought Ruth sadly, I've got my own teeth now and poor Dilys has got a false set.

Moreover, there was one thing about both Dilys and Sandra which secretly fascinated and frightened the infant Ruth. From time to time their arms and legs sported unexplained bruises, not the sort caused by falling down and scraping your knees in the playground. These were long narrow bruises and appeared in clusters. She never dared to ask Dilys about them.

How on earth did my father ever imagine I'd fit in at Lower Stovey Primary? wondered Ruth now, not for the first time. The teachers had been kind but it had made matters worse, causing her to be dubbed 'teacher's pet' and to have 'goody-goody' chanted at her. It was true she never misbehaved. She couldn't. She was the vicar's daughter and he had told her, as had her mother, that she must set an example. An example of what? At five you really don't understand. Ruth had interpreted it as meaning you always did as you were told and never opened your mouth without permission.

Originally she was to have suffered at Lower Stovey Church Primary until she was eleven. But one day, when she was nine, she had come home and innocently repeated some new words learned that morning in the playground. These words (she had no idea what they meant) were apparently so wicked as to necessitate her being taken away from the school almost at once. The day she'd walked out of the gates for the last time had been one of the happiest of her life.

After that she'd been dispatched, despite her tender years, to boarding school, a wind-swept institution on Dartmoor which might have shared much of its regime with the celebrated prison there.

From then on, Lower Stovey had only been visited at holiday times and later, in university vacations. Her mother's letters would occasionally mention some village event which would update Ruth on her former schoolmates. Sandra married a soldier and went off to foreign climes with him, something it was hard to imagine. Dilys got married too, but was abandoned by her husband within a year. She'd returned home to her parents, which suited them as Mrs Twelvetrees (who also, from time to time, had sported odd bruises), had been rendered housebound by an affliction of her legs. She died not long afterwards and Dilys stayed on to keep house for her ageing father. Her married name was abandoned by common consent and she'd become Dilys Twelvetrees again, as if her marriage had been a sort of blip and could be ignored.

So it had been until Ruth's return to Lower Stovey with her husband some twelve years earlier. Both her parents were dead by then. The vicarage was a private residence inhabited by Muriel Scott and Roger, then a boisterous pup of whom his mistress would blithely assure everyone that 'he'd quieten down as he got older'. If only! Age, in Roger's case, seemed to have disposed of what little canine reason he'd ever possessed. The school was on the verge of closing. Somehow, seeing Dilys on the doorstep that first morning, far from being unwelcome, had been almost a comfort. Something at least was the same. Probably exactly the same. Ruth wondered whether, in secret, Dilys still despised her.

Chapter Five

I

Dave Pearce stood before the bathroom mirror, his mouth opened as wide as was physically possible, and performed a series of stretches and contortions in an effort to inspect one of his own teeth. The mirror was inconveniently placed, not high enough for him. Tessa insisted that fixed any higher, it would be too high for her. It meant he had to half-crouch in an attitude hard to maintain. The light wasn't good enough. If he approached the mirror any closer, his breath steamed it up and he couldn't see at all. He hooked a finger into his lower lip, pulling it down, and wrenched his head sideways producing one more face which would have won him any girning competition. The tooth looked all right to him. So why, then, when he ate anything on that side, or drank anything very hot or cold, did it suddenly feel as if someone had jabbed a red-hot needle in his jaw?

He gave up the attempt and finished shaving. He supposed he could stop off at a dentist's surgery on the way to work and make an appointment. He clattered down the stairs. As he reached the hall, the front door opened and Tessa appeared, flushed of face, hauling a reluctant brindled lurcher in her wake.

'I've walked Henry,' she said in a voice which held layers of meaning.

'I said I'd do it,' offered Pearce lamely.

'Saying's not much good, is it? I didn't think you were ever coming out of that bathroom. I've just run round the playing field with him. But tonight you can walk him. It's your turn!'

'All right, I'll walk him!' Pearce's temper began to fray.

Henry collapsed on the floor, put his head on his paws and rolled his eyes upward, watching his owners with interest.

'I know why you were so long up there!' announced Tessa, arms akimbo. 'It's that flipping tooth. I told you to make a dental appointment.'

'I will, I'll make one,' he promised.

'Yeah, like you promised to walk Henry. You put everything off, David.'

He knew he was in trouble when she called him David.

'I promise you,' he said, 'that some time today, if I'm not too busy, I'll ring the dentist's and fix an appointment. And when I get home the first thing I'll do is walk Henry.'

'I'm going to be late for work,' she swept on effortlessly to a new grievance. 'You'll have to drop me off.'

'It means going out —' Pearce began but didn't finish. 'All right,' he said. 'Get your skates on or we'll both be late.'

'Get *my* skates on? You know, Dave, for someone with such a responsible job as you've got, you're not very good at taking responsibilities at home. You can't just switch off, you know, like a – a telly. One life inside the box, another out. I mean,' Tessa became aware that her simile was leading down a complicated path. 'Of course, I don't want you to bring your work home. I don't bring my work home, do I? I get loads of hassle at the building society. But I don't leave my sense of responsibility behind when I leave at the end of the day, either. Now you —'

'For crying out loud, get in the car!' exploded Pearce.

'There's no need to shout. You're not arresting me, you know. I've not some yobbo with a skinful of lager. If you'll just hang on a moment, I've got to change my shoes.'

'Can't you change them in the car?'

'I wouldn't have to change them at all if I hadn't had to walk Henry.

And I wouldn't have had to walk Henry if you hadn't been stuck in the bathroom messing with that tooth. If we're running late this morning, David Pearce,' Tessa finished this *tour de force* of logic, 'it's because you're scared of going to the dentist. So there,' she added.

Sometimes, thought Pearce, police work was a doddle compared with domestic life. He sighed.

Henry groaned in sympathy from the carpet.

II

Alan Markby sat at his desk. He'd been there since early morning, arriving while the cleaners were still at work. Yet when he'd picked up the phone he'd found that someone had arrived in Records though the off-hand tone with which the phone was answered, suggested whoever it was had just got in and was taking off his coat.

'What is it?' asked the voice curtly. It added loudly to someone else, 'Yeah, you can bring me a cup of coffee and a bacon sarnie.'

Markby identified himself and was mildly amused by the change in attitude and tone.

'Yes, sir. Sorry, Mr Markby, didn't know it was you. I just got in. What can we do for you?'

'You can look out an old file for me,' said Markby. 'It was a serial rapes case, unsolved, and the perpetrator was nicknamed the Potato Man.' He gave the date and location of the rapes.

'Get it up to you directly,' promised the voice.

Markby walked down the corridor and helped himself to a brew from the machine there. He presumed it to be tea because he'd pressed the button marked 'Tea' but without this clue, anyone could have been misled. Though normally he didn't take sugar he selected the sweetened version because it masked the usual taste of burnt cocoa which seem to dominate any beverage provided by this dispenser.

He carried it back to his office, his footsteps echoing in a building still half-empty. Back in his office, he stood with it in his hand, staring from the window, not seeing the asphalted parking area, the moving cars below like so many shiny beetles, and the ant-like clusters of men and women. He saw Stovey Woods.

Occasionally his gaze drifted from the scene outside to the top of his desk and the crumpled package lying there. He murmured, 'Who are you?'

Just bones? Or bones which could still speak to them? In the days before X-rays, a skeleton had been the symbol of mortality, the intricate and unlikely framework of the human body, only seen once its owner had long gone, dust to dust. It pranced, grinning, along the façade of many a medieval cathedral in a *danse macabre*, reminding the other revellers, the monk, the lady, the knight, the peasant, of that end to which all must come. That symbolism had faded in the glare of scientific advance. Yet perhaps true awareness of reality lay not with modern scientists and their machines but with the sculptor of long ago. Even the sad little collection on his desk represented a living, breathing being. Flesh had clothed those bones once. That jaw had moved up and down in speech, chewing food, singing a popular song, and he had to put a name to him or her. The necessity was like a nagging pain. It wouldn't leave him, the question would never cease to plague him morning, noon and night. Was he looking at the mortal remains of the Potato Man? Or at the pitiful remnants of one of his victims? Or, indeed, someone else altogether? He mustn't let himself become so convinced that the bones related to the old case that he ignored other possibilities.

Though the bones were few, they contained the lower jaw and that, in turn, contained something which might be the invaluable key to identity. He'd already been on the phone to his own dentist, confirming his suspicions. Expensive dental work ought to be traceable, especially that kind.

Markby allowed himself a wry smile. It wasn't the kind of dental work that a Lower Stovey villager might have been able to afford, all those years ago. If the jaw was that of the Potato Man, it suggested that the rapist had been from outside the village, after all, as the Reverend Pattinson had always insisted.

He sipped his tea, winced and sighed. He should have gone up to the canteen but his appearance there, so early in the day, would disturb things. From the window he saw Dave Pearce arrive, park his car, and stride purposefully towards the building. Dave looked a bit out of sorts.

Markby went into the outer office. 'Inspector Pearce is just on his way up,' he said. 'When he gets here, tell him I want to see him at once, will you?'

Pearce, the message received, made his way to Markby's office, wondering what was up and half welcoming a diversion which would take his mind off his own problems. Along the way, the tooth twinged, letting him know it wasn't to be forgotten so easily. After the detour to deliver Tessa to the building society, he hadn't had time to stop off at the dentist's.

He found Markby standing by his desk, staring down at a creased sheet of paper on which lay some not unfamiliar objects.

'Bones,' observed Pearce with professional detachment. Inside, he was feeling far less sanguine. Was that what this call to Markby's office was all about? That crummy collection of oddments? He wasn't going to be asked to make something of them, was he? Yes, he probably was. With a note of resignation in his voice, he added, 'You wanted to see me, sir?'

'Yes, Dave, and yes, bones. They were found in Stovey Woods at the weekend by a hiker.'

Pearce drew nearer and studied the gruesome collection un-enthusiastically. 'Old,' he opined. 'And pretty chewed about. Found in the woods? Then the damage will be down to foxes, most likely. Is that it? No more?' Even Markby couldn't expect him to conjure up a miracle of identification, surely, from this little lot?

Oh, yes, he did.

'Not as yet. The woods will have to be searched.'

Pearce drew a deep breath. 'It'll be quite something to organize. Those woods cover a fair area. You know we've got a bit of a manpower problem. Oughtn't we get the bones to a boffin first? They could be donkey's years old.'

'And you're obviously hoping they are. I'm hoping they're not, not relating to a time out of living memory, anyway.' Markby poked the bones with a long thin forefinger.

Pearce clearly resisted the urge to ask why, realising the danger that any information might result in yet more work. He stooped to low cunning. 'If animals are involved, the bones could've been carried from somewhere else.'

'Then check Lower Stovey churchyard,' suggested his boss mildly. 'See if any old graves have been disturbed. No one ever goes there and a disturbance mightn't be noticed. I was there myself at the weekend,' he added contradictorily.

'Why?' asked Pearce, genuinely curious this time and putting a hand to his jaw without being aware of the gesture.

'House-hunting. No, not in the churchyard. We looked at the old vicarage next door to it.'

'Any good?' enquired Pearce, suddenly seeing the faint hope of deflecting Markby from the bones.

'I'd say it'd got possibilities,' Markby told him. 'But it's on the large side.' He caught at the paper and rustled it. 'Without having had an expert look at these, I'd judge them to have been lying around for twenty years at least. But that, Dave, is still recent enough to interest us!'

'It'll be some old tramp, died of hypothermia,' Pearce persevered in the face of certain defeat.

'We can't assume that!' Markby told him severely. 'Take a look at the jawbone.'

The last thing Pearce needed was to study a set of rickety teeth. He picked up the jawbone gingerly.

'Notice anything?' the superintendent was asking.

Which meant there was something to notice, Markby had already seen it and Pearce had better see it quickly. He saw it.

'Some fancy dental work here. I've not seen anything like it.' Nor did he like the look of it, or the thought of it. Implanted in the jaw was a discoloured piece of metal resembling the popular image of a

Christmas tree. He sighed, seeing his hope that the remains were historical vanish. Nor did tramps usually have mouths filled with expensive dentistry.

'It's called a blade implant,' Markby informed him. 'This type is called a Christmas tree implant. I know this,' he explained, 'because before you came in, I rang my dentist and described the thing to him.'

Pearce wondered what time that morning Markby had arrived in his office. Very early, by the sound of it. Pearce had worked with Markby over several years. He knew that this early morning eager-beaver stuff usually meant Markby was dissatisfied about something, not necessarily to do with police work, and having another problem to worry at, got the dissatisfaction out of his system. It was probably the house-hunting, thought Pearce, not without sympathy. He and Tessa had suffered similarly before buying their house. He just hoped that domestic frustrations didn't lead to Markby pushing everything that came their way under his, Pearce's, nose. Especially, if it had anything to do with teeth.

'What's more,' Markby was saying, determined it seemed, to talk about teeth and nothing else. 'About twenty years ago – assuming that to be the age of the bones although that can only be guesswork at the moment – such dental work was comparatively rare and carried out only in a few places. So, we might be able to trace that particular effort. The metal piece has some sort of mark on it.'

'Oh, yes . . .' Pearce, forgetting his personal aversion, peered at the blade. 'Like a hallmark.'

'Manufacturer's mark, most likely. Get on to it, Dave.'

Just like that. He was going to be busy all day. Which meant, Pearce decided, he wouldn't have time to ring his own dentist about his own teeth. He gathered up the mystery bones. 'I'll get 'em over to the experts,' he said.

But Markby had something else for him. He picked up a file from the desk. It looked to Pearce to be a pretty old one. 'You might,' Markby said casually, 'like to read up on this old case. It might have some bearing.'

Pearce added the file to the parcel of bones in his arms. 'Right you are,' he said and edged towards the door before he could be burdened with anything else.

III

Someone else was having a frustrating morning.

'Hello again!' said the young man breezily.

He wore a white shirt and garish tie. His jacket hung on the back of his chair. He had one of those well-fed and well-pleased with life faces topped with hair cut and gelled in the fashionable spikey style. Meredith was pleased to note that, despite his age which was probably a good ten years younger than she was, he had the beginnings of what was popularly known as a beer-belly.

'Hello again,' she echoed, taking the chair opposite him.

He leaned his elbows on his desk and steepled his fingers. 'Well,' he said cheerily. 'Did you go and look at the Lower Stovey property?'

'We did. Mr —' Meredith glanced at the plaque on his desk. It read simply 'Gary'. 'Gary,' she began again. 'We went to see it. Tell me, have you seen it?'

He blinked. 'No, I don't think I did the valuation on that one. Let me see.' He shuffled papers. 'No, Cindy did that one.'

And how old is Cindy? Nineteen? snarled an inner Meredith.

'But I can tell you,' Gary was breezing on. 'That my colleague was very impressed by the property. Very impressed indeed.'

'By colleague you mean Cindy, I suppose,' said Meredith icily and without waiting for his acknowledgement, went on. 'Just as a matter of interest, what impressed Cindy in particular about the Old Vicarage, Lower Stovey?'

'It's unique,' he said solemnly. 'A quality residence on a practical scale.'

'It's huge. It has five bedrooms without counting the maids' rooms up in the attics.'

'The attics could be turned into a super recreation room. Snooker, ping-pong, a gym . . .' He beamed. 'Cindy thought you could get all that up there, lovely place. Enough room for a bowling alley.'

'I don't need to play snooker at home or bowl. As for a gym, I've got an exercise bike and it takes up very little room. I'm not so much bothered about space, in any case, more general condition. You know the central heating system is out of the ark and broken? I hate to think what the electrics are like.'

'It does need some modernisation,' he agreed reluctantly. 'But that is reflected in the price, Miss Mitchell.'

'The kitchen is out of Dickens.'

'But a lovely size.'

'It's got sash windows which stick.'

'Period features.'

'A garden which is completely overgrown.'

He had his answer ready. He beamed at her. 'I understood that Mr Markby is a very keen gardener! Plenty of scope for him there! Grow all your own vegetables,' he added, inspired. 'Organic, natural, full of flavour.'

'And Lower Stovey is totally cut off, down a road which leads nowhere, only to some woods.'

He jabbed his index finger at her. 'Got it. Entirely secluded and . . .' his voice rose in triumph . . . 'no risk of further development. The old drovers' way runs just behind the village and right through the woods. It's protected. It's, you know, historic. No one's going to put a motorway through there, are they? Or put up two hundred starter homes. Believe me, a location like that doesn't come on the market every day.'

Meredith sat back in her chair and heaved a sigh. 'Haven't you got anything else on your books?'

'Yes, lots,' he nodded. 'But not what you're looking for. Three bed semi? No problem. Detached with garage and room for extra parking? Show you two or three. Nice little bungalow?' He shook his head. 'But you don't want any of those, do you. You and Mr Markby, you want character. You want period charm.' He leaned across the desk and added in a hoarse whisper, 'You want to go up-market.' He made it sound like the last word in degeneracy.

'How about a biggish cottage?' she asked desperately.

He spread his hands. 'At the moment, not a chance. Wouldn't I like to be able to show you one? Of course I would. But they're like hot cakes, they are. Hardly touch the books. Word gets out one is for sale and I've got prospective buyers tripping over one another trying to get through that door first.'

'But they're not tripping over one another to offer for the Old Vicarage?'

Gary folded his hands. 'I'm sure,' he said confidentially, 'that Mrs Scott, the owner, would accept any reasonable offer.'

Meredith, although she knew it was a mistake, heard herself ask, 'How reasonable?'

He tapped the side of his nose. 'Leave it with me. I'll talk her down a bit.'

'Hang on!' Meredith protested, knowing she was being outmanoeuvred here. 'Let's leave Lower Stovey on the back burner for the moment. We're bearing it in mind.' She got up. 'In the meantime, we'll look further.'

He rightly interpreted this as meaning they were going to consult the books of a rival firm.

'Don't be hasty. Let me talk to Mrs Scott. While you're waiting . . .' he cast about and brightened, 'you could go and take a look at Hill House. It commands spectacular views over unspoilt countryside. Mind you, it's been empty two years and about a year ago there was a bit of trouble when some hippies broke in and camped in it for a month or two. Since then it's been boarded up. But it's a beautiful late Georgian house.'

'Forget it,' said Meredith.

'You let me talk to Mrs Scott,' he urged. 'And why don't you go and take another look round the property? I can tell you, once word gets out —'

'They'll be tripping over one another in your doorway, I know.' On the other hand, Hill House sounded immeasurably worse. 'Let me think about it,' she said.

IV

Meredith was still thinking about the lack of success she and Alan were having house-hunting as, the following morning, she journeyed up to London by crowded commuter train and packed Tube to her Foreign Office desk. Gary, she decided, had only told her about Hill House to make the Old Vicarage sound positively desirable.

At lunchtime a friend, Juliet Painter, rang. 'I haven't seen you in ages, Meredith. I was thinking, if you haven't got to rush off home after work today, we could have a bowl of spaghetti together somewhere.'

'Where's Doug?' Meredith enquired.

'Don't ask me. Working.' There was a touch of annoyance in Juliet's voice.

'That'll teach you to date a copper,' said Meredith unsympathetically. As Juliet was finding out and Meredith had already learned, policemen, like doctors, were apt to be called out at inconvenient times. 'Where do you want to meet?' she said more kindly.

The restaurant Juliet had in mind was in Soho, off Dean Street.

'Because,' she said, when she and Meredith were settled at a table, 'it's lively down here. You can watch the street life through the windows. See?' She pointed through the glass at the thronged pavement. 'Doug and I like it.' There was a touch of defiance in the last words, Meredith thought.

'This is getting very serious with you and Superintendent Minchin, isn't it?' Meredith studied Juliet. 'There's something different about you. Where are your specs?'

'Got contact lenses.' Juliet took one of the two menus a waiter was holding out to them. Her tone was suspiciously airy.

'I thought you couldn't get on with them.'

'They've got new types now. I'm managing better.' Juliet tilted her chin and tossed her single long plait of hair. 'It's not because of Doug, if that's what you're thinking. We're not that serious, thank you. Not as serious as you and Alan.' She was getting her own back.

Meredith glared morosely at the menu. 'If that's what I am. Alan's serious.'

'Hey, getting cold feet?'

'I suppose so,' Meredith admitted.

'It's all this talk of marriage,' said Juliet firmly. 'Look, I can understand your jitters, even if Alan can't. It's because he's been married before and he thinks in those terms. He must be forty-five now and it's a funny age. He wants to settle down. Now you and me, we're used to our independence. But life's got to move on. You're what, thirty-seven? Does Alan want kids?'

'I've never asked him! In any case, I don't think he's marrying me because he fancies sitting at the head of the table, gazing down at a line of scrubbed little faces. I should bloomin' well hope not. Anyway, I'm too old to start a big family. One child or two, I might – might! – be able to cope with. I'm not even sure about that. I've never had anything to do with babies. I'm an only child. Right now it just appears another complication and marriage, to me, already sounds complicated enough. I've never even lived with anyone, not under the same roof for any length of time. Whether it's been Alan or earlier relationships I've had, I've always insisted on my own space. When I was overseas with the Diplomatic Service, of course, I got my own flat as part of the job.'

She sighed. 'I did love my time overseas. For ages after I got back I tried to get posted out somewhere, anywhere, again. Now I know that's not going to happen and I'm stuck at a Foreign Office desk until pension day. I'll be honest. I did resent that. It made me very dissatisfied for a long time and poor Alan bore the brunt of it. It's been difficult for him. I can see that. I can also see that those years living abroad weren't the absolute good thing I thought they were. They cut me off from normal life. I was living a very satisfying, but distinctly peculiar, artificial life. It made me into a peculiar sort of person.'

'Who isn't?' asked Juliet.

'You know what I mean. This setting up together which everyone else seems to take for granted makes me feel odd. Look, Alan and I did try living together in his place whilst mine was being fixed up, but it just didn't seem – seem natural. To be frank, after years of a nomadic life, even the idea of putting down some real roots terrifies me.'

'You'd manage fine if you were married. You've just got to take hold of your courage and go for it, Meredith.' Juliet smiled brightly at her.

'It's all right you talking like an agony aunt,' Meredith defended herself. 'I love Alan, I do! It's just the idea of always being under one another's feet . . . Every evening coming home and asking, "How was your day, dear?" Having to check with someone else before you accept even a casual meal out with a friend, like this. Being, being beholden to someone. You see, that's Alan's idea of domestic bliss.'

'Give the poor guy a chance. He wants to look after you.'

'But I can look after myself, thank you very much, and I've been doing it for quite a while now. The habit's hard to break.' She sighed. 'I'm sure Alan suspects I'm deliberately dragging my feet over the house-hunting. But honestly, we've yet to view any house that makes me feel that I can really live in it – with or without Alan.'

The waiter arrived to take their order.

'The spinach and ricotta cannelloni,' said Meredith.

'For me the pollo milanese,' said Juliet. 'And a bottle of the house red. It's very good here, Meredith. We can manage a bottle between us, can't we?'

'The way I feel I could manage a bottle on my own!' retorted Meredith as the waiter left them. 'Juliet, in your line of business, don't you know of any nice houses which would suit us?'

'I'm not an estate agent,' Juliet reminded her. 'I'm a property consultant. I look out for houses for the rich and famous and sometimes for the even richer who take good care not to be famous. If I knew of anything, I'd tell you. But you want to be in the Bamford area, don't you? There aren't that many houses of the type you're after around there, not in good condition, anyway.'

Meredith told her about the Old Vicarage and for good measure, about Hill House.

'Forget Hill House,' advised Juliet immediately. 'I've seen it. It's as near derelict as makes no difference and would cost a small fortune to put right.'

'That rules us out, then!' said Meredith in relief.

'But this Old Vicarage place, that might be a possible. I think you ought to take another look. As for worrying about all those bedrooms, you haven't thought it through. Look, five main bedrooms, right? One you'll turn into a study for you so that you can work from home sometimes, everyone does. Another Alan will turn into his den. That just leaves three of them for sleeping in which is only what you'd have with a semi.'

'There are another five or six cubbyholes up in the attics! Apparently, Cindy, who works at the estate agent's, thinks someone might build a gym or gamesroom up there.'

'Cindy's got the right idea. Look, if Mrs Scott is keen to sell and if the central heating is on the blink and the windows stick and all the rest of it, she can't hold out for top whack. Hey, you can do business!'

'All right, then,' Meredith agreed, bowing to the force of Juliet's enthusiasm. 'I'll take a couple of days off next week and go and take another look.'

'If it's still on the market,' Juliet had a caveat.

'Believe me,' Meredith assured her, 'I've every confidence it'll still be on the market.'

V

'See you tonight, Grandpa!' said Becky Jones on Thursday morning.

She dropped a kiss on the top of the old man's bald head with its pattern of liver spots and fringe of white hair. He sat alone at the breakfast table, at the head where he'd always taken his place, in the same Windsor chair, its arms polished to the surface touch of silk by the grip of his hands over fifty or more years. But the authority this implied had long dwindled to a mere token. He was the last to finish as always, chewing slowly and methodically through his bacon, long gone cold, and thick slices of buttered bread.

'That's right,' he replied. 'Listen to the teacher, learn something.' He chuckled at his own wit.

He said the same thing every schoolday morning and his thirteen-year-old granddaughter made her reply absently as she picked up her books and stuffed them into her canvas bag. Her mother's voice came distantly from out in the farmyard, calling impatiently to her to 'hurry along, for goodness' sake!' Becky scurried out and scrambled into the front passenger seat of the family's elderly car.

Mrs Jones ground into gear and they lurched through the gate and down the track connecting the farm to the potholed road which to the right went to Stovey Woods, and to the left, to the village. Becky was a pupil at the Bamford Community College.

'Radio was saying there's extra traffic on the main road this morning,' Linda Jones said fretfully. 'Seems it's been diverted because of some road-works or other. I do wish you'd stir your stumps of a morning, Becky. You know I have to allow half an hour to get you to school.'

'I was only saying goodbye to Grandpa,' her daughter defended herself.

Linda sighed. 'There's another slowcoach. He takes so long over his breakfast, longer every day it seems to me. It makes your dad that cross.'

'Why should he be cross? It doesn't interfere with him. He doesn't have to clear up the breakfast things, you do.'

The car bounced over a rut out into the road through the village.

'It's not that, Beck. Your father's got a lot on his mind lately what with livestock prices being so low and everything. He's worried about your grandfather.'

'Grandpa's all right!' Becky's voice rose defiantly. There was an edge of tears in it. 'There's nothing wrong with him. He eats slowly because his teeth aren't any good.'

Linda glanced at her daughter and said soothingly, 'I realise that. I know he's all right, really.'

Which he most certainly wasn't, she thought sadly. Despite herself, an audible sigh escaped her lips.

Becky heard it. 'Is everything all right, Mum? I mean, apart from the lambs not fetching decent prices and all the rest of it. Dad's not been making a fuss about Gordon again?'

'Gordon? No!' Mrs Jones wrenched the wheel round to avoid a cat which had decided to settle down in the middle of the road. 'Nothing like that. He's been grumbling a bit about old Billy Twelvetrees.'

'Poor old Mr Twelvetrees,' said Becky.

'Poor old, my foot!' snapped her mother. 'He's a mischief-making old scoundrel, is Billy Twelvetrees!'

Becky conceded that Billy was a gossip and worse, a bit of a bore. 'But Dad wouldn't really throw him out of his cottage, would he?'

'Of course not. Not while your grandfather is still alive, anyway, and he wouldn't *throw* him out. But that cottage is worth a lot of money, you know, Becky, and well, if Mr Twelvetrees wasn't in it, we could do it up a bit and sell it on for a tidy sum. I won't say the money wouldn't come in useful.'

'Sell it to second-homers, you mean!' her daughter said scornfully. They were passing the church as she spoke and she added, 'I don't know why people want to buy a place in Lower Stovey. It's dead dreary.'

'It's quiet,' corrected her mother.

'It's the pits,' said the younger generation unrepentantly.

Linda didn't argue. They'd left the village behind and reached the junction with the main road. She could see there really was extra traffic today. They'd be stuck here for ages trying to get out.

Eventually when they did manage to pull out into the main stream of cars, she said, picking up the conversation, 'There's worse places than Lower Stovey.'

She knew her voice lacked conviction. The words were a mantra she'd been repeating for more than twenty years and she'd yet to be convinced by it. She'd hoped that, by saying it, bad things would be kept away. But bad things had come back, only just recently, with the finding of those wretched bones. Linda couldn't see into the future and told herself she didn't want to. She was already resigned to what it

74

would hold. Becky would fly the coop when she left school, just as Gordon had done. In five years' time, she and Kevin would reach that time she dreaded, when both her children would be gone, her father-in-law would very likely be dead, and she and her husband would be left alone together at Greenjack Farm, staring at one another across the table with nothing to say. All they'd have would be memories and they wouldn't want to discuss those.

Yet Kevin was a good man, loyal and hard-working. He did his best to look after her and Becky and his increasingly senile father. He'd looked after Gordon. She wished he got on better with Gordon. It was no fun for her being piggy-in-the-middle, trying to keep the peace and sympathize with both sides. Of course, Gordon didn't want to stay on the farm. Why should he? It'd be the same, even if Gordon had been —

Becky's voice broke in on her thoughts, eerily echoing them. 'Mind you, since they found those bones, life's got a bit more interesting.'

'Becky!' Linda's voice burst out, shrill, causing her daughter to start in surprise.

'Calm down, Mum. You've got to admit normally nothing happens. Since the bones were found in the woods, my friends are dead keen to know more about Lower Stovey.'

'Pity they've not got better things to talk about!' said her mother sharply.

They were into Bamford now and Becky abandoned the topic of the Stovey Wood Remains, as the local press called them.

'There's Michele! Let me out here, Mum. I can walk the rest of the way.'

Linda felt a surge of relief. 'I suppose you've got time and I've got to call by the supermarket.' She pulled into the kerb and waited while her daughter struggled to get out, hampered by her bag of books and efforts to signal to her friend.

When Becky finally reached the pavement she turned back, lowered her head by the still open car door, and asked, 'Can I come home on the later bus tonight, Mum?'

'No, my girl, you may not.'

'Oh, *Mum*!'

'I'll pick you up at the bus-stop, quarter past four, same as usual. You be there.'

The door slammed on her daughter's muttered response. Linda drove on. There was no convenient bus in the morning so she had to drive her daughter to school. But there was a bus later in the day which Becky could catch at four o'clock and which stopped just before the turning to Lower Stovey. It was a blessing because it meant Linda hadn't to drive all the way back into Bamford a second time. She simply drove up to the turn and picked up her daughter there.

The disadvantage was that Becky had no time after school to socialize with her friends unless she caught the bus which ran a full two hours later. Of late, she'd been doing this more and more and Kevin had put his foot down.

'Running round town with those silly girlfriends. You don't know what mischief they're into. Anyway, she ought to be back here at the farm, lending you a hand with the supper.'

Normally, Linda was more easily persuaded by Becky's pleas. But her daughter's words about the grisly find in the woods had annoyed her. She began to think Kevin was right and Becky was better not spending too much of her time with those addle-pated girls. If those after-school companions *were* girls and not boys. A cold fist closed on the pit of Linda's stomach. Becky was thirteen. She was pretty. *Don't throw your life away, Beck, oh, don't! And don't trust men.*

This early in the day the supermarket car park was half-empty. In the store itself the girls on the cash-tills chatted to one another as they waited for customers. Linda helped herself to a basket and went to the bread-counter where she pushed half a dozen loaves into the basket to stock up her freezer. Kevin took sandwiches out into the fields most days. In his youth, when old Martin had run the place, Linda's mother-in-law, long gone, cooked a meal every day at midday except at harvest-time. It wasn't just the time and trouble which had caused this custom to be dropped. It was economy.

Anyway, it made sense to eat of an evening when Becky had come home. She debated over doughnuts which today were 'buy one, get one free'. Eventually she bought the one plus one, a little treat for Kevin and the other for the old man, on the principle of it being a good offer. She didn't need one herself. On her way back to a till, she passed through the meat department, not because she wanted meat but to check on the prices. She picked up one cling-film-wrapped pack after another and put it back with a sigh. To think Kevin got almost nothing for the last lot of lambs and just look at the price of lamb chops here.

She drove home feeling depressed. As she passed through Lower Stovey, she saw a figure she recognised and tapped the horn. The walker looked up and waved.

'I wonder where's she's going?' mused Linda and almost immediately, forgot all about it.

VI

That Thursday Meredith came back to Lower Stovey. Fate worked in a funny old way. She'd often thought it. When she'd left here with Alan that day some hiker found bones in the woods, she'd privately resolved never to set foot in the place again. But back, before you could say Jack Robinson, she was.

Meredith pulled her car into the parking bay before the church and got out. The slam of the door echoed round about and sent jackdaws from their tower roost to circle her head in a cawing squadron of black shapes. There was a bit of a breeze today. It knocked the jackdaws off course and rustled the churchyard trees.

She had thirty-five minutes to spend before her appointment with Mrs Scott at twelve. She meant to spend it taking a proper look at the village. Even if, on second viewing, she decided the house was a possible, it wouldn't matter if she couldn't live in this village.

Meredith jammed her hands in the pockets of her fleece body warmer and strolled down what she supposed was the main street. There was no sign of life. Where were they all? She reached the end, turned and walked back, branching off down a narrow thoroughfare marked as Church Lane. It was lined with rows of cottages, nicely painted but apparently as deserted as the *Marie Celeste*. At the far end stood a very old, uneven building which appeared to be two or even three knocked into one. A house sign bore the name The Old Forge. Ruth Aston's house. Meredith remembered her invitation and wondered whether to knock at the door. Not a good idea, perhaps. She might get talking and be late for her appointment. She walked back to the main street and glanced at her wristwatch. Her perambulations had taken a mere five minutes. The door of the pub, the Fitzroy Arms, was ajar. They must serve coffee.

She crossed the road and pushed at the stout oak door. It swung open easily and a smell of stale beer, cigarettes and lavatory cleaner drifted out. Despite this, the bar looked comfortable enough. The walls were lined with sporting prints. The beams which ran the length of the room suggested the core of the building must be old. Someone, in an excess of enthusiasm for horse brasses, had tacked dozens of them to the beams.

She could see no customers but a movement at the rear of the bar took her eye. A middle-aged man stood there. His head was oval and his hair thin and flat. The skin of his face looked soft, pinkish and abnormally clean as if it had been subjected to some chemical process. It was quite unlined and the features seemed fixed as if the eyes couldn't blink or the lips move. When she'd been a child, Sunday morning breakfast had always been a boiled egg. When she'd finished her egg, she'd pass the shell to her father. He'd upend it in the cup and draw a funny face on it for her. Now she felt she was looking at one of her father's egg faces come to life. She didn't know if he'd been there when she entered and she'd failed to notice him or if he'd arrived later, attracted by the sound of her movements. He stood watching her, motionless but for his hands which moved methodically, as if of their own volition, to polish a glass with a cloth.

'Good morning,' Meredith offered.

'Morning,' he replied. His voice was as soft as his facial skin. The cloth continued to buff the glass. She thought, irrelevantly, that he'd have made a good undertaker. He was, she presumed, mine host.

'Do you serve morning coffee?'

'Don't get much call for it. But the wife will make you a cup.' He went into a rear room and she caught a distant murmur of voices. He came back. 'She'll be a couple of minutes. Make yourself comfortable.'

Meredith chose a chair by the unlit hearth in which a pile of dusty logs awaited winter. The landlord, to her relief, put down the glass he'd been polishing. He placed his palms on the bar counter and surveyed her in the same dispassionate way he'd had from the start. It made her uncomfortable and she hoped his wife would hurry along with the coffee and that she would prove a more lively person. The silence was unbroken and seemed to stretch out endlessly.

At long last feet clattered on a tiled floor and a small, bustling woman appeared carrying a tray. She scurried across the floor to Meredith and put her burden on the table.

'Coffee,' she said cheerfully. 'Milk, sugar. I thought you'd like a couple of digestive biscuits.'

'That's kind of you, thank you,' Meredith said.

The woman's head was almost as much a perfect round as her husband's was oval. She pushed it into Meredith's face, giving Meredith a close-up of the greying roots of her dyed hair. She had small, bright, squirrel's eyes. 'I like a digestive,' she said as if imparting a state secret. 'You can dunk 'em.'

With that, she retreated to whatever lair she inhabited at the rear of the place and Meredith was left alone with the landlord.

'You're not very busy at this time of the morning?' she asked in what sounded an abnormally loud voice. She hadn't meant it to come out like that.

'Twelve,' he replied and blinked at long last. 'They'll be in after twelve.' From where she sat, it looked as if he had no eyelashes. 'What's brought you here, then?'

He'd shown so little curiosity until then that the question startled her. Meredith opened her mouth to reply that she was just passing through, but remembered in the nick of time that no one passed through Lower Stovey as its road was a dead end. And they didn't come deader, in her book. 'I'm looking at property,' she said cautiously.

He moved his head in a curious sideways twist, like a parrot inspecting something new. 'Generally a house or two for sale around here. You've seen the old vicarage?'

'Yes. It's – it's big.' That was a daft reply, she thought. But for the life of her she couldn't think of anything better at the moment. She covered her confusion by sipping her coffee which was very weak but hot. Meredith nibbled at a digestive biscuit.

'One of those little houses in School Close is up for sale.' His mouth turned down disparagingly. 'No room to swing a cat. They should never have been allowed to build so many on the site. It used to be the school, you know.'

'You're a local man, then?' she asked.

His gaze slid away from hers. 'In a manner of speaking,' he said.

Whatever that meant, thought Meredith crossly. She was getting a bit fed up with this. If she and Alan moved to Lower Stovey – and the idea was becoming less attractive by the minute – they certainly wouldn't be drinking in the Fitzroy Arms, not if she had any say in it. Alan, however, had a liking for weird pubs. He'd probably love this one, spooky landlord and all.

He spoke again, disconcerting her once more. 'My mother was a Twelvetrees,' he said. 'That won't mean anything to you.'

'As a matter of fact, it does!' She had great pleasure in contradicting him and seeing the skin above his eyes pucker. He had no eyebrows to speak of to raise. 'I met an old gentleman called Billy Twelvetrees in your church the last time I came here.'

He nodded. 'That'll be Uncle Billy. He's always popping in and out of the church when it's open. Not that he's religious, mind. He likes to chat to the ladies who keep the place clean and tidy, Mrs Aston and her friend, Miss Millar. Nothing else for him to do, is there, at his age? Mrs Aston, she was Miss Pattinson before she married. She was the old vicar's daughter.'

80

'I've met Mrs Aston,' Meredith told him.

'Seems you've found out a lot about us, then,' he retorted.

She had the feeling he was annoyed. Good. He'd annoyed her. Let the boot be on the other foot, as the saying went. But she didn't want to linger here. Quit when you're ahead.

'Thank you for the coffee,' she said. 'How much do I owe you?'

He shrugged. 'I don't know. Fifty pence be all right?'

Meredith put down a pound coin on the dark oak counter. 'It hardly seems enough when your wife had to make it specially for me and gave me biscuits as well. I don't want any change.'

He stared down at the coin. 'Please yourself,' he said. 'It's up to you.'

She left the place with unseemly haste. Outside she saw with surprise that it was still only ten minutes to twelve. What was it about this place that it seemed able to suspend time?

'It gives me the creeps,' she muttered. She glanced across at the church. She had to waste at least five minutes before she could call at the Old Vicarage. Meredith decided on impulse to glance into the church. Perhaps Ruth Aston would be there.

She walked across the road and pushed open the lych-gate. As she passed under its wooden roof, she saw, in the far distance, a squat figure hurrying away among the graves and ramshackle tombs. The figure had a stick and hobbled but was making remarkable speed.

Meredith passed into the porch and opened an inner door made of chicken wire stretched over a home-made wooden frame which bore the words 'Please keep this door closed to prevent birds flying into the church where they might die of thirst.' The church was dark, except at the chancel end where sunlight coming through the Victorian stained glass window splashed coloured daubs across the choir stalls. It was cool, still and silent apart from a clatter above her head made by the jackdaws hopping about on the roof.

Meredith's eyes accustomed slowly to the gloom as she searched for the Fitzroy tomb. There it was. She walked to it. Here lay Sir Hubert, his stone features mutilated out of any semblance of humanity. Beside him for eternity lay the wife he'd not wanted beside him in life. Her face looked serene within its coiffed head-dress. Her long thin hands were pressed together in prayer on her breast. Someone had stuck a piece of chewing gum on her right sleeve. Meredith wished her Latin were good enough to decipher the inscription around the base. But lack of scholarship and what looked like more intentional damage meant that apart from 'Hubertus' and 'Agnes uxor sua' she could make out nothing. Even the years of their deaths had been obliterated.

Meredith turned away and, able to distinguish clearly now, saw that she wasn't alone, after all. A woman knelt in prayer in a pew on the other side of the church, beneath the tablet commemorating periwigged Sir Rufus. Her head was bent right forward, her forehead resting on the shelf for prayer-books fixed to the back of the pew in front. Meredith, embarrassed at disturbing such intense private devotion, began to tiptoe out. But at the door, she paused and glanced back. The woman was so still. There was something not quite right about her posture. Her hands weren't clasped but dangled loosely at the end of her arms which hung down straight by her sides.

The hair prickled on the nape of Meredith's neck. She walked rapidly towards the crouched figure. As she neared, she asked, 'Are you all right?'

There was no movement, no reply. The woman's slumped form lacked all bodily grace and Meredith couldn't see her face, only her coarse curling grey hair. Meredith put a hand out and gingerly touched her shoulder. Something warm and sticky smeared her fingers. She snatched back her hand and looked down at bright red blood. Stooping, Meredith tried to see the hidden face and met the unseeing gaze of one glazed eye half-open beneath a drooping frozen eyelid. Nausea rose in Meredith's throat and she stood up hastily. Round the woman's neck was wound a scarf patterned with geraniums but not all the scarlet splashes were printed flowers. There was a straight tear in the silky fabric. The blood had oozed into the scarf and from it, by a process of osmosis, down the woman's lightweight sweater. There was no doubt, no doubt at all, that she was dead.

Chapter Six

It wasn't the first time Meredith had seen a dead body. It wasn't even the first time she'd had the misfortune to stumble upon a victim of violent attack. This didn't make the experience less gruesome or shocking. In a sense, it added to the horror. Someone else might have pretended that the woman wasn't really dead. Meredith knew she was. Others might have persuaded themselves a bizarre accident had befallen the unfortunate. Meredith knew she looked at a murder victim. Yet there was disbelief mixed in with her reactions. Not an incredulity at the reality of what she saw, but that she should have been picked out by some capricious Fate to go through all this again.

At least, she thought, I know the drill. It struck her then that the murderer might still be in the church, crouched down among the pews or behind the huge Victorian organ with its forest of dusty pipes. Or behind that faded brocade curtain hanging over the arched doorway into the vestry. Her heart hopped irregularly in her chest as her ears strained for the soft intake of another's breath, the tell-tale creak of wood, and her eyes watched for the slightest movement of the curtain. Nothing. She was alone with the dead. Sir Rufus sneered down at her as if telling her this sort of thing would never have been permitted in his day. She went outside, took out her mobile and rang Alan, trying to force her voice to remain steady, knowing it wasn't and that it was pitched unnaturally high.

He took it calmly. He was a professional. He had been through it all before and it didn't surprise him that he had to face it all again. That, as he sometimes wryly said, was what he was there for. But she felt a rush of tenderness and gratitude towards him at hearing his clear, comforting but instructive tones. Wait there, by the door. Don't let anyone else enter. If anyone insists, go with them and make sure they don't remove or touch anything.

When Alan had rung off, Meredith remembered to call Mrs Scott, who was now waiting for her in vain at the Old Vicarage. She explained there had been an emergency and she was delayed. She might not make it that day.

'Emergency in the village?' asked Mrs Scott's voice sharply. 'Is someone hurt?'

Meredith was startled. How did the woman know where she was? But of course, she was where she was supposed to be that morning, in Lower Stovey. She had been wandering all over the place and although she had seen no one, that didn't mean no one had seen her.

'In a manner of speaking.' She borrowed the landlord's phrase.

'Where are you?' demanded Mrs Scott in a voice which brooked no evasion.

Meekly, Meredith told her, at the church.

'Ruth Aston hasn't fallen off that wretched stepladder, has she? It wouldn't surprise me.'

'No, no she hasn't. It's nothing to do with her.'

'Huh!' said Mrs Scott in Meredith's ear and slammed down the phone.

Within minutes the real thing stood before Meredith, bearing down on the church porch like an avenging angel weirdly clad in handknits and droopy skirts, long grey hair tossed wildly by the breeze.

'Now what's going on?' she demanded.

'I can't let you go in.' Meredith barred the entry by the simple expedient of spreading out her arms. 'The police told me to let no one in. I'm waiting for them.'

'Police?' Mrs Scott twitched an eyebrow. 'Not paramedics?'

'The police will send out a doctor.'

Mrs Scott placed her hands on her ample hips. 'Someone's snuffed it,' she said, sounding not displeased. 'Who is it?'

'Yes, someone's dead.' Meredith found it was a relief to confess the truth. 'I don't know who it is.'

'I'd better take a look, then.' Mrs Scott advanced towards her as steadily as a tank. 'And don't bleat about the coppers not letting anyone in. Of course you don't know who it is. But I probably shall, if it's anyone local, that is.'

This was true and the police would be keen to have an early identification. Though Meredith was unwilling to return to the scene, she said reluctantly, 'I'll have to come with you.'

'Naturally,' said her companion. 'Make sure I don't leave my dabs all over the place or pocket the evidence.'

Meredith made an inspired guess. Mrs Scott was a crime fiction fan. She had been reading about it for years and now, to her manifest delight, the real thing had happened on her doorstep.

'It's not like in books,' Meredith said firmly.

'Don't expect it to be. Come on.'

They entered the cool dark interior. The slumped figure was as Meredith had left it. They approached in silence and as quietly as they could as if their steps could disturb the crouching form.

When they reached it, Mrs Scott gave a gasp.

Meredith glanced at her. The woman's florid complexion had paled to a grey hue. Meredith felt an unworthy desire to say, 'I told you so'. She said instead, though it amounted to the same thing, 'I warned you it would be nasty.'

The other made an impatient gesture. 'I've seen nasty sights before. It's just, it isn't anyone I'd have expected it to be.'

'You don't know her, then?'

'Of course, I know her!' Mrs Scott snapped, rallying. 'It's Hester Millar who shares a house with Ruth Aston. What a bloody awful mess. Who'd want to kill Hester? What on earth for? A thoroughly harmless woman. Where's her bag?'

'Her bag?' For a second Meredith didn't catch on.

Mrs Scott pointed at a scuffed brown leather bag lying on the floor by the dead woman's feet. 'There it is. It doesn't look as if it's been opened. She wouldn't have had any money on her, anyway. The whole thing's a nonsense. He must be a madman, whoever he is.' She squinted at Meredith. 'You didn't see anyone about, I suppose?'

'I – no, not in the church.'

'He might still be here, hiding. Did you try the tower door to see if it's locked?'

To Meredith's dismay, she started towards a narrow door behind them.

Meredith grabbed her arm. 'We don't touch a thing! It'd be plain stupid to go up there, anyway. If whoever did this dreadful thing is hiding anywhere around here, he's not going to let either of us get in his way. You said before you came in you understood about fingerprints. If we stay here, we'll mess up the scene of the crime. We should go back outside right now. The police will be here in a minute and they won't be happy to find us in here.'

Mrs Scott allowed herself to be led back to the porch. There she turned on Meredith with much of her former hectoring manner. 'Someone's got to go and tell Ruth the news. She'll take it badly. They'd been friends all their lives, since young women.'

'Let the police do that.'

'Nonsense! Let a flatfoot barge into Ruth's home and tell her poor Hester has been stuck in the neck with a knife?'

'If that's what's happened.'

'You saw the blood,' said Mrs Scott truculently. 'You saw the hole in that scarf. You'll see, it'll have been a knife.' She put a hand to her own neck. 'Carotid artery,' she said. 'Bet my boots on it. Did you see how much blood had been pumped out of it?' She pursed her mouth. 'Once the police turn up, this entire village will be here to watch what's going on. Someone's bound to tell Ruth. She'll rush up here in a panic and find out it's Hester. I don't care what you or a bunch of coppers think. I'm going down Church Lane to let her know.'

With that she marched off.

Meredith watched her despondently. Mrs Scott was probably right. As soon as the official circus appeared over the horizon these apparently deserted homes would disgorge a crowd of curious beings. And speaking of curiosity . . .

Meredith let her gaze roam across the frontage of the cottages flanking the pub. In which one of these did Billy Twelvetrees live and where was he?

The arrival of the first police car put paid to her musings. It was followed by the police doctor and by the scene of crime officers. Then it was the regional serious crime squad in the familiar person of Dave Pearce and behind him another familiar face, Ginny Holding.

'Hello!' Pearce greeted Meredith. 'The super said you'd be here.'

'I found her,' Meredith told him bleakly. 'And I've got an identification for you.'

'Oh, right.' He looked surprised. 'Someone you know?'

Meredith shook her head and explained, 'I couldn't prevent Mrs Scott rushing off to tell Ruth Aston about it.'

Pearce said, 'In a place this size, this Mrs Aston would be bound to hear of it before we got to her. We'll need a statement from you and from Mrs Scott and Mrs Aston.'

He made off into the church and Meredith turned to greet Ginny. 'Hello, DC Holding.'

'Hello again,' returned Ginny amiably. 'I've made sergeant since we last met.'

'Sorry, didn't know. Congratulations,' Meredith apologized.

Holding shrugged. 'No reason you should know.' She lowered her voice to ask, 'Do you know this village well?'

'No!' Meredith retorted. 'And I don't ruddy well want to!'

She had surprised herself with the vehemence of her reply and she'd certainly impressed Holding, whose eyebrows twitched.

'As bad as that?' she said.

A blue and white tape printed with Police Crime Scene had appeared as if by magic across the churchyard gate and not a moment too soon.

The landlord and his wife had come out of the Fitzroy Arms as Meredith spoke to Ginny Holding. They stood, he impassive, she hopping with excitement, outside their front door to watch all the activity. Other villagers were appearing from all directions but among them, Meredith failed to distinguish the solid form of Old Billy Twelvetrees. Suddenly heads turned and the small crowd parted.

Ruth Aston, pursued by Mrs Scott, appeared running from the entry to Church Lane. She ran on under the lych-gate, breaking through the newly erected tape, dodging the young officer who'd moved to cut her off and arrived panting before them. Mrs Scott lumbered up in her wake.

'Where is she? Where's Hester?' Ruth demanded of Meredith.

'Inside the church, Ruth, but I don't think you can go in . . .' Meredith glanced at Holding and murmured, 'This is Ruth Aston who shared a house with – with the deceased. And that's Mrs Scott, the woman I told you and the inspector about.'

'I want to see Hester!' Ruth's voice rose. A supporting murmur came from the crowd.

'All right, dear, all right,' soothed Ginny Holding.

The raised voice had attracted Pearce who re-emerged from the church porch and unwisely chimed in with, 'All in good time, madam.'

'Don't patronize me!' Ruth pointed a trembling forefinger at him. 'I want to see my friend. Muriel Scott says she's lying dead in there. It can't be true.'

'It's true enough, I'm afraid,' said Mrs Scott behind her. 'Saw her myself. And she's not lying down, she's propped up in a pew under the monument to old Rufus.'

'Thank you, madam!' said Pearce loudly, cutting off the flow of information which was being eagerly mopped up by the listening crowd. He looked around him, harassed, and pressed his fingers to his jaw as he weighed up the pros and cons of a hysterical scene before an avid audience as against an extra person cluttering up the scene of the crime.

'I'll just take you as far as the door, Mrs Aston, but no further. And you mustn't touch anything, all right?' he conceded.

'I don't want to touch things. I want to see Hester!' Her voice rose plaintively like a child's.

'She'll break down . . .' Meredith couldn't help but murmur to Pearce.

Perhaps Ruth overheard because she made a visible effort to pull herself together. 'I am a churchwarden of this parish,' she said with dignity. 'As is Hester. We look after this church and its contents. If anything happens on the property or to it, I have to report it to Father Holland at Bamford in the first place and probably, after that, to the bishop.'

Pearce, with visions of having to appease a band of ecclesiastics, was made still more unhappy but gave a reluctant nod. 'I'll take you to see her but then we come straight out, understand? There's no question of you touching your friend, I'm afraid.'

Ruth repeated with infinite patience, 'I want to see Hester. I won't leave until I've seen her.'

Pearce led her into the church and Meredith and Muriel Scott slipped in behind them before Ginny Holding realised what they were about to do.

Ruth hurried towards the pew beneath the Sir Rufus Fitzroy tablet. 'Hester?' she was saying. 'Hester?' It was as if she still hoped that somehow a mistake had been made and now she was there, she'd be able to rouse that sad, huddled form.

Pearce hurried anxiously after her and caught her arm. 'Go easy!'

But Ruth had stopped, staring down at her friend's body. She repeated once, 'Hester?' Then she sagged at the knees.

Pearce grasped her as Meredith and Muriel Scott ran forward.

It was Mrs Scott who took charge. 'See here,' she said to Pearce. 'I knew this would happen. I live next door at the Old Vicarage. You can see the place from the porch. I'm going to take Ruth there – Meredith here will help me – and I'm going to make her a good strong cup of tea with a dram of something in it. Got that?'

'Er – yes,' said Pearce.

'If you want statements and things like that, you'll find us there, so don't worry you've lost us.'

'No,' said Pearce.

The two women, supporting Ruth between them, managed to get back to the porch. A sympathetic murmur rose from the crowd as they appeared. Holding signalled to the officer in charge of the gate who lifted the tape to let them through. The watching villagers parted in silence. Somehow, with Ruth stumbling and only half conscious between them, they reached the Old Vicarage. At the door, Mrs Scott stopped and addressed Meredith.

'You have to manage on your own for a couple of minutes. I've got to go and shut Roger in the cloakroom. If he jumps up at Ruth while she's in this wobbly state, he'll send her flying.'

She let herself into the house, squeezing through the door to prevent the exodus of Roger who could be heard whining and crashing into the hall furniture in his joy at her return. Sadly for him, his enthusiasm was rewarded with his being incarcerated in the cloakroom, whence soon echoed a dismal howl.

Muriel Scott reappeared panting. 'All right now. Come on.'

Ruth was rallying. 'I'm sorry . . .' she was muttering. 'I'm so sorry . . .'

'Buck up!' Muriel ordered her not unkindly. 'Let's get you indoors.'

They deposited Ruth on the ramshackle sofa in the sitting room. Muriel Scott rummaged in a cupboard and produced half a bottle of whisky and some tumblers. She put these on a coffee table and ordered Meredith, 'See to that,' before disappearing in the direction of the kitchen.

As she passed the cloakroom door, Roger scratched furiously at it making it rattle. Meredith wondered how strong the catch was. She poured three shots of whisky and handed one to Ruth.

'Don't like it much,' protested Ruth weakly.

'Think of it as medicine.'

Ruth obediently took the glass, sipped and winced. Meredith took a good swig of her own drink and was grateful for the peaty tang and the comforting sensation of warmth in her gullet. She sat down on the sofa beside Ruth and decided it would be best to forewarn the woman about the next likely events.

'The police will be here shortly, wanting to know things, asking questions about every conceivable detail. Some of it will be horribly personal. There's no such thing as privacy in murder investigations, I'm afraid.'

'You know about them?' Ruth managed a wry smile. 'But of course, from your friend, Mr Markby. Will he come?'

'I hope so,' Meredith told her. She longed to see Alan, to know that he was there, taking charge of all this. But she added, 'I've known Inspector Pearce, who took you into the church, for some time and he's a most capable chap.'

Roger burst into hysterical barking which indicated he'd heard his mistress returning. Muriel Scott bore a tray with steaming mugs of tea into the room.'

'This'll put you right,' she told Ruth. 'Feel cold? Want the fire on?'

'I am a bit chilly,' Ruth admitted.

'That's the shock. Hang on.' She stooped and switched on the gas fire in the hearth. 'You'll be better in a minute.'

'But I'm not going to be, am I?' Ruth contradicted her. 'Better in minute, I mean. Not in days or weeks or months. I don't know what I'm going to do without Hester. I'll go on, manage, all the rest of it. But it's going to be so hard. Not just the loneliness but the knowledge that she died like that.' She shook her head in bewilderment. 'I just can't seem to take it in. Someone *killed* Hester. Who? Why? It's just not possible. No one in Lower Stovey would do such a dreadful thing. Not to Hester, not to anyone.'

'Wouldn't they?' asked Mrs Scott unexpectedly. 'What about those bones they dug up in the woods the other day?'

Ruth put her hands over her face and moaned.

'Oh, for goodness sake!' snapped Meredith to their hostess. 'We don't need to talk about those now!'

Mrs Scott was unrepentant. 'The police will.'

'Why should they? Those bones are probably donkey's years old. Alan told me. They can't have anything to do with this.'

Whatever Muriel Scott might have replied was drowned out in a

91

crescendo of barking and scratching. The cloakroom door shuddered.

'Someone's coming,' said Mrs Scott.

She went out and could be heard opening the front door. 'Oh, it's you,' she said. 'Thought you might turn up. Come on in, then.'

A tall, familiar figure in a crumpled green Barbour filled the doorway to the sitting room.

'Oh, Alan!' said Meredith. 'Thank goodness.'

'Do you feel up to talking about your friend?' Markby asked Ruth gently.

They had spent some time on the civilities, drinking the tea and whisky, dispensing condolences and comfort. Now Alan, seated on a nearby armchair, leaned forward with his hands loosely clasped.

'We were friends since we were girls, students,' Ruth answered simply.

'How long had you shared a home?'

'Oh, that.' Ruth hunched her shoulders. 'Not so very long. Only about three years, no, nearly four. It was after my husband died. I made a rather late entry into the marriage stakes,' she added.

Markby caught Meredith's eye and saw her look away.

Ruth was still speaking. 'My late husband was a nice man. He liked surprises. You know, finding out what people liked and buying suitable presents or setting up little treats. I used to tell him, he liked to play Father Christmas. It was a little like that, really. Harmless enough, except that sometimes he got it wrong. He got it wrong about the Old Forge. He knew I'd lived in Lower Stovey as a child, that my father had been the vicar here. So when he found out the Old Forge was up for sale he went and bought it without a word to me. He thought I'd be delighted to come back here to live. Only I wasn't. I've never wanted to come back to Lower Stovey. But I couldn't tell him that. He was so pleased at what he'd done, so confident that I'd be as pleased as he was.'

Ruth hunched her shoulders again. 'So that's how we came back here to live. Then he died, Hester came to stay and – and never went away again.'

'Miss Millar wasn't married, hadn't been married?'

'Oh no, never. It was a pity, really. She was an awfully good cook.' Ruth sighed. 'We've got a larder full of jams and pickles and a freezer full of pies and cakes, pâtés and meringues, oh, everything under the sun. All Hester's work. I shan't be able to eat any of it, that's the trouble. Poor Hester. But I can't.'

'Yes, you will,' interrupted Muriel Scott. 'Can't let good food go to waste.'

'It would be like dining with a ghost,' said Ruth in a low, firm voice.

Markby cleared his throat and brought the conversation back to matters in hand. 'Would she have some relative, someone who would be next-of-kin and needs to be informed?'

Ruth shook her head. 'No one I ever knew of. I used to know her mother, many years ago, but she's been dead ages. Her father died when she was quite little. No brothers or sisters. She never got a Christmas card or birthday card from anyone. She never talked about anyone. I never asked her. I just assumed there wasn't anyone one. I think she only had me,' Ruth finished sadly.

'I see. Tell me about the church. I understand you and Miss Millar acted as churchwardens. Was it left open all day, every day?'

'Oh, no. From springtime onwards, now, when the visitors come – if if they do – we open it after breakfast, any time between nine and ten, and close it up at tea-time. In the winter months we don't open it unless we go in there to clean. Except when there are services, of course. On the first Sunday in the month when we get a visiting priest, the church is open all morning and afternoon. Generally Father Holland from Bamford comes or sometimes the Reverend Picton-Wilkes, who's retired but takes the odd service.'

'And so it would have been open today? For casual visitors, tourists?'

'Yes.' Ruth nodded. 'Hester went to open it, that is, she had a couple of errands in the village and that was one of them.'

'How many sets of keys are there? I mean, did Miss Millar have her own keys to the church? Or did you share a set?'

'Hester had a set and I had one. Father Holland has another. Those are the only sets I know of. Each set has four keys on a ring, one for the north door which serves as the main entrance, one for the west door which hasn't been opened in donkey's years, one for the vestry office and one for the tower. What used to be the south door was bricked up a hundred years ago. I don't know why. Not that either of us ever goes up into the tower. There's nothing up there except bats. They're a bit of a nuisance but we can't get rid of them, protected species, as you probably know.'

'I see,' Markby said. 'I wonder, could I borrow your set of keys? If you haven't got them on you, then I'll send someone round to your house later to pick them up. Naturally, I'll see someone brings them back to you in due course but we'll need them for a while to secure the scene of – of what's happened.'

Ruth began fumbling in her handbag. 'I should – yes, I have. Here are mine.' She thrust a ring of large old-fashioned keys at him. 'Take them. I don't need them. How can I – how can I ever go in there again?'

'Of course you will!' interposed Muriel Scott sternly.

Markby slipped the keyring into his pocket. 'So Miss Millar went out this morning to open up the church. What time would that have been?'

Ruth looked confused and clutched at her head, burying her fingers in her hair. 'Nine-thirty or thereabouts? We listen to Radio Four in the morning, the *Today* programme, and it had finished and the news summary which follows it. I wasn't paying much attention to the programme which followed that, someone being interviewed, I think.'

'Do you know what the other errands were? It would be useful to know if she completed them before going to the church.'

'I'm not sure,' Ruth admitted. She wrinkled her brow and began to look distressed. 'She had her leather shoulderbag with her as always and she may have been carrying something else, something small, but I'm not clear in my mind about it. I just wasn't paying attention. I'm so sorry. I ought to have asked her. But she just said she had a couple of things to do, including opening the church, and would be back in under an hour.' Tears filled her eyes and rolled down her cheeks. 'I didn't even turn round properly, I just glanced back at her over my shoulder and saw her standing by the door. I mumbled, OK or something like that. We didn't even make a proper goodbye.'

Muriel Scott was looking restless. Markby took the hint.

'Thank you, Mrs Aston. Perhaps we can talk again later, when you've had a chance to take all this on board. I realise it's been a terrible shock.'

He got to his feet. Meredith and Mrs Scott rose with him. Muriel moved towards Ruth and bent over her. Meredith followed Markby to the hall.

Roger, in his prison, scratched at the door, whined and then fell silent, no doubt listening intently.

'There is something I ought perhaps to tell you,' Meredith said in a low voice.

Alan raised his eyebrows. 'Yes?'

'When I first met Ruth, in the church the day we came to look at this house, there was an old boy there, a local man, a sort of oldest inhabitant. Ruth called him Old Billy Twelvetrees. She told me he watched out for her entering the church and then always came over to chat. The landlord of the pub here is apparently a nephew of Old Billy and he also mentioned to me that his uncle liked talking to the ladies when they came to the church. I'd just popped into the pub for coffee, by the way. It's a peculiar place. I didn't fancy it.'

'You're getting off the point,' he chided her.

'Right. Well, just before I found Hester, as I was walking up the church path, I saw someone in the churchyard. He was quite a distance away and of course, I wasn't close enough to make a confident identification. The man had his back to me, in any case. But he was the height and build of Old Billy. He limped and was helped along with a stick as Old Billy is. He seemed in a great hurry, scrambling over the graves, almost as if he wanted to get away from something.'

'Ah,' said Markby.

Meredith put a hand on his arm. 'That's not all. Once news got out about what had happened, people came from all over the place. You must have seen the crowd outside the church. Goodness knows where they were before. I didn't see a soul when I first arrived. But the thing is, Old Billy wasn't amongst them. So where was – is – he? For a real old nosy-parker as he struck me as being, it does seem odd.' She drew a deep breath. 'So I'm wondering if I really was the first person to find Hester.'

'I see.' Markby rubbed his chin thoughtfully. 'You think the old man saw the church was open, went in to see if either of the churchwardens was there so he could trap her in conversation, found Hester dead, panicked and scarpered. Now he's lying low.'

'I'm also wondering whether he saw anyone else around there – or if anyone else saw him. Perhaps you ought to try and find him quickly, Alan. I'm not telling you your job. I'm just concerned about the old fellow.'

'We'll make it a priority, don't worry. At the least, he seems a possible material witness.'

Markby turned back into the sitting room. Mrs Scott had joined Ruth on the sofa and was patting her shoulder in awkward sympathy.

'Sorry to bother you again,' he said. 'But is there someone in the village, an elderly person perhaps, who'd know all the gossip, someone who'd talk to me?'

'There's Old Billy Twelvetrees,' said Ruth, looking up from the crumpled handkerchief she'd held to her eyes.

'Old mischief-maker!' snorted Muriel Scott. 'If you talk to him, discount half of it. What he doesn't know, he makes up.'

'I'll bear that in mind,' Markby promised her. 'Where can I find him.'

'Second cottage down from the pub, to the left. He's got a daughter living with him, Dilys. If you can get past her, Old Billy will be pleased to see you.'

'That at least will make a change,' murmured Markby to Meredith as he went out. 'Most people, even the innocent, are usually displeased to see the police on their doorsteps!'

Woof, woof, woof, went Roger in support.

Chapter Seven

When Markby returned to the church he found a scene of some confusion. The crowd was as numerous as before and additional vehicles had arrived including one near which stood two sombre men, waiting patient and motionless. Though the sightseers were jostling for a good view of the church, around the van and the men there was a space. A *cordon sanitaire*, thought Markby with grim amusement. On the one hand the crowd was fascinated by a violent death. On the other hand, the formalities of death itself were too close to home.

Pearce appeared clad in protective clothing as Markby made his way into the porch.

'They won't disperse!' he said irritably. He put his hand to his jaw.

'Something wrong?' Markby enquired.

'What? Oh, no. I'm just fed up with that lot of ghouls out there. Why won't they go home?'

'It's never any different, Dave. They'll go home once the body's been taken away.'

Pearce sniffed. 'Dr Fuller's here.'

'Better go and have a word with him, then,' Markby murmured. 'Got a spare suit there?'

Inside the church lighting had been set up but the photographer was beginning to pack away his cameras. Fuller, the pathologist, teddy bear like in his one-piece disposable suit, was standing a little forlornly by the corpse.

'This is very inconvenient,' he said as Markby, now similarly clad, came up. 'You'll be wanting a post mortem as soon as possible and I've tickets for a concert at the Festival Hall tonight. My wife and I have been looking forward to it but it does mean travelling up there this afternoon. We had hoped,' Fuller continued, fixing Markby with a look which suggested all this was his fault, 'to stay overnight in London. My wife wants to do some shopping.'

'What about Streeter?' Markby named Dr Fuller's assistant.

'In Marrakesh,' returned Fuller.

'On holiday?'

'Not a holiday, a conference. Don't ask me why they chose Marrakesh.' Fuller turned his discontented stare on the hapless Hester Millar. 'This lady has considerably upset my plans. I shall have to leave Miriam in London and return on an early train to carry out this examination.'

Markby didn't know whether to be amused or cross. He'd known Fuller for years. Fuller's obsession with music and his family were famous. Nevertheless, the man was meticulous as regarded his profession. Markby knew he'd get the post mortem results through within a couple of days. Fuller was just letting off steam.

'Now you've seen her,' Fuller was saying, indicating the body. 'Perhaps we could take her away? The chaps are waiting outside.'

'I saw them,' Markby murmured. 'Unless Inspector Pearce has other ideas, let them take the body by all means.'

The undertaker's men arrived with their temporary coffin. They lifted the inert mass which had been Hester Millar gently from the pew. As they did something glinted on the ground by her feet.

Markby stepped forward and using a biro, hooked up a ring of keys.

Hester's body was zipped into a black body bag and deposited neatly in the coffin. Markby and Dr Fuller followed it from the church. The crowd fell silent as it appeared, was loaded into the van and driven away. Markby turned to the watchers.

'Right, you might as well all go home now. We'll be busy here for a long time but there will be nothing for you to see.'

They shuffled about but then began to go their various ways, several of the men disappearing into the Fitzroy Arms. Fuller had driven away.

'Thank goodness for that!' muttered a voice at his elbow and Markby turned to see Pearce. He beckoned the inspector back inside the church and held up the keyring.

'These were hidden by the body. She'd used them to open up. Then she walked over to that pew, put the keys down on the little ledge here and when she fell forward, stabbed, they were knocked to the ground.'

He held the biro with the dangling keyring towards Pearce who searched in his pocket, produced a small plastic bag, and slipped it over the keys.

'And,' Markby went on, producing Ruth's keyring from his own pocket. 'Mrs Aston has lent me her set. Have you checked the vestry, Dave?'

'We've been in there,' Pearce said. 'It's behind that curtain. There is a small area at the rear behind a screen, locked off. I was hoping to get some keys from Mrs Aston. I didn't fancy breaking it down, being a church. The tower's locked, too.'

'Then we'd better put Ruth Aston's set to good use.'

The two of them made their way to the vestry. It was empty of furniture except for an old wooden table scored with the initials of choirboys long dead. Rows of pegs along the wall were bare of the robes which might once have hung there. The screen to which Pearce referred was of blackened oak and rose nearly to the ceiling. The gap above had been filled in with what looked like chicken wire.

Markby inserted the key labelled 'Vestry' in the lock. It turned easily. 'Someone comes in here,' he observed. 'Oiled.'

But there was nothing in the tiny office behind the door but a box of candles, two tall wooden candle-holders, once gilded but now scratched and faded, and a tin of polish. A sepia photograph hanging crookedly on the wall depicted a nineteenth-century clergyman with muttonchop whiskers and a look of confidence which provided ironic contrast to the stripped surroundings.

'Perhaps they use it when someone takes a service here,' Pearce suggested, poking around in the candle box. 'Nothing here.'

Markby slammed the door of an empty cupboard. 'All the church records must've been moved out when the building fell out of regular use.' He pointed at a paler patch on the dusty floor. 'There must have been a safe there once.'

They relocked the vestry and went back to the nave. By common consent they made for the tower door. Here entry also proved easy. Markby peered at the lock.

'This has been oiled, too. That's odd. Ruth Aston told me they never climbed the tower.'

The door clicked open and swung silently inwards. Markby ran his finger over the hinges and showed Pearce the resultant smear of oil. A spiral of stone steps ran upwards, thickly coated with dust but showing clearly the imprint of footwear.

Markby pointed at the prints. 'Two people. Trainer soles, from the pattern. One set larger than the other. A couple of youngsters, one older? Or a man and a youngish woman, casually dressed?'

'Perhaps whoever it is chews gum,' Pearce said excitedly. 'We found a piece over there, stuck on an effigy on a tomb. But it was all dried out, been there a week or more. Still, perhaps they were up here when Miss Millar came into the church —'

'Then why not just wait until she left again?' Markby pointed at the line of footprints. 'Anyway, the prints have had time to gather their own dust, lighter than the surrounding grime, so they aren't so very recent. I'd say made at least ten to fifteen days ago. Your theory won't work, Dave, I'm afraid. It's been a week or more since anyone came up here, too, for whatever purpose. Time enough for fresh dust to settle. Hester Millar's killer wasn't hiding up here.'

Pearce, a promising line of investigation abruptly terminated, mumbled, 'Pity.'

The two of them climbed the narrow twisting stairs, taking care to keep to one side, clear of the trainer imprints. Pearce, treading in Markby's footsteps, thought ruefully he was like the page who followed that king who went out in the snow, in the Christmas carol. At intervals they passed window slits through which they could see across the surrounding churchyard and village street. At the top, they came out into a small room smelling strongly of age, damp mortar and bat urine. The bells hung above their heads, the ropes disappearing down through a square hole in the floor. Markby touched Pearce's arm to indicate caution.

But Pearce was looking at something in the corner. 'See there! Someone's been camping out in here.'

A candle stub in a pottery holder stood on the floor beside an old sleeping bag which had been unzipped and opened out flat. Markby stooped and picked up a small empty packet. He held it up so Pearce could see it.

'Here's your explanation. Condoms. Either the youth of the village have found this spot or someone was making a illicit tryst. Whoever it is must have found a key which would turn the tower lock downstairs. As soon as one of the churchwardens has opened up the church of a morning, whoever it is contacts his or her partner and they rendezvous up here.'

They retreated to the floor of the church and locked up the tower again.

Markby handed the keys to Pearce. 'You'd better keep these. I've told Mrs Aston we'll return them in due course.' He frowned. 'We'll have to find out who holds that other tower key, though just how I don't know. Our mystery lovers are hardly likely to come forward and admit to desecrating the church. They may just have an odd key which turns the lock. These old-fashioned mortice locks can sometimes be opened like that. My mother used to keep a whole boxful of odd keys for emergency use if one went missing. If that's the case, we don't have to worry. On the other hand, they may hold the entire set for the church, entrances and vestry, which would really put the cat among the pigeons. Yet Ruth says only she, Hester and James Holland have keys. I'll have to check that one out with James. The idea of a spare set of keys hanging around really muddies the water.'

Pearce grunted and pushed the keys into his pocket. 'How did you get on at the house, sir? With Mrs Aston and that other batty old dear with the striped sweater?'

Markby summed up the rest of his conversation with Ruth Aston and added Meredith's account of seeing someone leaving the churchyard at the far end as she'd approached the church.

'It seems likely that she saw this old fellow, Twelvetrees. He's the local gossip but he doesn't seem to have put in an appearance here. At least, I couldn't see anyone in the crowd who answered the description Meredith gave me. I thought I'd go along to his cottage and see what's going on there.'

'They're a funny lot,' observed Pearce of the villagers in general. 'What with shenanigans in the belfry and all the rest of it. Good luck.'

Markby was well aware that his short progress from the church to Billy Twelvetrees' cottage was being observed. It couldn't be helped. There was no way any investigations in this village could be carried out with any kind of privacy, much less discretion. The atmosphere of excitement all around him was palpable. It could only get worse when the commuting population of incomers returned that evening and made for the Fitzroy Arms to soak up details of the day's events. Mixed with the excitement was a kind of decent horror and even a sense of being offended that this could happen here in their quiet community.

Or am I, Markby asked himself, looking back to that last enquiry I conducted here and translating what I felt then to what I feel now? It was a curious feeling, he supposed one could call it *déjà vu*, to be knocking on doors in Lower Stovey again after a gap of more than twenty years. The physical appearance of the village had changed in the intervening time, as he'd noticed on his visit to the Old Vicarage with Meredith yet, despite the loss of shop and school, it looked prosperous. Nearly all the cottages in the main street had been painted up and garnished with carriage lamps and the like. He guessed at second homes.

In this line of gleaming prosperity, the Twelvetrees' dwelling stood out like a rotten tooth in an array of perfect gnashers. It hadn't been painted for years. Its thatched roof was dark brown and disintegrating, held together by a hairnet of chicken wire through which could be seen patches of moss and sprouting weeds. The wooden frames of the windows were crumbling but the panes were well polished as was the fox-head doorknocker. He lifted it and rapped on the door. He hadn't seen inside yet, but he could guess what he'd find.

No one came for a few minutes during which he heard a rattle above his head and knew someone was looking from the tiny window under the mouldering thatch to see who the visitor was. Eventually the door shuddered and was pulled open.

He found himself looking at a middle-aged woman in a pink overall, the colour oddly matched by her salmon-pink tightly-curled hair. Her face was round and snub-nosed. Her lower lip was fuller than her upper lip and overlapped it, suggesting what dentists call an 'overbite' when the lower jaw protrudes further than the upper one. Her expression was truculent and he was forcibly reminded of a surly bulldog. He held up his identification.

'We've got nothing to do with it!' snapped the woman.

He ignored this. 'Could I speak to Mr Twelvetrees? This is his house?'

'Dad's not in. He didn't have anything to do with it, either. How could he at his age and in his state of health?'

'Where is he?' asked Markby bluntly.

'I dunno. Gone out for a walk, like he does.'

'Where does he walk normally?'

She uttered a sort of hiss which issued from the sides of her mouth. 'Just round and about. He can't go far, not with his hip.'

'Oh?' Markby smiled innocently at her. 'I'm sorry to hear that. Does he have a stick?'

'He's got one of them.' She nodded her head and Markby was reminded of all the tinned salmon sandwiches he'd been obliged to eat as a child. 'But what he needs is one of them new hips. Doctor says so. Only he's obstinate, is Dad. He won't go in no hospital.'

She glared at Markby and in the ensuing silence, came a diversion.

From the far end of the narrow hall, behind a door, another door slammed. They could hear someone wheezing and a sound like a stick tapping on flagstones. There must be a back entrance, an alley or such running behind these cottages.

Markby smiled at the woman again, something which seemed to alarm her. 'It sounds as if your father's come home. Why don't you go and see?'

He moved forward as he spoke and she retreated allowing him to squeeze into the hall. As he did, the door at the far end opened and the sturdy outline of an elderly man appeared, filling the aperture. He raised his stick and jabbed it aggressively at the stranger.

'Who's this feller, then?' he asked.

'Policeman, Dad,' said his daughter. 'Don't know what he wants. Well, he says he wants to talk to you. Can't think why.' This was accompanied by a sidelong contemptuous glance at Markby. 'I suppose they've got to look as if they're doing something. There's been a bit of bother, someone's died. I told him, you've got nothing to do with it.'

'Murder,' declared the old man with some satisfaction. 'I met someone on my way home as told me about it. Well, Mr Policeman. You'd better come into my parlour, as the spider said to the fly.' And disconcerting Markby considerably, he burst into a cackle of laughter.

His daughter shot forward and bundled him back into the kitchen. 'You got to take them dirty boots off, Dad!' she said loudly. Over her shoulder to Markby, she added, 'You go on and wait for him. He'll be with you direct.'

Markby obediently went into the parlour. The room in which he found himself spoke of poverty, not a recent lack of income but a generations-long want. Poor people begetting poor people, trapped in a narrow existence not only by lack of cash but by lack of education and a deep mistrust and fear of the outside world. He wasn't surprised Billy Twelvetrees didn't want to go to hospital. He suspected the very idea was terrifying to the old man. He'd lived here for his entire life and he had no wish to be surrounded by strangers at this late stage.

He knew he had a few minutes to examine his surroundings. Billy and his daughter would be exchanging information and arguing what was the best thing to do with the visitor. Billy's curiosity might make him eager to chat. His daughter's instinct would be to tell him to button his lip and get rid of that copper, that it was nothing to do with them. The woman was a not unfamiliar type. It would be a mistake to think that because of her appearance and manner she didn't have a sharp brain. She also had the instincts of her type, which were to round up and protect her young at any hint of danger from an intruder by physically placing herself between the threat and her charges. Her elderly parent had become, due to age and infirmity, her child. It was that curious and sad reversal of roles so often observed when the carer becomes the cared-for.

The room was cramped and full of furniture, all of it rickety. By the fire was an armchair with faded loose covers and the look of having been much sat in. Billy's chair, he guessed. Above the mantelshelf hung a sepia portrait of a man in First World War uniform. Beneath it, along the shelf, stood further photographs. There was one, also sepia, of two children, a boy and a girl, dressed in their best and staring miserably at the camera. Next to it, in complete contrast, was a recent picture of a plump woman, bearing some resemblance to the one who'd opened the door to him, but better dressed in a floral skirt and white top and beaming happily at the lens. The building behind her looked unreal, an extravaganza of turrets. Markby was peering at it in an attempt to identify it, when the door opened. He turned guiltily.

Billy Twelvetrees stomped in, banging his stick down on the worn carpet. Behind him hovered his daughter but he soon dismissed her with 'You go and bring us some tea, Dilys.'

Dilys went and Billy sat down in his armchair. If there'd been an argument in the kitchen, Billy had won it. Markby, guessing he wouldn't be invited to sit, sat down anyway on a straight-backed Edwardian dining chair which didn't feel too safe under him.

'You were looking at our pictures,' said Billy with a certain pride. He raised his stick again and used it to point in the manner of an old-fashioned schoolmaster. 'That big 'un, that's my father. That one there is me and my sister, Lilian. Her son, Norman, he runs the pub here now. Done well for himself, Norman. That one is my elder daughter Sandra taken in Flor-ee-da, at Disneyland. That one on the end is my wife and my kids, took when my boy was just starting school. We had a school in them days. It's houses now.'

Markby looked at the photo which showed a plump sullen woman holding a baby on her lap. To either side of her stood two other children, a boy about five and a girl a little younger. The baby must be Dilys.

'Your daughter, the one I've met, she lives with you, Mr Twelvetrees?'

'Lived with me for years. I gave her a home. Her husband, Ernie Pullen, done a bunk. He was gone six months after their wedding day, run off with the barmaid at the Fitzroy Arms. Never saw hide nor hair of either of them again. I don't know why he married our Dilys in the first place. She was never no oil-painting.'

The door opened as he spoke and Dilys entered with the tea. Her red face indicated she'd overheard his disparaging remarks. She put the tin tray down with unnecessary force on a small table and withdrew silently.

Billy chuckled. He picked up a mug and sipped from it though the amount of steam rising from it suggested it was very hot. Markby touched his mug tentatively and withdrew his hand.

'Hester Millar, as I hear,' said Billy, abruptly introducing the reason for Markby's call. 'Dead murdered.'

'That's correct. You would know her, of course.'

The old man nodded, slurping more hot tea. 'Her and Mrs Aston, they look after the church. Mrs Aston is the old vicar's daughter.'

'You like to go in the church and talk to them, I hear.'

'Did you?' Billy glared at him. 'And where did you hear that, I wonder?'

Markby only gave a bland smile.

'I might do,' Billy agreed grudgingly.

'When did you last talk to one of them in the church?'

'That's a bit of a daft question, ain't it? I don't know. Maybe yesterday, maybe the day before. One day's much like another to me. You'll find that out when you get to my age.'

'But not today?'

'No,' Billy's small malevolent eyes met Markby's without flinching. 'I wasn't in there today.'

'Did you see Miss Millar outside the church, say walking towards it?'

'No, why should I?'

'Because I understand you were in the churchyard.'

'No, I wasn't,' said Billy promptly.

'A witness saw you hurrying away from the building, over in the far corner of the churchyard.'

Billy scowled. 'Who's your witness? He wants spectacles, whoever he is.'

Markby waited silently. Billy turned the matter over in his mind. 'I might,' he said. 'Only might, mind you! I might have cut across the corner of the churchyard on my walk. I often do that. I can't recall exactly. At my age, your memory gives out. But I know I never went near the church itself. And I never saw no one.'

Billy appeared pleased with this somewhat contradictory statement. 'That's it,' he said and picked up his mug again.

'Does anyone else have a habit of dropping in the church?' Markby asked him.

'No.' Billy shrugged. 'Unless it's visitors. They come to see the monuments. We got some very good monuments. They was nearly all put up to the Fitzroys. They used to be the big family around here. There's none of 'em left now. There was a visitor in only the other day, tall good-looking woman. She and her partner, as she called him . . .' Billy sniggered, 'they'd come looking to buy the old vicarage. Wants their heads seeing to, darn great place like that. It's what you'd call a white ellyphant.'

'Yes,' said Markby, discomfited. 'I don't think we need count them. No one else?'

'Who else,' countered Billy, 'comes to Lower Stovey? It's the end of the world is Lower Stovey.'

'But you've lived here all your life?' Markby contemplated him.

'It used to be a good deal livelier,' Billy grumbled. 'Before they took our school away and never replaced the old vicar. We had a couple of little shops, and all. They've gone. Now a feller comes a couple of times a week with a van selling groceries. He charges the earth. Mrs Aston, she takes Dilys with her into Bamford once a week and Dilys does our shopping then. Dilys cleans for her. She's a nice lady, Mrs Aston.'

'And Miss Millar? Was she a nice lady?'

'She was.' Billy sucked his discoloured teeth. 'But she wasn't a local. Mrs Aston, she's one of us.'

Whether poor Ruth Aston liked it or not, reflected Markby, she was for ever to be associated with Lower Stovey in the minds of its native population.

'She went to the village school for a bit,' went on Billy. 'She went to school with our Sandra and Dilys.'

Markby couldn't help but think that time had dealt more kindly with Ruth Aston than with Dilys, who must be the same age but looked ten years older.

'I remember when the village had a school,' he said.

Billy stiffened. He put his mug down slowly. 'How's that, then?'

'I was here before, oh, a long time ago. Twenty-two years. You still had the school then and a post office.'

'Oh, yes?' said Billy, treating him to a wary look. 'They never ought to have taken away our post office. I got nowhere to draw my pension. Dilys has to draw it for me when she goes to Bamford.'

There was a note of genuine resentment in his voice. Markby wondered if this meant that having got her hands on his pension money first, Dilys put most of it towards the housekeeping, and doled out tiny amounts to her father which limited his spending power in the local pub.

'There were a number of attacks on women in Stovey Woods,' he prompted Billy. 'That's why I came here before.'

'So they said,' mumbled Billy, gazing into his empty mug. He looked up and his withered lips twisted in an unkind smile. 'I never reckoned to it. Them girls give it away and then they took fright in case they found themselves in the family way. They made up that story. You ask anyone in the village.'

Markby well remembered this attitude at the time. It angered him as much now as it had then. He snapped, 'Two of the victims were from outside the village, a hiker and a cyclist on the old drovers' way.'

'There you are, then,' returned Billy unrepentantly. 'What were they doing up there, all alone, a couple of young girls like that? Not decent. Asking for trouble and they got it.' He jabbed a finger at Markby. 'The police never found anyone, did they? Stands to reason they didn't. There never were no Potato Man.'

'You remember his nickname then,' Markby observed drily.

' 'Course I do. But that don't mean he ever was real. He weren't. Ever since I was a boy there's been stories about Stovey Woods. People used to reckon it was haunted. They said the old Green Man was up there. You know about him?'

'I've heard of the Green Man,' Markby told him.

'Right, then you've heard all you need to. Folk have always believed there was something in those woods and when those girls started telling their stories, people remembered the old tales. Only instead of Green Man, they called him the Potato Man. But it's the same feller and just as much twaddle.'

Billy pointed at the photograph of Sandra outside Disneyland. 'It's all as real as anything you'd see at that place. Dwarves and fairies and the like. In the old days, people believed anything. They was simple,' concluded Billy, dismissing his forebears. 'Daft as a brush.'

Markby got to his feet. 'I don't think you're daft as a brush, Mr Twelvetrees. I want you to think carefully about today, about your walk, about the churchyard, about whether or not you went into the church or saw Miss Millar or anyone else. The police will call on you again. Not me, probably, but someone else.'

'I'll tell him the same as I told you,' said Billy sourly. He brightened. 'Here, tell 'em to send one of the young policewomen!' He gave Markby a cunning sidelong look. 'I might talk to one of them.'

'I'll let myself out,' Markby told him, ignoring this suggestion. What an unpleasant old devil he was. And lying through his teeth. He either saw Hester outside or inside the church. Markby would bet his bottom dollar on it.

The hall was empty but he could hear Dilys moving about in the kitchen. He tapped on the door and pushed it open. He was rewarded with a view of Dilys's pink nylon rear as she bent over a chipped enamel pedal bin. He cleared his throat.

Dilys jumped up and the lid of the pedal bin clashed down. She whirled round.

'I'm leaving,' said Markby.

'Right you are, then.' She looked relieved. 'Dad didn't have anything to say to you, then?'

'I expect he'll tell you all about it. I understand you clean for Mrs Aston – and Miss Millar.'

'I work for Mrs Aston,' returned Dilys pedantically. 'Miss Millar only lived there. It wasn't her house.'

'Were you there today?'

She shook her head. 'I don't go every day this time of year, only Tuesday and Friday. I do a bit extra in the winter because of the stove in the old hearth. They burn logs in it. The ladies make no mess. I just go over there and do the rough work, such as it is.'

'You went to school with Ruth Aston, your father tells me.'

She blinked. 'Only for a couple of years. Then the vicar took her out of our school and sent her off to some fancy one. Don't know why they ever sent her to our school in the first place. But the old vicar, he was full of ideas like that. You know, he thought he was being one of the villagers.' Dily snorted. 'Him? I often thought he ought to have been a schoolmaster himself, always with his head in books as he was. He had all kinds of daft ideas, always wanting to know about what he called local legends.'

'Like the Green Man?' Markby asked.

'Oh yes, he was very keen on the old Green Man. He'd knock on people's doors and ask them if they knew any stories. What he called folk memory. No wonder half the village thought he was crackers.'

Markby held out his hand. 'Thank you, Dilys.'

She looked at his outstretched palm in dismay but nervously placed her stubby fingers on his. 'No trouble I'm sure,' she said in with an assumed prissy gentility.

Back in his car, Markby stretched his hand out to put the key in the ignition and saw, to his surprise, that his shirt cuff was stained with a pinkish smear. He'd been careful to touch neither the body nor anything in the area where it had been found. He frowned, peered at the offending stain, sniffed at it and finally, cautiously touched it. It was sugary, something he'd brushed against in Dilys's kitchen. It would probably be difficult to remove. Dilys, in her own way, had had the last word.

Having left Pearce conducting investigations in Lower Stovey, Markby drove back to Bamford. As he put distance between himself and the village, he felt as if he drove out of thick cloud into sunshine. It was a feeling which had nothing to do with the weather which was mild and unremarkable. It was the atmosphere which clung to the place. But he couldn't distance himself from what had happened there that day completely. He had a call to make.

Bamford vicarage was familiar to Markby and the vicar, James Holland, an old friend. But he wasn't normally given to calling on James unannounced. As he walked up to the front door later that day he reflected that the vicar would guess it was police business of some kind as soon as he saw who stood on his doorstep.

'Alan!' exclaimed James with a flattering note of pleasure in his voice, before adding, as Markby had known he would, 'Something wrong? Come on in and tell me about it.'

The vicar led the way to the antiquated kitchen, filled the kettle and plugged it in, then turned to his visitor. 'Tea or coffee?'

'Tea, please, if it's all the same to you.'

'Comes out of the same kettle,' returned James placidly, unwittingly reminding Markby of the drinks dispenser at Regional HQ.

James' tea was, thankfully, a big improvement on the brew dribbled out by the dread machine. They carried their mugs into the study and sat, facing one another, in large, rickety, comfortable armchairs. To Markby's right were french windows giving on to the overgrown garden. The early evening sun bathed them in a warm orange glow.

'This is a nice room,' he said appreciatively.

James nodded. 'It's a nice house or would be, if it were done up. No chance of that. The bishop is still keen to sell it and put me in a modern three-bed box somewhere on one of the new estates. The PCC is fighting him tooth and nail and Bamford Council isn't keen for fear of what might happen to what is a well-known building in the town. So I continue to sit here and the place continues to crumble about my ears.'

'Meredith and I have been to view a former vicarage,' Markby told him. 'Out at Lower Stovey.'

'The house-hunting, how's it going? Lower Stovey,' James went on meditatively. 'Bit remote, I'd have thought.' He drank some tea and as he did, his mug half vanished into his bushy black beard.

'Its souls are in your charge, I believe.'

The vicar nodded. 'I only get out there once a month. Sometimes old Picton-Wilkes takes a service for me there. He's retired, over eighty, but likes to keep his hand in. The church is called St Barnabas and is quite a fine building. But it represents a problem to the diocese.'

'Surplus to requirements?'

Another nod. 'There's hardly any congregation and the place is kept up by the dedicated efforts of a pair of ladies who act as churchwardens. One of them, Ruth Aston, is the daughter of the last incumbent. He died, let's see, eighteen years ago but the problems had already begun. The population of the village was dwindling, few young families. Frankly, Pattinson, the vicar, was gaga for the last year. The decision was taken not to replace him and to attach St Barnabas to our church here in Bamford. The same thing happened to Westerfield church. So now I run the joint parishes. As regards Lower Stovey, a few new homes have been built there in the last five or six years, most when the old school was sold off for development. But it hasn't made any difference to the community. The backbone of that was broken long ago.'

James sighed. 'Mrs Aston is in her late fifties, as is her fellow-warden. They won't want to carry on for ever. Within the next five years the crunch will come.'

'I'm afraid, James, that the crunch has already come,' Markby said, putting down his mug. 'But not in any way you could have anticipated. One of your churchwardens, not Mrs Aston, the other one, Hester Millar, is dead.'

His words were met with shocked silence. Then James asked quietly, 'How?'

Markby told him. 'As it happened in the church, I've come not only to inform you, but to pick your brains.'

Father Holland stirred from the deep thought into which he'd been plunged since Markby began his tale. 'About Lower Stovey? I'm afraid there's little I can tell you about the place. To my shame my monthly visits are all I see of it. Ruth Aston could tell you —

He broke off and shook his head. 'But poor Ruth won't be in a state to tell you anything. She and Hester were very old friends. After Gerald Aston died, Hester moved in with Ruth. My own acquaintance with Hester dates from then. She was a practical sort, no nonsense and absolutely no malice in her. I liked her but I can't say I knew her well. Look, of course you'll need to talk to Ruth, but anything to do with the church I'd rather you discussed with me. As for Ruth, I doubt she'll make much sense in the circumstances.'

'There's something else I should tell you which you may or may not wish to tell Mrs Aston,' Markby told him apologetically. 'There are signs that someone has gained access to the church tower for – er – romantic reasons on at least one occasion.'

'What?' James sat up straight in his chair. 'Fornicating in the church?'

'It looks like it. In the belfry room to be exact. We found a packet of condoms and a sleeping bag up there.'

'That does it,' said James grimly. 'We'll have to rethink having the church open during the day. It looks as if we'll have to keep it locked all the time. I'll discuss it with Ruth when – when she's over the initial shock of Hester's death. But in the end, it's my decision, and after what you tell me —'

'I was hoping,' Markby interrupted him, 'that you could tell me if there are any sets of keys to St Barnabas other than the one you hold and those held by the churchwardens. Whoever has been using the tower for unofficial purposes uses a key to unlock the tower door.'

James paled. 'Someone has a key? How is that? The only other set I know of is held by Harry Picton-Wilkes. I hardly think he's been misbehaving in the tower.'

'Then could I ask you if you'd kindly find out on my behalf where the reverend gentleman keeps his keys and whether they're accessible to anyone else. Are they hanging up in a pantry or something like that?'

'Yes, of course I will. I need to know, too!' James looked flustered.

'Do you know whether Hester Millar had relatives?' Markby brought the subject back to the victim.

Again a shake of the head. 'I can only repeat I know – knew – little or nothing about Hester. What I know of Ruth is really only through her connection with the church and of course, through Gerald, her late husband whom I knew slightly. I'm afraid I can only refer you to Ruth for details of Hester's background.'

Markby looked through the small square panes of the french windows at the untrimmed hedges and weed-choked borders. What he wouldn't give to get his hands on this garden.

'Just now you spoke of the backbone of the community of Lower Stovey as being broken. Were you referring only to the population drift away?'

He was aware of James Holland's intelligent gaze fixed on him. The vicar took his time before replying. Eventually he said:

'I understand that there were some very unfortunate happenings there more than twenty years ago, before my time.'

'A series of rapes,' Markby said. 'We never caught him.'

'More's the pity, and not only because such a monster must be caught in any circumstances. In a small community like that, such a terrible thing can shatter it and nothing can put it together again. Did the police suspect anyone? A village man?'

'We had no suspects. He might have been a villager but equally he might not. Two of the attacks took place on the old drovers' way. He might have been a tramp, a wandering psychopath. Perhaps someone who'd been in trouble elsewhere and had taken to the road on the run? We don't know.'

'And because the police never nailed him, the villagers were left harbouring suspicions about their neighbours,' James said. 'The old trust and reliance on one another were destroyed. That's what broke the back of Lower Stovey. It's probably what did for Pattinson's mental faculties. They couldn't cope and neither could he.'

'That's when I first visited the vicarage there, in the course of those enquiries,' Markby told him. 'I had a long chat with Pattinson. I remember him as an old-fashioned, bookish sort of chap. He certainly wasn't gaga then. Not quite in tune with the modern world, perhaps.'

The vicar's beard moved indicating that beneath it he was pulling a wry grimace. 'I hadn't realised you were involved, Alan. I didn't intend to sound as if I blamed Lower Stovey's collapse on any failure on the part of the police.'

'But we did fail,' Markby said. 'And when we fail, communities do suffer. An unsolved serious crime is like an open sore, never healing.'

'And now you have a murder, Hester's murder,' James said.

'Exactly. I don't mean to fail Lower Stovey a second time.'

Something more than ordinary resolution in his tone had worried the vicar who frowned. 'Don't take it personally, Alan. You're a professional, as I am. You know as I do that sometimes you don't win or you can't rearrange matters. You and I both deal with cases which move us deeply. We're human beings and we get angry, distressed, depressed. But we can't help others if we get carried away ourselves.'

Markby burst out energetically, 'I *do* take it personally!' He flushed and added, 'Sorry. I know you're right. It's just . . .' His voice tailed away.

James was nodding. After a moment he said, 'Didn't someone find bones in Stovey Woods recently? I read something in the local paper.'

Markby's gaze was on the garden again. 'Oh yes, the bones. I wonder, if they hadn't been found, whether Hester Millar would be alive today.'

He had shocked the vicar for a third time in their conversation. 'You think there's a connection?' James Holland frowned.

Markby put his hands on the arms of the chair and pushed himself upright. 'Who knows? Probably not. I had no reason to say that and perhaps I shouldn't have. But I don't like coincidences, James.' He smiled sadly. 'You probably try to see the best in people. My problem is that I tend to see the worst. I'm like an old-time seafarer whose charts are marked by sightings of mermen and sea-monsters. I float precariously on a world seething with dangers, known and unknown. I see evil, James. I'm attuned to it. I smell it. I pick up its vibes. I scent evil in Lower Stovey.'

Ruth Aston sat at the kitchen table in the Old Forge and watched the shadows lengthen as the sun went down, touching the sky with rose-coloured fingers. Everything about the kitchen was familiar and ought to have been reassuring. But there was only emptiness and pain in every aspect. Hester's well-thumbed cookery books were stacked on a shelf. Hester's cooking implements hung in a neat row beneath. In the larder was half an apple pie made by Hester the previous day and intended to be finished at lunchtime today. But by noon this day Hester lay dead.

The whole thing seemed unreal. She sat in a world in a different dimension to that inhabited by everyone else. Ruth found herself thinking: *The door will open in a minute and Hester will come in.* But the door wouldn't open for a long time and, when it eventually did, whoever walked through it wouldn't be Hester. The most likely next arrival at the kitchen door would be Dilys Twelvetrees. Tomorrow was one of her cleaning days. Ruth wondered whether she should walk up to Billy's cottage and push a note through the door, asking Dilys to give the next day a miss. She really didn't want the woman there, clumping round in her stolid way as if everything was normal, which it wasn't. The Twelvetrees had no telephone and the effort of writing out a note and walking the short length of Church Lane to deliver it, seemed a task of Herculean proportions. Besides which, she might meet someone who'd want to talk about Hester and what had happened. Worst of all, she'd see the blue and white ribbon the police had placed across the entry to the churchyard. The church, which had been so much a part of her childhood and for the last few years her life here in the Old Forge, had become a Scene of Crime, tainted for ever.

At this point, with a pang of guilt, Ruth remembered Father Holland at Bamford. St Barnabas was in his care. He ought to be told what had happened. It was her job as churchwarden to inform him. But perhaps the police had already told him of the dreadful desecration? She wished she knew. She should have asked Markby or that other man, Pearce. Would it require some kind of cleansing ritual before it could be used again as a house of prayer? Would she, Ruth, ever be able to set foot inside it again?

Not only lunch had been missed. She'd eaten nothing all day since breakfast-time, it seemed a lifetime ago. Aware of a sinking feeling in the stomach, Ruth got up and went to fetch Hester's apple pie. She couldn't throw it out. Hester would be so upset. Neither did she feel like eating any of it. But it was the only thing available which didn't require defrosting. Even a sandwich required preparation which she felt was beyond her. It was ironic that, with a full freezer and larder full of jars, she had nothing she could just pick up and eat.

She cut a small wedge of apple pie and put it on a plate. But after two mouthfuls, swallowed with great difficulty, she gave up. Saying aloud, 'Sorry, Hester, I really am!' she picked up the pie and her uneaten wedge and tipped the whole lot into a plastic bag. She rolled it up, took it outside, and deposited it with the greatest care and reverence in the dustbin feeling like a worshipper laying an offering before an altar.

Ruth went back inside and had just put the pie plates in the dishwasher when the phone rang. She'd been remiss in not switching it over to the answering machine. She had to pick it up. It might be the police. Ruth lifted the receiver gingerly and managed to say, 'Yes?'

'Ruth?'

She recognised the voice as belonging to James Holland and heaved a sigh of relief. 'Oh, James, I was thinking about phoning you. Have you —?' She broke off.

'Yes, I've heard about it. Superintendent Markby came to see me. I'm very sorry, Ruth.'

She'd be hearing the last words a lot over the coming weeks with varying degrees of sympathy and sincerity. James, at least, meant it. 'I've been wondering,' she said, 'about the church. Whether it will have to be rededicated or anything.'

It crossed her mind that he'd think it odd that she'd be worrying about such a detail at a time like this. But it was better than talking about Hester or directly about the dreadful deed that had taken her friend from her.

He probably understood. She believed he was a sensitive man for all his hirsute appearance and his fondness for roaring round the country-side on a motorcycle. He was also a good priest. He was phoning her because she was a bereaved parishioner, not because she was a churchwarden in whose charge the church had been so foully violated.

'We'll worry about that later. Are you alone, Ruth? I'll come out there straight away.'

'No!' She feared her voice was too sharp. 'Thank you, James, but I'm fine, really.' Ruth paused. 'No, not really, but I can manage. You know what I mean. I'd rather be alone this evening.'

'Then I'll come over first thing in the morning.' His voice was both competent and soothing. 'Don't worry about the police activities, Ruth. I'll deal with whatever I can, make 'em go through me wherever possible. Though you must brace yourself to answering questions, I'm afraid. They will want to know as much about Hester as you can tell them.'

She tried to answer but it only came out as a suppressed sob.

118

Anxiously, he was asking, 'Look, I'm very concerned about you. Have you eaten, Ruth?'

'Yes,' she lied. Well, not a complete lie. The two mouthfuls of pie lay heavily on her stomach. She strongly suspected that before long she'd throw them up again.

'Have a drop of brandy,' he advised.

She lied again, promising she would, and hung up.

It was nearly dark now and she switched on a lamp before going to the window to pull the curtains. Outside Church Lane was poorly lit. Yet it seemed to her that opposite the Old Forge, in the dark recess between two buildings, something moved. Her heart jumped in alarm. It wasn't just her overwrought imagination. There was someone there. Someone watched the house. A police officer? The murderer, knife in hand? No, there was something familiar about the figure.

Ruth's heart leapt in sudden hope. She did something completely irrational about which she was afterwards deeply embarrassed. She ran to the front door, pulled it open and called out, 'Hester?'

As the name passed her lips, she realised how foolish she was being. There were no ghosts. It wasn't all some ghastly mistake. Pulling herself together, she called, 'Who's there? Who is it?'

The shape became a squat form moving towards her with quiet resolution. The light fell on the visitor's face and she recognised Dilys Twelvetrees.

'Oh, Dilys!' Ruth gasped, half relieved and half dismayed.

'I come to see if you were all right,' came Dilys's voice.

Ruth realised that she was framed in the doorway, lit by the lamp behind her. Anyone else watching would have a good view. Unwillingly she stepped aside to let Dilys over the threshold. She saw, as Dilys lumbered by, that the woman was carrying a small earthenware casserole.

'I brought a bit of stew,' Dilys said. ' 'Cos I thought you'd probably not eaten anything. You need to keep your strength up.'

'Thank you,' Ruth replied weakly, stretching out her hands to take the dish.

'I was watching out front,' Dilys went on, 'because I wasn't sure if you'd gone to bed already. The house was all dark. But then you switched on a light. I didn't come to the back door because I didn't want to give you a fright but I dare say I did that, anyway.'

'No, not at all.' Ruth reflected that she was telling a lot of lies this evening. Had Dilys heard that despairing cry, heard her call to a friend now gone beyond hearing?

'Dad said as I should come and see how you were doing. He thinks a lot of you, does Dad, you being the old vicar's daughter and all.' Dilys tut-tutted. 'Mr Pattinson wouldn't have liked any of this, in his church, too.'

'None of us likes any of it!' Ruth almost shouted at her. She controlled herself and added, 'But it's kind of you, Dilys, and kind of your father to be concerned. Give him my thanks.'

Dilys nodded. 'I'll be in tomorrow morning, same as usual.'

Ruth opened her mouth, lost courage, and said meekly, 'Yes, Dilys.'

'You pop that in the oven straight away.' Dilys indicated the casserole.

'I will.' Ruth finished her evening of lies with yet another. It was getting easy.

Dilys departed. When she was sure the woman had left Church Lane, Ruth went back to the kitchen, found another plastic bag and tipped the stew into it. It flowed glutinously, mud brown, dotted with yellow scraps of carrot, and smelling strongly of onions and Oxo cubes. Ruth put the plastic bag inside another and then wrapped the whole lot in newspaper.

Fearing she'd be observed and a report reach Dilys, she switched off all the lights before opening the back door and slipping outside. Moonlight fell palely over the garden. The field beyond was a watery silver lake. Only Stovey Woods were a dark forbidding mass on the horizon.

Ruth found her way back to the dustbin and pushed the parcel of stew deep down inside beneath other rubbish. The bag containing Hester's pie, lying on top, looked startlingly white in the moonlight. Ruth, in a kind of revulsion mixed with fear, pushed it also deep down beneath the garbage, so that neither of them should know, neither Dilys nor Hester.

She went back indoors and slowly got ready for bed, wondering how many more lies she'd be obliged to tell before all this was over.

Chapter Eight

The following morning, Friday, Meredith rang her Foreign Office department and explained she wouldn't be coming to work.

'Are you sick?' asked Lionel, the colleague she'd reached, in his familiar nicotine-laden growl.

'No, I'm a material witness in a murder case. I need to be on hand if the police want to go over my statement.'

There was a pause. 'Anybody you know?'

Meredith interpreted this query as referring to the victim. In the commercial world, her reason for absence might have been received with more scepticism, shock, excitement, morbid curiosity and so on. Lionel, a grizzled veteran of a wandering life in the service of HM Government, was inured to sudden alarms and out of the way occurrences. His first reaction was to establish the degree of consolation she might require, followed by a mental assessment of what action would be required of her and – eventually – how much inevitable paperwork.

'I didn't know the person. I just happened to be in the wrong place.'

'Bad luck. Take whatever time you need. Keep in touch.' With a note of mischief he added, 'Do you want a character reference?'

'Not yet,' she told him. 'But you never know.'

By the end of the day she was beginning to wish she had gone up to London and got away from it all. She'd expected to find herself giving her statement to Dave Pearce but found herself instead closeted with a sergeant she knew but only slightly, Steve Prescott. An amiable giant, he'd taken her through her statement an unnecessary number of times, or so it had seemed to her. His explanation was that 'something might come back to her'. Eventually even Prescott was persuaded that nothing new was likely to surface in her brain by this method and that his interviewee was growing mutinous. Meredith was allowed to scrawl her name on a typed version of her statement and told she could go home. So eager was she to get through the door, she'd raised only a token objection to the way in which Prescott had translated some of her words into a form he thought more suitable. She did strike out 'observed' as in 'I observed the figure of a woman' and replaced it with 'saw' but left it at that. However she phrased it and whatever the vocabulary, she couldn't add anything to the stark reality which had been Hester Millar's blood-soaked scarf and pale, frozen eye. She thought the sergeant, too, looked relieved at having the encounter over.

Alan reappeared in the early evening on her doorstep, looking equally frazzled. They slumped in facing (and mis-matching) armchairs in Meredith's tiny sitting room.

'This will never do!' Meredith said suddenly. 'Come on, let's go out and eat somewhere.'

'We haven't booked,' he objected in the voice of a man who having found somewhere quiet to relax and nod off, was less than keen at the idea of being chivvied out of it.

'Friday won't be as busy as Saturday. It's not seven yet. I'll give the Fisherman's Rest a ring.'

'You aren't too tired – not, um, stressed?' he asked wistfully.

'Listen,' she told him. 'It's been a very tiring and stressful week, let alone today. We need to put it behind us. Dozing in front of a television screen all evening will make us feel worse.'

Later, at the restaurant, she was beginning to doubt this was quite the bright idea it'd seemed at the time. That Alan was still preoccupied was obvious. For her own part, she was still unable to rid her memory of that silent huddled form in the church, something she'd spent the day talking about and hoped this outing would wipe away if only for an evening. Around them the air was heavy with the smell of food and noisy with the chatter of voices. It had begun to make her head ache and the food odours which normally she would've found enticing now only made her nauseous. She toyed with her *saumon en croûte* and noticed that Alan was making only slighter better headway with his steak *au poivre*.

They sat in what had once been the snug of a public house. But, as the nature of menu made clear, the Fisherman's Rest hadn't been that kind of pub for some years. No fishermen had crossed its threshold for a long time, neither for rest nor sustenance. Nor was it the sort of place local people dropped into for a pint. Most of the people present that evening, Meredith guessed, had driven some miles to be there, as she and Alan had done. The Fisherman's Rest was well known, both for its food and its situation. They'd been here several times before and both of them liked it. Tonight, however, it was failing to work its usual magic.

The restaurant sat atop the river bank, looking out across the gentle landscape of the Windrush valley. By this time of the evening the further bank was veiled in the mist creeping across the meadows and swirling in wraith-like tendrils across the water. The string of lights decorating the façade of the restaurant were reflected in the rippling river surface. The building itself, at least two hundred years old, was painted white and as the daylight faded it seemed to glow eerily in the dusk.

Inside it was warm, attractive, in every way welcoming. Every other patron was having a wonderful evening. Only she and Alan sat, monosyllabic, picking at this excellent dinner.

Eventually, Meredith asked, 'Is it the house-hunting or the murder which is worrying you?'

He was immediately apologetic as she'd known he'd be and it made her feel guilty. Her own input into the conversation had been minimal.

'In a way it's neither,' Alan was saying. He looked up, caught her eye and set down his knife and fork. 'I shouldn't be doing this, but I can't help brooding over the investigation I conducted in Lower Stovey years ago. It's Friday evening and I should be taking advantage of the free weekend to which my illustrious rank entitles me. Taking work around with me in my free time is something I've always tried to avoid. Taking it around with me in *your* free time is inexcusable.'

Meredith abandoned the salmon, pushed her plate aside and rested her clasped hands on the table. 'I shouldn't have dragged you out here. I thought it would help. But like you, I'm still brooding. It can't be helped and I was stupid to think we could either of us just set it all aside. Can't you tell me about the old case? Was that when you had reason to interview Ruth's father, the Reverend Pattinson?'

'That's right. James Holland tells me Pattinson was gaga in his last years but when I saw him he was lucid enough and really quite vehement in defence of his flock.'

'Who were accused of what?'

'None of them was ever accused of anything. We never even got that far.' And he told her about the Potato Man.

'Nasty,' Meredith said soberly. 'And very, very scary. To think of him stealing something from each of those poor women, taking it home and gloating over it. It's sick.'

She pushed back her thick brown hair in a gesture which Markby knew betokened thought. 'I wished you'd told me all about it before.'

'Hardly the stuff of pleasant conversation. You've got enough on your mind already.'

'You've had this bothering you for the last twenty-two years. You know, Ruth made a remark about bad things happening in Stovey Woods and that must be what she was talking about. But there's no connection, surely? Not with what's happened now? Twenty-two years is a long, long time.'

'A connection with the death of Hester Millar? Probably not, at least not directly. But who knows? Or a connection with the bones Dr Morgan found in Stovey Woods? That sounds more of a distinct possibility on the face of it. But I don't want to jump to conclusions. It all depends what the experts have to say about the bones themselves, how long they'd been there before the good doctor fell down a bank and stuck his head in a fox-hole.'

He paused. 'I don't like coincidences. I told James Holland so. Nothing of a criminal or startling nature has happened in Lower Stovey to my knowledge since the Potato Man vanished all those twenty-two years ago. A long time, as you say. Now, within a fortnight, someone finds human remains in the woods and a local resident, a blameless lady who appears to have had not an enemy in the world, is found stabbed in the church. Hester clearly had no connection with the Potato Man. She wasn't living in Lower Stovey at that time. But the finding of those bones may well have given someone in Lower Stovey a severe fright. Someone who has something to hide. And that brings it up to the present day and the unfortunate Miss Millar. Though I still,' he added disconsolately, 'can't imagine what she could have discovered that might have made her a threat to anyone. Still, it may, in some tortuous fashion, all connect up.'

'I've been wondering, too,' Meredith confessed. She tucked a swathe of hair behind one ear. It promptly fell forward again. She put both hands up and tucked the hair on both sides of her face behind either ear. One side stayed put, the other fell forward again.

Markby reached across the table and took her hand. 'You're fidgeting with your hair. It means you're going to come out with some theory.'

'No. But I've been thinking about Hester, too. I did find her body.'

He wrinkled his forehead in dismay. 'It was a terrible shock for you. I shouldn't have mentioned Lower Stovey.' He sighed. 'Sorry, this outing tonight is falling pretty flat, isn't it?'

'It was my idea to come,' she pointed out. 'I thought it'd take our minds off everything.'

'Exactly. You're trying to blot out what you saw. That's normal and I should have been aware of it!' He released her hand after a brief squeeze of her fingers and added wryly, 'The thing is, on a personal level I'd like to help you forget it. On a professional level, the last thing I want is for you to blot out that picture altogether. You are, you see, my witness.'

Meredith said slowly, as someone laying out a mental puzzle as she might the pieces of a jigsaw. 'Of course I've been wondering about Hester though I haven't come up with any theory as yet, sorry to disappoint you. That's because I've nothing to go on. I didn't see Hester die. I didn't know Hester although I knew of her existence because Ruth had mentioned her to me. So when I saw her – saw her body there, I didn't know who she was. Muriel Scott told me. There was something really weird about Muriel's reaction. She seemed –' Meredith paused.

'Yes?' Alan was watching her intently.

'She seemed surprised without being shocked. In fact, until she saw who it was, her manner was quite brisk. It was strange, somehow. I don't know how to describe it better. From the moment I told her I'd called the police, she seemed to have no doubt it would turn out to be what you'd call a suspicious death. It didn't seem to cross her mind that it might be a case of heart attack or a lump of masonry falling off one of those monuments and clonking someone on the head. Then, when Muriel saw who was dead, she said, "It's not anyone I'd have expected to see." It left me wondering if there was someone she *wouldn't* have been surprised to see lying there dead. It's particularly odd because Hester, of all the people in Lower Stovey, was regularly in the church and Muriel shouldn't have been surprised to see her there, alive naturally. It wasn't that Hester was *dead*, but that *Hester* was dead, which seemed to throw her. It was the emphasis in her remark. Do you follow?'

'I follow. It's intriguing, I admit. However, a shocked person can make some odd, even garbled, statements. Whatever you say, to find Hester Millar stabbed in St Barnabas's was enough to shake the sang-froid even of the redoubtable Mrs Scott.'

'Poor Ruth Aston, of course, was horribly shocked, devastated,' Meredith continued. 'The real thing bugging me is another perhaps trivial detail. I keep wondering what Hester was actually doing in the church when she was attacked. I mean,' she added hastily, 'I know that she, along with Ruth, was a churchwarden. I understand that she'd gone to open up the building. My mind's working in a more literal way. What action was she actually engaged in? You see, from her attitude she'd been kneeling in a pew praying when the assailant struck.'

Alan smiled faintly. 'People do still pray in churches.'

'Yes, and probably Hester was just doing something she always did when she visited the church. But it might be worth asking Ruth if Hester was in the habit of kneeling in prayer for a few minutes when she went into the church. We know why Ruth looks after the church. Her father was its last vicar. It means a lot to her. But it has – had – no personal association for Hester. So, was she a particularly religious woman? After all, it looks as if she was a churchwarden because Ruth was one and it must have been convenient for the two of them to share duties, keeping an eye on the church. I was wondering, you see, if she was kneeling in prayer because something was worrying her and she didn't know what to do. She was seeking guidance. The other thing that occurred to me – and probably already has to you, too – is that whoever approached Hester near enough to attack her either did so very quietly, so that Hester didn't hear them and look up or move, or was someone Hester knew and whose presence she felt she could ignore.'

He nodded. 'It had occurred to me, if for no other reason than that murderer and victim very often are acquainted. Why kill someone who means nothing to you? It would be motiveless. Unless the killer is drunk, drugged or crazed, in which case anyone might be attacked by an outsider with no discernible motive. Such cases are rare, however. Danger lies in our nearest and dearest, not in strangers. And no one,' Markby smiled drily, 'has so far mentioned seeing any strangers in Lower Stovey recently – except you and me.'

'Lionel asked me if I'd need a character reference,' Meredith told him. 'Perhaps I'd better take him up on that.'

He grinned. 'Oh, I'll vouch for you!'

The waitress arrived to remove their plates. She was very young, fresh-faced and pretty despite the braces on her teeth. She was probably a college student and this was an evening job. She looked anxiously at the amount of food left.

'Something wrong?' she asked tentatively.

129

They assured her in unison there wasn't. She looked unconvinced but then asked brightly, 'Would you like the dessert trolley?'

They exchanged glances. Meredith shook her head. 'No, thank you,' Alan told the waitress. 'We'll just have coffee.'

When the girl had gone, Meredith said, 'I know you want me to remember things. I've tried to remember everything I saw. In fact, the person I find myself thinking about as much as I've been thinking about Hester, is Ruth. I thought I might drive out and see her some time tomorrow. She must need support. I don't suppose she's got many friends in that village. Unless you count Muriel Scott who, I imagine, is a bit of mixed blessing at a time like this. Well-meaning, you know, but clumsy.'

'And I, in my sneaky policemanly way, wouldn't mind you having a chat with her. She might open up to you.'

The coffee arrived and there was a break in conversation. When Meredith took it up again, it was to ask, in response to his last remark, 'Open up and tell me what?'

He hunched his shoulders, stirring his coffee. 'I don't know. Nothing, something, any little thing.'

'I don't want to grill her. She's probably had enough of that already.'

'I fancy Dave Pearce intended to send Ginny Holding out to talk to her and get a statement today. Holding is good with nervous witnesses. No grilling. Lots of TLC.' He hesitated. 'I'll let Dave know you're going to see Ruth. This is his case.'

'Sure.' Meredith added with a touch of her usual spirit, 'I'm not pulling chestnuts out of the fire for the police. I'm going to see Ruth just to give her a shoulder to cry on if she wants one. I won't be a – a mole.'

'Of course you're not,' he soothed. 'But people sometimes tell you more when you don't ask them questions – and if you don't come from the police.' Unexpectedly he chuckled. 'Anyway, moles are shy, reclusive creatures. Not your style.' He pushed his empty cup away and signalled for the bill.

* * *

Outside, it was nearly dark but the length of riverside path near the Fisherman's Rest was lit with lamps strung from the trees lining the car park.

He held out his hand. Meredith took it and they strolled cosily along the quiet track. Here at least the modern world with its bustle and trouble was kept out. The twilight soothed the eye and the sounds of the night were pleasant on the ear. To their left the river chattered softly to itself and scraped watery fingers along the bank which had been reinforced to protect the pub from the risk of flood. A black shape flew out of the trees and flapped across the river to the further bank and farmland beyond. Traffic on the main road to their right passed at intervals, unseen except for the rake of headlights along the trees.

'It does seem to me,' Alan said, 'as though our house-hunting is jinxed in some way. We can't go to view a place without it ending with us being mixed up in this mess.'

'I didn't find Hester on purpose.' She sighed. 'Perhaps the whole thing is just jinxed. Perhaps I'm jinxed.'

'Hey, hey! Cheer up! We'll find somewhere, though I don't, somehow, think it will be in Lower Stovey.'

'Gosh, no, Alan. It's a weird place. Even if it weren't, that house, the Old Vicarage, is far too big. I don't care what Juliet says.'

'Juliet?'

Damn! thought Meredith. She hadn't told him of her meeting with Juliet Painter.

'I saw in in London. We had lunch. She asked about the house-hunting, being in that line of business herself.'

'But not an estate agent!' he said.

'Most definitely not! She does hate being called that. She's still dating Superintendent Doug Minchin.'

'Hope she's got him wearing a more tasteful line in shirts by now.'

'She's wearing contact lenses, not specs. That's for Doug, I fancy.'

'The things we do for love. You told her about the house, then?'

'I asked her opinion. She was all for converting the attic and having separate studies in two of the spare bedrooms. It's the sort of thing her clients would do. But since her clients are nearly all pop music millionaires or oil-rich sheikhs, as far as I can make out, she would think along those lines.'

'Blimey!' he observed.

Meredith laughed. 'Well, you know Juliet.'

They turned and walked back to the car. As Meredith was buckling her seat belt, she said, 'I know Hester Millar didn't live in Lower Stovey at the time your Potato Man was active. But Ruth's family did and I imagine she visited them even if she wasn't living at home by that time. And I suppose it's possible Muriel Scott lived in the area.'

He switched on the ignition. 'It's something to think about, certainly. But not tonight, not any more. We've hashed it over more than enough. As the saying goes, my place or yours?'

'Yours,' she said.

A fine drizzle was falling when Meredith returned to Lower Stovey on Saturday afternoon. The scene of crime technicians appeared to have finished at the church. There were no vehicles outside, no uniformed constable guarding the approach. The blue and white tape which had cordoned off the area lay trampled into the wet muddy ground. The church door, when Meredith tried it, was firmly shut. She craned her neck looking up at the tower but even the jackdaws were sheltering out of the rain. Meredith walked round to the side of the building. High under the roof the Green Man gazed out at his erstwhile domain, Stovey Woods. Water trickled down the funerary monuments of the churchyard, collecting in the nooks and crannies of the carved angels and draped urns. She went back to the car.

Across the road, at the Fitzroy Arms, Norman the landlord was standing in his doorway in conversation with a young man in a raincoat holding an open notebook. The press had arrived in Lower Stovey.

As Meredith drove slowly away, Norman looked across at her car. She waved a greeting but his pale face remained expressionless and he made no signal of acknowledgement. Nevertheless, she was sure he'd observed her movements around the church and classified them as meddling. Possibly, she thought wryly, he blamed her in some way for what had happened.

She drove on and turned into Church Lane. Here a young woman was knocking energetically at a cottage door. Receiving no answer, she moved on to the next. Wisely, the inhabitants were lying low.

At the Old Forge a lamp was lit in the sitting room despite the early hour. Meredith got out of her car and knocked at the door. Ruth's face appeared at a window and disappeared. Seconds later the door opened.

'Do come in quickly,' Ruth begged. 'Or that dreadful girl will see me.'

Meredith obligingly nipped through the narrow aperture allowed her. The door was promptly slammed behind her.

'You mean that reporter? The one knocking on doors?'

'Yes. She's been once and I pretended I wasn't here. But she'll know I'm here now because she'll have seen you arrive. Anyway, I switched the lamp on because it's so gloomy in here this afternoon.' Ruth was leading the way as she spoke.

The sitting room was comfortably furnished, almost a model for a room of its type with its black-painted oak beams and ingle-nook hearth in which logs crackled sending out welcome warmth.

'You'll think it odd,'Ruth went on, 'for me to have the fire going at this time of year. I was trying to cheer the place up and besides, Dilys Twelvetrees was here again this morning, which I could have done without. She doesn't normally come on Saturdays. I suppose she's trying to look after me and I should be grateful. Asking her to set the fire at least gave her a job and stopped her plodding round after me asking, of all things, what I intended to do about Hester's funeral. She kept on about ham sandwiches here or Norman at the pub having a functions room. If he has, it's the first I've heard of it. I dread to think what it's like. Anyway, who is there to invite back afterwards? There's only me and James to conduct the service which I don't even know will be in the church. I mean, how can you conduct a burial service for someone who's been murdered in the very pews . . .'

Meredith touched her arm consolingly. 'Don't fret about it. Dilys meant well, I'm sure. There may be more people wishing to attend Hester's funeral than you think. Villagers will want to show their respects. The police usually send along someone in these cases. Alan and I will be there. James can always hold the service at Bamford Church. Have they, the police I mean, indicated when they'll release the body?'

'No, not yet. I don't like to think of Hester lying in the morgue, but frankly, just at the moment I don't think I can cope with the funeral either, let alone Dilys's ham sandwiches.' With grim humour Ruth added, 'Which will be real old doorsteps, you can bet. With horrible home-made piccalilli, I shouldn't be surprised, strong enough to crumble the fillings in your teeth! Anyway, I sent her home immediately after she'd set the fire. As you say, she meant to be helpful. I should be grateful, I suppose, for her support. Though I never thought the day would come when I'd turn to Dilys Twelvetrees in my hour of need!' Ruth rubbed her pale fingers together. 'I still seem to be feeling the cold.'

'It's shock,' Meredith told her. 'Drink a lot of hot drinks.'

'I'll make us tea in a minute,' said Ruth as if interpreting this as a hint, to Meredith's embarrassment. 'Do sit down.'

'I only came to see how you were getting on,' Meredith told her. 'I won't stay if you don't want me to.'

'I do want you to. I need to talk to someone. I can't talk to anyone else here, except Muriel and she, poor dear, is so desperately bracing. The sort of person who tells you to pull your socks up. She hasn't told me that yet, but I feel she will at any minute.' Ruth slumped into the corner of chintz-covered sofa. 'Besides I couldn't deal with Roger today.'

'I've yet to meet Roger.'

'That ghastly dog,' said Ruth without malice, 'is a menace. Muriel dotes on him. I do like dogs,' she added. 'But I like 'em well-behaved. My personal opinion about Roger is that he's the canine equivalent of bonkers.' She sighed. 'Perhaps I'll get a dog myself now, for company. My parents always kept a dog, a labrador.'

'Don't rush into any decision,' Meredith urged. 'Give yourself time.'

'Time's all I've got now, isn't it? Time on my hands, as they say. I'll have to take up tapestry or something like that. Not that I'm any good with a needle. I suppose I'll have to carry on being churchwarden at least for a while because no one else will do it. But just now, I can't go near the church. I've told James Holland so. He's says, not to worry.' Ruth made a rueful, dismissive gesture.

'I believe the police came to see you yesterday.'

'Oh, yes, a nice young woman came along in the morning. I couldn't answer any of her questions. Hester and I don't have – didn't have – any enemies. We weren't involved in any disputes. To my knowledge, no one has been hanging round the church and there's nothing in the building to steal. The officer did keep asking about that. It seems lonely churches are targeted by unscrupulous people who hack out statues and remove paintings and decorated panels. They market the goods through the murkier corners of the antiques trade using false provenances. She asked if I thought it possible Hester had disturbed a thief. But I told her, all the brass altar furniture, candlesticks, the lectern and the Bible on it, all that kind of thing, were all removed after my father's death into the safe keeping of the diocese. When James comes out to take a service, he brings an altar cross and candlesticks with him. The rest of the monuments are solid marble and stone, well attached to the walls or the floor. Anyway, Hester was kneeling in the pew. She wouldn't have been doing that if she was confronting someone. She wouldn't even have done it if some stranger came in and was wandering about the place. As a matter of routine, we always kept an eye on anyone who was in the church when we were there. People who came in when we weren't, of course, could do what they liked. But we never had any trouble.'

'No,' Meredith said. 'And Hester wasn't having trouble of that sort if she was kneeling in the pew, you're right.' She wondered whether it had yet struck Ruth that the murderer might have been known to Hester. It appeared not.

She put the question she'd told Alan was bothering her. 'Did Hester usually say a prayer when she went in the church?'

Ruth raised her eyebrows and shrugged. 'Not when we went in together to clean. She might have done when she was alone in there. I don't know.'

'Was she what you'd call religious?'

'She was a practising Anglican, if that's what you mean.' Ruth went on, 'The officer kept asking me about Hester's plans for the morning. I could only tell her Hester went out to run a couple of errands including opening the church. However,' here Ruth took a deep breath, 'so far, it seems, no one else has come forward to say they saw her. No one saw her open the church door. No one saw her anywhere else in the village. I'm beginning to wonder if the police suspect me.'

'Of course they don't!' Meredith exclaimed in horror. 'They don't suspect anyone yet. It's early days and in any case, why should they suspect you?'

'Because I was apparently the last person to see her alive. Because I'm the only one able to give any account of her movements that morning and I've no one to back me up. Because poor Hester wasn't connected in any way with any one else in Lower Stovey.'

Alan's words, that danger came from our nearest and dearest and not from strangers, echoed uncomfortably in Meredith head.

'One of the things the police will be doing,' Meredith said, 'is investigating Hester's past. This could have to do with something which happened years ago, before she came to live here.'

The result of her words was startling. All colour drained from Ruth's face. 'They won't go back that far, surely?' she whispered.

'Far enough, I suppose.' Meredith added as gently as possible, 'Ruth, is there something in Hester's past?'

'No, not a thing!' Ruth's voice became sturdily decided. 'Hester didn't have a past. She taught for years until she retired and came here.'

'She had no family, either, I gather, except you,' Meredith probed.

'I told your friend, Mr Markby, and I told that woman officer Friday morning. Hester didn't have anyone.'

Conversation was interrupted by a rat-tat at the door.

'It'll be that girl!' whispered Ruth. 'Ignore it.'

The rat-tat sounded again.

'Let me get rid of her,' Meredith offered. She got up and went to the door, opening it the barest crack.

The young woman she'd seen earlier knocking on doors was on the step, smiling brightly despite the rain which made her long fair hair cling damply round her face.

'Mrs Aston?'

'No, I'm a friend. Mrs Aston is indisposed. You'll understand, I'm sure, she doesn't want to talk to the press.'

'How about you?' the girl persisted. 'How is Mrs Aston taking it? Do you have any theory? Can I have your name?'

'No, you can't.' If this eager-beaver ever found out Meredith had discovered the body, all hope of peace would be gone. 'No one has anything to say to you. Please, go away.'

Meredith shut the door.

'She'll be back,' she warned Ruth as she returned to the fireside where Ruth huddled in the corner of her sofa. 'She or one of her mates. Shall I make the tea?'

When she came back with the tea, Ruth was kneeling in front of the hearth, putting another log on the embers. Without looking up, she said, 'I'm going to sell this place, you know.'

'Honestly, Ruth, I meant what I said just now. Don't rush into any decision,' Meredith urged.

'I never wanted to live here, for goodness sake! It was my late husband's idea. If it hadn't been for Hester, I wouldn't have stayed after he died. Hester liked this house. I'd even left it to her in my will —' Ruth's voice quavered briefly. 'Now I want to shake the dust of Lower Stovey off my boots for ever.' She looked up now, over her shoulder. 'So, if you and your friend do want a place here, The Old Forge will be on the market.'

Something in Meredith's face must have betrayed her feelings.

Ruth gave a smile with was half commiserating and half triumphant.

'You see, you don't want to live in Lower Stovey either. And I don't flipping well blame you.'

There was no sign of either of the young reporters and the front door of the Fitzroy Arms was firmly shut when Meredith left Ruth's house. On an impulse, she turned her car into the pub's small car park and got out. It had stopped raining now and she picked her way through the puddles to the rear of the building where, as she'd hoped, there was a sign of life. The back door stood ajar and from within came voices. Meredith knocked and before anyone could reply, pushed the door open and stepped inside.

She was in a large kitchen. Norman and his wife were seated at the kitchen table. Between them lay some unwashed dishes and all the signs were they'd been having a vigorous discussion about something, if not an outright argument. Even Norman's pale visage was flushed and animated. When Meredith appeared, both of them stopped talking and sat, open-mouthed, staring at her.

Norman's wife rallied first. 'Hello, dear,' she said. Her round face split in a meaningless grin and her small eyes shone with fright.

His wife's voice acted as a spur to Norman who scrambled to his feet. 'Evie, you go and check the bar. We'll be opening in an hour.'

Evie obediently trotted away and Norman faced Meredith.

'We're closed,' he said. 'Thought you'd have seen that.'

'I don't want a drink,' she replied. 'I just wanted a few words.'

His expression was tight and angry. 'The whole world and his wife wants a few words with me, it seems. First the coppers, then the press. Now you. What do you want to talk about, then, as if I didn't know?'

'You know I found the body,' Meredith said.

' 'Course I bloody know it. Everyone knows it. What were you doing, poking your nose into the church? Trying to get in there again earlier, weren't you? I saw you. You can't leave well alone, can you? You're the sort that always causes trouble.'

Meredith realised that she'd been quite right. He did blame her for what had happened.

138

She ignored his direct question and asked instead, one of her own. 'Did you see me go into the church on Thursday morning, when Miss Millar died?'

If he'd been expecting a question, it hadn't been that one. It threw him. 'No,' he said after a perceptible pause. 'How should I?'

'The pub is pretty well opposite. You saw me today when you were standing on your doorstep. You were in your bar-room on Thursday morning. I came in here for coffee. It would be natural if you looked through the window after I left.'

'Why should I do that?'

'To see where I went,' she said calmly.

Norman put his head on one side. 'I didn't give a tinker's cuss where you were going. And I didn't see you.'

'Nor anyone else? Your Uncle Billy, for example?'

'You leave Uncle Billy out of this.' Norman took a step towards her. 'He's eighty and got trouble with his hip and the angina. The last thing he needs is people bothering him. He's already had one copper round there asking him a lot of damnfool questions.'

'But did you see him?' Meredith insisted. 'Because I thought I did, in the far corner of the churchyard.'

She'd opened an escape route for Norman. 'Ah, then!' he said triumphantly. 'I wouldn't have been able to see him from here, then, would I? I can see the church, yes, but I can't see round corners. I'm not Superman, am I? I can't see the churchyard except just the little bit by the road.'

Meredith realised she'd mishandled that one. She changed the question. 'Did you see Miss Millar enter the church?'

Norman thrust his unattractive features into her face. 'No. The police have been here asking that. I told them no. I've told you no. I told that whippersnapper from the tabloids no. I'd tell the Pope no if he was to turn up and ask me.'

'Did you see her at all that morning, see her walk by, perhaps?'

'Why're you asking me?' he demanded.

'Because you were in your bar!' Meredith snapped back.

'And what was I doing there? I'll tell you, my girl. I was working. One of the pumps had been playing up and I had to fix it. Then I cleaned up the mess and had just finished when you waltzed in wanting cups of coffee. If you run a pub, you don't have time to look out of windows *or* stand talking with interfering outsiders who come here and cause trouble.'

'I didn't cause trouble!' Meredith argued. 'That's unfair.'

'Of course you caused it. Everything was all right until you came, finding bodies.'

'Someone would've found her, sooner or later.'

'It didn't have to be you, did it? Ruddy outsider. If one of us —' Norman broke off, his face scarlet and eyes bulging.

'Go on,' she invited him. 'If one of you had found it, what would you have done?'

'Called the police!' he retorted. He drew a deep breath. 'And now,' he said. 'You can just clear off.'

Meredith cleared off.

'I went to see Ruth,' Meredith said that evening, peering dubiously into a pot of boiling pasta. 'She's bearing up well, all things considered. She thought your Sergeant Holding was nice, but she couldn't answer any of the questions she was asked.'

'It's early days,' Markby said absent-mindedly. 'Perhaps Ruth will start remembering things in a day or two, when the shock subsides.'

'It doesn't look as if there's anything to remember. Neither of them had enemies, according to Ruth, and it's hard to see how they could have done. They don't appear to have much to do with anyone. Neither of them has any family.' She hooked a piece of pasta from the pot with a fork and held it towards him. 'Try this and tell me if you think it's *al dente.*'

'It's hot!' Markby juggled the piece round his mouth. 'It's about right, I think. Here, I'll drain that.'

He carried the saucepan to the sink. Meredith waited until the boiling water had splashed away down the plughole.

'Alan?'

'Mmn?'

'You don't think Ruth killed Hester, do you?'

He turned in surprise, the colander full of pasta dripping on to the kitchen floor. 'We don't have a suspect. Why should I think Ruth killed her friend?'

'I don't know. But Ruth seems to think she's your number one suspect – because she was the last person we know saw Hester alive.'

'So far. Someone else may yet come forward who saw Hester later. Ruth's not our number one suspect. We don't have such a person.'

'But she's on your list of possibles?'

Alan had set the colander on the draining board and was mopping up the spillages. She could only see the top of his head and a mop of fair hair. From beneath it came his voice, 'Everyone's on my list of possibles.' He straightened up. 'Put it this way. You found her. I might suspect you. Don't look at me like that! She'd been dead about an hour and a half when you walked into that church, or so Fuller reckons.'

Meredith stared at him. 'She was all that time in the church, dead, and no one else had found her?'

'Ah,' said Markby. 'Isn't that the sixty-four thousand dollar question!'

'It does bring us back to Old Billy Twelvetrees, doesn't it? I saw him, Alan. I'd swear it was him.'

'He denies it and he's sticking to it. But I believe,' Markby scowled at the colander of pasta as if it might put up some argument, 'that Old Billy is an untruthful person. I mean, his distinction between what's correct and what isn't is formed entirely by what suits him. He wouldn't call it lying, that's the awkward thing about dealing with such people.'

'But you and I would call it lying?'

'Upright citizens that we are, we probably would. I have no doubt he's lying, but what about? About not being in the church? Or about something else altogether?' He sighed. 'The trouble with such people is that often, they simply can't tell you the facts. They lie for no reason. So, has the old man got a reason? Or is he being plain bloody-minded?'

PART TWO

Chapter Nine

The investigation into the murder of Hester Millar was now taking up much of the available manpower resources. That was probably why, on Monday morning, the switchboard decided to route the call from the laboratory through to Markby's office, or so he first thought until he was connected.

'Superintendent Markby?' The voice was female and somehow familiar though he couldn't place it for the moment. He confirmed his identity and it went on, 'It's Ursula Gretton. Do you remember me?'

'Of course I do!' he exclaimed. An image of her leapt into his head, a tall young woman in muddy jeans standing by a ramshackle trailer on the site of an archaeological dig. 'This is a surprise!'

'It's about your bones.' She giggled. 'You know what I mean. The bones we received from the police.'

'From which I deduce, being a detective, that you don't work for the Ellsworth Foundation any longer.'

'No.' Her voice was suddenly sober. 'Not for a while now, not since that business – you know.'

He did, indeed. Murder. A woman's body lying in the sun amid piles of household rubbish. A death which, for Ursula, had struck very close to home.

'I needed to take a new path in my career. Sometimes one does.'

'I understand. Good to hear your voice, Ursula.'

'How's Meredith?' she asked.

Markby told her Meredith was fine and hoped she hadn't noticed any doubt his voice. 'House-hunting,' he added, in case she had.

'Rather you than me,' said Ursula. 'No luck, I take it?'

'Not yet. Right now it seems ill-fated to tell you the truth. No doubt,' he added with forced heartiness, 'we'll find just the thing any day now.'

'Of course you will. I've got my report all printed out nicely for you, but I thought you'd might like to know the bare facts right away. An excuse to touch base, anyway.' He heard the rustle of paper and her voice continued, 'I understand they were discovered in woodland which makes sense. I estimate they'd been lying there about twenty years.'

Markby heard himself exclaim, 'Ah . . .' on a long breath.

She had heard it. 'Was that what you were hoping?'

'They may be connected with an old, unresolved case,' he admitted. 'Male or female?'

'Oh, I think this is a male in his late thirties. You've noticed, of course, that he'd had some distinctive dental work?'

'I had. Absolutely no sign, I suppose, of what might have caused his death?'

'No, sorry. No sign of disease or injury. A lot of teeth marks, they've been well chewed by animals, but no saw or knife marks, nothing to suggest deliberate dismemberment. Soil, leafmould, traces of microscopic insect life. There aren't enough remains, I'm afraid, to tell you much more. But that jaw, I'm sure, is a male jaw. I'll pack them up and send them back to you.'

On impulse, Markby said, 'No, I'll come over to Oxford and pick them up.'

Ursula's department lurked behind the respectable red-brick façade of a North Oxford Victorian villa. Her office was at the rear of the building, overlooking what had once been a garden but was now a tarmacked area, partly taken up with prefabricated huts and cluttered with stacks of boxes. A bicycle rack sheltered by a corrugated roof managed to be a particular eyesore among the rest. Markby wondered briefly how the garden had looked in its heyday when it had been a family home and there had been lawn and flowerbeds out there, and ladies in long skirts and large hats taking tea.

The bones were in a box on Ursula's desk. She came from behind it to greet him, hands thrust into the pockets of her unbuttoned white lab coat. Her long dark hair was brushed back and secured with what Markby understood from his young niece to be called a scrunchie. He hadn't forgotten how striking were her cornflower blue eyes but even so, the effect of them was considerable. He found it hard to imagine there wasn't a man in her life. Even a broken heart usually mends sufficiently for its pain to be contained, even if it isn't forgotten.

'Long time, no see,' she said. She took her right hand from her pocket and extended it.

He admitted it ruefully, clasping her proffered fingers. 'Meredith and I have both been busy and so, I see, have you.'

'Time flies when you're having fun,' she returned drily.

'Doesn't it just?' He was unable to prevent himself replying a trifle sourly.

She pulled a comic face. 'Oophs! Have I put my foot in it? I thought you sounded a bit depressed on the phone.'

Markby pulled himself together. 'Everything's fine, really.'

'Well, there are your bones. And the report is in the folder. There's little to add to what I told you on the phone.'

'You were very helpful.' He glanced at his wristwatch. 'It's nearly one. Let me take you to lunch?'

'That'd be lovely. Thanks. I don't normally get much in the way of lunch, just an apple and a bag of crisps. There's a pub not far from here which does bar snacks.'

The pub was a fairly typical Oxford hostelry with much dark oak, a cramped interior, and numbered a good many tourists amongst its clientele. They settled for scampi and chips each, a white wine for Ursula and a tomato juice with a dash of Lea and Perrins for Markby, who had to drive back to Regional HQ.

'Everything is all right between you and Meredith, I hope,' Ursula said, sipping her wine. 'I'm not being nosy. It's just that I've always envied you two. You seem so well suited and happy.'

He found himself mildly embarrassed. 'We've been house-hunting. I had no idea it would turn out so stressful. We can't seem to find the right property and then, unfortunately, Meredith stumbled across a body. It's triggered a murder investigation.'

'That's a bit of rotten luck.' Ursula put down her glass. 'She must be upset.'

He reflected. 'I think, in a way, she's more annoyed. But yes, of course she is upset, too. The victim was an apparently blameless lady of a certain age, a retired teacher.'

Ursula sat back in her chair and surveyed him. 'This isn't the murder case reported on the local news? The one which happened at Lower Stovey, where the bones came from?'

'That's the one. The victim's name is Hester Millar. There's no obvious motive, and there's no connection as yet with the bones, in case you're wondering. Not one we've found, anyway. Hester was unmarried and lived with an old friend, Ruth Aston. We had hoped Mrs Aston would know of the next-of-kin. But it seems Hester wasn't in touch with any relatives, if she had any. Her parents died years ago. There were never any tell-tale Christmas cards, that sort of thing. She was one of those people who don't have any family and seems to have had precious few friends and acquaintances apart from Ruth. There are any number of middle-aged women like that around the country. What a typical example like Hester could possibly have done which would make someone else want to kill her, is beyond me. I really think we're going to be up against it on this one.'

Ursula said slowly, 'I think she may have had at least one relative.'

Surprised, he stared at her.

She flushed. 'Someone I work with mentioned the murder this morning. He'd heard it on the news. He said he thought that Hester Millar might have been related to Dr Amyas Fichett, the distinguished historian, you know.'

'To my shame, I don't know. But what gave your colleague this idea?'

'Oh, well, he – Peter, my colleague – has a wife who visits Dr Fichett. He, Dr Fichett, is ancient and has been retired for yonks. He rattles round on his own in an old house not far from here. He's got a woman who comes and cleans and does his shopping. Otherwise he's only got Peter's wife, Jane, who calls in once a week, just to make sure he's all right. They were neighbours once and she always got on well with the old boy. The reason Peter connected him with Hester is that from time to time, Dr Fichett gets out old photograph albums and reminisces with Jane about the people in the snaps. Jane is sure he called one of the little girls pictured his niece, Hester Millar, his sister's daughter, and said he believed she lived near Bamford though he wasn't in contact. Jane offered to get in touch for him, apparently. This was about a year ago. But he said there wasn't any point in it. He can be obstinate so she let it go, though she thought it a pity as he hasn't anyone else.'

'Right,' said Markby, trying to keep the excitement from his voice. 'Could you ask Jane where he lives? He does look as though he might be next of kin.'

Ursula pursed her mouth then dived into her bag, pulling out a mobile phone. 'The old chap must be ninety. Even if he wasn't in touch with Hester, it'll be a shock to hear of her death. I doubt he's heard already. The modern world and all its works, according to Jane, stop at his front door. It would be best if I call Jane and arrange for you to meet up with her first. She can take you along and introduce you to Dr Fichett. It's likely he'd refuse to see you, otherwise, and it really would be best if Jane were on hand when you break the news to him.'

As she waited to be connected, the mobile pressed to her ear, she leaned across the table and whispered, 'I always hate it when people use mobile phones in pubs, don't you?'

Markby chuckled. The scampi arrived as she was speaking to Jane. Ursula put the phone away and picked up her fork. 'All fixed. I'll take you to Jane right after lunch.'

'I'm really grateful, Ursula. We probably wouldn't have got on to the old fellow, otherwise. Good job I came to see you!'

'Anything I can do.' She looked up from her meal, transfixing him with those startling blue eyes. 'I owe you and Meredith a lot.'

'No, you don't. Would it be tactless of me to ask if you've someone special in your life now?'

She shrugged. 'I'm not good at relationships. I think my judgement is probably at fault. Look at that disastrous one I got into with Dan. Since then, I've met nice enough blokes, but I don't know . . . Perhaps my line of work doesn't help. It would be nice,' Ursula said, 'to meet a man who doesn't spend his day with mementoes of the dead, whether it's bones or fossils or preserved bits of things. I spend a lot of time,' she finished calmly, 'in the company of bones.'

'Don't take up with a copper, then,' he advised.

'Now, before I take you to see him,' Jane Hatton said, 'I ought to tell you that he can be a very naughty old man.'

'Good grief. In what way?' Markby asked.

Mrs Hatton was a plump young woman with a great deal of frizzy blonde hair. When Markby had arrived at the house, he'd found her surrounded by a lively brood of infants, but these had been shooed away in the care of an au pair and he had been installed in a very old and rickety armchair in order, he had discovered, that Jane might interrogate him.

'I need to know what sort of person you are,' she'd told him frankly. 'Before I take you to Amyas.' After a lengthy question and answer session, she said, 'When Ursula said you were a policeman I was rather fearing the worst. But you're very nice and sensible and he'll like you. I'll take you.'

'I'm much obliged and much relieved,' he'd replied and she had burst into hearty laughter.

It had faded almost at once as she'd added, 'I'll give him a ring and let him know we're on our way. I'd be going anyway because someone's got to tell him about his niece and I suppose it's got to be me. I doubt he's heard about it yet.'

Now she clasped her hands and adopted a deeply earnest expression.

'In answer to your question, I don't mean he chases me round the parlour. I mean he can act up. Sometimes he pretends he's deaf. He's not. Or he pretends he can't remember. He can. He is really the most frightful old gossip. The only thing is, having been shut up in that house on his own, more or less, for years, all his gossip is out of date. He knows all the scandal in the University of forty years ago. He can tell you all any number of stories about Famous Persons who were here as undergraduates. He rarely watches his television, though he knows who people in the news are, I mean like the Prime Minister or an Olympic Gold Medallist, but I'm afraid he finds the modern world tedious. He gave up taking a newspaper because there was never anything in it he wanted to read about. All the people he was ever interested in are dead, or nearly dead, poor old boy.'

'He sounds,' said Markby, 'very like my late Uncle Henry.'

The other thing about which Jane warned him on their way to see Dr Fichett, was that his house was 'a real museum'. It was certainly that. Whereas most of the huge rambling nineteenth century properties in the area had been turned into something else, language schools, B & B's or places like where Ursula worked, Amyas Fichett was still living in his almost comically over-large accommodation. Jane had a doorkey and let them in, calling out as she did to warn the old man of their arrival. In response came a squawk from near at hand.

'He's in his study,' whispered Jane and led the way down a gloomy corridor and into a dark, book-lined, high-ceilinged room which smelled fusty and was filled with a jumble of furniture. The curtains were half-drawn, which made matters worse. There was illumination of sorts, a green-shaded desk lamp. But when Markby looked towards it, he found that the contrast with the surrounding darkness made anything beyond the reach of the lamp impossible to see at all. So when, from the shadows behind it, a voice piped up, he was startled.

'To what do I owe the honour?'

'This is the gentleman I phoned you about, Amyas. You know you haven't forgotten.'

Jane Hatton had gone to the window as she spoke and yanked the curtains apart allowing daylight to seep into the room. Markby found himself looking at a tiny figure, a little bird of a man, with a bald pink dome surrounded by a fringe of white hairs and a look which really was very like that of a naughty child. Dr Fitchett rose from behind the desk and came round to Markby's side of it. He moved with a curious bobbing gait.

'Sit down, sit down!' he trilled at them, indicating a pair of massive Victorian armchairs. When they were seated he took a seat in a worn velvet chair of the Queen Anne model, and beamed at them. 'Company,' he said. 'How very delightful. We shall have tea.'

'I'll make it,' said Jane, rising from her chair.'

'Biscuits in the tin!' he called after her as she went out, giving Markby a conspiratorial look as she did.

Alone with him, Markby relaxed in his vast chair, crossed his legs and observed, 'It's very good of you to see me, sir.'

'Jane tells me you are a police officer.' Dr Fichett squinted at him. 'You must therefore keep fit.'

'Er – yes. It's a requirement,' Markby said.

'I myself keep very fit. I jog round my garden, twenty times round, every morning.'

'That's very good indeed.'

'Yes, isn't it? I eat healthily. No meat. I haven't eaten meat for years. Fish, yes. Eggs, yes. Do you eat meat?'

Markby admitted that he did.

Dr Fitchett shook his head in sorrow. 'You are making a great mistake. My dear boy, do consider giving it up. What is it you wish to see me about?'

The move from one subject of conversation to another was so sudden it disconcerted his visitor who realised that this was exactly the object of the exercise. Dr Fichett, as Jane had warned, was beginning to 'act up'.

'I'm afraid I have some not very good news for you, sir. But perhaps we should wait until Mrs Hatton comes back.'

'Ah,' said Dr Fichett. 'You're the bringer of ill-tidings, are you? It was customary once, in some cultures, to kill the man who brought bad news.' His sharp little eyes glittered at Markby in malicious glee.

Markby, who'd been worried about bringing bad news to a nonagenarian, decided that the old man would take it fairly well when it was broken to him. He was a tough old bird. Nevertheless, he waited for Jane to come back, which she did almost at once, carrying a tray with the tea things which were made up of assorted mugs and a brown-glazed teapot with a chipped spout.

'Now then, my young fellow,' said Dr Fitchett when they each had a mug of tea and a chocolate Viennese Whirl. 'Out with your bad news! Are the barbarians at the gates, eh? Has Rome fallen? Has the council complained again about the oak tree in the garden? It is perfectly safe. I won't have it trimmed.'

'Amyas,' said Jane. 'This is serious. You may not have heard this, but someone, a woman, has been found dead in a church at Lower Stovey.'

'Where's that?' he asked, biting off a piece of Viennese Whirl and showering crumbs down his waistcoat which seemed to have already had a collision with egg earlier that day.

'Near Bamford. You remember telling me you thought you had a niece who lived near Bamford? Hester Millar?'

He gave them a mistrustful look and mumbled, 'I don't remember.'

'Amyas, you *do*. Please,' Jane begged him. 'Don't tease. Not at a time like this. Oh, this is dreadful.'

Intelligence gleamed in the elderly eyes fixed on her face. 'Are you trying to tell me that this unfortunate woman was Hester?'

As he spoke, Dr Fitchett froze, half a biscuit in one hand and a pottery mug emblazoned with the coat of arms of Ramsgate in the other. 'Little Hester? Are you telling me she's dead?'

'I'm afraid so, Amyas. I'm awfully sorry.'

Dr Fitchett meditated briefly on the news and appeared to slot it into some revelant pigeonhole in his memory as he chewed thoughtfully on the rest of his biscuit. 'Dear me. Strange news indeed. How old was she?'

'Fifty-seven,' Markby told him.

'I dare say she ate meat,' said Dr Fitchett.

'She didn't die naturally, sir. She – er – she was stabbed.' Markby found himself forced to say.

'In a church?' Dr Fitchett sounded a little like Lady Bracknell. 'How extraordinary, like the unfortunate Becket. Who stabbed her?'

He darted a sudden keen look at Markby who thought that sitting in a tutorial with Dr Fitchett in his active days must have been a disconcerting business. He fully realised the old fellow was using tricks on them he'd once practised successfully on hapless undergraduates. On the other hand, these same tricks helped this aged person cope with distressing news.

'We don't know yet, sir. It seems you are her only relative and next-of-kin.'

'I don't know that I care to be that!' Dr Fitchett said immediately and shook his bald head. 'No, no, that won't do at all. You'll take care of it for me, won't you, Jane?' He gave her a coaxing sideways glance.

'Your solicitor would be better, Amyas. I'll call by and tell him about it.'

'Just so long as I'm not required to go anywhere. I won't go to any inquest.' His voice, already high-pitched, rose to shrillness.

'That won't be necessary,' Markby reassured him as Dr Fitchett had begun to show signs of genuine distress, not at the news, but at the idea of leaving his own property. Markby wondered when he had last done that. 'What I was hoping was that you could tell me something about your niece.'

'Not a thing, dear fellow.' The old man relaxed at the assurance he wouldn't be required to venture out into a modern world he despised and did his best to ignore. 'I last saw her when she was, oh, about thirty, if that. She was always a very plain girl. Jane, do bring me the album, won't you, my dear?'

Jane, who seemed well-aquainted with all the arrangements in the house, obediently fetched a large leather-bound album from a shelf. Fichett turned the pages slowly until at last he found what he wanted.

'Here you are.' He tapped the photograph with a wrinkled finger. 'It will have been taken the first year Hester was up at Oxford. The other girl is a young friend who was holidaying at my sister's house.'

The album was passed to Markby. It was so heavy he almost dropped it. The photograph had been taken in high summer. It showed two young women in light dresses. One was unmistakably a very young Hester. She had been plain though not without a healthy kind of attractiveness. Both girls had that innocent glow which marks those who've just left school and ventured into a new world, in their case the exciting one of the university. They were leaning against a drystone wall but he couldn't place the location.

'It will have been taken,' said Dr Fitchett, as if he could follow Markby's mind, 'in the Yorkshire Dales. That is where my sister lived. Don't ask me why.'

But Markby had glanced at the girl with Hester. He peered more closely at the photo. The other girl was pretty, very pretty, but fragile-looking. That prettiness had faded with the years but enough of it remained to make him sure he'd seen it recently. He held the album open under Dr Fitchett's nose.

'Can you identity the other girl?'

The old man glanced at the photo and looked up at Markby. His eyes were sparkling again with that malicious glee.

'Oh my, yes. That's little Ruth Pattinson, the vicar's daughter! You know the rhyme, Superintendent? *There was a little girl and she had a little curl, right in the middle of her forehead. When she was good she was very, very good, and when she was bad* – she got into trouble!'

And Dr Fitchett laughed so much he choked and had to have first aid rendered by both his visitors.

'A baby?' Pearce looked surprised then shrugged. 'It happens all the time, I suppose.'

'We're talking about 1966, Dave, and the girl came from an ultra-respectable clerical family. The father of the child had declined to marry her. It was the year before the Abortion Act came into being and

155

even if it had been in force, I doubt Ruth Pattinson with her religious upbringing would have sought a termination under it. An illegal abortion would have been dangerous and she probably wouldn't have known where to go to get one. Just as well. She couldn't turn to her own parents. They would've been deeply shocked and disappointed in her, especially her father who'd have considered that a vicar and his family should set a good example to the rest of the parish. So, at all costs, she wanted to keep the knowledge from them. One wonders what she'd have done if Hester and her mother hadn't offered her a home in that difficult time for her. Would she have been driven to face her own parents, after all? Or would she have been unable to do that and taken some desperate action?'

Markby shook his head. 'I was warned that Dr Fitchett was a real old gossip. He's just that. The point is, all his gossip *is* old. He might have forgotten about his niece's young friend, along with a lot of other ancient history, if anything else had happened to interest him in the last thirty years. But he lives in the past and it's more real to him than the present.'

'Who was the father?' asked the practical Pearce.

'Ah, that we don't know. All we know is what Dr Fitchett can tell us. Ruth Pattinson became pregnant during her last year at university. Somehow she managed to conceal it until the end of the university year, sitting her final examinations meanwhile. However, faced with going home she panicked and confided in her best friend, Hester Millar. Hester had the solution. She took Ruth to Yorkshire with her where Hester's mother, who was of an understanding nature, agreed that the girl could stay with them until the baby was born. I don't know what they told the Reverend Pattinson and his wife to explain Ruth's continuing absence. I dare say the two girls cooked up some story. That Hester's mother was ill, for example, and the two of them were looking after her. The child was born in Yorkshire and Dr Fitchett believes was adopted immediately. Ruth went home and nobody was the wiser. The old chap knows about it because his sister did have a few doubts about the deception and asked his advice. Amyas Fitchett was wise in the ways of undergraduates and the scrapes they got themselves into. He also had some slight acquaintance with the Reverend Pattinson who, apparently, was apt to fire off long letters about his researches into myths to any unfortunate historian whose address he could get hold of. Amyas considered him a crank. He told his sister that informing the Pattinsons of their daughter's predicament would, to use his words, "only make matters worse." Better Ruth had her child secretly and the Pattinsons were left in blissful ignorance. Mrs Millar, satisfied once her brother had supported her decision, was happy enough to go ahead and let Ruth stay with her. Amyas, incidentally, put forward another reason to me for his attitude. "A very bright girl who'd just achieved a good degree," he said. "No need to let her mess up her life at that stage".'

Pearce thought about this for a while. Eventually he said, 'What's it got to do with Hester Millar's death?'

'As far as we know, nothing. But it explains why Ruth offered a home to her friend. She owed Hester a debt.'

Pearce brightened. 'Perhaps Hester Millar was about to go public and tell about the child!'

'After thirty-five years? Would it matter now? Anyway, tell whom? There's no one the slightest bit interested now except you and me,' Markby pointed out.

'And the kid,' Pearce countered. 'Wherever it is. He or she might have been asking around. Was it a boy or a girl?'

'Dr Fitchett thinks it was a boy, but isn't sure.'

'So, he'll be thirty-four now, this lad, you say? Perhaps he has been trying to trace his mother? Perhaps he'd got as far as Hester Millar? Perhaps —' Pearce began to sound excited. 'Perhaps he thought Hester Millar was his mother! He tracked her down in the church and accused her of having abandoned him. She denied it and —'

'Calm down, Dave,' advised the superintendent. 'This isn't *East Lynne*.'

'Who's she?' queried Pearce.

'It's a book, Dave,' Markby said with a sigh. 'A Victorian story which was made into a successful stage play containing the line, "Dead, dead, and never called me Mother!" The only line anyone remembers. Well, enough of that. The murder mustn't make us forget the bones found in the woods. Perhaps we could concentrate on that for a moment. You've seen Dr Gretton's report?'

Pearce indicated that he had. 'We're doing our best to trace that fancy tooth filling.' He paused to explore the side of his own mouth with his tongue.

'Got a bit of tooth trouble of your own, Dave?'

'Nothing to speak of,' lied Pearce.

'Right, then think about this.' Markby ticked the points off on his fingers as he enumerated them. 'Twenty-two years ago the Potato Man was active in Stovey Woods. The bones are of a young male and have been lying in the woods for twenty or so years. We know they aren't one of the Potato Man's female victims, so —'

'Are they the bones of the rapist himself?' Pearce finished. 'He did disappear from the scene sudden-like, you said.'

'He did, but we mustn't leap to conclusions. In addition to following up that dental implant, have someone check missing persons. See if any young male disappeared in the area between twenty and twenty-five years ago.'

'Young males are always disappearing,' said Pearce gloomily. 'Like looking for a needle in a haystack.' He then looked himself very like a man who wished he hadn't mention the word 'needle'.

'By the way,' said Markby casually that evening. 'Ruth wasn't quite right in saying Hester Millar had no living family. We've traced an elderly uncle.'

Meredith looked startled and then puzzled. 'Oh? Ruth couldn't have known about him.'

'Possibly. Or, given that he's ninety-one and hadn't been in touch with his niece for twenty-seven years at least, Ruth might reasonably have supposed he was dead, if she ever knew about him. Or,' Markby added, 'she might know about him and not have wished us to talk to him.'

'Why not?' Getting no reply, Meredith asked, 'Alan? Is there a secret in Hester's past?'

'Yes and no,' he told her aggravatingly. 'And it's confidential information.'

'Do you or do you not want me to help?'

'I told you I'd be grateful if you could worm anything out of Ruth. But now that we've successfully traced the uncle, perhaps you needn't worry about it. We'll manage without your undoubted sleuthing skills!'

'Sometimes,' Meredith told him, 'you sound positively smug!'

'That's because I'm pleased with myself for finding the old boy. Oh, I saw Ursula Gretton today. She it was, actually, who put me on to Hester's uncle, via a friend of hers. Ursula dated the bones in the woods for us.'

'Ursula did? How is she?'

'Got a new career but not, I gather, a new love in her life.'

'That's a shame.' Meredith shook her head.

'Yes, yes it is a shame. She's a very attractive woman. We had lunch.' Markby wondered if he was overdoing the casual tone. He feared he was beginning to sound idiotic.

'Oh? Right. Well, that's nice.' This enigmatic reply told him nothing.

Their eyes met. There was a quizzical look in Meredith's. Rumbled! thought Markby.

'So,' asked Meredith, 'how old?'

'How old what?'

'Was the man whose bones were in the woods?'

Markby abandoned his laid-back manner. 'They are the bones of a man in his thirties and have been lying around in Stovey Woods for about twenty years. Scientists always allow themselves leeway when dating things. The bones might have been there as long as twenty-three or four years but probably not less than eighteen or nineteen. Don't ask me if they belong to the Potato Man because I don't ruddy well know!'

Chapter Ten

'You want to see about that tooth, Inspector,' said Ginny Holding reproachfully on Tuesday.

'Don't you worry about my tooth,' retorted Pearce, 'you worry about the teeth in that jawbone and tracing that Christmas Tree implant. Mr Markby wants to know who our mystery man of the woods is.'

'Oh that,' she replied unruffled. 'I think I've got something on that.' She tapped her computer keyboard. 'You know you asked me to chase down missing persons as well?'

Pearce edged closer and peered at the screen. 'What have you got?'

She pointed. 'Him,' she said. 'Simon Hastings. He was a thirty-five-year-old botanist on a walking holiday.'

'Don't tell me,' Pearce muttered. 'He was walking the old drovers' way.'

'That's right, all on his own. I pulled the file from records.' She tapped a folder on her desk. 'On the evening of the twenty-third of August he stopped off at the Drovers' Rest and took a room for the night. The Drovers' Rest is a pub in the middle of nowhere which does B & B and makes its trade from the people who use the old way for recreational purposes. Robert and I have been in there.'

Robert was Ginny's partner. A police-dog handler by profession, he rejoiced in the nickname of 'Snapper' but no one used it in Ginny's hearing. Both Snapper, sorry Robert, and Ginny were keen cyclists.

161

Pearce could imagine them pedalling merrily along the old way.

'Nice place, is it?' Pearce asked blandly. He'd given up riding a pushbike the moment he'd got old enough first for a motorbike and then a car. Not that the machines ridden by Snapper – must remember to call him Robert – and Ginny merited the derisory name of pushbike. Space age technology they were.

'Yes,' she returned brightly. 'It's a pretty nice spot. You and Tessa would like it. Of course you can't get up there by car. It's actually on the old drovers' way itself, donkey's years old, really atmospheric. You know, creaky and creepy. The sort of place you'd really expect to see ghosts. But you could park near the way and then walk. You've got a dog, haven't you?'

Pearce felt vaguely insulted by the implication that neither he nor Tessa would go anywhere they couldn't visit by car nor take a walk voluntarily unless accompanied by Henry, the lurcher. Perhaps they should take more exercise, he and Tess. Tessa went to her aerobics class, of course. But that didn't involve fresh air. One of these weekends, when the weather was nice, he'd get Tessa to walk a little along the old way. Where they'd probably be overtaken, as they slogged along on foot, by Snapper and Ginny, ringing their bells as they swooped past.

Ginny had got back to the matter in hand and recalled Pearce from his imaginative detour.

'Hastings was unmarried but had recently become engaged. He made two telephone calls that evening from the Drovers' Rest. One was to his fiancée. They talked about their forthcoming marriage. The other was to his mother. He told them both he was feeling fine and enjoying the fresh air and the scenery. There was absolutely no indication of any problems. He talked of going to visit Mum when he got back from his walking break. The following morning he set off again. The landlord saw him leave. It was the last anyone ever saw of him. He disappeared into thin air. He's never turned up since, nor any trace of him.'

Pearce was interested enough to forget the insistent throb in his gum. 'Where did he live?'

'He lived in London. There's his address. He lived in SE19. That's

Wimbledon. He worked for and was a shareholder in a company producing herbal beauty products.'

'Poor chap,' commiserated Pearce.

'Those companies make a packet,' said Holding knowledgeably. 'So he had no business or money worries. No reason to do a bunk.'

Pearce grunted. 'Well, see if either his fiancée or his mother is still around. The fiancée is probably married and has got another name. You might have trouble running her down. Try his mum. She'll probably be in her seventies but it's more likely she's still going by the same name. If you find her, ask her if she remembers the name of his dentist.'

'I've got the name of a good dentist,' offered Holding, giving him a wicked look.

'Thank you, Ginny, there's nothing wrong with my teeth!'

As sometimes happened, two lines of enquiry turned up trumps at the the same time. Simon's erstwhile fiancée proved untraceable, as Pearce had feared, but Mrs Hastings was contacted easily enough in Goldalming. She hadn't moved house since her son's disappearance. She remembered he'd always used the family dentist, a local practice, even after he'd moved away to live in his own place. The dentist had retired, but his son ran the practice and, an unexpected bit of good luck, had kept a lot of very old records, stuffed into boxes in the attic. A diligent search by local officers and the shifting of a great deal of dust had discovered Simon's dental records, yellowed but complete. As a result of an injury playing rugby, Simon had required extensive dental work. It had included a blade implant of the Christmas Tree type.

At the same time, the manufacturer of the distinctively shaped implant was traced and the hospital where the operation had been carried out. The record had been kept because of the rarity at that time of the treatment. X-rays of Simon's jaw were still used as illustration of the technique when lecturing to students. So not only had they dental records, they had an actual X-rays of the teeth to compare with those surviving in the jawbone. The match was unmistakable.

'That seems about it, then,' said Pearce to Markby. 'Our bones belong to the missing hiker, Simon Hastings.' He gave Markby a somewhat apologetic look. 'But it doesn't seem likely he was your Potato Man, sir. I mean, he lived in London. He was in the area just briefly on his walking holiday. He couldn't have been miles away in London during the weeks beforehand, making his herbal facepacks, and roaming Stovey Woods, looking for women on their own, at one and the same time. I did check the dates of the attacks. I thought, if they'd all taken place at the weekend, it might just be possible that Hastings had something to do with them, but they didn't. Some were in the morning, others in the afternoon. The village women were attacked on weekdays, mostly late in the day. The same goes for the two girls from outside the area, the walker and the cyclist. They were there in vacation time and they were attacked on weekdays. In fact,' concluded Pearce thoughtfully, 'it's as though the rapist avoided the weekend. Why do you think that was?'

'Too many people using the area recreationally,' Markby said shortly. 'Strong chance a woman's scream might be heard or he'd be seen in the area.'

'Or he had a job which kept him busy at weekends? Anyway,' Pearce shrugged. 'It rules out Simon Hastings who spent his weekdays, nine to five, in his laboratory working out how to stop women's faces wrinkling.'

'I take the point,' Markby returned irritably. 'But when he disappeared, the Potato Man disappeared, and don't tell me there isn't a connection. We just don't know what it is, that's all.' He then added more mildly, 'Well done, anyway. And tell Holding, good work.'

In view of their success, the inquest on the bones, which had been opened and adjourned to allow police to follow enquiries, was reconvened.

The night before it was held, the gusting wind, which had been absent since the onset of the rain, returned and rampaged until the early hours of the morning. In Lower Stovey its wild rattlings and whistlings echoed with particular savagery. Perhaps it was that which kept the inhabitants from their slumbers, or it may have been other things troubling their minds, as the wind troubled the roof tiles and chimney stacks and even succeeded in bringing down a tree on the edge of Stovey Woods themselves.

Ruth Aston lay awake and listened to the wind howl round the eaves of the Old Forge. At one point she got out of bed to close the window because the curtain billowed crazily and the bar threatened to spring loose at any minute and let the casement fly open and slam against the outer wall. She pulled it shut and the noise of the wind was lessened. From her window she could see the clouds scudding across the night sky and the garden and fields beyond bathed in pale moonlight, bounded by the mass of the woods. Squatting on the horizon as they did, it seemed too easy to feel Stovey Woods possessed a single personality, a dark force from an ancient past. Ruth imagined how the wind must roar among the trunks and bring down debris, branches and birds' nests. Into her head unbidden came the old nursery rhyme: *When the bough breaks the cradle will fall, down will come baby, cradle and all.* Something was about to come tumbling down. She felt it, sensed it, heard it in this wind, a force which would tear aside every pretence and reveal old secrets, large and small.

She knew that in view of the inquest there was something she ought to do and knew, too, that she lacked the courage to do it. She went back to bed with a wretched conscience.

Billy Twelvetrees lay awake in his cottage and wondered if the rotting straw above his head would withstand the buffeting. The roof needed a complete re-thatch. But the owner, Jones who farmed under Stovey Woods, steadfastly refused to entertain the idea, though he had put the wire net over it to hold it together. Landlords were supposed to maintain property in a fit way, Billy grumbled mentally to himself. But he was in no position to cross swords with Jones who could turn him out of here if he took a fancy to. He'd promised, of course, he'd promised Billy could live here until he died, or had to leave for some kind of residential home, something Billy would be hanged if he'd ever do. But promises had a way of being forgotten and at the very least, Jones might increase the rent which was a nominal amount. He'd worked for Joneses all his life, thought Billy angrily. This Jones who was young Kevin and before him for his father old Martin Jones, who was still alive but did nothing very much about the farm now. And that was the problem. The promise had been made by Martin, but the decisions these days were being taken by young Kevin.

The noise of the wind made Billy uneasy. He could barely hear the ticking of the ancient alarm clock on the table by his bed. The groaning of the roof timbers didn't quite blot out the snores of his daughter in her room across the passageway. Take more than this to keep Dilys awake, he thought in disgust. She always slept like a log. Another gust of wind rattled the crumbling windowframes. Billy pulled the sheet up over his head and gave himself over to rancorous thoughts about Kevin Jones until he fell asleep.

In their private flat on the top floor of the Fitzroy Arms Norman and his wife both lay awake in their cramped bedroom. They argued fiercely but in low voices as if there were anyone to overhear or the wind itself might seize their words and hurl them into the night sky for anyone to catch. After a while, Evie began to cry in an awkward, unattractive fashion, snorting and gulping. Norman told her to stop her noise, for goodness sake.

She mumbled resentfully, but as one who knew her point of view would always be disregarded, 'It's all your fault. You don't have cause to blame me. They'll find out.'

'No, they bloody won't if'n you don't tell them!'

'It's disgusting. In the church, too.'

'It wasn't in the church,' said Norman wearily. 'It was in the tower.'

'Well, that's part of the church, isn't it? And that stupid girl, no better than she should be. Young enough to be your daughter.'

'Oh, stop belly-aching,' snapped Norman. 'It was only a bit of fun.'

'She might go gossiping.'

'Don't be daft. Who'd she tell?'

'Kids boast. They tell each other things you mightn't tell anyone because you're not a kid,' Evie said waspishly. 'Sex in the church, that's something she might brag about.'

Norman told her again not to be daft, but he sounded less confident. 'I'll have a word with her.'

Evie returned, with a wisdom which startled Norman, 'If you do that, you'll never get rid of her. She'll have you pinned down like a cat with a bird. She'll know how scared you are.'

'I'll fix it, I tell you! Go to sleep.'

'Oh, you're a great fixer, you are!' was the sarcastic retort. 'You've fixed yourself into all kinds of trouble. You should never have kept them. Did you get rid of them?'

'Yes, I told you! There's nothing to tie me into it, nothing!'

A sniff and a change of tack. 'Here, what did the police want to talk to Dilys and Uncle Billy for?'

'How do I know? Will you shut up or what?' roared Norman.

Evie knew the time had come to close the conversation, before Norman closed it with his fist. But she also sensed that for once, she had the advantage. 'Young enough to be your daughter...' was mumbled again, followed by 'Don't know what a young girl like that could see in an bald old bloke like you.' Then, in triumph, 'Sex in the church! You'll go to hell.'

'See you there, then,' returned her ever-loving husband.

At that moment a dustbin overturned with a crash and began to roll about the car park. Evie screamed.

In the morning, the main street was littered with bits of thatch, twigs, leaves and the rubbish that had come from the dustbin. The rest of the contents lay strewn about the car park. All in all, it took Norman an hour to sweep it up. Over in the churchyard, the stone angel had tilted to an even more precarious angle. But the wind had dropped and in the stillness Lower Stovey wondered what would come next.

In the circumstances, the inquest on Simon Hastings ought to have been a routine affair attended by a handful of interested parties, and taking only minutes. But Lower Stovey was in the news now, following Hester's death. The press, sensing a story, turned out in number, mostly local papers but with representatives from at least two national tabloids and one broadsheet. The journalists had been doing their homework, as Markby quickly found, and had unearthed the twenty-two-year-old reports of the rape cases.

'Do you think these are the remains of the rapist, Superintendent?' a dozen voices asked eagerly as he pushed his way into the room where the inquest was to be held.

'This is a simple inquest and nothing more!' he snapped back.

It wasn't a very big room and with the press and those who were drawn to a local story with such gruesome features, it was packed. Markby, glancing round, saw that Lower Stovey had sent what might be termed a deputation. The landlord of the Fitzroy Arms, his gloomy visage singularly appropriate for the occasion, sat a little way from Muriel Scott. Markby was surprised to see Ruth Aston sitting next to Muriel. Now, what brought Ruth here? At that point another villager he might not have expected to see emerged from the direction of the ladies' cloakroom and took a seat self-consciously next to Norman, the landlord.

Dilys Twelvetrees, he thought, by all that's wonderful. She was wearing what he guessed was her best coat, its lilac colour clashing somewhat with her salmon-coloured hair. The coat was well-worn at the cuffs and edges but carefully brushed and adorned with a brooch of glass 'stones'. Norman took no notice of her but presumably she'd come with him. They were, after all, Markby recollected, cousins. He was distracted from the Lower Stovey-ites by the arrival of an elderly well-dressed woman with fine bone-structure and expertly coiffed silver hair. She moved to the front of the court room and sat, bolt upright, her eyes fixed on the coroner except when Guy Morgan gave his account of finding the bones. Then she looked down at the gloves she'd pulled off and held tightly clenched on her lap.

Pearce gave evidence as to their identity. The coroner concluded that as there was no evidence of foul play, it seemed likely Simon Hastings had met with some accident or died of natural causes. He noted the occupation of the deceased and the likelihood, therefore, that he'd been following some botantical investigation in the woods at the time of his death which was why his body had lain there, and not on the old way itself.

The coroner then cleared his throat and directing his words towards the press contingent added, 'I understand that attempts have been made in some quarters to link this unfortunate happening to an old, unsolved case. I must stress that this court has heard no evidence to suggest any such connection and unwarranted speculation can only cause distress to the family.'

When the coroner had left the room, a loud buzz of animated chatter filled the air. Pearce approached Guy Morgan and thanked him for his contribution.

Guy was looking past him at someone else but turned his head politely back to Pearce. 'Not at all, Inspector. I'm glad you've been able to put a name to him. Tell me, who is the distinguished-looking elderly woman?'

Pearce glanced towards the silver-haired woman and said quietly, 'Mother.'

'Oh, I wondered . . .' Guy said. 'I noticed, when I was giving my evidence, that she gave me one quick look and then kept her eyes fixed on her hands. I could see that listening to me was painful for her. I'm glad she didn't have to give any evidence.'

'It wasn't necessary, in the circumstances,' Pearce told him. 'Once we identified the dental work in the jaw we knew we had Simon Hastings.'

Markby had turned to look for Ruth Aston, but now she and Muriel had disappeared towards the ladies' cloakroom. The elderly woman he'd observed earlier was approaching him. The mother, he thought. He must say a few words to her.

She spoke first. 'I understand you're Superintendent Markby.' Her voice was educated, pleasant and dignified. When he confirmed that he was, she went on, 'I'm Daphne Hastings, Simon's mother.'

'Yes, Inspector Pearce pointed you out to me. I'm very sorry,' Markby went on. 'This must have been quite an ordeal for you.'

A muscle twitched in her heavily-powdered cheek. 'It's been an ordeal for me, Superintendent, for more than twenty years, since my son's disappearance.'

'Have you come from Godalming?' he asked suddenly. 'Look, would you like a cup of coffee? There is a little café down the road here.'

'Thank you.' She inclined her head. 'I think I would like a cup of coffee. It was a long journey because I had to change trains in London.'

He was pleased to find the café half empty and particularly pleased that none of the journalists who'd been at the inquest had found their way there. They were probably all in the pub. The café was the sort of place where you went to a counter and fetched your own food and drinks. He established Mrs Hastings in a corner and went for the coffees. When he carried them back to the table, she'd taken off her black suede gloves and hung them neatly over her handbag. She'd unbuttoned her coat, but not taken if off. Now he could see she wore a black dress beneath it and pearls which looked to him like the real thing. He found himself wondering if this mourning attire had been donned since the discovery of her son's remains or whether she'd been wearing black in his memory for some years now.

She thanked him for the coffee, picked up a spoon and began to stir it round and round in the cup. 'I should wish to give my son proper burial,' she said. 'I have been in touch with the coroner's office. They are content for me to take the – to take Simon.' She gave a dry smile. 'I got the impression they were glad someone was offering to take responsibility. The girl I spoke to suggested I clear it with you, with the police. Will you need to retain —?' She broke off and raised her fine eyes to his. There was the imprint of tragedy in them.

Markby said quickly, 'No, we don't need to keep anything. Of course you may take – take your son's remains back to Godalming. I assume that's where you mean to bury him?' She nodded and he went on, 'A local undertaker here will be able to make the necessary arrangements to transport him. I recommend Jenkins in the Market Square. He's pretty good.'

She still seemed unwilling to drink any of the coffee and until she lifted her cup, he felt he couldn't drink from his.

'I know,' she said in the voice of someone forcing herself to speak painful words, 'that I haven't my son's complete – that I only have a few bones. But they are Simon's and I do have something to bury. I can't tell you how hard it's been, just not knowing. One always hopes, you see, when there's no body, that somehow, somewhere, one day . . . One consoles oneself with explanations of amnesia, kidnap, nervous breakdown . . . Anything, however unlikely, that might account for his just vanishing as he did. One thinks that one day he might just walk through the door again. That's why I've never sold my house. I thought, foolishly, that he might come home and I'd not be there, strangers might open the door to him. So, I stayed.'

'Mrs Hastings,' Markby said, deeply moved. 'I wish we could have found your son sooner. I have looked up the file. The police did search the area extensively at the time of his disappearance. But it's heavily wooded. We don't know exactly where – The place the bones were found is unlikely to be the exact spot he died. I don't know why they couldn't find his body then. I do know they tried.'

Yes, dammit! They had tried and they hadn't found him. Why? Markby wondered angrily. Of course it had been a difficult area to search. If the bones had been moved by animals, as seemed the case, Simon could had died anywhere along that length of the old way or in the woods on either side of it. But was there a more sinister reason why he hadn't been found? Was it because someone had made a good job of burying him somewhere in Stovey Woods? And why, oh why, had the attacks by the Potato Man ceased at the time of Simon's disappearance?

At last she was drinking her coffee and he was able to sip his.

'It will be a great relief,' she said, 'to be able to hold a funeral service. Of course in my heart I've recognised he was dead for some years. But one can't mourn without a funeral. All this, though it's been a shock, has also been a release. I think that tonight, Superintendent, for the first time in twenty-two years, I shall sleep soundly.'

The door of the café opened and two more customers came in, two women. Markby looked across and saw Muriel Scott and Ruth Aston. He was sure they hadn't seen him or Daphne Hastings.

The two newcomers consulted together and Muriel went to the counter. Ruth looked round for a vacant table and saw then who else was there. She flushed, hesitated and then came over to where they sat.

She glanced guiltily at Markby and addressed his companion. 'Mrs Hastings? You don't know me. But my name is Ruth Aston and I used to be Ruth Pattinson before my marriage. I was a student at the same time as your son. I am very sorry.'

'You knew Simon?' Mrs Hastings' face lit up. 'Do sit down.'

'Well, I'm with a friend —' Ruth gestured towards Muriel Scott. 'I just wanted to express my condolences.'

'That's very kind of you, my dear.' Mrs Hastings put out a hand and rested it on Ruth's arm. Markby thought Ruth twitched at the touch. It struck him she looked as if her nerves were in a bad way. Dark circles under her eyes indicated she hadn't slept well. She was a poor colour, very pale.

'Simon was a brilliant student, wasn't he?' Mrs Hastings was saying. She turned to Markby. 'And he was very popular. Everyone liked him. When he went into business, he was doing so well at that. It was as though he had a golden future.' She stopped speaking abruptly.

Ruth muttered, 'Yes, he was a brilliant student. I see my friend is bringing our coffee. Do excuse me.' She moved away.

'I must be going,' Daphne Hastings said. She sounded suddenly exhausted. 'I must go and see this undertaker, Jenkins, you say?'

'I'll take you there,' he offered.

She shook her head. 'You've already given up your time. I'm sure I shall find it. Is the Market Square very far from here?'

'No, it's only at the bottom of the road. How are you getting back to Godalming?'

'I came by train,' she said. 'As soon as I've made arrangements with the undertaker, I shall be going to the station. There are plenty of trains to London this evening, I understand.' She began pulling on her black suede gloves, smoothing down each finger individually.

'You've great courage,' Markby heard himself say suddenly.

She paused in the rhythmic movement of stroking the gloves and looked up, eyebrows raised and a half-smile on her face.

'Oh, no, Superintendent. Not at all. You were right in saying today was an ordeal. When that young doctor was giving his evidence I found it too painful even to look at him. Not because he described finding Simon's bones, something for which I'm grateful to him, but because he was much of the age Simon was when he disappeared. He was about Simon's height and build and he'd been hiking, as Simon was then. Just such a young man as my son was in every way. It was as if a ghost spoke to us.'

He opened the door for her and watched her walk steadily down the middle of the pavement in the direction of the Market Square. He remembered his thoughts on broken hearts when talking to Ursula Gretton. Mrs Hastings had been successfully maintaining a brave front for over twenty years. There was no doubt whatever that beneath it, her heart was broken.

He made to leave the café but heard his name called and looked back. Ruth had left the table she shared with Muriel Scott and came hurrying towards him.

'Mr Markby,' she said urgently in a low voice. 'I must talk to you but not in front of Muriel. I don't want to go to a police station. Can you come and see me? And bring Meredith with you?'

'Yes, of course,' he said. 'We'll come out this evening, if that's all right with you?'

'Thank you.' She twitched again. 'You see,' she said. 'I think I may have committed a criminal offence.'

Chapter Eleven

'What could she possibly have meant?' Meredith mused as they drove towards Lower Stovey that evening. 'Didn't she give any clue?'

There were few cars on this stretch of the early evening road. They must have hit that fortunate window between people hurrying home from work and those hurrying out again on evening pursuits. She thought Alan looked a little tired and definitely sombre. Sensitive to changes in his mood, she picked up on his inner tension and the not altogether successful way he was trying to disguise it.

She'd been on the train on her own way home from London when she'd received his call on her mobile. He suggested he drive over to her house and if she was willing, they'd go to see Ruth at her request. He'd explain when he saw her. She'd replied simply, 'Of course I'll come.'

She'd had no time other than to effect a quick change of clothes and run a brush through her thick brown hair, grateful for the amenable bobbed style which meant minimum fuss. He'd arrived as she'd just burned her mouth on a too-hot mug of instant coffee. In the car he'd given her a brief account of the inquest and of his meeting with Daphne Hastings, followed by Ruth's request. In answer to Meredith's question, he now said, 'Not directly. But as this urge to confess appears to have followed on the inquest I suppose it may have something to do with that. She was particularly anxious I bring you along.'

Markby slowed as they neared the turning which indicated 'Lower

Stovey. No Through Road.' 'There is one thing I should perhaps mention to you before we get there. There's no need for Ruth to know I've told you if the subject doesn't arise, but I fancy it will and I want you to be prepared.'

And as he turned down the single-track road and they bumped their way over the uneven pitted surface between high hedges, he told her about Ruth's baby.

'I didn't mention it before because it was by way of confidential information,' he added apologetically.

'Of course I understand that!' Meredith returned indignantly. 'But why should Ruth want to talk about it now?'

'Because she'll have to be told we've spoken to Dr Fitchett and it would be unfair and unwise to leave her in an agony of suspense over whether the old chap has let the cat out of the bag or not. And because I suspect that Simon Hastings was the father of her child. If he was, then I'll have to ask her where she was the weekend he disappeared.'

'So long ago, how can she be expected to remember?' Meredith asked indignantly. 'Alan, for goodness' sake, be careful. The poor woman already thinks you've got her marked down as Hester's murderer. Don't make it sound as if you're thinking she had a hand in another death.'

'I don't think it. I told you, I don't think anything right now. We don't know how Simon died. I'm merely observing and making notes to keep tucked away in a corner of my brain. I've made a note, for example, that two people have died in the neighbourhood of Lower Stovey and both were connected with Ruth Aston. But that's all it is at the moment, a mental note. It was Ruth herself, I'd remind you, who told me she thought she might have committed a crime.'

Meredith was prevented from comment because at that moment they encountered a tractor coming towards them. As the banks were steep and there was no passing room, Alan was forced to back his car until he reached a spot where enough space had been scooped out of the bank to allow him to pull over. The tractor, its huge wheels caked in mud, grumbled its way past. It was being driven by a weather-beaten man in a pullover and a battered cap who raised a laconic hand in acknowledgement as he passed.

'Kevin Jones,' said Markby. 'I went to their farm twenty-two years ago when we were investigating the Potato Man. Not for any particular reason, just routine. We called at all the farms and asked if they'd noticed any signs of anyone sleeping rough on their land. It was Martin Jones running the place then, Kevin's father. Kevin was there, too, waiting to take over when his father retired. That must have happened by now. Martin must be —' Markby frowned as he calculated. 'At least seventy. Kevin must be forty or so now. He was a young man in his early twenties then and I guessed chafing at not being able to run the farm in his own way. I've run into him a couple of times since. I got the impression he was in charge now.'

'He looked older than forty-something on that tractor,' Meredith said. 'Not that I got a good look at him.'

'Farming's a tough business these days with a lot of worries. I wonder if Kevin is as keen to run the farm now as he was in his twenties,' Alan returned drily. 'But perhaps we were both a lot keener on our chosen professions back then. I was only twenty-five.'

'You made inspector early,' she observed.

'They thought I had promise.' He allowed himself a brief grin.

'And they thought right!' she declared.

He gave a snort of derision. 'Did they? The very first case they handed me, the Potato Man, I failed to solve, didn't even turn up a likely suspect. There must have been a few of the top brass who had second thoughts!'

They'd reached the village. The Old Forge looked attractive in the dying evening sun. The last rays caught the upstairs windows, making them sparkle, and even the garden, littered with leaves from the previous night's storm, looked peaceful.

But it was clear Ruth herself wasn't at peace. She greeted them nervously, twisting her hands and rushing her phrases.

'Come in, do. Sorry to hustle you but the neighbours will have seen you arrive. I never used to worry about neighbours' gossip, but now it's different.'

She urged them ahead of her towards the ingle-nook hearth where seats had been drawn up round a low table on which stood a tray with a bottle of sherry and glasses.

'It's all I've got,' apologized Ruth. 'Except wine.'

'Sherry would be very nice,' Alan told her. 'Shall I pour?'

She gave him a timid smile and followed it with a little laugh. 'Is it that obvious I should be all fingers and thumbs?'

'You do look as if something's worrying you, Ruth,' Meredith told her.

'Yes, it is. Well, you wouldn't be here if it wasn't, would you? Thank you both for coming, by the way. You, Meredith, in particular are being very kind. I do realise you've probably been busy in London all day.'

They sipped at the sherry while Ruth sorted out her next words. 'I understand you've found old Amyas Fitchett, Hester's uncle.'

Markby nodded. 'Yes, I've spoken to him.'

Ruth looked reflective. 'How odd, he must be ancient. I thought he'd be dead.'

'He's in his nineties but remarkably well for his age. He doesn't leave his own house and garden, that's the only thing. That has nothing to do with a mobility problem. It's by choice. I don't think,' Markby smiled, 'Dr Fitchett has much time for the modern world.'

'Oh, he was like that years ago,' said Ruth dismissively. 'He always spoke with contempt of the world outside his own little academic island. He had a very brusque, almost inquisitorial way with him, I remember. Hester used to say he was really very kind and I suppose he was. Certainly, when Hester's mother asked him whether she was doing the right thing in helping me, he told her she was.'

Ruth looked full at them. 'You do know what I'm talking about, don't you?'

'The birth of your baby,' Markby said gently.

'That's right. A very nice woman called Mrs Hatton got in touch with me and warned me old Uncle Amyas had told you about that. To use her phrase, "told the superintendent details of my personal life which I mightn't have wished disclosed." She was very embarrassed and apologetic. She felt, because she'd taken you to see Amyas, she was responsible. I assured her she wasn't and that now Simon's remains have been identified, it seems destined to come out, anyway.' Ruth turned her head to look at Meredith. 'Has Alan told you about it, Meredith?'

Meredith confessed that he had. 'But only on the way here because he thought you'd mention it. He wouldn't have told me otherwise.'

'That's very gentlemanly of you,' Ruth said drily to Markby. 'Though it's not the scandal now it was then. Nobody cares about me now. Then it was different. Then I was the Reverend Pattinson's daughter and that kind of behaviour wasn't expected of me.' She gazed sadly into the hearth where the fire had again been lit. The flames flickered up and sent pink fingers of light playing across her face. 'I was very young, very stupid and in love. Or I ought to say, I'd been in love and I'd just found out that love plays some nasty tricks on you.'

'And the father of the child was Simon Hastings?' Markby prompted in the same quiet voice.

'Yes. You heard his mother talk about him today in that café.' Ruth glanced at Meredith. 'You weren't there to hear it, but she was going on about him as if he was Mr Perfect. She was right to say he was popular and very clever. But he certainly wasn't without his faults! But then, I wasn't without mine, if ignorance can be counted a fault.'

One of the half-burned logs in the hearth fell in with a crackle and sent a shower of sparks into the air.

'I realise now,' Ruth went on, 'that I'd had a peculiarly sheltered, isolated sort of life until I went to university. When I was young I lived here at Lower Stovey and then they sent me to boarding school in the West Country. That was out in the sticks, nothing much around for miles. I got through it all right. I made friends of a sort but the first real friend I ever made was Hester when I got to university. One sort of person I'd never had anything to do with was young and male. I didn't know any boys. Most of the girls at school had brothers or male cousins and as they got older they claimed to have boyfriends at home wherever that was. Some got letters which they carried round hidden in their junior bras because they were afraid a member of staff would find them.'

Ruth sighed. 'Not me. I was quite incredibly green and ignorant. I thought some day the right man would just appear in my life and after some initial sparring, it would all end happily, like a Georgette Heyer novel.'

'It doesn't work like that,' said Meredith soberly and felt Alan's gaze rest on her.

'No, of course it doesn't! But I didn't know that. When I met Simon I just fell in love. He seemed to return my love. I didn't doubt him, why should I? It was immensely flattering to have his attention. He was quite a catch. Other women students envied me. It was all very heady while it lasted. It ended quite abruptly the moment I told him I was pregnant. I'd been living in a fantasy where we'd get married and it would all be fine. But when I saw his face — ' Ruth broke off and swallowed. It was a moment before she continued and they waited in silence. Only the fire whispered softly to itself in the background.

'He was horrified,' said Ruth baldly. 'No other word for it. He suggested I "get rid of it somehow". That was his phrase. He was talking about his own child. I realised, when I heard him speak those words, that not only did he not love me and never had, but that I didn't love him any more. From thinking him Mr Wonderful I went to despising him in an instant. He went on to make it worse, obviously terrified he'd be forced into marriage. I wasn't going to tell my parents, was I? he asked. He'd no intention of telling his. I assured him I'd make no claims. I'd hide it from my family somehow. I had no idea how.'

Ruth looked up at them, her eyes huge and tragic in her pale face. 'You can't imagine the state I was in. I got to the end of the academic year somehow. To this day I don't know how, perhaps by concentrating desperately on my books to keep my mind off the one great problem. But then it was the end of term and time to go home. My pregnancy was beginning to show. I wore big floppy sweaters and loose shirts. It got me a reputation for being eccentric because everyone else was in mini-skirts. Sooner or later, someone would twig.

'I confided in Hester. I was at my wits' end. Hester, bless her, came to the rescue, taking me up to Yorkshire. The baby arrived, it was a boy, and put up for adoption. I went home and – and life continued. The strange thing is that a part of me still wanted to believe Simon had loved me once, that it was only the pregnancy which had frightened him off because he hadn't been prepared for that. That was my pride at work, I dare say. I didn't want to believe I'd been a complete idiot from the beginning! I even kept his letters until the other day. I used to read them from time to time. They'd lost their power to hurt but I kept thinking they must hold some clue to his real feelings. I was like an archaeologist trying to make sense of an ancient inscription. If I could just find the key word, the rest would fall into place. I burned them the day the bones were found. I panicked. I didn't want my link with Simon known. But I knew it would be, if ever the bones were identified and the police are so clever about that sort of thing nowadays, aren't they?'

'Not us,' said Markby wryly. 'The scientists.'

Ruth looked thoughtful. 'You know, I honestly think he did love me for a little while before he got bored with me. He was a very shallow type. In his defence – there, you see – I'm still seeking to defend him!' Ruth gave a mirthless laugh. 'On his behalf, then, I know that being so popular, so clever, good at sports, everything, he was surrounded by people who wanted to be his friend and who never, ever, would have criticized anything he said or did.'

'Turned his head,' said Meredith.

'Yes. He'd never had to overcome any kind of obstacle or adjust his thinking to anyone else's needs. I believe he felt that by putting an obstacle in his path, I was behaving unfairly by him.'

She heaved a deep sigh and sat back in her chair.

'How,' Markby asked her, 'did you know – or what led you to suspect – the bones belonged to Simon Hastings? I assume that by the time he disappeared, you'd already been out of touch with him for years. He lived and worked in London. Why should he turn up in Stovey Woods?'

She poured another sherry which she picked up with a trembling hand. 'You're right. I hadn't seen him for years, not until August, 1978. I was by then thirty-five, unmarried, teaching English. It was the summer vacation and I came here to Lower Stovey to visit my father. I was worried about him. My mother had died six months earlier. He was a very unworldly man and had always depended on her. She did everything, not only ran his house but ran his parish affairs, kept his diary. She was a sort of general factotum in our house. She was very capable, you see, and he wasn't. So when she died, he was lost. He couldn't keep his own diary. He kept forgetting to turn up at PCC meetings or for baptisms or even weddings. There was a frightful hoohah on one occasion when he had to be fetched from his study while the poor bride waited at the church door! Her father was most upset and wrote to the bishop. The bishop got in touch with me. He thought perhaps my father was in need of rest and recuperation. He suggested he go on retreat and sent me the address of a convent where they made a speciality of running restorative breaks for harassed clergy.'

Ruth made a gesture of resignation. 'I knew what was wrong with my father and that it would take more than a week in secluded surroundings with meditation and plain cooking to repair it. It wasn't something that could be repaired. I knew he could never manage alone. I made the mistake of expressing my doubts to the bishop and that got me another letter, hinting that it might be the answer if I could find it in my heart to return home, give up my teaching career, and stay here as my father's housekeeper.'

Ruth smiled. 'Hester talked me out of that. She said it was a Victorian idea. She pointed out, quite rightly, that if I agreed, within weeks I'd be in need of rest and recuperation myself. I'd probably have a nervous break-down. So there I was, not knowing quite what to do, staying with my father while I tried to find a solution which would suit us both. He, poor dear, was oblivious of any problem. I had to stop him wearing odd socks.'

Ruth broke off and in a sudden change of subject asked, 'You won't have eaten dinner, will you? Would you like something? I could do us all scrambled eggs on toast.'

182

'I'll do it later,' Meredith said. 'When you've finished.' She thought Alan gave her a slightly apprehensive look. She wasn't noted for her culinary expertise. Still, she ought to be able to manage scrambled eggs.

'It was late summer,' Ruth began her story again. 'The weather was very hot, I remember. My father was calmer now I was there but still getting muddled. He sometimes called me Mary, my mother's name. He'd had a terrible upset in addition to her death. There had been some attacks on women in the area of Stovey Woods and the old drovers' way. Really vicious attacks, rapes. The police had been to the village asking everyone questions and they'd come to visit my father and ask him if there was anyone who'd been acting strangely or anything he'd noticed or been told that was odd. My father assured them it was out of the question that anyone living in Lower Stovey could have anything to do with it. He thought the police accepted his word but he was badly shaken.'

'I'm the officer who spoke to him,' Alan said. 'I remember our conversation. I'm sorry if he was upset by my visit, but it's the nature of police enquiries to upset people. It wasn't a question of accepting his word. I'd no doubt he quite genuinely believed no local man was involved. He may even have been right. But we didn't know that and we still don't.'

'Was it you? How odd,' Ruth said. 'It is a small world, isn't it? Just like they say?'

'For what it's worth,' Markby added, 'I found your father a little eccentric but coherent. He defended his parishioners with great energy.'

'You didn't know him as well I as did. You couldn't be expected to notice the deterioration. After your visit – I'm not blaming you, please don't think that, but it sort of tipped him over the edge. After that, it was downhill all the way, I'm afraid. He got worse and worse. Despite everything Hester had said, I began to think I would have no choice but to stay on. My father had a dog, a labrador, which had been my mother's pet. That afternoon when it happened —' Ruth paused again.

Markby prompted, 'The afternoon Simon Hastings disappeared.'

183

She flushed then gave a rueful grimace. 'You're ahead of me, aren't you? There's me trying to explain and I dare say you half know what I'm going to tell you. I wanted to get out of the vicarage for a while, give myself some space to think. I took the dog and walked up towards Stovey Woods. I knew about the attacks but I didn't intend to go into the woods, just amble round the perimeter across Mr Jones's fields. But the dog ran ahead. She ran into the woods and I had to chase after her. I'd called her until I was blue in the face and she took not a bit of notice. Poor dog, I think she was so delighted to be out and running around. My father never remembered to walk her.

'So I followed her into the woods and after a few minutes I heard someone talking to her, a man. There, ahead of me, was someone sitting on a fallen trunk, a rucksack by his feet. The dog was standing in front of him and he was scratching her head. One of the hikers who walk the old drovers' way, I thought, and I called out a greeting. It never occurred to me it might be the rapist, in case you're wondering, because it was so obviously a hiker. He looked up and I saw it was Simon. For a moment we just stood there, staring at one another. The dog stood between us, panting. It sounded so loud, I remember. Then Simon said, "Ruth? What are you doing here?"

'I told him my father lived nearby. He said he was walking the old way. He'd got a business in London making natural beauty products from plants and was doing very well. He was looking around in the woods for ideas for new preparations. He was a botanist by training. Eventually – after he'd talked extensively about himself – he remembered to ask what I was doing. I told him I was teaching. I waited for him to ask about our child but he said nothing. So then I got angry and asked him, "Don't you want to know about the baby?" He said, "Baby?" in a blank way which really riled me.

' "Yes, baby. I had him adopted," I told him. And do you know what he said? He said, "Oh, that's all right, then."

'And then,' said Ruth. 'I really lost my temper.'

'I'm not surprised,' Meredith couldn't prevent herself commenting.

'It surprised him,' Ruth told her. 'He stood there while I ranted and raved at him. I can see his face now. He looked stunned, foolish, even a bit frightened. I can't remember all I shouted. "Don't you want to know what happened to your son?" was one of the things I yelled. "Don't you even remember he'll be twelve years old now?" Eventually I ran out of steam, turned and fled. I just couldn't bear looking at his face with that stupid, gawping expression. I think he might have called after me but he didn't run after me. He let me go. I went running on until I was out of puff and found myself way out in the middle of Jones's fields with a surprised-looking horse staring at me. The dog was running alongside me, jumping up and trying to get my attention because she could see I was unhappy. It was almost funny in a grotesque way. There I was in the middle of nowhere with a worried dog and a puzzled horse for company. I found I was crying, tears of rage, running down my face. There was a stream running along the edge of the field so I made my way there, knelt down and splashed my face and tried to repair the damage. The dog and the horse followed me. The dog, being a labrador and loving water, jumped in and began to swim about. Eventually, I got up and said to the horse —'

Ruth broke off and added apologetically, 'I know this sounds quite mad, but that's what I did. Perhaps I had gone just a little mad for a while. So I said, "I'm all right now." And the horse gave a little snicker as if he understood. I called the dog and we started to walk home. I prayed we wouldn't meet anyone but of all people, we met old Billy Twelvetrees, only he wasn't so old then. He worked for Mr Jones. He asked me if there was anything wrong and I said very sniffily, "No, of course not!" He gave me a knowing sort of look and said, "That right, then?" So, to make an excuse for my red face and puffy eyes, I told him I'd been thinking about my mother. He said he'd been very sorry to hear about Miss Mary's death. Miss Mary was what he and all the villagers called my mother. He made a little speech saying she'd been a proper lady of the old school and presented me with his condolences, very formally. I said, "Thank you, Mr Twelvetrees," and then I went home.'

Ruth sat back exhausted. 'I now know I was the last person to see Simon alive.'

185

An icy finger ran down Meredith's spine. Could Alan be right to include Ruth on his 'list of possibles'? In this same room Ruth had told her she had been the last person to see Hester alive. In Ruth's case, lightning would seem to have struck twice in the same place. Or was it simply bad luck? Had Ruth in her own words 'gone a little mad for a while' and, in her anger, struck out at Simon? Had he slipped and struck his head on the tree trunk on which he'd been sitting? She tried to force these thoughts away, saying, 'I'll go and make those scrambled eggs now, shall I?'

She made her way into the kitchen and began to look around for the necessary utensils and plates. Ruth called out to ask if she needed help and she called back that she didn't. After a moment she could hear Ruth and Alan talking again. The door stood open and their voices floated through.

'Why?' Alan was asking. 'Why did you tell me you thought you'd committed a criminal offence?'

'Because shortly after that, Simon went missing. Well, he went missing that day, didn't he, the twenty-fourth? It was in the local press and on the news. I should have come forward and told the police I'd seen him, but I didn't want to. I was afraid I'd have to make explanations. Anyway, I told myself, it wouldn't have helped.' There was a pause. Ruth added, 'Would it?'

'It might have done. We should have been able to pinpoint the exact spot he was last seen and narrowed our search to that area. Is that what you meant by your criminal offence?'

'It's half of it. When the bones were found, I had another chance to come forward and tell about that day, but I still didn't. There was an outside chance you wouldn't be able to establish whose bones they were. So instead of coming forward, I burned his letters, destroying evidence, if you like. I hoped and prayed you wouldn't identify him. But you did find out who he was.'

'It was by the purest good fortune,' Markby interrupted. 'Because he'd had distinctive dental work and the jaw was one of the bones found.'

'See? It was meant. So then I knew I really ought to come forward because what I knew was relevant to the inquest. But I didn't want to testify at the inquest. I just couldn't do it. Later, when I met his mother in that café and heard her talking about him, I felt so guilty. Poor woman, all those years wondering what had happened. Perhaps I could have shortened her agony if I'd come forward years ago. Morally, I shouldn't have withheld my evidence and in practical terms I probably broke the law, did I?'

Meredith heard Alan say soothingly, 'I'm not going to arrest you! I think you should have spoken up when he disappeared and we were appealing for any sightings of him. But as we didn't then, nor have we now, evidence that any crime had been committed connected with his disappearance, you weren't technically withholding evidence in a criminal matter. You were being unhelpful, that's all, and possibly caused some waste of police time as the wrong areas were searched. I'm not saying we would have found Simon, mind you, had you given us your information. We don't know the circumstances in which he died. The inquest is a little different. Strictly speaking, a lawyer would argue your evidence wasn't relevant since the identity of the bones wasn't in dispute. We had forensic evidence they belonged to Simon Hastings. The fact that you saw Simon in the woods is circumstantial. It wouldn't, in itself, have meant the bones were his, though it would've raised the possibility. But given the forensic report, we didn't need it. In any case, don't worry about it. Nothing you say now adds significantly to what we already knew, that he was walking the old way when he disappeared.'

Meredith heard Ruth heave a sigh of relief. 'Thank you. I've been so worried and my conscience has been troubling me.'

It was at that point Meredith realised that the eggs were sticking to the bottom of the pan. Her eavesdropping had distracted her from attending to stirring. She scraped the mixture off as best she could, leaving the brown burnt bits. The toast popped up obligingly from the toaster. She set it all out on the kitchen table and went to call the others.

She thought Alan looked a bit relieved when he saw the eggs, though he did glance towards the pan soaking in cold water. Ruth had disappeared into her larder and came out with a bottle of white wine. That a weight had been lifted from her shoulders was obvious. She looked quite cheerful.

'This is the wine I mentioned earlier. We'll have it with the eggs, shall we? Can you open it, Alan?'

After they'd eaten and had carried the remaining wine back into the sitting room, they settled themselves around the log fire. Meredith thought Ruth looked peaceful. It had been a relief, Meredith realised, for Ruth to have been able to speak at long last of something that had been a secret for so many years.

She heard herself asking, 'Looking back, do you think now that perhaps you could have told your parents about the baby? That they might have understood? Your father was a parish priest, he must have had people confide all kinds of things to him.'

'Oh, he'd have understood. He knew about human frailty,' Ruth returned. 'But he'd have been deeply disappointed and worse, he'd have felt guilty.'

'Why on earth should he do that?'

'For failing to bring me up so that I could resist temptation!' Ruth gave her a wry smile. 'I don't think he'd have coped very well, not with a scandal in his own family. Dealing with other people's problems is so much easier than dealing with your own, I always think. That was my experience as a teacher. I was always ready with good advice for my pupils. But look what a mess I made of my own life!'

Markby, who'd been staring at the whispering logs, leaned forward and picked up the poker to push to safety a piece of charred wood which was threatening to topple from the grate. 'You had one unsuccessful relationship. That wasn't entirely your fault. It's certainly hardly making a disaster of your life. You had a successful teaching career. You married later, someone else.'

'And here I sit,' said Ruth, 'with nothing. All I had in the end, you see, was Hester.'

Meredith started to ask, 'Have you never —?' but broke off in embarrassment.

188

'Never what?' Ruth asked calmly.

'None of my business, sorry.'

'Let me guess.' Ruth smoothed a wrinkle in her skirt. 'Have I never tried to trace my child? Is that it?'

'It was, yes.'

'And what would I say to him, if ever I found him? No, I like to think he's happy and successful somewhere.'

There was a long silence. It was broken by Markby, who asked suddenly, 'What arrangement did you eventually come to about your father, Ruth?'

'Oh, my father, yes, that was another problem I didn't know how to solve. But then I had a bit of luck. I saw Mr Jones a few days after – after that business with Simon. That's old Mr Martin Jones who farmed Greenjack Farm then, not young Kevin who farms it now. Only Kevin isn't so young now and back then, Martin himself wasn't so ancient. We were chatting and he told me he had a niece who'd just been widowed young and left in very difficult circumstances. No money, he meant. "She'll have to get a job," he said. "And find herself somewhere cheap to live."

'Do you know,' Ruth said earnestly, 'it was like being in one of those baroque ceiling paintings where a ray of sunlight streams out of clouds and strikes some kneeling saint. I said, "Mr Jones, if things could be worked out, do you think your niece would be interested in coming to live at the vicarage and keep house for my father?" He said, yes, he was sure she would. So I went to meet his niece and she was a good, practical sort with no children and very keen on coming to Lower Stovey to be near her uncle. So she did. She stayed with my father until he died and it made the world of difference to him. He got regular meals. She supervised his laundry. She kept a check on his diary and made sure he was where he ought to be. He was able to carry on being the vicar here until he died, entirely because of her.'

Ruth sighed. 'In the meantime, though, the parish had dwindled. The school had closed. To leave my father *in situ* looking after the remaining inhabitants had been all right. They knew him and he'd been so long here it would've been unreasonable to uproot him. But there was really so little for him to do. After he'd gone, the decision was taken not to replace him here but to join St Barnabas to Bamford church. In view of this, the church commissioners decided to sell the vicarage. As the housekeeper had remained living in it until a decision was made on its future, they decided that she could have it, if she wanted, on very generous terms. A knock-down price, in fact. They wanted rid of the place. It was a white elephant and in need of a lot of renovation. She'd been living there, bed and board supplied plus her wages, for some time and she'd been saving up so she was able to buy it. I think her Uncle Martin may have helped her out a bit with the asking price, too.'

Markby set down his wine. 'Just a sec. The housekeeper bought the old vicarage? When was this?'

'Yes,' said Ruth. 'It was in 1982 or early 1983 and she's still there, Muriel Scott.'

Chapter Twelve

'Come on, Henry!' urged Pearce.

He'd enjoy walking the dog this nice mild morning in the normal way of it but present circumstances were working against him in every department of his life. The tooth, which he'd been trying to treat with a course of mind over matter, hadn't responded and was undeniably worse. Moreover, he was well aware that they were getting to that stage of a murder case when the trail starts to go cold, at first imperceptibly but with growing obviousness. 'Three days,' many of the old hands said. 'You've got three days to come up with a really good lead or you're in trouble.' But twice that number of days had passed since Hester Millar's murder. As time went by, possible evidence was damaged or lost. People forgot. Worse, they began to remember differently. In many cases the murderer had skipped out and could be anywhere in the world.

Pearce didn't think this murderer had left the scene. He, with Markby, felt sure he or she was still there, in or around Lower Stovey. An absence from the small community would be missed, especially one which came about suddenly. But no one had unexpectedly upped and left, thought Pearce. They were all still there and among them . . .

'Henry!' he repeated with growing impatience. Some mornings Henry could be very obliging and they made their circuit of the playing field in record time. Sometimes, however, Henry seemed to go into a meditative phase. He would stop for no clear reason and stand, staring into the far distance (where Pearce could distinguish nothing), deaf to entreaty. He appeared, or so Pearce fancied, to have quite a glazed look in his eyes on these occasions. He was doing it now, still as a statue, communing with something unseen or unheard by man.

'Ruddy dog!' grumbled Pearce. 'I'll be late.'

And he had wanted to be early. He'd told Tessa so, arguing that with such an important case he needed to put in the extra time. 'Just think, love, if I can crack it without the old man's help, it'll do me a power of good career-wise.' The 'old man' – Markby – fortunately wasn't there to hear this unkind description of himself.

Tessa, who had heard it, had gone straight to the heart of the matter, saying briskly, 'I'm not walking Henry again this morning. It's your turn.'

So Pearce had set out, plastic bag in pocket, dog on leash. So far they'd met no one else, which was unusual. There were generally a few other dog walkers around. Both Pearce and Tessa kept an eagle eye open for those who hadn't equipped themselves with the necessary plastic bag. Pearce had once drawn a man's attention to the notice at the entry to the field, reminding people that allowing dogs to foul the area was an offence. The fellow, a weedy little chap with a pointed nose who had borne a marked resemblance to the dog he was walking, had proved stroppy. 'Mind your own business, mate!' he'd told Pearce. 'It is my business, I am a police officer,' had retorted Pearce, gaining the withering reply, 'Then why aren't you out investigating things? No wonder the crime rate is what it is. Wasting your time following people who are walking their dogs when other people are being burgled!'

The observation, that he was wasting his time when he ought to be investigating things, had come back to haunt Pearce this morning. Fortunately Henry had decided to move on but before they'd got much further there was a rustle in the hedgerow beside which they walked. Henry's somewhat blunted hunting instincts were aroused. He leapt towards the noise. The extendible lead ran out full length before Pearce could prevent it. Henry wriggled through a small gap in the tangled hedge, got the lead wrapped round a projecting branch, and was brought up abruptly, stuck. He whimpered pathetically.

'Serves you right,' muttered his unsympathetic owner. He joggled the lead but it didn't come loose. Pearce was obliged to scramble over the ditch, up the low bank and, twigs and thorns catching at his clothing and hair, extricate Henry backwards. During this operation, Pearce put one foot down in the ditch which was full of cold muddy water and Henry, who objected to being hauled away from something interesting, had to be dragged, still backwards, down the bank leaving scored tracks where his paws had scrabbled for a hold.

'That's it,' said Pearce to dog. 'We're going home, right now.'

He set off uncomfortably for his house. At the gate of his house he unclipped the lead from Henry's collar to allow him to run ahead, and took off his wet shoe. He'd have to change both his shoes and his socks now before he went to work. Sodden shoe in hand, Pearce limped towards the back door. As he reached it, a shrill cry broke the air.

'Dave Pearce! What do you mean letting the dog run in with muddy paws? He's gone all over my clean kitchen floor!'

Pearce paused at the door and cast his eyes heavenward. 'Please,' he muttered. 'Please let something go right today.'

His plea had been heard. When he eventually got into work, fifteen minutes late, he was greeted by Ginny Holding.

'We've got a response,' she said. 'To that appeal we put out on the local news. A woman's rung in to say she saw Hester Millar the morning she was murdered.'

'Who? Where?' demanded Pearce eagerly, reaching for the sheet of paper Ginny was waving at him.

'In the village, Lower Stovey, at about twenty minutes to ten. The woman is a Mrs Linda Jones. She and her husband farm just by Stovey Woods at a place called Greenjack Farm. She's got a thirteen-year-old daughter she drives to school every morning and she was on her way back. She passed Hester walking along the main street.' Ginny rolled her eyes. 'She says she's only just remembered.'

Pearce's grip closed triumphantly on the sheet. 'I'll go out and talk to her right away.'

Greenjack Farm lay at the end of a track leading off the rough roadway which itself led from Lower Stovey to the edge of Stovey Woods. The farm buildings nestled in a dip, a collection of grey stone and wooden structures. The house itself was a low, unpretentious, rambling place. It formed three sides of a square with an open shed with a corrugated roof to the left and old stables to the right. There was no one in the yard.

Pearce got out of his car. Rooks wheeled overhead and he could hear a tractor in the distance as he made his way to the front door of the house. It stood ajar. He tapped on it and called through the gap, 'Hello? Anyone at home?'

The footsteps which approached in response were slow and cautious. The door creaked open and he found himself looking into the faded blue eyes of an elderly man wearing an ancient-looking brown suit over a green pullover and shirt. His hair was thin and white and his complexion pink.

'Who are you?' asked the man, not aggressively but with a childlike curiosity.

'Inspector Pearce.' Pearce held up his ID. The old man took no notice of it, only stared at Pearce as if something about his appearance amused him. 'I was hoping to speak to Mrs Linda Jones,' Pearce said more loudly. He didn't know if the old chap was deaf. He might be.

'Linda's my daughter-in-law.' The old man, having bestowed this information, seemed to think that was enough and Pearce wanted to know no more. 'Nice to see you, lad,' he said and made to shut the door.

Pearce stuck his foot in it. 'Can I see Mrs Jones?' Not deaf, just daft, if you asked him.

The old man looked down at Pearce's foot and frowned. 'You got your foot in my door.'

'I know, I want to speak to Mrs Jones!' Pearce said desperately.

'You didn't say that.'

'Yes, I did. I said – look, is she at home?'

194

Fortunately, at that moment, a woman's voice was heard asking, 'What are you up to there, Dad?' The door was pulled open and Pearce saw a weather-beaten woman in jeans, check shirt and a sleeveless jacket. Her fair hair, streaked with grey, was coiled on top of her head and pegged in place with a couple of large hairpins. Strands of hair had escaped and hung round her face which was devoid of make-up. She was, despite this, an attractive woman. Pearce thought she was probably in her early forties.

'Mrs Jones?' he asked hopefully. 'I'm Inspector Pearce. You rang us and said —'

She interrupted him. 'I didn't expect you'd come all the way out here.'

'I'm really keen to talk to you, Mrs Jones.'

She looked undecided. 'I don't know. I told the person who answered the phone all I know. I saw Hester Millar the morning she was killed. A dreadful business it is, too.'

'He wants to talk to you, Linda,' said the old man, catching up on the conversation a little late in the day.

'Yes, Dad. You go on back indoors and sit down. I'll make a cup of tea directly.'

The promise of tea seemed to do the trick. He turned and disappeared back inside the house.

'Come through to the kitchen,' Linda Jones said. 'Though there's nothing more I can tell you.'

A little later, settled at the kitchen table with a mug of strong tea and a slab of solid cake, Pearce was able to ask his hostess, 'Did you know Hester Millar well?'

She shook her head. 'No, not well. I knew her to talk to, just to exchange the time of day. She was always pleasant. I knew she lived with Ruth Aston and she and Ruth took care of the church between them. It's a crying shame the way we've got no vicar now. Ruth's father was the last vicar here. You know that?' She fixed Pearce with an interrogatory look.

'Yes, I knew – know. You sound as though you're a local woman, Mrs Jones.'

'That's right. I've spent my entire life in Lower Stovey.' Linda Jones paused and when she spoke again the bitterness which had touched her voice as she had spoken these words had been carefully eradicated. 'My parents farmed Church Farm, right next door to this one.'

'I see. So, on the morning of Miss Millar's death, you were doing what?'

'What I always do of a weekday, school holidays excepted. I drove my daughter into Bamford. She goes to the Community College. They stopped running the school bus. Not enough children living out this way. There's a regular schedule bus in the evening she can catch back again. I pick her up at the top of the lane then.'

'So,' persevered Pearce, picking his way through the superfluous information. 'So you were driving to Bamford and it would be before nine o'clock.'

'No, I was driving back from Bamford and it was about half past nine or a little after. After I dropped off our Becky, I called into the supermarket. Let's say, it was about twenty to ten by the time I got to the village. Yes, that would be it. When I got back indoors here it was not quite ten. I was in a bit of a flap because I was running a few minutes late and you know how it is, you never catch up if you start doing that at the beginning of the day. I saw Hester as I drove through the village. She was walking past the church. I sounded the horn and waved and she waved back. We didn't speak.'

Pearce leaned forward. 'She was walking past the church, not turning into it? Are you sure?'

She was sure.

Pearce asked, 'Which direction was she coming from?'

'From Church Lane where she lived, like you'd expect. I mean, one of them always opened up the church about that time in the summer months. I often saw one or the other, her or Ruth.'

'But she wasn't turning into the church to open it up as she or Mrs Aston normally did?'

'No, I didn't give it much thought, but you're right. She wasn't.'

Linda paused to scour her memory. 'No, definitely not. She was walking from Church Lane past the lych-gate. I remember now, it did strike me as odd and I wondered where she was going.' She took the lid off the teapot and stared into its belly. 'This'll take a drop of hot water. You want another cup?'

'I'm fine,' Pearce assured her hastily. 'How did Miss Millar look?'

'Look? Like she always did. Normal.'

'Not distressed or worried?'

Linda stared at him. 'No. Not that I'd have noticed. I didn't look that close. After I saw her, I forgot all about it. Then when they made that appeal on the local news, I suddenly remembered.'

'And you are absolutely sure it was that morning you saw her, the day she died? It wasn't another day? You did say, it wasn't unusual for you to see either her or Ruth.'

'Absolutely,' Linda Jones said firmly. 'Because it was the day there was a warning of extra traffic on the main road to Bamford because of some diversion or other and I tried to hurry Becky along a little earlier when we left. Only that was a waste of time. You can no more hurry Beck that you can my father-in-law.'

Pearce swallowed the last of his cake as he considered her information. 'Can you remember how she was dressed?' Witnesses often insisted they were right about the day and to be fair, Mrs Jones appeared reliable and the detail about the traffic congestion on the main road leant credibility to her tale. But it never did any harm to check.

'Dressed?' Linda's eyes popped at him in amazement. 'Why on earth should I notice that? This is Lower Stovey, not in town where people put on their best togs to go out. We all dress much the same here, day in and day out. She was wearing her grey cord trousers, I think. She wore them a lot. But there, I could be wrong about that. She'd some kind of pullover and was wearing her bag slung crosswise over her chest to leave her hands free —' Here Linda stopped abruptly.

Pearce felt a tingle between his shoulder blades. 'Free for what?' he prompted.

'She was carrying something,' Linda told him, frowning. 'But for the life of me I couldn't tell you what it was, something small.'

From the yard came a new sound, the roar of a motorcycle. Linda looked up. Her eyes brightened and she flushed. 'It'll be Gordon!' She caught Pearce's eye and explained, 'It'll be my son come visiting.'

Blast! thought Pearce. Just when she was starting to tell me something which might be interesting. Good job this son didn't turn up earlier or I wouldn't have got that far.

Linda had risen to her feet. The kitchen door was pushed open and a stocky young man came in. His ginger hair was clipped short and he had the reddish complexion which sometimes goes with that hair colour. He wasn't a handsome youth, with his snub nose and wide mouth, but there was a kind of healthy youthful attractiveness about his face. He wore a leather jacket and carried his motorcyclist's helmet. Seeing Pearce, he put the helmet down and nodded a greeting to the stranger before going to kiss his mother's cheek.

'Hello, Mum.'

She reached up and put a hand on his shoulder. 'Your dad's about the place somewhere.'

Pearce saw the cheerful expression on the youngster's face fade. 'Is he? I really came to see you. I wanted to tell you about next Tuesday. It's all fixed up, the disco and everything.'

'I don't know why you want such a noisy thing,' she said affectionately. Turning to Pearce, she went on, 'Gordon will be twenty-one next Tuesday and he's having a bit of a party in Bamford where he lives. I know they get the vote at eighteen now, but they still celebrate twenty-one, don't they?' She turned back to her son and flowed on effortlessly, 'I don't think I'll persuade your dad to come to a disco. But Becky and I will be there. Becky's looking forward to it.'

'So long as you're there,' Gordon Jones said. 'It doesn't matter about Dad.'

Pearce noticed the stricken look which crossed his mother's face as the boy spoke. So father and son didn't get along and the boy lived in Bamford. A big strong lad like that, they could do with him at the farm. Had that been what the quarrel had been about? The young man had refused to follow in the footsteps of father and grandfather. Gordon Jones was looking at Pearce, a question in his eyes.

'Inspector Pearce, Regional Serious Crimes Squad,' Pearce introduced himself.

'Oh, yes? You'll be investigating our local murder, will you? What are you doing here?' There was antagonism in the youngster's voice but Pearce was accustomed to that from young males.

Linda spoke before he could. 'I phoned the police, Gordon, to tell them I saw poor Miss Millar the day she died, early on. I was coming back from dropping off your sister. So Mr Pearce here wanted to talk to me but I couldn't tell him much.' To Pearce she said, 'Bit of a waste of time you coming all the way out here.'

'We always follow up information,' Pearce said. 'Especially in a matter like this.'

'Stuck, are you?' asked Gordon insolently.

'No,' returned Pearce evenly. 'Not yet. Not by a long chalk.' The young man looked disconcerted and taking advantage of it, Pearce made his farewell to Mrs Jones.

As he was opening the door of his car, a tractor came rattling and rumbling down the track and into the yard. The driver, a weather-beaten man with thinning hair and a face which looked as if it might be permanently creased into an expression of discontent, climbed down and greeted Pearce with, 'Who're you, then? A copper?'

'Yes. I look like one, then, do I?'

A snort greeted this. 'What do you want?'

'You're Mr Jones?' Pearce asked.

'Course I bloody am.' Jones stared past him and scowled again at the motorcycle. 'See you're not the only visitor. What's brought you?'

'Just to have a word with your wife regarding her information.'

Jones's jaw dropped. 'What information?'

Oh dear. She hadn't told him. This was, Pearce decided, by way of being a dysfunctional family. But if so, he didn't think it was Mrs Jones's fault. 'Just a sighting of the murdered woman, Miss Millar, on the day of her death. Your wife remembered seeing her in the village around half past nine or a few minutes afterwards.'

'And she phoned you about that?' Jones snorted again. 'Waste of bloody time.'

'On the contrary,' said Pearce. 'It's extremely valuable to know it. She's the only person so far who's come forward to say she saw the victim.'

Jones stared at him. 'You won't get him, though, will you? The bugger that killed that poor woman. You coppers never catch anyone – not unless it's a speeding motorist.' He walked away towards the kitchen door.

'Nice type!' muttered Pearce. He drove out of the yard, wondering what kind of family reunion was taking place in the kitchen behind him.

As he drove back through the village he was suprised to see a second motorcycle, propped up outside the church. The door was open. Pearce pulled up, got out and walked quietly under the lych-gate roof and up the flagged path to the old oaken door with its iron bands. He paused outside and listened. He could make out the murmur of voices within, a man and a woman. He pulled open the door, crossed the porch to the chicken wire door. The inner wooden door behind it had been hooked back and he could see through into the church. The man and woman were seated in a pew in earnest conversation. Pearce had made no noise but perhaps a draught of air had alerted the talkers. The man looked round and Pearce saw it was James Holland, the vicar of Bamford. The woman was Ruth Aston.

Pearce pushed open the wire door and from the top of the steps down into the church, called apologetically, 'Sorry, Reverend! I saw your bike outside but I didn't know it was yours, if you see what I mean. The church was open and I though I'd check it out.'

Father Holland got to his feet and came towards him. 'Inspector Pearce, isn't it? Thank you for taking the trouble. Mrs Aston and I are discussing what to do about the church.'

'Let you get on with it, then,' said Pearce. 'Good morning, Mrs Aston!' he added.

Ruth returned his greeting but didn't leave her place in the pew.

Pearce left them there and went back to his car. He had been a little surprised to see Ruth Aston sitting there so calmly in the church, a few inches only from where her friend had been murdered. But then, he thought, sooner or later she had to go back inside the place, if she was still a churchwarden.

Inside the church, James Holland had returned to his place beside Ruth. She said, 'I wonder why he came back.'

'The inspector? In pursuit of his enquiries, I imagine. You're still all right sitting here, Ruth? You wouldn't rather go elsewhere?'

She shook her head. 'No, I've known this church all my life and I can't let myself be kept from it now by what's happened. Besides,' she hesitated. 'I feel close to Hester, somehow, here.' She cast him a guilty look. 'I'm not a naturally religious woman, you know.'

Her companion raised his bushy eyebrows.

'I know,' she went on hastily, 'that people, village people, think I am. But despite being a vicar's daughter and a churchwarden and coming in to clean out the church and all the rest of it, I wouldn't class myself as religious. All those things I mentioned, they're part of a way of life. Some people take up flower-arranging and some take up the church. What would I do if I didn't look after St Barnabas? I lack what I suppose I'd call a spiritual quality.'

'Do you?' he asked gently. 'What is a spiritual quality?'

'Now you're going to be clever,' she reproached him, 'and tie me up in theological knots. I can't describe it. But I know some people have it and some, like me, don't.'

'We each bring our gifts to the altar,' he said. 'All are valid. Dusting and polishing too. Not everyone, thank goodness, has visions.'

She gave a little smile. 'I wouldn't like to have a vision. I wouldn't know what to do.'

'Like the Victorian child who was asked what he'd do if he opened the door and found Jesus on the step. "I'd ask him in," he replied. "Offer him a glass of sherry and send for the vicar".'

This time Ruth laughed.

He patted her arm. 'I'm pleased you feel you can carry on as churchwarden, Ruth, for the forseeable future, anyway.'

'Until I leave the village,' she reminded him. 'I told you, I mean to sell up.'

'Of course. I don't know what we'll do about the building then. Without you and Hester, I suspect it will have to be closed up all week. We may, in view of what's apparently been taking place in the tower, have to keep it closed anyway. I'm sorry I had to distress you with that information, Ruth.'

She made a gesture with her hand, waving away his apology. 'Hester and I weren't doing such a good job, after all, were we? Still, now it's been discovered, perhaps that's the end of it. Especially now the lock's been changed on the tower door.'

'Even if the church is kept locked, it will be opened of a Sunday when either I or someone else comes out to take a service. I don't mean to let the church fall into complete disuse,' he told her.

Ruth smiled at him. 'It's a long way for you to come for such a small congregation.'

He hunched his broad shoulders. 'No, no. I follow it up by going over to the Manor and taking a service there for the residents.'

At this mention of the Residential Home for the Elderly, which had formerly been Fitzroy Manor and her mother's childhood home, Ruth sighed.

'I haven't seen the old manor house in years. Even when I was a child, we seldom went there. My maternal grandparents were dead and the house closed up. It was on the market and waiting for a buyer. Occasionally my mother would put me in her little car and drive over there and open it up just to check on the place. It was an expedition which, frankly, I dreaded. The house was so dark and musty-smelling. Most of the furniture had been taken out. We had one or two pieces of it in the vicarage, dark Victorian stuff mostly, except for a nice little Regency card-table which I've still got. The best of the rest had gone to the saleroom and the only things left in the house were things the saleroom didn't want and my mother used to say the vicarage hadn't room for. That meant, she didn't want them, either. Her other excuse was that the estate agent wanted some furniture left in the house because it looked better that way than empty. I don't know why he thought that. The first thing you saw, as you walked into the big entrance hall, was a stuffed owl in a glass case! That and some stag's antlers on the wall. Grisly. Our footsteps echoed as we walked about inside and I clung to my mother like a limpet. I remember one occasion when she took me upstairs and showed me a room with bars at the window. She said it had been the nursery. I was horrified. It looked like a prison and I said so. She laughed and said, oh no, just a Victorian precaution to prevent the children tumbling out. I remember being so glad I never had to live there or sleep in that barred room!'

'Times change,' James Holland said with a smile. 'Children aren't barricaded away in a distant nursery now until they're old enough to behave in adult company!'

'My mother never spoke much about her childhood,' Ruth said. 'They kept horses in my grandfather's day. She mentioned a pony she'd had called Patch. Otherwise, I can't remember her telling me anything about those days.'

'Sometimes it's painful to talk about things you've lost,' the vicar said.

'Like talking about Hester? I don't find it painful to talk about her.' Ruth stared round the church at the various monuments. 'I've been thinking a lot, James, since Hester died.'

'I dare say you have.'

'Not just about her. About all sorts of things.' She glanced at him and gave a wry smile. 'My father brought me up to see the best in everyone and believe me, I tried! I was a teacher, too, and one always tries to find something positive about the most unpromising pupil. It's hard though, when you feel yourself wronged, to see the best in the other person. Or when you see a great crime committed to forgive or try to understand the person responsible.'

'Have you forgiven the father of your child for deserting you both?' he asked.

'In as much as I feel sorry for him now, rather than hate him. Simon wasn't a wicked person, only flawed. Did it surprise you when I told you all about that?'

'I'm seldom surprised.' It was his turn for a wry smile. 'And as you'd told Alan Markby and Meredith, I suppose you thought it prudent to tell me.'

'In case they mentioned it? They wouldn't. They're a very – very discreet couple, aren't they?'

James laughed. 'Alan is, certainly. I don't know that Meredith is always entirely discreet but she's prudent.'

'At the inquest,' Ruth said hesitantly, 'I did just for a moment wonder if, after Simon had spoken to me, he went off into the woods and did something silly in a fit of remorse.'

'Ah. Suicide.'

'But then I thought, don't be silly, Ruth. Of course he didn't. Someone would've found his body and anyway, I did know him well enough to know that wasn't his style. Besides, he was engaged to be married to someone else, so they said at the inquest. He'd found somebody he wanted to marry at last. I can't say that didn't hurt me when I heard it. But that was Simon's way. He shook off disagreeable experiences or unpleasant facts and went on his way rejoicing. I think,' said Ruth, 'the term "water off a duck's back" might have been coined for Simon Hastings.'

Father Holland nodded. 'Met people like that myself.'

She darted another glance at him. 'Don't ask me to forgive Hester's killer. I can't.'

'As an abstract concept, of course you can't. Give yourself time. When we know – well, when the police have finished their enquiries, hopefully with success, that's the time to start trying to come to terms with it, as you've come to terms with being deserted as a young girl.'

'Find the murderer, you mean. How can there be any kind of success,' Ruth asked, 'with Hester still dead?' She flushed. 'I ought to think of Hester at peace, didn't I? But I'm selfish enough to want Hester here with me. She didn't deserve what happened to her.'

'No,' he said. 'She didn't and perhaps Simon Hastings didn't derserve what happened to him, whatever it was. Life often seems full of injustices. We all find that hard to understand. Perhaps we even find it harder to understand nowadays when there's a notion about that the world is perfectible. We can tinker with society, we can discover medical treatments, we can put everything right, so it seems to us. In fact, we can't, and when we're brought up sharp against the fact, we resent it.'

'You think someone might have killed Simon,' Ruth replied. 'I wonder about that too. Do the police think it?'

'The police are bound by the ruling of the inquest. There was no evidence of any kind that Hastings met his death in an unnatural manner. Young, apparently fit, men do drop dead. Had the body been found at the time and a proper autopsy —' James broke off. 'Sorry,' he said again.

'That's down to me, too, isn't it?' was Ruth's direct reply. 'Because I didn't come forward and say I'd seen him, when he disappeared. It meant he wasn't found.'

'They still mightn't have found him, even if you'd spoken up. If, and it's a big if, but if he was murdered, the killer would certainly have concealed the body. That no one found even a handful of bones until recently does indicate it was hidden. But whether intentionally, that's another matter. He could have rolled under bushes as he fell dead. A storm such as we had the other night might have brought down branches and covered him. There are any number of explanations.'

Ruth considered this. 'Tell me, do you believe in evil?'

'Yes,' he said quietly. 'I do.'

'Do you believe there's a force of evil loose in Lower Stovey?'

'I don't know,' he said honestly. 'But there's a lot we don't know yet, Ruth. We have to wait. It's hard, but we have no option.'

'And it will show itself? Is that what you mean.'

Soberly he replied, 'If it does, when it does, we shall know what it is.'

Chapter Thirteen

That Markby had discovered the existence of Amyas Fitchett and with it, Ruth Aston's past history, rankled in Pearce's heart. This was the case in which he'd hoped to shine. So far he seemed to be trailing in the superintendent's wake. Determined to make it clear that he, too, was having a measure of success, he presented himself in Markby's office on his return from Greenjack Farm to announce that he'd found a witness to Hester Millar's movements on the morning of her death.

'She was walking straight past that church,' he told Markby. 'She ought to have been turning in to it, to open it up like she said she was going to.'

'And she did do,' said Markby aggravatingly, 'because she died inside it.'

'Ah,' pointed out Pearce triumphantly. 'But before she opened it up she went somewhere else and I mean to find out where. I mean, it's only a little village. There can't be many places. Someone,' said Pearce grimly, 'in that village is holding out on us. She visited someone early on Thursday before she went to open the church. Why hasn't that person come forward?'

'What are you intending to do about it?' Markby asked him.

'Knock on every ruddy door in that village. Of course,' he added hastily, 'we've already done that once, but we'll do it again, and go on doing it until someone tells the truth.' It made a fine, ringing sentence. Pearce was quite pleased with it.

Markby made no comment but he was thinking Pearce was being optimistic if he was hoping to prise information from the inhabitants of Lower Stovey. He'd had experience of asking questions in that benighted neck of the woods all those years ago and he didn't anticipate Dave having better luck now than he'd done then.

'By the way,' he said. 'James Holland tells me the Reverend Picton-Wilkes keeps his set of keys to St Barnabas locked in a drawer in his study. He is, apparently, mildly obsessive about security and hotly resented any suggestion his keys could have been borrowed for illicit purposes.

'I prefer to think whoever holds the mystery keys lives in the village. Someone who wouldn't be noticed as a stranger going into the church. Those missing keys bedevil this enquiry. There's always the possibility the killer let himself into the church, re-locked the door from the inside and was waiting for Hester. Against that, we've not discovered even the slightest motive that anyone might have to want to harm Miss Millar!' Markby snorted. 'I hate apparently motiveless crimes! She wasn't a villager as such, she was an incomer. Her dealings with the villagers were superficial. She lived quietly with Ruth Aston and Ruth Aston is held in high esteem in Lower Stovey. To harm Hester was to distress Ruth and leave her alone in the world. I'd have said that Hester Millar could've done just about anything and Lower Stovey would've tolerated it for Ruth's sake. But Hester didn't do anything, did she? Except toddle down to that church and open it up.'

'I told you,' said Pearce. 'They're a devious lot those villagers. I'll ask about the keys, too, even if no one will tell me.'

Markby muttered agreement. Inevitably, his mind turned to the personal aspect of events. The more he thought about it, the more he was obliged to admit Meredith had been perfectly right. There was absolutely no way they could live in that village, either in the former vicarage, which in his mind appeared more unsuitable with every passing minute, or anywhere else. He must have been mad to take her out there to view it.

On the other hand, if he hadn't, he wouldn't have seen the police car going up to the woods and very likely, information about the discovery of the bones might never have reached him. It'd have landed on someone else's desk and been consigned to oblivion. Ruth Aston's touching faith in police efficiency had been misplaced. Every police force in the country suffered from lack of manpower, time and resources. Once the bones had been established as having been lying in the woods for over twenty years, that there were no more of them than a grisly handful and above all, that there was no sign of deliberate violence on them, the chances that anyone would persevere in identifying them would have been slight. Only he, with his memory of Stovey Woods to spur him on, had insisted on tracking them down. Only the amazing good luck of finding distinctive dental work had made it possible. Even so, he suspected that somewhere, the question had probably been asked, was it worth it? Had he been justified in devoting so much of limited means to something which resulted in no more than a perfunctory inquest and foreseeable verdict? Mrs Hastings, the mystery of her son's disappearance at least partly solved, would say yes. Authority would probably say no.

Pearce had returned to his theory and Markby reluctantly abandoned his own thoughts to concentrate on what he was saying. He realised he'd missed some of Dave's assertions and came back at the moment the inspector was declaring, 'And there's another thing. Hester was carrying something, something small.' Pearce made a shape with his hands indicating some spherical object. 'Linda Jones doesn't remember what. Hester didn't have anything with her in that church except her handbag with the usual sort of contents. She didn't have anything that she'd have had to carry in her hand. So between Mrs Jones seeing her and Miss Mitchell finding her dead, that something disappeared.' Pearce scowled. 'Mrs Jones reckoned she couldn't remember what it was but I think, if that son of hers hadn't turned up prattling about some ruddy disco for his twenty-first, she might have come up with something.'

Markby, who'd been fiddling with a biro lying on his desk, looked up. 'What's that again?'

Pearce blinked. 'Which bit?'

'The son with the twenty-first birthday.'

Now why, thought Pearce, should the old man be interested in that bit of trivia? 'The lad's name is Gordon,' he said. 'Chippy yob with carrotty hair and a motorbike. The message I got was that he doesn't get on with his dad. He doesn't live at the farm. He's twenty-one next Tuesday and he wanted his mum and sister to go to a party he's got fixed up here in Bamford. That's the disco and what do you bet, the kids will be popping pills, high as kites, and underage drinking will be the norm?'

'If his friends are his age, they won't be underage drinkers. As for the drugs, if adult members of the family are there —'

Pearce was having none of it. 'Mrs Jones reckoned Mr Jones wouldn't be up for a disco. The lad seemed not to care that his father might not go. Rather hoped he wouldn't, I suspect. I tell you, sir, that is one seriously odd family. There's an old man who's potty and —' Pearce broke off to squint curiously at the superintendent's desk.

Markby had picked up the biro as Pearce spoke and appeared to be doing sums on a notepad. 'Twenty-one next Tuesday, is he? We've reached the Millennium, 2000. (Or not, if you want to be purist about it!) At any rate, this young chap, Gordon, was born late in April 1979. Which makes him conceived in the earlier part of August 1978. I'm assuming Mrs Jones had a normal forty-week pregnancy.'

Pearce, startled at this unexpected foray into gynaecology, asked, 'So what?'

'So, could be significant,' was the aggravating reply.

Annoyed, Pearce growled, 'He's got no connection with Hester Millar that I've come across. The bloke doesn't even live in Lower Stovey. I suppose we can track him down and ask him for his movements, if you think we should. I wouldn't expect to learn anything from him.'

'I'm not interested in talking to Gordon,' said Markby. 'I'm interested in his mother. Sorry to confuse you, Dave. You're quite rightly thinking about Hester. I'm thinking about a twenty-two-year-old rape case. When I went out to Greenjack Farm in 1978 in the course of our hunt for the Potato Man, I met young Kevin, as he was. He wasn't married then.'

'He was probably courting,' said Pearce wisely. 'Linda's parents farmed Church Farm next door. They mightn't have been married at the time but they were probably having fun in the hayloft.'

'Indeed they might. Has Mrs Jones got red hair?'

'What?' Pearce blinked again and then looked wary. 'No, she's fairish. The sort of blonde who goes grey and you hardly notice it.'

'Nor does Kevin have red hair and I don't recall Martin Jones having red hair, either.'

Pearce absently touched his jaw where the tooth had given a malicious twinge. 'There's another kid, Becky, goes to Bamford Community College.'

'It'd be interesting to know if she's got red or ginger hair,' Markby said.

There was a silence. 'Now, let me get this straight,' Pearce began cautiously. 'You think young Gordon might be a cuckoo in the nest?'

'It would explain a certain coolness between him and his supposed father.'

'Does it matter to us?' Pearce asked, puzzled.

'Any child born after an encounter in Lower Stovey in late summer of 1978 about whose parentage there's any doubt, is of interest to me.' Markby retorted. 'Do you know anyone who's a pupil at that school?'

'Tessa's kid sister,' said Pearce.

'Do you think you could find out from her without rousing suspicion what colour hair Becky Jones has?'

'Better if Tessa asks,' said Pearce immediately. 'It's going to look weird, not to say dodgy, if I start asking about red-haired schoolgirls.'

'Point taken. Would Tessa oblige?'

Tessa, of late, had been anything but obliging. But she'd be intrigued. 'I should think so,' Pearce said. He hesitated. 'Do we need to know who Gordon's real father might be, always supposing he isn't Kevin's son?'

'Think, Dave!' Markby said irritably. 'August 1978! What happened then?'

'Both Simon Hastings and the Potato Man disappeared,' said Pearce. 'Crikey, you don't think —'

'I'll tell you what I think,' said Markby. 'I think there were more attacks than ever were reported. We don't even know that Mavis Cotter was the first, only that she was the first we heard about. Let's suppose, just as a theory, that Linda, then a young girl, was one of his victims but never came forward. If that were so, she becomes a very important witness indeed. Don't forget, I believe and have always done that the Stovey Woods rapist was a local man.'

'Look, sir,' Pearce began cautiously. 'I know you'd like to have solved that case. But twenty-two years on —'

'What's twenty-two years in a community like Lower Stovey? Oh, there have been incomers over the years, I grant you. New houses where the old school stood. Cottages sold to second-homers. But the core of the village, the old families, they'll still be there. One or two members might have moved out, as Gordon Jones has moved out. But the families, Dave, they're still there and village families are mighty close and clannish, as you've already found out.'

'You're not thinking the rapist might still be living there?' Pearce sounded even more dubious. 'Oh, come on, sir. It's a bit far-fetched. Even if it's true, we can hardly ask Linda Jones about it. If she kept quiet then, she's not going to speak up now, is she? Not with the boy just about to celebrate his twenty-first birthday! Wouldn't be much of a present for him, would it?' He met Markby's eye and added hastily, 'I'll get Tessa on to asking round about Becky Jones.'

Pearce set off back to his office. Before he reached it, he was waylaid. Ginny Holding appeared before him, flushed in the face and apparently unable to decide whether to look grimly professional or just burst out laughing.

'You'd better come, sir, if you've got a minute.'

'I haven't got a minute,' said Pearce despondently. 'I never have a minute. If ever I do, he —' His gaze drifted towards Markby's office. 'He finds something to fill it with. What is it? Can't you deal with it?'

'It's about the things you found in the tower at that church. You know, the sleeping bag and —'

Pearce snapped to attention. 'Yes, I know what we found.'

'A Mrs Spencer is here. She's come in with her daughter, Cheryl. They're down in the interview room. I asked them to wait. They've made a statement. Well, the girl has. But I thought you'd like to hear it yourself.'

Mrs Spencer was short, square, red-faced and belligerent. Cheryl was pale and spotty but not unattractive. Her pale blue, slightly protruding, eyes glanced over Pearce dismissively as he came in. Her jaws continued to move rhythmically.

'I already told this officer!' declared Mrs Spencer. 'And Cheryl, she signed a statement.'

'So I understand. I appreciate your waiting. My name is Inspector Pearce.' Pearce had not missed the dismissive look and it rankled. 'I'm investigating the events in St Barnabas Church, Lower Stovey.'

Cheryl didn't exactly sneer but she remained unimpressed. Her mother, however, leapt to her daughter's defence.

'Cheryl didn't have anything to do with any murder!'

Ginny moved in on the conversation, addressing the gum-chewing Cheryl. 'No one's saying she did. But the inspector needs to know everything that's happened in that church recently. Just tell the inspector what you told me, Cheryl.'

'I'm not under-age,' said Cheryl. 'I know what I'm doing. It's my business and no one else's, right? Mine and Norman's. You can't touch us.'

'I can!' snarled her mother. 'When I've finished with Norman, he'll wish he'd never been born!'

'Who's Norman?' asked Pearce.

'Norman Stubbings. He runs the pub, the Fitzroy Arms.' Cheryl paused to remove a putty-coloured wad from her mouth, survey it frowning and look round for somewhere to put it. Holding indicated the ashtray on the table. Cheryl dropped her gum into it. 'He's my boyfriend.'

'No, he isn't,' argued her mother. 'He's a married man and you ought to know better.'

Cheryl ignored this. 'I used to work there evenings, washing up glasses. I live in Lower Stovey. It isn't half a dump,' she added in parenthesis. Pearce wondered whether there was anything and anyone other than the absent Norman that Cheryl didn't despise.

'Evie, that's Norman's old woman, she doesn't like me. She was always picking on me. She kept snooping round trying to catch me with Norman. Norman didn't want her making trouble with the brewery. So I started working up at the Drovers' Rest, on the old way, instead. It's nice up there. You get interesting people, cyclists, walkers and that and they've got a dishwasher. I was sorry not to see so much of Norman, of course.'

'Wouldn't you think,' demanded Mrs Spencer, 'that a girl her age – she's only just turned nineteen – would find a young man and not go wasting her time with someone old enough to be her father and married, at that? You silly slut!' she admonished her daughter.

'Oh, give over, Mum. You don't know Norman.'

'Don't I? Then that's just where you're wrong, my girl! Norman Stubbings was in the primary class when I was in the top class at the old school. Nasty, sneaky little kid with a runny nose, always standing by himself in the corner of the yard because no one would play with him. I remember his mother, a real old besom. Hardly ever sober. She used to stand outside the school and shout at the teachers. We always reckoned she was barmy.'

Holding cleared her throat as a hint. Cheryl obligingly took up her tale. 'Not working at the Fitzroy Arms any more, it was difficult for me to see Norman, like I said. Then he had this really good idea. See, the pub's opposite the church. The church is open most of the day but no one goes in it much. Norman, he'd got the keys. He could go in there any time.'

'Where did he get the keys?' Pearce asked startled.

'He'd always had them. Well, they were his dad's. Ages ago when it was a proper church and had a vicar, it had a bell-ringing team and Norman's dad was the captain. He had the keys so that they could all get in there and practise. When it stopped being a proper church, there was no more bell-ringing, but no one asked Norman's dad for the keys, so he kept them. When he died they were among his stuff and they'd been lying round in a drawer at the pub for years. One of the keys lets you into the tower. There's a little room at the top. So when I wasn't working at the Drovers', he'd give me a call on my mobile, and I'd slip over to the church and wait for him there. As soon as he could get away from Evie, he'd come over and open up the tower and we'd go up there. At first it was really cool.'

'It was downright disgusting!' said Mrs Spencer.

'When?' asked Pearce. 'When was the last time you and Stubbings rendezvoused in the tower?'

Cheryl was nonplussed by the term 'rendezvous' and enquired if that meant having if off?

'In your case,' said Pearce, 'it probably does.'

'Ooh, sarky!' retorted Cheryl. 'Is that why they made you inspector? Because you knew some long words?'

'Stick to the point, Cheryl,' advised Holding hastily.

'The last time I met Norman in the church – *rendezvoused* – was before that old woman got stabbed. At least two weeks before that. We'd stopped using the tower. Evie had got so suspicious, he found it harder and harder to get away. He said we should vary our routine, that's what people should do if they're being watched, and he said we shouldn't go there again. I didn't mind because by then I'd gone off being in the tower. It was fun at first, you know, exciting. But after a bit I got fed up with hanging around in the churchyard with all those graves, and when I could get inside, it was worse. It's not much fun being on your own in an empty church with all those stone carvings looking at you. I didn't mind it when Norman was there with me. But on my own, it gave me the creeps. Norman said not to worry, he'd think of somewhere else.'

'And did he?'

'Yeah, Norman's clever, he thought of the old shed at the back of the car park.'

'Which,' said Mrs Spencer, 'was where I found them last night. I knew that girl was up to something. I heard her muttering on that mobile phone of hers. She's always got it glued to her ear. I knew she was up to no good from the sound of her voice, whispering all excited. I followed her and I caught 'em at it. Norman, the little toad, he ran off. I made our Cheryl tell me everything. In the church, I ask you. Then I reckoned we ought to come and tell you, because you've been investigating in that church. Evie, she's a spiteful cow, not but what she's got good reason for it. But she might go telling you she'd seen Cheryl going in there. Just to get her own back, see?'

'You did quite right, Mrs Spencer and you, Cheryl.'

Cheryl took a fresh stick of gum from her pocket and unwrapped it. Popping it in her mouth, she observed, 'Norman's not going to like this.'

Mrs Spencer assured them in bloodthirsty tones that you bet Norman Stubbings wasn't going to like it, not one bit.

Pearce went back to Markby and gave him the news that the mystery of the tower's visitors had been solved and it didn't appear to have anything to do with Hester's death.

'By the time Hester was killed, Stubbings and the girl had given up meeting in the tower. They were using some old shed. That Mrs Spencer's a real old battleaxe. If we find Norman Stubbings with a knife sticking out of his back, we'll know who did it!' Dave concluded.

He then drove out to Lower Stovey and proceeded to give the landlord a wretched half-hour.

It was always nice when one could tie up loose ends and Pearce went home happy. Tessa, also in a good mood, proved surprisingly obliging when asked if she'd like to make a few discreet enquiries of her sister regarding Becky Jones. In fact, she was alarmingly keen to do a bit of detective work, as she put it. Pearce was afraid she might get carried away and watched her depart for a visit to her family with some trepidation. He wished the superintendent appeared more interested in who had murdered Hester Millar and less in catching the rapist after twenty-two years. Pearce still doubted the offender had remained in

Lower Stovey, if he'd ever lived there. He certainly didn't believe the Potato Man had come out of retirement after so long simply to stab Hester Millar.

Tessa, while her husband was meditating on these things, was sitting in her sister's bedroom. She had listened patiently to a long tale of Jasmine's dramatic break-up with her latest boyfriend, and now that Jaz had got that off her chest, Tessa made her move.

Staring in the dressing-table mirror, she tugged at a strand of her long, pale yellow hair and announced, 'I'm thinking of dyeing it red.'

'What, your hair?' asked Jaz, momentarily distracted from her broken heart. 'What for?'

'For a change. Why not? It might suit me.'

'Dave wouldn't like it,' said Jaz sapiently.

'Don't see why he shouldn't.' Tessa clutched her hair and piled it on top of her head. 'I want a new look.'

'Most people want to be blonde,' said Jaz enviously, studying her own mousy locks, reflected over her older sister's shoulder.

'But there are fewer red-heads,' argued Tessa. 'How many girls at your school have really red hair or ginger hair? I bet, not many.'

Jaz considered this and said, 'Michele King has and she hates it. She's got the freckles that go with it and she can't sunbathe or anything. She goes bright red. When her family goes on holiday to Spain, she has to cover right up, long sleeves and everything. She wore a bikini one year and she said she ended up looking like a lobster.'

'But I haven't got that sort of skin, have I? Anyway,' said Tessa, 'not all red-heads have that problem. Isn't there another kid in your class, Becky something or other, with reddish hair?'

Jaz frowned. 'The only Becky is Becky Jones and she hasn't got red hair. It's light brownish, sort of a bit like mine.'

'Oh, right, I'm thinking of someone else, then. Anyway, I think I'll have my hair cut really short.'

'You're barmy,' said Jaz.

Markby was on a trail of his own. Among the photographs on Old Billy

Twelvetrees' mantelshelf stood one of the late Mrs Twelvetrees and three children. He'd seen Dilys. Sandra he'd no idea where to find and wasn't much bothered. He was interested to find, if possible, young Billy Twelvetrees, the eldest of the trio of glum infants in the picture. Dilys was of an age with Ruth, who was, he knew, fifty-seven. Young Billy must now be in his early sixties. Which meant that twenty-two years ago, he'd have been just on forty. But there was no record of an interview with him in the file on the Potato Man. Since every other man in the village had been quizzed, how had they missed Young Billy? If he hadn't been in the village, where had he been?

Tracking down Young Billy wasn't difficult, as things turned out. The surname was unusual and its owner hadn't moved far. He lived in Bamford. The house was a narrow terraced one with a pocket-sized front garden which was obsessively neat. Everything in it was to scale, that is to say, small. The principle, Markby supposed, was that you thus could get in everything a bigger garden might have. Bonsai-sized shrubs surrounded a tiny square of grass in the middle of which was a stone basin not bigger than a large dinner plate, filled with pebbles over which dribbled an amount of water you'd be pleased to clean your teeth with. A row of miniature red tulips stood like toy guardsmen in a strip of earth which could hardly be called a bed. It looked more like a tyre-track. On one side of the front door was a Grecian pot the size of a milk saucepan in which was planted a miniature rose. On the other side of the front door crouched a small stone frog, painted green. Markby felt like Gulliver among the Lilliputians.

The door was opened, unsurprisingly, by a small neat woman without a hair out of place. William, she told him, was in the back garden. Markby was invited to just walk through.

By now as curious to see the garden and the gardener, Markby walked down the narrow hall, through the pint-sized but amazingly tidy kitchen and out on to a patio. At least, he supposed that was what it was meant to be. The back garden wasn't much bigger than the front one but obviously designed by the same hand. Thus the patio was four

small paving stones long and three wide. On it stood two tiny uncom-
fortable-looking white plastic garden chairs. The rest of the back garden
was laid out in immaculately-hoed square plots, each handkerchief-
sized. In each a label announced what kind of vegetable would shortly
be poking its head above ground, except for one which was laid out
mathematically with onion sets. At the furthest point from the house,
reached by Markby in half a dozen strides, a man was carefully
arranging six bamboo canes in a wigwam shape.

'For my beans,' he informed Markby as the visitor came up. 'When
I get 'em planted. I got 'em under glass at the moment, waiting for
'em to shoot.'

Markby supposed 'under glass' referred to a shoebox-sized cold
frame. Even the enterprising Young Billy – or William, as his wife
preferred – hadn't yet found a way to squeeze a greenhouse in this
garden. Give him time and he probably would. It was odd to be
thinking of a man of sixty-one or two as 'young' but Markby could
see why people found it necessary. Young Billy bore a remarkable
resemblance to Old Billy, being short and square. He was still
muscular whereas his father's muscle mass had atrophied, and still
had a countryman's weather-beaten skin. It looked as though whatever
jobs he'd held in life, they'd all been out of doors. A battered flat cap
was wedged on his head, a fringe of white hair showing round it. He
wore an aged but clean showerproof bomber jacket over a hand-
knitted pullover. His hands, deftly securing the canes, were large and
knotted.

'Good idea,' said Markby of the bean seedlings. He held up his ID.
'Mind if we have a chat?'

Young Billy squinted at the ID and said, 'I ain't got my glasses.
You'll have to tell me what it says.'

'It says I'm Superintendent Markby. I'm from the Regional Serious
Crimes squad.'

'Oh, ah?' Young Billy was engrossed in winding string round the
bamboo canes.

'You come from Lower Stovey, I understand, Mr Twelvetrees.'

'Oh, ah. When I was a boy. I ain't lived there for more than forty years.'

'We're investigating certain matters in Lower Stovey.'

'Woman got stabbed, I heard.'

'Yes. Do you visit your family there?'

'No. Never got no cause to.' Young Billy shook his head.

'You don't visit your father and sister?' Markby asked.

'Them?' Young Billy finished tying up the bamboo canes to his satisfaction and turned his attention fully to his visitor. 'Last time I saw the old boy was Christmas. I don't have no car, no more does he. But my neighbour was going out that way and give me a lift. Our dad hadn't changed. He's the same miserable old devil he always was. Don't know how our Dilys sticks it. She pops round to see us sometimes when she's shopping in Bamford. That woman she cleans for, Mrs Aston, she gives her a lift in. She don't change, Dilys, either,' reflected Billy. 'She was always a great lump. Good worker, mind.' This last was added in case Markby should think he sounded disloyal.

Markby didn't think Young Billy was disloyal. He was realistic. You can choose your friends but not your relatives, as the saying went. But poor Dilys did seem singularly unappreciated by her family.

'I was in Lower Stovey years ago,' he said in a conversational way. 'We were investigating some attacks on women in and around the woods.'

Young Billy squinted up at the sky and then at Markby. 'That'll be the old Potato feller.'

'Yes, you remember, I see.'

'My wife wrote me about it. It was in the papers, she said. Made Lower Stovey famous, that did!' Young Billy chuckled hoarsely.

'Wrote to you? Where were you living then?'

'I were on the high seas.'

'What?' Markby was surprised into exclaiming.

'I were working on the cargo boats at that time. I liked that, you know. I like being at sea. Lizzie wrote me all about it and I got the letter when we reached the Windward Islands. Bananas, we took on board there. Thousands of 'em.'

Young Billy paused and ruminated on that lost period of his life. 'I liked it, but not my Lizzie. She didn't like me being away so much. When I left Lower Stovey I took a room as lodger in Lizzie's parents' house. That's how I met her. We got married at eighteen, just as my dad and mum had done. But we turned out happier than they did, thank goodness. We've had our Ruby Wedding. Not bad, is it?'

Markby agreed, wondering whether he and Meredith would ever celebrate any anniversary.

'Anyhow,' said William Twelvetrees, 'because she didn't like it, I gave it up and came ashore. I got a job down the quarry. I still got a job down there, watchman, though I don't work full time now. But I don't mind that. It gives me time for this.'

During his time afloat Young Billy had probably learned to stow things neatly in small spaces and it might explain his ingenious use of his garden. It also deleted him from the Potato Man enquiry.

'Right,' said Markby heavily. 'Thank you. I'll leave you to your gardening.'

Two steps forward, one step back. But somewhere he was on the right lines, he was sure of it. He just couldn't see where. It would be difficult, but he had to speak to Linda Jones.

The train rocked slowly out of London. Meredith found herself trapped, cramped in a corner seat, next to a sweaty young man reading a paperback novel. The jacket illustration depicted people living in some mythical past when clothing consisted either of rags or elaborate armour and no one had invented anything in the line of smart casual. As the young man read he chewed gum and breathed through his mouth at the same time, no mean achievement. Meredith had tried to ignore him and concentrate on the *Evening Standard* crossword but that had been difficult because she couldn't move her arms. Nor could she move her feet which were imprisoned against the side of the train by the formidable boots worn by a long-legged tough-looking girl sitting opposite. The girl was reading too, *Captain Corelli's Mandolin*. The fourth occupant of their quartet of seats was a middle-aged man in a business suit who'd fallen asleep the moment the train started.

Well, at least it was Friday once again. The weekend had come around almost before the previous one had gone out of mind. At least it meant two train-journeyless days. What, she wondered idly, did these people do at the weekend? What about the Amazon with the romantic heart? And what about Chewing-Gum-Man here? He wore a wedding ring so it was a fair guess part of his weekend would be taken up with the family weekly shop. As for the business type over there, his head now lolling in a familiar way on the oblivious shoulder of the tough girl, no prizes for guessing he planned a round of golf. And me? she thought. Do any of them wonder about me and what I'll be getting up to during these precious two days of freedom? Some freedom. I shall spend it viewing undesirable properties with Alan, both of us getting tetchier by the minute. She sighed. That was when her mobile phone began a frenzied rendition of the opening notes of *Eine Kleine Nachtmusik*.

Meredith scrabbled in her briefcase and retrieved it. Mobile phones had been going off all over the carriage since they'd started but hers caused a minor stir among her immediate companions. The tough girl became aware of the businessman's shoulder and pushed his head away. He woke up, harrumphed, and stood up to take down his coat from the overhead rack. The gum-chewer put away his paperback and made similar moves indicating he was getting off at the next stop.

'Hello?' Meredith asked the mobile.

The caller was Ruth Aston, which surprised her mildly, before she remembered she'd given Ruth the number of her mobile at the close of the visit she and Alan had paid to The Old Forge. 'Give me a call if you want to chat,' she'd invited and Ruth had taken her up on it.

'I was wondering, Meredith. I dare say you and Alan have plans for the weekend, but if you had time, would you like to come to tea tomorrow? The thing is, Hester made a lot of cakes which are sitting in the freezer. I can't eat them alone. I can't throw them out. I've given a couple away but it made feel guilty. So, I thought, if you and Alan have a hour to spare around half-past three or four, say?'

Ruth's voice tailed away on a hopeful note. It couldn't hide the underlying despair. She's been crying to herself over Hester, guessed Meredith. She wants the company.

'Of course, we'll come,' she said. 'Or I will, anyway. I'll have to check with Alan.'

Ruth was embarrassingly grateful.

'I couldn't refuse. I did tell her to ring me,' Meredith said, twisting her head in the crook of his arm to look up at him. His head was propped on the sofa back and his eyes closed.

'It's all right,' he mumbled. 'I've got to go out to Lower Stovey sometime, anyway. I want to check on something at Greenjack Farm. Why don't I drop you at Ruth's at three-thirty? I'll go on down to the farm and come back to Ruth's when I've finished there. I shouldn't be long.'

Meredith said hesitantly, 'Ruth may expect you to report some progress. How's Dave Pearce getting on?'

Alan opened his eyes at that. 'Slowly. But James Holland at least will be a happy man.'

'You've found the missing tower key?' Hastily she added, 'Am I not supposed to know about it? James told me.'

'I didn't tell him not to. Quite the opposite, I asked him to check everywhere he could to find the key. Half Bamford must know about it. In the end, we turned up a complete set of keys about which the church authorities had known nothing.'

'Who had them?'

'Would you believe it? Norman Stubbings, landlord of the Fitzroy Arms. Seems he's the local Don Juan and was in the habit of taking his latest conquest to the tower to have his wicked way.'

'The thought,' Meredith said, 'makes my skin creep. Not the tower so much as Norman Stubbings's amorous embrace. Well, Norman and the tower together. Just imagine, Norman creeping about the belfry like Quasimodo. I always thought that man seriously weird. You don't think he might have had something to do with Hester's death?'

'He has no motive and I can't put him in the church at the time.' Alan chuckled. 'He got a scare when Dave turned up, demanded the keys and threatened to charge him with withholding evidence. He handed them over as meek as a lamb. His wife, little fat woman —'

'Evie,' Meredith informed him.

'Evie, then. Evie was hopping about in the background insisting Norman couldn't have been in the church the morning Hester died because he'd been on the phone to the brewery on and off for the best part of an hour from nine onwards. Dave checked that out and it's true. After that, apparently, Stubbings had to fix one of the pumps and didn't leave the bar.'

'He said something about that to me, not on the day of the murder, on the Saturday when I called by his pub after I'd seen Ruth. Just before he threw me out.' Meredith was loath to support Norman's story but was impelled by a sense of fair play.

'He has a witness for the day itself. A friend of Evie's popped in for a chat and saw him at work. It seems he was quite abusive towards the visitor who described him to Pearce as "a miserable old git." Norman doesn't have many friends but he does have an alibi. I'm glad we can rule the keys out of our enquiry but I was never convinced it was a lead. The footprints in the tower were old and dusty and it's so easy to hare off on a false trail, getting too excited about things like that. Investigation into big crimes has a way of turning up a host of small sins.'

'Pity you can't arrest him for something,' she said wistfully.

He chuckled. 'Not worth the time or trouble, even if we managed to find a charge. It's like I said. You trawl a net hoping it'll snare a big fish. If you pull out a minnow like Norman Stubbings you just have toss him back in the river.'

'He broke into the church tower!' she pointed out.

'Not technically. He had a key.'

'He was trespassing.'

'Not of itself a crime.' Markby shook his head. 'He misbehaved up there but he didn't do any damage to the place nor did he steal anything.

If the bishop wants to proceed with a civil action for trespass, that's up to him. I'm after a killer.'

'So you're back at square one?'

'Did we ever leave it?' he asked wryly. 'However, Dave's a tenacious sort of copper. He's found a witness who saw Hester in the street outside the church.' He frowned. 'His witness says, Hester was carrying something. Ruth had the same impression and it might be worth asking her if she's managed to remember what it was.'

On this low-key note they arranged their return to Lower Stovey.

Chapter Fourteen

Markby pulled up outside St Barnabas church, Lower Stovey in mid-afternoon, the following day, Saturday. 'Wind's getting up again,' he observed.

Meredith peered through the windscreen. The tips of the trees surrounding the churchyard bent and swayed. The inn sign of the Fitzroy Arms rocked agitatedly on unoiled hinges. It carried a faded heraldic representation, the most distinguishing feature of which was a small animal of vague species, apparently a rodent. It seemed particularly apt. Norman the landlord had been standing in his doorway, alone and palely loitering, but identifying Markby's car, he scurried back indoors.

Meredith said, 'Doesn't he look like something you find when you turn over a stone?'

Markby grinned. 'Between the police and one of the village women, the mother of his latest dalliance, Norman's got good reason to keep his head down. I'll drop you here and go on to the farm. Tell Ruth I shouldn't be long.' He glanced past her towards the church. 'Why do you want to go in there before you see Ruth?'

'It's just something I feel I have to do. I have to go in there and see it's all right now, just an empty building with no dead bodies except in stone effigy. If I don't, the last image I'll have of the interior of the place will include Hester slumped in the pew. I don't want it to be that.'

She paused. 'Ruth told me the church was built as an act of atonement for a murder so it's as if history has come round to repeat itself. You can't help, somehow, getting an odd feeling when you're walking round it, outside and inside. Inside you're under the eye of all those Fitzroys and outside you're under the eye of the Green Man, up there on the wall. What do you think the medieval masons thought was over there in those woods?'

'I don't know what they believed,' he said a little sourly. 'But as far as I'm concerned, whatever's been there or is there, is human.'

But even I, he thought, have had moments of doubt, if I'm to be honest. Superstition has deep roots. We all pretend we're not affected by it. We're all just that little bit afraid of what we don't know.

Meredith had pushed open the door and swung her legs to the ground. As he drove away towards Stovey Woods, he could see her in the windscreen mirror, standing by the lych-gate, watching his car.

A little before the road ran out at the edge of the woods, he came upon a wooden board with the name Greenjack Farm burned on it in pokerwork, at the entry to a turning on the right-hand side. Several cattle in a field beyond the sign were lying down. Folk wisdom believed that meant rain. He glanced at the sky appraisingly as he jolted the short distance down the track to the farm gate.

Twenty-two years. Could it really be so long? What had happened in the meantime? He'd married and divorced. He climbed to the rank of superintendent. He'd never become a father but he was the uncle of four, thanks to the efforts of his sister and her husband. He had met Meredith, something which still filled him with wonder as a man who had unexpectedly, and undeservedly, been offered a second chance. So why, when life so manifestly went on, opening new horizons, couldn't he let go of this old puzzle?

'Because,' he said softly to himself, 'I believe that in some way I can't yet fathom, it has to do with the death of Hester Millar. Because I feel I'm on the edge of knowing. That I do, in the back of my mind, already know.'

And that other death? That of Simon Hastings? To say nothing of the sense of failure which had dogged him for all those years. Would the former ever be explained or the latter exorcised?

He got out of the car, pushed open the gate and went through, taking care to close it behind him. A black and white border collie dog ran towards him barking but not aggressively.

Markby said, 'Hello, old fellow!' and the dog wagged its tail and accompanied him, making figure-of-eight movements around the visitor's feet as he continued on his way.

There was someone in a former stable building on the right. The doors of the end loosebox had been removed and part of the stone wall knocked out to make a wider opening. It was from in there that he could hear intermittent rattling and a voice uttering sounds indicating physical effort. Curiously, he poked his head through the gap.

Inside it was dark and it took a moment to accustom his eyes to the gloom. Ancient straw was piled in the corners, a hayrack was used as a receptacle for junk, strings of cobwebs dangled from the roof. Pride of place belonged to a Victorian pony-trap, its shafts resting on the ground. It'd once been painted blue and red and although the paintwork was damaged now and dull the trap was still clean. Someone was engaged in buffing it up still more. He was an elderly man, working slowly but doggedly, a cloth gripped awkwardly in a hand with knuckles distorted by arthritis. He looked up as Markby's shadow filled the opening into the yard and straightened with an effort and another mumbled exclamation. Markby, realising that with the yard light behind him the old man could see nothing but a sinister dark outline, was obliged to step inside and make himself properly visible.

'Good afternoon,' he said.

The old man stood, rag in hand, and contemplated him.

'I seen you before,' he returned at last. He chuckled and shook the rag at Markby. 'Yes, I know you. I've seen you before.'

'Yes, Mr Jones, you have, but it was a long time ago. I didn't think you'd remember me.'

Martin Jones came towards him, head tilted to one side, faded eyes scrutinizing the newcomer's face. 'I disremember your name, though. You'll have to tell me.'

Markby told him and added, 'It was twenty-two years ago I came here asking about the Potato Man.'

A long sigh escaped old Martin. 'You still looking for him, then?'

'Yes, and for the murderer of Miss Millar.'

Puzzlement crinkled the old man's features. 'I don't know her.'

'She lived in Lower Stovey with Mrs Aston. Mrs Aston used to be Miss Pattinson, the vicar's daughter.'

'I remember little Miss Pattinson. She was a pretty little thing. But she doesn't live in Lower Stovey no more.'

'Yes, she does, Mr Jones. Only she's called Mrs Aston now. Miss Millar was her friend and she died, she was killed, in the church here.'

He wasn't sure he was right in talking to Martin about the death. It was possible his son had decided not to worry the old man with the grim news. But the idea of death was less worrying to Martin than the location in which it had occurred.

'It don't seem right,' Martin waved the cleaning rag back and forth as if wiping away a stain. 'Not killing that woman in the church.' He began to look distressed.

Markby decided on distraction and moved nearer to the pony-trap. 'Going to take it out for a spin?'

At this Martin perked up again, the death in the church immediately wiped from his mind. 'No. Only pony on the farm now belongs to young Becky and that's a riding animal. Put him between the shafts and he'd likely bolt away. But it's a good conveyance. I'm minded to sell it. You never know, someone might want it.' He gave the nearest wheel another rub with his rag. Then turning his head so that he could see Markby, he added, 'Becky's my granddaughter.'

'You've got a grandson, too, I believe, Gordon?'

Martin frowned. 'I haven't seen him in a while.'

'He didn't come the other day to see his mother? On his motorbike?'

'He may have done. The days all seem one to me now.' He squinted at Markby. 'I remember you, see. You look much the same, you do.

Some folks change. I remember the Potato Man and all kinds of things that happened back then. But I can't seem to keep in my head things that happen nowadays.' He frowned and as if there was a necessary time delay between absorbing a question and focusing on it, went on, 'That's a noisy thing, that motorbike. When I was his age I drove this trap here into Bamford. I didn't need no motorbike. Kevin don't like that motorbike either. He don't like Gordon bringing it in when there's beasts in the yard.'

'Where is Kevin now?' Markby asked.

A shake of the head. 'I don't know. I don't recall seeing him today. He's likely about the place.'

'What about Mrs Jones, Linda?'

The old face brightened. 'She's a good woman, Linda. She'll be over to the house.' He turned back to the trap. 'You don't know someone as wants a good conveyance like this 'un, do you?'

Markby said apologetically that he didn't. The old man nodded and returned to his polishing. It seemed the conversation was over.

'Nice to have seen you again, Mr Jones,' he said to him, but got no reply.

If Mrs Jones was in the house she was probably in the kitchen. Markby made his way round to the back door and sure enough, it was open and he could see the figure of woman moving in the dim interior. He knocked on the door jamb and she looked up in surprise.

'Superintendent Markby,' he said quickly and held up his ID.

She came towards him wiping her hands on a tea-towel pinned round her waist and he saw that she'd been making pastry.

'Never another one!' she said, not crossly but in a mild amazement. 'I had a feller here the other day.'

'Yes, Inspector Pearce. May I come in and have a word, Mrs Jones?'

She shrugged. 'You can come in. I don't know what word it is you're going to have. I've told all I know. I only saw poor Miss Millar as I drove past the church. I didn't see where she was going. My mind was on other things. I do wish, though, that I'd stopped and had a word with her. You never know, it might have made a difference somehow. But then, it might not. You never know about these things, do you?' She pointed with a floury hand at a chair. 'Sit down, why don't you?'

Markby sat down and she returned to the table and rolling out her pastry.

'I'm just making a few little sausage rolls and fancy bits,' she said. 'Cheese straws and that sort of thing.'

'Would that be for your son's twenty-first party?' he asked.

She was startled. 'How'd you know about that? Oh, right, Gordon came when your inspector was here. Yes, for the party. Gordon was for getting it all from a shop but I don't reckon to shop-bought sausage rolls. I've made the cake and all.' She pointed proudly at the nearby dresser on which sat a large fruit cake. 'I've got to decorate it yet,' she explained. 'I'm going to put twenty-one on it in icing in the middle and pipe "Happy Birthday, Gordon" round the edge.'

'Very nice, too.' Markby paused then said, 'I saw your father-in-law in the barn. He's cleaning up a pony-trap you've got in there.'

She clicked her tongue against the roof of her mouth. 'That old trap. He's always in there messing about with it. Still it keeps him occupied. Did he try and sell it to you?'

'Not really. He just asked if I knew someone who wanted a conveyance, as he called it.'

She laughed. 'He usually tries to sell it to people. He's not, you know —' She tapped her forehead. 'He's not gaga, but not quite in working order up there, either. His mind goes along its own road, if you understand me.'

'I understand. He remembered me, though.'

Her hands stopped working. She rested them on the flat disc of dough and her eyes searched his face in a level, thoughtful gaze.

'You've been here before? I don't remember you.'

'It was twenty-two years ago.'

The level gaze faltered. She turned her attention back to her work, picking up a knife and cutting the rounded edges from the pastry so that she was left with a neat square. 'Surprised he remembered you,' she said, her voice muffled. 'He doesn't remember much.'

232

'But he remembers what happened a long time ago better than last week,' Markby observed. 'He even remembered why I came here. It was when we were enquiring into the attacks on women in and around Stovey Woods. The Potato Man. Do you remember that case, Mrs Jones?'

The hand holding the knife shook. 'Barely. Is that what you've come about, after all this time? Haven't you got enough to do with the murder?' Her voice was harsh.

'Enough, certainly. But sometimes one thing leads to another and it can take years for everything to work itself out. You do remember the Potato Man, then?'

She put down the knife and collapsed abruptly into a chair, making it scrape noisily on the flagged floor. 'I was only a girl, seventeen.'

'Were you engaged to Kevin Jones then? I met Kevin at the time. I seem to remember he wasn't married.'

'We were courting.' The words were almost inaudible.

'And you got married soon after?'

She raised her gaze briefly to meet his then dropped it again.

'I always believed,' Markby said softly, 'that the rapist was a local man. I've also always believed there were more rapes than were ever reported.'

'Do you now?' she said dully. She made a visible effort to pull herself together. 'I wouldn't know about that.'

Markby leaned forward, resting his clasped hands on the edge of the table. 'You know, it's funny thing,' he said conversationally. 'But many a witness doesn't come forward because he or she believes what he or she knows, isn't important. Or that he or she knows nothing. Yet when we do find these people and talk to them, it's amazing what they start to remember.'

Linda Jones made no reply and he went on. 'I'm not seeking to stir up old pain, Mrs Jones. I'm not seeking to make anything public. But I believe he's still here in Lower Stovey and I mean to have him yet.'

Something in his voice, a touch of steel, had frightened her and she looked up, shying her head away from him like a nervous beast.

'Don't be alarmed,' he urged. 'I told you, I don't mean to make anything public. Just now, you said you wished you'd spoken to Hester Millar when you passed her. It might have made a difference, you said, or it might not. But you did right to tell the police about it. Because whether it makes a difference is something the investigating officers will decide. So many witnesses,' Markby added with a pleasant smile, 'try to second-guess us. They tell us what they think we want to know and leave out things they fancy aren't important.'

She said very quietly, 'If there were other women who were attacked by that man, women who haven't come forward ever, it will be because they have spent more than twenty years burying that memory. They wouldn't be able to tell you anything. None of them saw his face. All they heard was a footstep, a breath and then that horrible earthy-smelling sack —' She put her hands over her face and after a moment, took them away.

'Mr Markby,' she said, her voice shaking a little but still filled with resolve, 'I can't tell you anything. I – I wish you weren't still looking for him and I can't say I hope you find him. All it will do is stir up old trouble, memories no one wants recalled. Those women who didn't come forward, they had their reasons. They were maybe going steady with a young man and were afraid that he might not want them any more, if they were dirtied in that way.'

He hadn't meant to interrupt at this moment when she'd at last begun to speak, but he couldn't prevent himself exclaiming, 'It wasn't their fault. The women themselves had done nothing wrong.'

'Does that matter?' she asked simply. 'The result's the same. They might have been told by their families not to go near the woods, it wasn't safe. They might have gone there anyway and then been afraid to own up. They'd be blamed because they disobeyed. The family would say, the girl had brought it on herself.' Her gaze met his briefly, 'There's no way out,' she said. 'Not living in a small place like this. Clever people living in towns might say differently. But here, well, certainly twenty-two years ago, we all knew each other so well. We all had to live cheek by jowl. No one wanted to believe there was something –

someone – so evil here, in Lower Stovey, so they had to believe it was somehow the victim's fault, do you see?'

He did see. After a moment, Markby said, 'The young man, the girl's boyfriend, you spoke of, he might have guessed what had happened?'

She gave a faint travesty of a smile. 'Oh yes, he might have guessed. And he might have said, so long as no one knew, he'd not speak of it again and I – the girl wouldn't speak of it and it'd be forgotten.'

'And has it been forgotten?'

'No,' she said quietly. 'The knowledge is like some kind of growth, like a fungus that you get on rotten wood. It gets bigger and smells fouler and you can't do anything about it because you've agreed to pretend it's not there. After a while, you can't speak of it but you're aware of it, oh, you're aware of it there at your shoulder all right. I can't speak of it, Superintendent, I'll never speak of it.'

Markby's gaze drifted to the birthday cake.

'Oh yes,' she said. 'It's possible, but I don't know, no more does Kevin. You see, we were courting at the time and we – well, we were going to get married anyway when I was eighteen so we sort of jumped the gun, if you like.'

'So that's another thing between you that you never speak of?'

She gave that sad smile again. 'How can we, now?'

Markby got to his feet. 'I'm truly sorry to have bothered you.' He hesitated. 'It's just, I've been remembering the Potato Man for over twenty years, too. He's never left me. I failed to find him. That matters to me. Because I failed to find him after the first reported attack, on Mavis Cotter, other women became his victims. It is, if you like, on my conscience. It's the thing at my shoulder which doesn't go away. I'll follow up any small clue, even now. Goodbye, Mrs Jones.'

As he reached the door he thought he heard a muffled sound behind him, as if she'd spoken, and he looked back.

She had taken sausage meat from a bowl and was rolling it into a long snake.

Without looking up at him, she said, 'He had a working man's hands.'

'You're sure of that?'

'Oh yes. And they weren't young hands, if you see what I mean. They'd calluses on them from years of work.'

Old Martin Jones was still in the barn as Markby passed by but he didn't look in. He'd no wish to buy a conveyance. He got in his car and drove slowly down the track to where it joined the road. There, instead of turning left up towards the village, he turned right and drove the remaining two hundred yards to where the road terminated and the woods began.

Switching off the engine, Markby sat back and stared through the windscreen at the dark mass of the woods, shivering in the wind. Meredith would be at Ruth's by now and they'd be waiting for him. He didn't want to be involved in tea, cake and chatter. He had to come here again. The woods drew him to them, the woods and their secret. He was right. He'd begun to work it out on the day of Hester's death, the conviction growing ever stronger, just the details blurred. But what he hadn't got was any kind of proof. And would he ever get it? Which was worse? Not knowing? Or believing he knew and not being about to prove it? And why Hester? If anyone had died, should it not have been Ruth Pattinson Aston, the local girl?

Markby got out of the car, slammed the door and made for the stile. He climbed over it and jumped down on the damp earth. He sniffed, able to smell the rain. The noise made by the wind in the trees was so loud now, it sounded like the angry roaring of some creature roaming in there. He had to force away the idea, remembering with a wry grimace his words to Meredith, that whatever lurked in the woods had only ever been entirely human. Markby turned up the collar of his jacket and set off down the narrow track between the trees.

When Alan's car had disappeared from sight, Meredith turned in under the lych-gate and walked towards the church door. It was unlocked. Ruth had been here today. Ruth had courage. Before she went into the porch Meredith turned her head and glanced back at the Fitzroy Arms. No one stood in its doorway now but she fancied something moved behind one of the windows. She didn't doubt she was being observed and another black mark being put down against her.

She opened the wire door and went down the few steps into the old church. It was cool and smelled a little musty, the odour of dust in old fabric hangings and piled up in nooks and crannies where Ruth's duster couldn't reach. By the place where Hester had been found someone had put flowers in a vase. Hester's story would become part of the story of this church, related to visitors in years to come.

The Fitzroy monuments in their splendour looked forlorn, forgotten, out of their time and their place. In their boastfulness of a lost grandeur, they put Meredith in mind of Shelley's 'Ozymandias'. Nothing lasts for ever, she thought, not a great name nor great wealth nor a social system which put the squire securely at the top of the local heap. She tried to imagine Sir Rufus in his periwig, proceeding majestically to his appointed seat between obsequious rows of other worshippers, the majority of whom would've depended on him for their livelihoods. Or, to go further back, wicked old Sir Hubert, wheeling and dealing with the bishop, offering a church for a pardon. 'I can't say better than that, your grace, now, can I?' And the bishop, knowing he'd got Hubert on the run, insisting that the new church must be large, splendid, well-appointed. Seen in the context of all the past, Hester's murder was just one more event to be absorbed by St Barnabas and relegated in time, like the others, to history.

Outside the church again, the wind ruffled her hair and the uncut grass growing long on the untended graves swayed like a hayfield. Meredith walked around to the south side and stared up at the carving of the Green Man. There was a look of malign mischief on his face still, even though the stone was weatherworn. Meredith shivered, perhaps because of the carving, perhaps because the wind pierced the thin fabric of her shirt. Then she heard behind her a sound which wasn't the wind or the rustling grass, a heavy, laboured breathing.

The hairs on her neck prickled. Meredith turned slowly and looked around her. The churchyard appeared empty. But she could still hear that eerie breathing. It came from the direction of a mossy tomb. For a few seconds she froze in pure panic. What was in there, trying to get out? Then, pulling herself together, she told herself firmly that it was in the middle of a Saturday afternoon and whatever was making its presence known in this deserted place, it was of this world and no other. Of course the sound didn't come *from* the tomb. It came from *behind* it. Cautiously she picked her way towards the spot.

Behind the tomb, slumped on the ground, his back to the monument, was Old Billy Twelvetrees. His stick lay on the ground beside him. When his eyes fixed on her, he opened his mouth, but then abandoned the attempt to speak, merely pointing feebly at his chest.

He suffered from angina, Meredith remembered Ruth telling her so. She stooped over him, 'Don't worry, Mr Twelvetrees. I'll get help. I've got my mobile and I'll call an ambulance.'

Alarm crossed his face. He waved his hand in a gesture of negation. His mouth opened again and he wheezed, so quietly she had to stoop right down beside him to catch the words, 'I don't want – to go to – no hospital.'

'You can't stay here, Mr Twelvetrees.'

'I – got – my pills. All I want – are – my pills.' His hand dropped to his side and he tapped the pocket of his jacket.

'Are they in your pocket?' Meredith hunkered down and prepared to search his jacket pocket. She didn't particularly relish pushing her hand down among the fluff and bits of sticky rubbish but there was a small bottle. She pulled it out and held it up. 'These?'

He nodded.

Meredith scanned the wording on the bottle, opened it and tapped out a small white pill on her palm. 'Just open your mouth a bit, can you?'

She pushed the pill through his withered lips.

The muscles of his face moved as he sucked on the pill. After a bit he wheezed, 'I can get up now if you —' Another wave of his hand.

'I'll help you. Look, here's your stick and you can brace yourself against this tomb.'

Somehow she got him upright. A flush of colour had returned to his cheeks. He said, more clearly than before, 'I get took sometimes like it. I just sat down for a minute because it come on bad.'

'Perhaps we can get you home, Mr Twelvetrees, and then I can phone your doctor.'

'I got pills,' he repeated stubbornly.

'Yes, I know, but I still think – let's get you home first, shall we?'

With his stick to support him on one side and leaning heavily on her arm on the other, he progressed slowly to the path and down it, under the lych-gate, out into the street.

'I live along there,' he gasped, indicating the left hand row of cottages.

At that moment, Evie appeared in the pub doorway. 'Summat wrong with you, then, Uncle Billy?' Her round face wrinkled in alarm.

'He's had an angina attack,' Meredith called to her. 'Do you know his doctor?'

Evie gaped at her. 'Oh, it'll be Dr Stewart.'

'Can I bring your uncle inside?'

Evie dithered and then stood back as if to allow them into the pub. But Old Billy gasped, 'I can get to my house.'

'If you're sure,' Meredith told him doubtfully. To Evie she called, 'He wants to go to his house. Can you call Dr Stewart's surgery and tell them what's happened? I think someone should call on Mr Twelvetrees today.'

Evie blinked at her, then turned and went inside, with luck to ring the doctor.

She and Billy made an ungainly progress to his ramshackle cottage. Meredith propped him against the wall by the door and rapped the fox's head knocker as loudly as she could. No one came.

Old Billy said, 'Dilys will be about somewhere. You can leave me here.'

'No, I can't, Mr Twelvetrees. Haven't you got a key?'

'Don't need no key. Back door will be open.'

Meredith's gaze searched the row of cottages, seeking some access to the rear. She spied a narrow alley, little more than a wide crack, between the next cottage down and the one after that.

'Down there, Mr Twelvetrees?'

He nodded. 'Gimme a minute or two and I'll be able to get myself round the back.'

She couldn't abandon him, not in this state. 'You stay here. I'll go round and if I can get inside, I'll go through the house and open the front door for you.'

'No – Dilys —' he began and grasped at her arm but let it drop to put a hand to his chest. 'It's coming on again.'

Meredith didn't wait. She ran to the alley and squeezed down it, her shoulders rubbing the rough stone walls of the cottages to either side. It led between the two gardens and then, sure enough, at the end debouched into a muddy lane which ran past the rear of all the cottages in the High Street. Meredith turned right and found the rear of the Twelvetrees' home. It was secluded from the lane by a ramshackle fence of corrugated iron sheeting and a wooden door. To it was nailed, as if some ghastly talisman, an old, dried and dirty hairy object which she realised was a fox's brush. She shuddered. To what purpose had it been fixed here? To keep away what unwished visitation? Avoiding it, she pushed the door. It creaked open and she hurried across the garden which appeared entirely given over to cabbages and smelled pungently of rotting greens. She fumbled at the back door.

It swung open beneath her touch and she found herself in the kitchen. The air there smelled of fried bacon. She called, 'Dilys?'

There was no reply. She was half-way across the kitchen and almost at the door into the hallway, when her eye caught a jumble of objects on the kitchen table. Despite the urgency of her errand, curiosity made her turn aside to see them better.

All appeared to have been taken from a battered cardboard shoebox which lay to one side. The objects had been laid out in a kind of pattern as if some human version of a bower-bird had been setting out its hoard of bright-coloured garnerings to lure a mate. There was a string of beads. It had broken and the ends roughly reknotted. Beside it lay a very nice male signet ring, another ring with a large fake stone, a pearl earring, a woman's wristwatch, a copper bangle and a blue plastic hairslide shaped like a butterfly.

The kitchen seemed unnaturally quiet. Meredith picked up the signet ring. It was heavy, expensive. On the shield was engraved, in Gothic lettering, *SH*.

She put it back gently, as if it might break. As if in a trance, she walked down the hallway and pulled open the front door. Old Billy still stood where she'd left him, propped against the doorjamb.

'You'd best come in, Mr Twelvetrees.' Her voice sounded distant, not her own.

She took his arm and led him into the hall and after a momentary hesitation, into the tiny parlour to the right, which gave on to the street.

Old Billy subsided into his armchair and leaned back with a sigh.

'I'll be all right now. You don't need to stay. Dilys will be here in no time. She won't have gone far.'

'You're sure?'

'I'm sure!' He raised the stick and gestured towards the door. 'You go on! Our Dilys, she won't be far away, just nipped out to see a neighbour most like. I've got me pills. I'm all right now, sitting here quiet.'

She left him, going out of the front door and pulling it shut behind her. A glance up and down the street showed no one but an elderly woman, unknown to her. She didn't think that could be the absent Dilys who, Alan had told her, was Old Billy's daughter. That old dame was at least seventy. The woman went into another cottage and shut her door. So that was that. Dilys cleaned for Ruth Aston. Could she have gone there?

Meredith wrestled with conflicting responsibilities, her mind reeling. In Old Billy's interest, she ought to go back to the pub to tell Evie that she'd left Mr Twelvetrees alone and check that the woman had called the doctor. But time was of the essence. She knew that the person she wanted to see was Alan and that it was imperative she see him as soon as possible. She had to get him back here before anyone else came, Dilys, Evie, Dr Stewart, anyone. Any of them might tidy away the

241

objects on the kitchen table. Alan had to see them there, just as they were.

He'd driven to that farm, Greenjack. Meredith fumbled in her bag for her mobile phone and rang his. For some reason she was unable to make contact. She pushed the phone back in her bag and thought furiously. If she walked in that direction, towards Stovey Woods, she'd probably meet him driving back. Meredith set off down the street.

Soon she'd left the houses behind and the track led on between the drystone walls towards the woods, dark and hostile on the near horizon. The wind ruffled her hair. It carried a few spots of rain on it. Meredith stepped out briskly.

Chapter Fifteen

The distant woods had seemed nearer to the naked eye than they were in reality. As Meredith trudged along the uneven single track road, they began to take on the characteristics of a mirage, always just ahead. There was no sign of Alan's car coming towards her as she'd hoped. The further she got from Lower Stovey, the lonelier it became. The wind whipped across the open fields and buffeted her face and clothes. Even the sheep huddled under the shelter of the drystone walls. The rainspots were getting more frequent and stronger. She hadn't so much as a scarf and was going to get soaked. A curious and unpleasant sensation was assailing the spot between her shoulderblades, as it can do when one senses one is being followed. She began to glance behind her but the road was as empty behind as before. A couple of times her attention was taken by the sheep, suddenly uttering loud bleats and scattering across the field in a panic. Perhaps the sight of her had alarmed them, though she couldn't think why. She had the feeling, and couldn't get rid of it, that she was being watched. By whom? Only the sheep. The few cows were all lying down, chewing placidly as they awaited the rain. They had no interest in a solitary human hurrying along the road. 'Get a hold of your nerves!' she told herself sternly.

There was no avoiding the rain now. It had begun to fall steadily. She had to put up with it as the animals were doing. It trickled down her face, her shirt became wet and her jeans clung unpleasantly to her thighs. Meredith strode out determinedly, making the best time she could, but discomfort was adding to the frustration of not seeing the familiar car approaching. Where was Alan? How long was he taking at that farm?

There was a turning ahead and a wooden sign. At last! She scanned the words 'Greenjack Farm' and turned down a muddy track. The farm-gate appeared barring her way forward and holding for her all the significance of a frontier post for a refugee. But her heart sank when she found no one in the yard and most significantly, still no sign of Alan's car. Meredith frowned, puzzled. She hadn't encountered him on the only road back into the village. He appeared to have dematerialised. She picked her way cautiously across the yard avoiding the more obvious cowpats but certain her shoes were fouled up with odiferous slime, the memory of which would linger long after the footwear itself was scrubbed.

Her ring at the farmhouse door was answered by a woman about forty. She stared at Meredith in some surprise as well she might.

Meredith, knowing that her drenched appearance out of nowhere probably begged explanation but unable to give it, simply asked, 'Is Superintendent Markby here?'

The woman, still staring bemusedly at Meredith, shook her head. 'No, he left about, oh, ten minutes ago.'

'*Left?*' Meredith could help but sound incredulous. 'But I didn't see him on the way here from the village.'

The woman blinked. 'Do you want to come indoors?' she asked. 'You're getting fair drowned there.' She peered past her. 'Where's your car?'

'I – I walked. I won't come in, thanks. I came with Alan, with the superintendent, and I've really got to find him.'

Another surprised blink. 'Well, perhaps he'll come back. Or I can run you back to the village, if he doesn't. You'll be a policewoman?'

'No.' Meredith pushed back wet hair from her eyes. 'Look, you're sure he left? He's not around the farm somewhere?'

'Only if his car's still there.'

'It's not.'

'Then he's left.'

This conversation was going round in circles, getting nowhere and Meredith felt herself growing desperate.

'Then where could he have gone?' she insisted, still believing Alan must be here somewhere here.

The woman gave her an odd look. 'If you didn't see him on the road, then he must have turned right and gone down to the woods.'

The woods. Of course, he'd been drawn back to the woods by his obsession with the Potato Man.

Meredith muttered, 'Thank you! Sorry to have disturbed you . . .' and turned away.

The woman exclaimed, 'You're never going down there! It's not a place to go – it's not a place for a woman on her own.'

'I have to find him, it's urgent.'

The woman was looking at her in distress. Seeing Meredith was adamant, she said, 'Hang on, then, I'll give you a brolly if you must go!' She pulled a battered umbrella from a stand in the hall and handed it to Meredith. 'I still think you'd do best to wait for him here. If he is in the woods, then he's still got to drive back past the turning to the farm. If you were to wait down there, you'd see him and he'd see you. There's no need for you to go down to the woods.'

Her obstinate insistence that Meredith shouldn't go alone to Stovey Woods seemed disproportionate to the circumstances. Meredith would hardly get wetter waiting at the side of the road, by the sign to the farm, than walking to the woods. Come to that, she could hardly get any wetter, anyway. She was drenched to the skin already. Even the offer of the umbrella seemed superfluous but it was kindly meant and it would be churlish to refuse.

'Thanks for the umbrella,' Meredith gasped. 'I can't wait.'

She hastened back across the yard, aware the woman stood in her doorway, watching her retreat with the same distressed expression.

The umbrella, which was a large old-fashioned model, made progress a little drier but no easier. The wind caught at it and threatened to turn it inside-out if she kept it upright. If she lowered it in front of her, the force of the wind pushed her back. At the end of the track to the farm, Meredith abandoned her attempt to make use of the brolly, refurled it and propped it against the farm sign where it could be seen, turned right and began to jog towards the mass of the trees ahead. She was so wet now, it no longer mattered.

Eventually she reached the end of the road and the edge of the woods. There at long last she saw, parked to one side, the welcome sight of Alan's car. But he wasn't in it and when she tried the door, it was locked. She took out her mobile again and tried his number, still without luck. He was in the woods and communication with him impossible. It must be a dead spot in there. She could wait here like a drowned rat or go into the woods after him. In among the trees it would at least be sheltered. However, if she did that, there was just a chance they'd miss each other and she'd return to find he'd driven off. Meredith tore a scrap of paper from the notebook in her bag and printed on it, *I'm in the woods. Wait for me.* She stuck it under the windscreen wiper. That should do it. Meredith scrambled over the stile and plunged into the trees.

Once among the tall trunks she was protected from the worst of the weather, though she could hear the rain rustling in the branches above her. Every minute or so it found its way through and splashed down on her head. At least the wind didn't permeate the mass of trunks. She cupped her hands round her mouth and shouted, 'Alan!'

Her voice was swallowed up by the trees. She went a little further on, following a narrow deer track, and tried again but with as little luck. He couldn't be far, surely? Where could he be making for? Perhaps for the place where Dr Morgan had found the bones. But Meredith didn't know where that was.

She had left the comforting glimpse of the open fields at her back and was now deep in Stovey Woods. Far from a sense of loneliness now, she had the feeling she was surrounded by watching eyes. The impression that she'd had on the road was redoubled. She spun round. Nothing. Still the eerie sensation was growing until the moment came when, with absolute certainty, she knew she wasn't alone. Something – someone? – was there, every instinct, every nerve in her body told her so. She couldn't see it, couldn't hear or smell it, but her skin tingled and she had a heightened awareness of her own progress. Evolution was sloughing away and she had begun to move differently, placing her feet carefully on the pine-needle strewn ground, head high and casting about for movement in her immediate surrounds, ears straining for the slightest indication as primitive instincts long dormant were awakened by the need of this oldest of survival techniques, that of hunter and hunted. She was both, hunting Alan and in turn herself being hunted – by what? She regretted having abandoned the umbrella. It would have given her some kind of weapon, some means of keeping whatever it was at bay.

She shouted Alan's name again, trying to keep the panic from sounding in her voice. Very, very faintly she thought she heard an answering call and her heart leapt as a feeling of relief swept over her. He was ahead of her. He wasn't far away. She wasn't alone but it was Alan who was there.

And then she heard it to the right. A crack of twig as if something had stepped on it. Meredith froze, her heart beating wildly. She called, 'Hello?'

No reply. There were animals in these woods. It was a deer perhaps. Yes, almost certainly. She hurried on. *Alan was ahead.* She repeated the three words like a mantra. He'd heard her call. He'd be coming towards her.

Yet behind her, somewhere over to her right, it was still there, keeping pace with her. Look intently among the trees though she might, she couldn't catch sight of it. But more twigs snapped. She began to fancy she heard laboured breathing. It had to be fancy. She told herself it *must* be fancy.

Suddenly she found herself in a small clearing. It came upon her with disconcerting suddeness. Before there had been trees sheltering her but now she was out in the open and standing on the rim of a depression. If there was any living thing behind her, it could see her clearly. Staked out, she thought grimly, like a goat awaiting the tiger. Around the rim of the hollow, deer tracks ran off it in all directions into the surrounding trees. She had no way of knowing if Alan had come this way, or if he had, which one path he had taken. She called desperately for the last time, '*Alan!*'

Then it was upon her, leaping from the dark mass of trunks, crashing across the intervening space, breathing stentoriously. She spun round, throwing up her arm in an automatic gesture to protect her head. Her opponent was there, no longer a tracker, but face-to-face, in appearance both confusing and terrifying. 'It' was revealed as female, a woman not young, a woman wearing slacks and a waterproof jacket. A woman with oddly-coloured pinkish hair and staring eyes, gaping mouth. A woman brandishing a carving knife.

The knife slashed through the air, just missing Meredith's shoulder. The arm was raised again. Meredith grabbed it and tried to twist it and force her assailant to drop the weapon. But the woman was strong, unbelievably strong. With all her own strength Meredith pushed her away and eluding the flailing knife, began to run back the way she'd come. She was younger and lighter. She had to be able to out-run whoever this was. But the sheltering trees she sought betrayed her. She tripped on a protruding root, flung out her arms in vain to save herself, and sprawled full length with her face in the carpet of pine needles. Rolling over on to her back, scrabbling for a handhold, she looked up and saw the woman looming over her. The knife was raised again. The round face with its staring eyes shone with a wild triumph.

Then, from one of the other tracks into the trees, something else came bounding out and across the clearing towards them. To Meredith's terrified gaze it was an apparition as fearsome as the one standing over her. It was a beast and one which for a split second seemed out of time, leapt from some medieval past. Then she saw it was a huge shaggy hound, dark in colour and the size of a Shetland pony. Ears and red tongue flapping, it covered the clearing in a split second and launched itself at Meredith's assailant.

Under its weight, the woman went down as if poleaxed. The knife flew out of her hand and landed inches from Meredith who grabbed it and scrambled on to her knees. The hound had placed its great paws firmly on the fallen assailant's chest, pinning her down, and was enthusiastically licking her face. Helpless beneath its weight and the assault of the rough tongue on her features, the assailant was cursing the animal and struggling vainly to push it away.

From out of the trees in the wake of the hound came a familiar figure in long skirts, rainbow-hued pullover under a grubby body-warmer, and a plastic rain-hat. She lumbered across the clearing towards them, shouting: '*Roger! Roger! Leave it! Bad dog*!'

'No!' shouted Meredith. 'Tell him to stay right where he is!'

Muriel Scott panted to a halt beside her. 'Why?' she asked in a practical voice.

Meredith held up the knife. 'She tried to kill me. She killed Hester.'

Mrs Scott peered at the figure on the ground. 'Dilys did? Why?'

Meredith gasped, 'I saw the things in the kitchen, I saw the Potato Man's collection.'

'Did you?' said a new, male voice.

They all looked towards the sound. Alan Markby had arrived and was standing a few feet away.

He stepped forward and grasped Meredith's shoulders. 'You're all right? Not hurt?'

'Yes, yes!' She pointed a shaky finger at the glowering prostrate Dilys. 'She – she – She frightened me out of my skin!'

'It's over now. I'll take care of it,' he said and she felt the panic seep out of her.

He held out his hand. Meredith passed him the knife, remembering belatedly to hold it by the tip of the blade, and watched him take his handkerchief and carefully wrap it round the handle.

'Right, Dilys,' he said to the figure on the ground. 'If Mrs Scott will kindly call Roger to heel, you can get up. Then we can all go back to Lower Stovey and have a word with your father.'

The short journey back to Lower Stovey in Alan's car had to be the strangest Meredith had ever made. Unable to fit in Roger, Muriel Scott had set off to walk him back home. After a brief discussion Meredith declared herself recovered enough from her fear to drive, at a snail's pace, the short distance to Lower Stovey. She was all too aware of Markby sitting in the back seat alongside a silent Dilys Twelvetrees. The woman's face was impassive now. Her workworn hands lay folded on her knees. She stared straight ahead. Markby had phoned Dave Pearce and told him to meet them at the Twelvetrees' cottage but it would at least twenty-five minutes before he got there.

At the cottage, Markby drew up, and they all decanted themselves into the street.

'Alan —' Meredith touched his sleeve. 'Before I came down to the woods, the old man had a bad attack of angina. I helped him home. He mightn't be fit enough to answer questions.'

He nodded. 'We'll see. Key?' he asked Dilys.

Sullenly she pulled it from her jacket pocket.

'Open up, then, please.'

Dilys obeyed grudgingly.

'Go in first, if you would. Tell your father I'd like a word.'

Dilys glared at him and, still silent, went into the cottage. They followed her and waited in the narrow hall.

Dilys had gone into the parlour. They heard her say, 'Dad?' There was no reply and after a pause and they heard her coming back.

Alan swore softly under his breath and put out a hand to throw back the parlour door.

Their line of sight was blocked by the solid form of Dilys, standing before them, something of the look of triumph back on her face.

'You won't be talking to him,' she said. 'Not now, not never.' Her eyes gleamed mockingly.

Markby pushed past her. Old Billy still sat in the chair where Meredith had left him. His stick was propped against his knees and his right arm hung over the chair. Beneath his dangling hand, the little medicine bottle lay on the carpet, the pills were scattered across it. His eyelids drooped over glazed eyes.

Markby drew in a sharp breath. To the end the Potato Man had eluded him.

Behind him, Dilys, quietly exultant, said, 'See? I told you. You ain't never going to get him now.'

Chapter Sixteen

At that moment they were all startled by the unexpected sound of someone clearing his throat behind them.

A youngish man in a sports jacket was standing in the doorway. He was carrying a medical bag.

'Dr Stewart,' he introduced himself. 'Come to see Mr Twelvetrees.'

'Your patient is in here,' Markby told him. 'But I'm afraid you're a little too late.'

As they all were.

Stewart uttered an exclamation and hurried past him into the parlour.

As he passed Dilys, she spoke for the first time. 'No use hurrying yourself, doctor. He'll wait for you.'

Her voice was swallowed up in the noise of a car drawing up. Pearce's voice could be heard calling, 'Superintendent? Are you in there?'

Markby went into the hall and found Pearce just ducking his head beneath the low lintel to enter. Behind him stood Ginny Holding and in the background, a uniformed man.

'Where's the woman?' Pearce asked bluntly.

Markby jerked his head towards the parlour. 'In there with her father who's just died. You'll have to tread carefully, but I think we can be sure we've got the murderer of Hester Millar. As to why, I'm sure we can work that one out now.'

Meredith came out of the parlour, pale-faced. 'I feel dreadful. I should never have left the poor old chap alone. He insisted. He said his daughter would be coming in soon. I'd told the woman at the pub to call Dr Stewart and I – well, I was desperate to find you and tell you about the things in the kitchen. Are they still there?'

'Damn!' Markby muttered. He ran down the hall and into the kitchen. The table was bare. He swore loudly and forcefully.

Meredith appeared at his elbow. She glanced at the bare table-top and observed, 'I really screwed this up, didn't I? I should have stayed here until I could get you on my mobile, kept an eye on Billy and made sure the box of oddments wasn't moved. Sorry.'

He hunched his shoulders. 'Don't apologize. You reacted naturally given the shock you'd had. Either Dilys before she set off after you or the old man himself before he collapsed hid the evidence. Let's hope it was the old man. He couldn't have moved far and it's probably still on the premises. Dilys, on the other hand, might have got rid of it anywhere between here and Stovey Woods. It's easy to guess what happened. She came home moments after you left her father, heard from him that you'd brought him home and you'd gained entry to the cottage via the back door and the kitchen. She knew you couldn't have missed his box of trophies and you were bound to tell me about them. She set out after you, determined to reach you before you reached me.'

'She nearly did,' Meredith said with a shudder.

'Yes.' Soberly he added, 'I should have thought of that. I'd been putting it together in my head slowly for the past week, but after I'd spoken to Linda Jones I was sure. Old Billy Twelvetrees was the Potato Man of twenty-two years ago. I should also have realised that Dilys must know and have known for years.'

'And have kept silent?' she stared at him incredulously.

'Would you have spoken up in her situation? She lives in this village. She has nowhere else to go. Besides, twenty-two years is a long time ago. She'd believed it buried and forgotten.'

He shook his head and added, 'You know, the problem with meeting for the first time people who are already very old, is that it's hard to imagine them younger and even more difficult to imagine them involved in violence. You knew Twelvetrees only as an old fellow, lame and using a walking stick, wheezing with breathing problems. How could he ever have been a threat? Even to suspect him of anything must seem uncharitable. I or someone else must have interviewed him years ago when we talked to all the village men, but he was so changed that even I saw him as a totally different person, a new acquaintance. I only recognised Martin Jones because I saw him in his own stables. Out of his familiar environment, who knows, I probably shouldn't have recognised him, either!

'I see now I made a mistake too, back then and again now. I was assuming that rape would be the crime of a much younger man, someone in his twenties. Yet Ruth had tipped us off, had we had ears to hear. She told us, if you recall, that running from Stovey Woods where she'd encountered Simon Hastings, she almost ran into Twelvetrees. But, as she pointed out to us, he was a lot younger then, not "old" at all, only in his late fifties, hale and hearty. He worked for Martin Jones right by Stovey Woods. No one would ever give a second thought to seeing him around there. Ruth didn't. It was where he was supposed to be.'

'Ruth!' exclaimed Meredith. 'She must be wondering where on earth we are!'

As they hurried out of the house they passed Dilys being ushered into a police car by Sergeant Holding.

'Tell the inspector we've gone to see Mrs Aston,' Markby ordered her.

Dilys looked up and for the first time some emotion other than the maniacal triumph entered her flat features. Genuine regret touched them before she shook her head and resignation replaced it.

'You tell Mrs Aston,' she said to Meredith. 'That I'm sorry. But it couldn't be helped. She'd seen what you saw.'

'You mean, Hester Millar saw your father's box of trophies,' Markby said. 'Where is it now, Dilys?'

'I don't know. Maybe,' her glance at Markby was both mocking and vindictive, 'maybe you should ask Dad?'

Meredith saw a nerve jump in his jaw but he returned calmly, 'Why did Miss Millar come to the cottage that morning?'

'Brought us some jam,' said Dilys with a sniff. 'She was always making the stuff.'

'Jam!' exclaimed Ruth. 'That was it. That was what Hester was holding in her hand when she came to tell me she was leaving. A pot of jam. It was such an ordinary thing I didn't pay any attention. I clean forgot about it but now you tell me, I can see her standing there, holding it. She didn't say she was going to Old Billy's cottage but she must have been. It was my idea —'

Ruth broke off and after a moment added quietly, 'So I did kill her, didn't I? Morally, anyway. It was my idea she take the jam to the old man in person. Because she did that, she walked in on the old wretch gloating over his box of trophies.'

'She wouldn't necessarily have known what they were,' Meredith objected. 'They were just a jumble, a string of beads, a man's signet ring and so on.'

'A man's?' Markby asked her with a frown.

'Yes, I realised straight away it was the odd item in the group. All the other things he'd taken from women, beads, earring, hairslide. But this ring was a big heavy thing, definitely a man's —' Meredith looked nervously at Ruth. 'It had the initials SH on it.' To Markby she added, 'I was going to tell you about that. I hadn't got round to it.'

'I gave that ring to Simon,' Ruth said quietly. 'I showed it to Hester before I gave it to him. She would have recognised it. She knew bones had been found in the woods. I'd told her about meeting Simon there that day. She knew the ring must have come from him and she must have let it be seen that she knew.'

'But she didn't know how it got to be in that box,' Markby took up the story as Ruth fell silent. 'Old Billy had got the ring in the woods, for sure. But had he taken it from a man he'd found dead? Or a man he'd killed? She went to the church and knelt in the pew, seeking guidance. She knew she'd have to tell you, Ruth. And she knew that you and she should tell the police. It was going to take a lot of courage on your part. The story of your child would become known. She'd protected you before, all those years ago when you were pregnant. But she couldn't see a way of protecting you now.

'Dilys had followed her to the church. Hester might have glanced up as Dilys came in, we don't know, but she wouldn't have feared Dilys, even in the circumstances. She knew her too well. She might even have thought that Dilys didn't know where her father had got the ring.'

Ruth stirred on the sofa where she'd been sunk in thought as Markby was speaking. 'I still find it hard to believe,' she said now. 'But perhaps I shouldn't. The Twelvetrees family was always beyond the pale in Lower Stovey. It's funny, isn't it? Every village has one family which is tolerated but disapproved of.'

'Probably for good reason, even if it was the sort of reason no one spoke of. Perhaps Old Billy was the local drunk?'

'He certainly drank but whether more than the other men, I don't know.' Ruth bit her lip. 'But looking back, I can see he was violent, even then. Domestic violence they'd call it now. Back then they probably just said he knocked his wife and kids about. Mrs Twelvetrees cleaned for my mother. She often had bruises. The girls had them, too, when they came to school. But they weren't badly marked enough for a teacher to start making enquiries. I suppose that if they ever were, they were kept home until the bruises had faded. There were days when Dilys didn't turn up. When she came back she always said she'd had a cold, but I never saw her sniffing.'

'At school,' Markby mused. 'Dilys and Sandra Twelvetrees, two little red-haired girls.'

'Yes,' Ruth said in surprise. 'They did have red hair. Dilys still touches hers up with hair-colourant because she started to go white quite early.' She raised her eyebrows. 'How did you know?' she asked.

'Guessed,' he said enigmatically, thinking of family photographs on the Twelvetrees mantelshelf. Three small children, all red-haired, and the later picture of Sandra née Twelvetrees posing for the camera in Disneyland, the sun setting fire to her auburn curls.

The duty solicitor, a pale-faced and earnest young man, looked unhappy. 'My client wishes to answer your questions frankly and freely. Nevertheless, I shall point out to her when she is not obliged to do so.'

'Fair enough,' Pearce told him shortly. The tooth was beginning to nag again. He explored it with the tip of his tongue and winced. Beside him, Ginny Holding gave him a knowing look.

Pearce forced his mind from the tooth and concentrated on matters in hand. 'Right, Dilys. Let's start at the beginning. When did you realise your father was the rapist of twenty-two years ago?'

'You don't need to answer that!' said the solicitor immediately to Dilys. To Pearce he said, 'You have no evidence the late Mr Twelvetrees was responsible for the attacks. Why should my client think that he was?'

'The box,' growled Pearce.

'What box might this be? It seems to have disappeared. It was, by the description, if it ever existed —' The duty solicitor allowed himself a smirk. 'Merely a collection of *objets trouvés*. The old gentleman might have picked the things up anywhere, lying on the ground, things lost in the woods.'

Pearce gave a faint groan. It was going to be one of those days. Again.

But Dilys chose to ignore her legal adviser. 'I didn't realise nothing. I always knew it. It was when my mother was bedridden it began. She couldn't do a thing, not wash herself, hardly feed herself. She got enormous and Dad, he hated her for it. He's stand in the bedroom doorway and call her filthy names. But he never got any further than the doorway, I saw to that. I'd come back home to live because my husband had left me. He went away with a barmaid, brassy floozy who worked at the pub in the village. Good luck to her, I say, and good riddance to him. I had nowhere to go so I had to go home. Ma had taken to her bed, anyway. Someone had to look after her and him, the old blighter. In that way, it sort of worked out. But that's when he started that caper in the woods.'

'Mrs Pullen . . .' pleaded the solicitor. 'This is very unwise and unnecessary.'

'How did you feel about your father, Dilys?' Ginny Holding asked in her soft voice.

'He was an old devil. And when he was young he was a young devil. We were all terrified of him, all us kids. You only had to catch his eye and it got you a clip round the ear. When he came home from the pub in drink, he'd come upstairs and pull us out of bed to thrash us.'

'Is that all he did, Dilys? When he came up to your bedroom?' Ginny asked softly.

Dilys glared. 'Wasn't it enough? Ma would be hanging on his arm, begging him to leave us be, and he'd turn and smash his fist into her face. My brother William, the one they call Young Billy, he cleared off at seventeen and went to sea, got out of it. My sister, she married a soldier and went off to live in Germany. But me, I drew the short straw, it seems.' Dilys's gaze, as hard as marbles, met Pearce's. 'That kind of fear doesn't wear off when you get older. I might have been too big for him to wallop me but I was still scared of him. See, he had another weapon. I needed to live there. I had no place to go. I had to put up with all his nonsense.'

Dilys's voice sank and her gaze moved to her hands, resting on the table-top. 'I knew when he'd been out fooling with those girls. I could smell it on him when he come home. I smelled it on his clothes when I did the laundry, I saw the stains. He showed me those things he took from them. He liked to see the look on my face. He liked knowing that he could tell me and I couldn't do a thing about it. He was a nasty old bugger and that's a fact. But my concern was for Ma, that she shouldn't learn about it. He'd led her a dog's life. She was just worn right out and she couldn't do with any more trouble. I didn't have time to worry about those girls.'

Holding asked, 'And did he also bother you in that way, Dilys?'

Dilys's small eyes moved their stony gaze to her. 'He didn't fancy me, most like. I was never anything but a big lump who could cook and clean.'

'Nevertheless, you were there, under the same roof. You were in no position to protest, as you've said. It wouldn't be surprising if he'd taken advantage of that, if you know what I mean.'

'I know what you mean!' Dilys's mouth snapped shut like a trap.

There was a silence. Dilys gave no sign of saying any more. Her eyes were blank. Pearce nudged Ginny. It wouldn't do for Dilys to clam up now.

'What happened after your mother died?' Ginny prompted.

Dilys blinked and shrewd suspicion returned to her expression. 'After Ma died? What should I do? I stayed there, cooking and cleaning for him. Not that I ever got a word of thanks. I still needed a place to live and as long as Dad was alive and living in the cottage I had a roof over my head. I knew old Mr Jones wouldn't throw Dad out and I knew young Kevin wouldn't, not while his father was alive. But old Martin Jones was getting older and so was Dad. If old Jones died, young Kevin might decide to get us out. Or if Dad died, it'd be easy. I wasn't the tenant. Dad was. I knew Dad wouldn't ever agree to go to a retirement home. He wouldn't even go to hospital. So it was in my interest to look after the old blighter and keep him alive, wasn't it?' Her flat gaze returned to Pearce's face.

Pearce felt a deep depression settle over him. 'All right,' he said, 'Tell me about Simon Hastings.'

'Dad never killed that chap!' Her voice was vehement. 'Not intentional, not like you mean. It was an accident. Could've happened to anyone.'

'Go on.' Dilys had stopped as if she'd expected Pearce to agree with her. 'Why was it an accident?' Pearce asked.

The solicitor interrupted again. 'My client can't tell you that because she doesn't know. She wasn't there when Simon Hastings died.'

'I know what Dad told me!' said Dilys truculently to him.

'Yes, Mrs Pullen, but you don't *know* it happened that way. You weren't a witness. Your father's account may have been flawed.'

'He was telling me lies, you mean?' Dilys glared at him. 'So what am I supposed to do? Sit here with my mouth shut and let these coppers think Dad killed that hiker? Well, he didn't. He told me so and I reckon he told me right. How do I know? Because he was that scared, that's why. Something had happened he hadn't counted on, see? You didn't know my father and I did. You didn't see him that evening when he come home and told me about the hiker and I did. Fair shaking in his boots, he was, and as white a sheet.'

She turned her attention back to Pearce and Holding. 'Dad had met Miss Pattinson, as she was then, hadn't he? Coming from the woods and crying. Dad knew she hadn't met the Potato Man because he was the Potato Man. She said, she was crying for her mother who'd just died. But Dad thought different. He was curious. He went up to the woods and he came across this chap, a hiker. The feller looked odd, Dad reckoned, as if upset about something and angry. Dad asked him if he was the reason Miss Pattinson had run out of the woods in a fair old state. And the feller just went for him, went for Dad. Swung a haymaker of a punch at him and Dad, he ducked it and fetched him a cracker in return. The hiker went down and hit his head on a fallen tree. That was it. Dead as a doornail. Dad took fright when he saw he was stuck there with a corpse on his hands. He pulled a lot of branches and stuff over him and came home. That night he went back with a spade and buried him. And I know that's right,' Dilys added with a glower at her legal representative, 'because I was there that time! He took me with him.'

The solicitor broke in with desperation in his voice. 'Mrs Pullen, do you realise —'

Dilys turned on him. 'You don't need to keep on calling me Mrs Pullen. I'm Dilys Twelvetrees. That's what I was born and that's what I'm still.'

'Did you divorce Mr Pullen?' Holding asked her.

Dilys stared at her scornfully. 'What for? He was gone. What's the point in divorce?'

'Then technically you are still Mrs Pullen,' Holding said.

'I'm Dilys Twelvetrees,' she repeated obstinately. 'It was never a name to be proud of but I'd rather have it than Pullen, any day.'

'I don't think it matters if Dilys chose to resume her maiden name,' Pearce said firmly, with an irritated look at Holding. 'So, you went back to Stovey Woods that night with your father and helped him bury Simon Hastings?'

'Mrs – Twelvetrees!' said the solicitor loudly. 'You don't have to answer that. You've said quite enough already.'

'You keep quiet,' Dilys said to him. 'I know what I'm minded to answer and what I'm not.'

'We discussed this, Mrs Pu – Twelvetrees! I explained —'

'I know what you explained.' Dilys returned her attention to Markby. 'Dad needed me to hold the lantern. Anyway, he knew that if I helped him, it'd be difficult for me to go telling anyone about it. I was in it, too, wasn't I?'

Her expression grew reminiscent and when she began to speak again there was a change in her voice. It had gained the mesmerising quality of a traditional story-teller, softer, inviting the audience in to listen. Pearce realised they were all leaning forward, even the solicitor, hanging on her every word, knowing they were to be told something that would lodge in their own minds for ever.

'Dad was pretty sure he could find where he'd left the hiker. But it was pitch black in those woods. You couldn't see a hand in front of your face and not one thing looked like it did in daytime. We only had the lantern, an oil-lamp, it was. It made the shadows jump around in the trees like a lot of mad creatures dancing around us in the dark. We made a couple of false stops before we reached where Dad thought it should be. He said, "Tis around here someplace, Dilys. Do you go and take a proper look round." Well, I wasn't going poking about in those trees, not knowing what was there, and very likely falling over a dead man. So I held up the lantern high and swung it round. And bless me, there it was.'

The solicitor drew in his breath slightly. Holding was frozen in an attitude of rapt attention. Pearce felt a frisson of anticipation.

'You saw the body . . .' he whispered.

Dilys gave him a curious, mocking look. 'I saw the hand.'

'Hand?' gasped the solicitor.

'Yes, hand. You deaf? I saw an arm, and the hand on the end of it, pointing up into the trees. It was poking out of the leaves and branches Dad had dragged over him, pointing up like a signpost to tell us where he lay. I said to Dad, "You buried the chap alive! He's moved. He's been trying to dig himself out!" But Dad said, "No, he ain't." Leastwise not that he knew of it. "It's the rigor".'

The solicitor muttered, 'Good grief!'

Dilys, perhaps interpreting his comment as lack of understanding, went on to to explain it to him. 'Rigor, that's what sets in when something dies. Dad had seen in it cattle and sheep. The limbs go stiff and stick up all awkward. This hiker's arm had just risen up in the air like of its own accord. The leaves Dad threw over him weren't heavy enough to keep it down.

'But Dad was put out because he couldn't bury him easy with the arm sticking up like that. So he took a great swing at it with his spade. I heard the bones all crack but it didn't fall because the muscles kept it upright. So Dad went at it like a madman, bashing it until it lay flat. Then he bent down and pulled off the signet ring that was on one of the fingers. He said it would do to go with the other things. I told him he was a fool. It was evidence. He just told me to shut up. But I was right, wasn't I?' Dilys put the question suddenly to the solicitor. 'It was evidence?'

'You were right,' he told her faintly.

She seemed pleased, nodding her head. 'So, Dad dug a grave in another place and we rolled him in there and covered him over. Dad and I pushed the fallen treetrunk on top to stop anything digging him up. We were careful to move dry leaves and such over the place where the tree had lain before, so that no one should see it had been shifted. But in time, something must have dug up bits of him because that doctor fellow found the bones in a fox-hole, so I heard him tell the coroner. And the coroner agreed it'd been an accident, didn't he? He said there was no evidence of foul play. Now you're trying to make out different, but coroner's already said there wasn't. We went home, Dad and I, and for the first time, I stood up to him. In fact, I fair laid into him. I told him there was to be no more nonsense with the women up there in the woods or on the old drovers' way. If it ever all came out, I told him, no way would the police believe the hiker had died by accident. They'd believe Dad killed him because he'd seen Dad up to something with one of the girls. And Dad, for all he put a bold face on it, had had such a fright he gave in without a squeak. So that was the end of the Potato Man.'

Pearce found he'd been holding his breath. He expelled it in a long sigh. 'Tell me about Hester Millar.'

Dilys gave an echoing sigh and her shoulders slumped. 'Oh, that. That was a bit of bad luck, that was. She was a nice lady. I had nothing against her. But she walked in that morning and found Dad messing with the things in that old box. He would never throw it away. He liked to take them all out and put them on a table. He'd pick them up, one by one, turning them over in his fingers and remembering the girl he'd taken it from, chuckling to himself all the while. I hated him doing it. I was always afraid one day someone would walk in on us and I was right about that, too! Because Miss Millar did just that.

'She just appeared out of the blue that morning early. She came the back way, straight into the kitchen without so much as a by-your-leave, calling out, "It's only me!" She'd brought a pot of jam for us, dropped in on her way to open up the church. She was a dab hand at the jam-making. She put it on the table where Dad was sitting with the box, looking all pleased with herself. Then she saw what he was at, messing with those bits of jewellery and such. She asked Dad, what all those things were. Dad said, just things he'd found in the woods. But then she picked up the ring and she asked, in a funny sort of voice, "Where did you get this, Mr Twelvetrees? Did you find this in the woods, too?" And I knew, just knew, from her way and her voice that the ring meant something to her. She'd recognised it.

'My heart was in my boots. I thought that if I didn't silence her, she'd go blabbing. It would all come out, after all those years, Dad would be taken away. Everyone in the village would know the truth. Kevin Jones would move me out of the cottage. So I had to follow her over to the church and keep her quiet. She was kneeling saying her prayers when I went in. I called out that it was only me, Dilys, and she didn't turn round. It was easy. I've had more trouble killing a chicken. I didn't like doing it, mind! But the way I saw it, it had to be done. Then I went home and told Dad I'd done it, that he hadn't to worry she'd tell about the ring.

'Dad, he called me a stupid great turnip and asked me what I'd wanted to go killing her for. I told him, because of him, that's why. It was his fault. He said, I never did do anything right and what if she was only wounded and someone took her to the hospital? She'd know it was me done it. We waited for a while, to see if anything would happen over at the church like someone find her. But nothing happened and Dad got restless. He went over to the church to look, but she was dead all right, so he got out of there. See, Dad didn't want to be the one to find her and have to answer questions. He got away only in the nick of time because that friend of the superintendent's turned up and she found Miss Millar. So I had managed it all right, hadn't I? You'd have thought the old devil would've been grateful. I reckoned I'd handled it pretty well. If Dad had had more faith in me and not gone over there prying, that Miss Mitchell wouldn't have spotted him in the churchyard and Mr Markby wouldn't have come to the cottage asking questions. I told Dad, after he'd gone, that from then on he was to leave it all to me. I reckoned I sorted things out pretty well.'

'Surely you're not claiming that murder is justifiable?' Ginny Holding asked incredulously.

Dilys sniffed. 'Well, it would've been, wouldn't it? If that had been the end of it. But I had bad luck as usual and that wasn't the end of it. People prying, that's what causes trouble. That friend of Mr Markby's, she did the very same thing as Miss Millar did. It's like you've got no privacy in your own home. Dad was took queer in the churchyard and she helped him back to the cottage. She went through the kitchen to open up the front door. Dad, silly old fool, had left the back door unlocked and left all the things on the table. I came in not three or four minutes after she'd gone. Dad was sitting in his chair. He told me he'd had a bad turn but the lady had brought him indoors. I knew she'd got in through the back door and she must have seen everything. I ran outside and I saw her in the distance walking towards the woods. I followed her, kept down on the other side of the stone walls and went along the fields. A couple of times the sheep nearly gave me away, running off spooked. But it was raining that hard I reckon the superintendent's friend was more worried about that than the antics of a few sheep.'

Holding asked in a despairing voice, 'And it was worth killing one woman and trying to kill another to protect someone like your father?'

Dilys looked affronted. 'You haven't been listening! I told you about losing the cottage. How'd you like to lose your home? Besides, I thought perhaps I'd be in trouble because I knew about the women all those years ago, and didn't tell. I helped bury the hiker, too. But that wasn't my choosing. It was Dad's idea.' Her gaze met Pearce's, level and almost serene. 'None of it was my choosing,' she said. 'It was all Dad.'

After a moment's silence, Pearce said hoarsely, 'Thank you for telling us about it, Dilys. You did the right thing.'

But Dilys had something to ask. 'Shall I go to prison?' She didn't sound worried, rather curious.

'If you are convicted.'

'Because I've been thinking,' Dilys said placidly. 'Now Dad's dead, Kevin will have me out of that cottage for sure. But if I'm in prison for a nice long time, it'll be a roof over my head, won't it?'

'I'd like a word in private, Inspector!' snapped the solicitor.

In the corridor outside the interview room, the solicitor button-holed Pearce with a fierce gleam in his eye. 'I wish it to be made quite plain that my client spoke to you so freely against my advice. I warned her against making a confession and I shall be advising her to withdraw it.'

'Why?' Pearce asked bluntly.

'Good heavens, man! Need you ask? Her reasons for making it are extremely suspect. She wants to go to prison because, as she put it, it will give her a roof over her head! If you expect to go to court on the basis of that confession, I should tell you I shall make sure that a jury knows that is her reason. If a judge hears her talking like that, he'll probably tell the jury to disregard it!'

Pearce was inclined to agree but didn't say so. Instead he said, 'You can't deny she attacked Miss Mitchell.'

'She may have attacked her. She didn't kill her. That she killed the other woman, Hester Millar, is something we only have her word for. The old father probably did it. He was always going in that church, she told me so. He liked to chat to the churchwardens of which Miss Millar was one. You can't rely on anything she's told you, and that's the top and bottom of it. As for that business of burying the hiker in the woods —'

'Don't tell me all that grisly detail came out of her imagination,' Pearce interrupted.

The solicitor looked momentarily disconcerted. 'Yes, well, we still can't believe that she witnessed it, just because she said so. The old man could equally have come back and told her about it. Just as he could have come home and told her he killed Hester Millar. Or possibly neither of them killed her. Can't you see, Mrs Pullen is desperate not to find herself homeless? Now her father's dead, she sees prison as a safe refuge. The woman's mind is scrambled.'

'We'll leave it to a jury, shall we?' Pearce suggested.

The solicitor snorted. 'The whole taradiddle rests on the existence of that box of trophies.'

'Which Miss Mitchell saw and can describe.'

'But,' said the solicitor nastily, 'can't produce.'

Pearce eyed the solicitor suspiciously. 'Tell me, why are you so keen to get her off?'

'It's my job,' retorted the solicitor silkily.

'There's more to it than that.'

The young man gave him a dirty look. 'All right. She's poor and uneducated. She's middle-aged, unattractive and totally unaware of the impact of what she says. She was a battered child who grew up in fear under the thumb of that wicked old man. Despite her evasions, I believe he abused her and her sister sexually when they were children and probably abused her after her mother's death. You'll have noticed she avoided straight answers to any question about that kind of abuse being inflicted on her either as a child or later. He beat the kids up, that's all she'd admit.'

Pearce said thoughtfully, 'If she doesn't want to tell, she won't. Don't plan on making that part of your defence.'

The solicitor fixed him with a glittering eye. 'When people like her fall foul of the law and get into the system, they can't defend themselves. Everything they say or do makes it worse. They make a poor impression on a jury. Yes, I'm going to do my damnedest to get her off that murder charge! And you know perfectly well you have to do more than rely on a confession. You've got to have proof.'

He stalked off.

Pearce trudged upstairs to Markby's office. The superintendent looked up as he appeared and asked, 'Things not going well, Dave?'

'Look at it this way,' returned Pearce gloomily, rubbing his jaw. 'She's confessed but it's just our luck that her solicitor is a crusader.'

He explained, summarising what had happened in the interview room.

'Doing his job, Dave,' said Markby. 'Like he said. And we're going to do ours.'

'Patronising, public-school ponce!' growled Pearce. 'Sorry, sir, I meant the solicitor. I didn't mean you.'

'Thank you, Dave. I appreciate you making that clear.'

'I mean,' Pearce pursued the point. 'I don't suppose Dilys would have liked to hear herself described the way he described her. Anyway, he's wrong. He's talking as if she's simple. She's not. She's a cold-blooded killer and she's what my grandma used to call as artful as a cartload of monkeys. She'd run rings round that solicitor any day if she put her mind to it. And now she's running rings round us.'

'You mean the remark about wanting to go to prison,' Markby said.

'That's it. Confession? It's worthless. She made it worthless the moment she said that about going to gaol to have a roof over her head. What's more, she knew it and didn't need the solicitor to tell her so!' Pearce snorted.

Markby nodded his agreement. 'A confession without evidence to back it is, in any case, worthless. We must find that box with the old man's collection in it.'

'We're turning that cottage inside-out,' Pearce protested.

Markby sat silent. The Potato Man had escaped justice. Left to the eager-beaver solicitor, the Potato Man's daughter might yet beat a murder charge, unless they could come up with some tangible evidence.

'And we had it,' he said softly. 'We had it and I didn't realise it. Jam! I had jam on my shirt cuff when I left that cottage. She was bending over the pedal-bin throwing something away. She was throwing away that pot of jam! If Ruth had just remembered, while I was talking to her at the vicarage, that Hester had been holding a pot of jam, I might have got on to Dilys straight away!'

It hadn't been the only indication. Hindsight was a wonderful thing and Markby reflected ruefully on what it was telling him now. Another image had filled his head, that of Dilys opening the cottage door to him when he came to seek her father and her immediate declaration on seeing him that, 'We've got nothing to do with it!' He might well have asked her, there and then, with what? For Dilys hadn't been among the spectators at the church so how had she known what to deny? Of course, she might have popped her head out of her front door and a neighbour given her the news. But her denial, when she'd been asked no question, told its own tale. It was the reaction of her type to any suggestion she might be responsible for anything meaning trouble. He should have twigged that her defensive reaction to the mere sight of him meant she had something to hide, that the use of 'we' meant they both did, she and the old man.

There was a rap on the door. 'Sir?' It was Ginny Holding's voice, and seconds later her excited face peered round it. 'Sorry to interrupt but thought you'd like to know.'

Ginny wasn't without enjoying a moment of triumph. She paused then threw open the door wide so that she was revealed clasping a soot-streaked shoebox. 'They just brought it in, sir! They found it stuffed up the chimney. All the things are in there, the ring, everything.'

A smile broke on Markby's face. 'Well done, Ginny.'

'Great!' said Pearce in a muffled voice.

Markby looked at him. Pearce was holding his hand to his jaw again.

'For crying out loud, Dave,' Markby said wearily. 'See a dentist about that tooth first thing tomorrow morning. And when you have, come in and see me. We've got another line of enquiry to open up.'

'What?' Pearce gazed at him baffled.

'Come on, Dave. You said yourself the woman is a cold-blooded killer. Mr Pullen and his girlfriend, the barmaid, both disappeared overnight and were never seen again. Dilys never bothered to file for divorce. She wouldn't need to, would she, if she knew he was dead? Look, the same scenario has been replaying itself at that pub for weeks now. Norman Stubbings, tired of his wife Evie, has been fooling around with Cheryl Spencer. The difference is, Evie hasn't taken a kitchen knife to Norman – yet. Well, go on, then, get to it.'

Outside his office, a dismayed Dave Pearce turned to Sergeant Holding. 'He's not serious, is he, Ginny? I haven't got to dig up those bloody woods again?'

Chapter Seventeen

Roger was in the garden when Markby got out of his car before the old vicarage. Seeing a visitor, he let out hysterical barks of welcome and pounded towards the gate. When he reached it he stood on his hind legs, hung his huge paws over the topmost bar, and dribbled happily.

Markby patted his head, which seemed to drive Roger delirious, and told him, 'I'm just coming to see your mistress, if you don't mind getting down off the gate.'

Roger barked expectantly and showed no sign of moving. He was too heavy to push. Fortunately, his owner had heard the commotion and was coming towards them.

'Oh, it's you,' she said on spying Markby. 'Hang on, I'll let you in.' She threw her arms round Roger's neck and hauled him away from the gate. 'Come on, then!' she panted.

Markby hurriedly open the gate, slipped through and closed it securely behind him. Roger wriggled furiously in the headlock Muriel Scott had on him.

'Go indoors!' ordered Mrs Scott. 'The front door's unlatched. When you're in, I'll follow and shut Roger out here.'

He wasn't sure quite how she was going to manage that. Markby opened the front door, went in, pushed the door back ajar, and waited in the hall. After a moment and sounds of combat the door flew open. Muriel catapulted inside and slammed the door in Roger's face. He responded by attacking it. His claws could be heard scraping teeth-grindingly on what was left of the paintwork.

'There's no harm in him,' declared his breathless owner, leaning back against the door. 'He wants to be friends. The only reason he laid Dilys Twelvetrees out flat in the woods, the day she went for Meredith, was because he'd recognised her and wanted to say hello.'

'I'm very glad he did. He saved the day.'

'You're sure Dilys killed Hester, then?' Muriel stared hard at him.

'I believe so and we'll work hard proving it.' He eyed her curiously. 'Meredith told me that when you saw Hester dead in the church you appeared more surprised at the identity of the corpse than at its presence. Had you expected it to be someone else?'

She sniffed and said promptly. 'Norman, from the pub. Either him or one of those daft girls he's always fooling with. I thought Evie might finally have snapped and taken a carving knife to him. I wouldn't have blamed her if she had.'

Surprised, Markby asked, 'You knew he took his girlfriends to the church tower?'

She had the grace to redden and avoid his eye. 'Not exactly, well, I did suspect. His dad had been bell-ringer, you see. That would probably have given him the idea.'

Markby blinked. 'And you said nothing?'

Mrs Scott rallied. 'To whom? To Evie? Didn't she have enough troubles? That family, Twelvetrees – Norman's mother was a Twelvetrees, did you know? They always did look on women as punchbags.' She met his gaze now. 'Or worse,' she added.

There was a silence as both contemplated the crimes of the late Old Billy Twelvetrees.

Muriel Scott broke it to say, 'I don't know why we're standing out here. Come in and sit down.'

He followed her into the untidy drawing room and took a seat on the horsehair sofa. Muriel flopped into an armchair and asked, 'Do you want a cup of tea?'

'Please don't bother. I really can't stay long. I felt I had to come and explain to you that we shan't be making an offer for the house.'

She gave a mirthless hoot. 'I didn't think you would! After all that's happened? The last place Meredith wants to live is Lower Stovey, I should think.'

'She isn't keen on the place, I admit.' She wasn't keen on the house, either, but if Muriel liked to think their objection was to the village, rather than the vicarage, that suited him.

'If I don't sell it to you, I dare say I'll sell it to someone else eventually,' Muriel observed. 'I'll have to bring the price down. Just so long as I get enough to buy a little place somewhere for me and Roger.'

'Roger would prefer the countryside, I imagine.'

'I wouldn't take him to the town. He'd hate it and so would I.' Muriel tapped her fingers on the arm of her chair. 'You know, years ago, when I came to this house to look after the Reverend Pattinson, I was really thrilled. I was widowed, broke, homeless, rather as poor Dilys was after her husband bolted with the barmaid. But I'd better luck that she did. When they told me that Miss Pattinson, as she was then, had asked if I'd keep house for her father, it was like a miracle. I wrote straight away to accept. I met Miss Pattinson and the old reverend and we all got on like a house on fire. It seemed meant, somehow, that I should come here. He was no trouble, Reverend Pattinson. A bit absent-minded and living among his books, like I said. But he ate whatever I put in front of him, was always polite to me, followed instructions. If I told him to go and change his jacket he'd toddle off and do it. He was a nice old chap.'

'And you had relatives in the village, another reason to be here.'

She raised an eyebrow at him. 'Yes, I did. How did you know?'

'Ruth Aston told me Martin Jones is your uncle. That he told her you were available to keep house and it was to him she made the suggestion you come here.'

'That's right. But Kevin wrote me the letter because Uncle Martin wasn't used to writing letters. Kevin, of course, is my cousin. Not that I go over to the farm much. I can't take Roger there. He misbehaves all over the place. It's a funny thing. My Uncle Martin always said Old Billy had been the best farmworker he'd ever hired. The Reverend

Pattinson never spoke badly of the family, either, because Mrs Twelve-trees had once been the cleaner here. But then, the reverend was a man who couldn't see what was under his nose half the time. He had a problem distinguishing between what was real life and what he'd like life to be. Do you understand me?'

'I do indeed,' Markby told her. 'There are a lot of people like that.'

'He spent too much time with his head in books, that's what,' concluded Muriel.

'You know,' Markby said to her, 'I think I may have met you twenty-two years ago when I came to this house to talk to Mr Pattinson. A woman showed me into the study but to my shame, I can't remember if it was you.'

'It would've been me but I don't remember you, either. I remember a copper coming to call about the rapes in the woods, but not his face.'

Markby said ruefully, 'My memory ought to have been jogged when you opened the door to Meredith and me and remarked we might have thought you the housekeeper. Not now you're not. But you were then. I should have remembered.'

There was a silence. Then Muriel added soberly, 'So it was Old Billy Twelvetrees, after all. It makes sense when you think about it, but when I remember him tottering up the village street with his stick – well, it's hard to adjust to it.'

'He wasn't old then. He was fit, strong and sexually, he was frustrated. His wife was an invalid and marital relations had ceased. But he was also disposed to domestic violence. He saw no reason why he shouldn't take what he wanted elsewhere. He worked right alongside the woods. Yes, it does all make sense.'

'Living here all those years among us,' Muriel shook her head. 'Knowing what he'd done. I wonder he had the nerve. He couldn't have had any conscience.'

'I don't suppose he did. He was a nasty piece of work. Nor was he afraid his daughter, who alone knew what he'd been up to, would tell. She was cowed by his authority and frightened of losing her home. Besides, if he'd left, where else would he have gone? This was his village, his was a local family. All his life had been spent here. He worked at the farm and had no other skills. He lived in a tied cottage. He'd lose all that. What's more, if he'd ever considered running away, he must have realised it would arouse suspicion in itself. That a man with his roots so firmly in Lower Stovey would suddenly pack his bags and go, that would have had tongues wagging. He kept his head. There were no suspicions of him. He stayed. In fact, he became pathologically afraid of leaving.'

Muriel nodded. 'He cheated us all at the end, too, didn't he?'

'Us?' Markby enquired gently.

She grimaced. 'I do have a personal interest. I wasn't one of his victims, don't go thinking that! But I had other relations here besides Uncle Martin when I came. You investigated the Potato Man business. You'll remember Mavis Cotter.'

'I do. She was the first, or the first we knew of.'

'Poor kid. She was a sort of cousin of mine, too. In villages like this one, we're all pretty well related. Only I'm not kin to the Twelvetrees, thank God! Tainted bloodline that, if you ask me.' She looked up at him. 'They put Mavis away, you know, after that affair in the woods.'

'Put her away?' Markby was startled.

'Yes, in an institution. Her mother reckoned she couldn't be responsible for her, not after what had happened. She said Mavis might go roaming off and something else happen to her. Mavis had no sense. Bit simple. But she was a nice girl, pleasant, hard-worker, biddable. Never any trouble. She had a very loving nature. But she couldn't look after herself. So, in the end, away she went. It was wrong, wasn't it, to do that to her?' Muriel's sharp gaze rested on Markby's face.

'Yes,' he said. 'It was wrong.'

'She wasn't crazy. She wasn't a danger. She was just a bit backward and her mother couldn't cope with it. So away she went, locked up with a lot of strangers, looked after by strangers. She would have had no idea why. They did that in those days. It was as if they punished the victim.'

'I'm sorry,' he said.

'Not your fault,' she replied. 'That's life, isn't it? Something goes wrong and then things keep on going wrong. It can happen to anyone.' She looked thoughtful. 'It'd been nice if the police could've nabbed him back then. But at least we know what happened and people here know that poor Mavis didn't make it all up.'

'I'm glad,' Markby told her, 'you see it that way. It is, I suppose, some small consolation even for me.'

From outside came a dismal howl.

'I'll have to let him in,' said Muriel.

'I have to go. I have to pick up Meredith at the church and then we mean to look in on Ruth before we leave.'

Muriel scowled alarmingly not, as it turned out, in wrath but at the working of memory. 'Ruth, glad you reminded me. Tell her, will you, that I've got some papers of her father's for her. I've been turning out. Got to, now the place is up for sale.' She gestured vaguely towards the study. 'I should have put everything of his together when he died and handed it all to his daughter then. But Ruth wasn't living here then, so I pretty well left everything where it was. Later Ruth did move back here with Gerald, her husband. He was a nice bloke,' Muriel added in parenthesis. 'Pity he didn't last long. Cancer, you know. Anyway, I remember I told Ruth I had some stuff here if she wanted it and she said something about coming over and going through it all. But she never did, what with Gerald being ill and so on.'

'I'll tell her. What sort of papers are they?'

A sniff greeted this. 'What he used to call his research. He was very keen on ancient legends and that sort of thing. He had a bee in his bonnet about the Green Man. Hang on.' Muriel got up and lumbered out of the room. After a moment she returned and handed Markby a battered cardboard folder. 'This is a typical example. Give it to Ruth, will you, so she can see the sort of thing it is. Tell her, there another three boxes full of it.'

There was another amiable battle with Roger on the way out. Markby got into his car and put the folder on the front passenger seat. He reached out with the ignition key, but then curiosity overcame him. He flipped open the folder and pulled out the top sheet. It was hand-written in a cramped, old-fashioned style.

'Yesterday my wife persuaded me to go with her to a garden centre. I was surprised to find there (among all the other very expensive ornaments for gardens) a plastic mask of the Green Man. Or that's what it claimed to be. It should have been labelled as foliate head, because its expression was far too benign for the old Green Man! It looked quite jolly. Where were the sly features or the tormented ones? Where the eyes filled with ancient wickedness and the knowledge of unspoken, dreadful sin?'

Markby pushed the sheet back into the folder. The late Reverend Pattinson had been misled. Because features were benign, it didn't mean some awful memory didn't lurk behind them. Only consider Old Billy Twelvetrees, a mischievous old fellow, a local eccentric, but no harm in him to all outward appearances. But unspoken sin? Oh, yes!

Meredith had left Alan to tell Muriel Scott they didn't want the house. She hadn't wanted to rehearse the episode in the woods again. She was grateful to Muriel and grateful to Roger but it wasn't something she wanted to relive.

She pushed open the church door and stepped into St Barnabas's cool dim interior for the last time. She saw at once she wasn't alone. A young man was studying the Sir Rufus Fitzroy monument, a tourist, she supposed. He turned his head and smiled at her.

'Imposing old fellow, isn't he?'

She felt impelled to carry on Ruth's tradition of welcoming visitors. Meredith walked over to stand beside him and looked up at Sir Rufus. 'He looks a tough old chap to me, too,' she agreed.

'They were tough days. Survival of the fittest. Just to stay alive you had to be incredibly strong. Disease, poor sanitation, half the food you ate already on the turn, operations without anaesthetic or dis-infectants . . .' He gave another, slightly deprecating smile. 'I'm a doctor,' he said. 'I think about these things.'

'You're not Guy Morgan, are you?' Meredith asked. 'Who found the bones?'

He looked astonished. 'Yes. You are —?'

'Meredith Mitchell. I was visiting Lower Stovey that day with Alan Markby, Superintendent Markby.'

'Oh, right. Yes, he was there when the other coppers and I came out of the woods with the bones. I'm glad they were able to put a name to them.'

'I should have liked to attend the inquest, but I had to be at work that day.'

At the mention of the inquest, Guy frowned. 'The dead chap's mother was there. I wanted to go and speak to her, condolences and all that, but she wouldn't look at me. She avoided my eye in a very definite way, so I left it. I guessed my finding her son's remains was something she found difficult, a real stopper to any conversation.'

'Alan told me Mrs Hastings was very – well, not happy, that's not the word – that she was satisfied that her son's remains were found. It was a great consolation to her so I'm sure in a way she was glad you did find him. To lose a child must be terrible, no matter how old he is at the time.'

'I suppose so.' Guy turned his head away and looked up at Sir Rufus. 'My mother gave me away, but I dare say she had her reasons.'

'Gave you away?'

'Yes, put me up for adoption. I expect I was illegitimate. Looking round this church and seeing all these people belonging to one family is odd to me. I don't have any blood relations and I can't imagine what it's like. I've got my adoptive parents and they are my parents as far as I'm concerned. They've been loving and supportive and understanding. No blood parent could have been better. They'd been unable to have children and so saw me as a wonderful gift. I realised, even when I was very young, that I was very special to them.'

Meredith asked, 'So you've never tried to trace your birth mother?'

He shook his head. 'No. What would be the point? What would we say to one another? She's made her life without me and I've made my life without her. Let sleeping dogs lie. Or, as an elderly patient once said to me, "It's best not to go stirring up the water, there's sometimes nasty things lying in the mud at the bottom of a pond.'" He turned to go. 'Well, I'll be on my way. I wanted to come and look at this place, what with it being in the news after I found the bones in the woods. Give my regards to the superintendent. Nice to meet you.' He shook her hand briefly. 'Cheerio.'

She watched him walk out, his stocky figure briefly silhouetted against the sunlight in the open door before it fell shut behind him, leaving her alone with Sir Rufus, Hubert and Agnes, and whatever ghosts inhabited this old church.

'Well, now, Mr Pearce,' said the dentist. 'We haven't seen you for a while.'

'Um, no,' said Pearce. 'I've been busy.'

'I read about it in the papers. The murder at Lower Stovey. Nasty affair. And that business of the bones someone found in the woods. It's all go with you, isn't it? Are the teeth giving you trouble?'

Pearce's mind, for an instant, scrambled the question so that he almost replied that the teeth had been a clue to the jawbone's owner. But of course, he was here for his own teeth, or particularly, one tooth.

'I've been having a few twinges,' he admitted.

'Then let's have a look. Open wide, please, wide as you can . . . Ah, yes . . .'